OTHER

An Anthology of
Science Fiction and Fantasy

CANADAS

Edited by John Robert Colombo

D0930150

McGraw-Hill Ryerson Limited

Toronto   Halifax   Montreal   Vancouver

Other Canadas: An Anthology of Science Fiction and Fantasy

Copyright © J. R. Colombo, 1979

Note: Pages 357-360 constitute an extension of the copyright page.

ISBN 0-07-082952-7 (Trade Edition)

ISBN 0-07-082953-5 (Education Edition)

1 2 3 4 5 6 7 8 9 10 D 8 7 6 5 4 3 2 1 0 9

Printed and bound in Canada

Canadian Cataloguing in Publication Data

Main entry under title:

Other Canadas

ISBN 0-07-082952-7

1. Science fiction. 2. Science fiction, Canadian (English).*
I. Colombo, John Robert, date.

PN6071.S33084   808.83'876   C79-094475-8

To

S O L

The Spaced Out Library

The world's largest public library of science fiction and fantasy
Established by Judith Merril

Maintained by the Toronto Public Library System

May SOL Never Set

And perhaps the attempt to see our turbulent world against a background of stars may, after all, increase, not lessen, the significance of the present human crisis. It may also strengthen our charity towards one another.

Olaf Stapledon in *Star Maker* (1937)

In his old bustling world there were the works of man's hands all around to give a false impression of man's power. But here the hand of God had blotted out life for millions of miles and made a great tract of the inconsiderable ball which was the earth like the infinite interstellar spaces which had never heard of man.

John Buchan in *Sick Heart River* (1941)

"Now," said Joe, "I'm going to show you the stars!"

Robert Heinlein in "Universe," *Astounding Science Fiction*, May 1941

CONTENTS

vii

PREFACE

Canadian science fiction and fantasy—is there any?

Time and again I was asked this question when word got out that I was compiling the present anthology. Now I am able to answer the question in the affirmative and prove what I have always felt, that there is a Canadian science fiction and fantasy, and that it is worth a serious reader's serious attention.

By Canadian science fiction and fantasy (hereinafter SF&F) I refer to writing in prose or poetry form by all of the following: Canadian citizens, new Canadians, former Canadians, even non-Canadians (when their work is set in Canada). The body of writing produced by such a diverse group of writers may lack a distinctive character all its own, but in my view it does possess some distinguishing characteristics. *Other Canadas* is the first anthology of such Canadian science fiction and fantasy. It is meant to be both an entertaining collection of writing and an intriguing, speculative look at Canada, its alternate pasts, parallel presents, and possible futures.

The reader will find in this anthology: excerpts from four novels, seventeen short stories, twenty-seven poems by thirteen poets, two critical articles, one prophetic essay, a film script, and a brief annotated bibliography. I believe that all of these works are characteristic of the country's fantastic writing and that they are works that bear reading and rereading.

Unlike space, which appears to be infinite, anthologies are known to be finite creations. It has, therefore, been impossible to include here all the writers who have made contributions, especially in the area of pulp fiction, or to represent featured writers as fully as they deserve. As well, the historical approach I have taken has limited the number of contemporary writers I could include. By opting for the chronological arrangement, I was able, to some extent at least, to represent the evolution of fantastic literature itself — from a cosmic voyage written in the seventeenth century, through tales of Utopias and Bug-Eyed Monsters, to urban folklore, and ultimately to a fantasy set so far in the future that Thor Heyerdahl is but a legendary figure who sailed an insignificant sea on an almost-forgotten planet.

Before suggesting some of the characteristics of Canadian SF&F, let me mention that, contrary to what most people think, activity in this area has been extensive. There are over six hundred separate books that fall into this category, written by Canadians or set in Canada by non-Canadians, so it is possible to generalize somewhat. The four characteristics are, of necessity, inherent in the genres of science fiction and

1

fantasy; yet all four seem to me especially relevant to any study of that body of fantastic writing that could be identified as Canadian.

The first characteristic theme is that of the POLAR WORLD. Amid the ice and snow of the Far North lie marvels and wonders: lost civilizations, prehistoric creatures, bases for UFOs, etc. The North Pole may be an erupting volcano (as in the excerpt from Jules Verne's novel), or it may be a "polar opening," an entranceway to the world inside our planet (represented here by the excerpt from James De Mille's novel). American writers have been quick to mine the possibilities inherent in the Arctic, but there are Canadian writers who have been attracted to the polar possibilities too.

The second characteristic theme is the NATIONAL DISASTER SCENARIO, in which in the near future the country is falling apart, blowing up, being invaded, invading, or otherwise succumbing to some superior force. The disaster may be a political one, with Quebec leaving Confederation or Alberta opting out of it, or the Dene Indians seceding. Richard Rohmer has made this theme his speciality with such novels as *Ultimatum* (1973) and *Separation* (1976). On a more limited basis, a writer focuses on the collapse of a single city, the contamination of a region, or the unravelling of the social fabric of the country. In this anthology, stories by Margaret Laurence, Hugh Hood, and Yves Thériault represent this concern.

The third characteristic theme is that of the ALIENATED OUTSIDER. Although specially poignant in Canadian SF&F, this theme is common enough in contemporary literature. The sense of being on the outside of society (or the world) and of looking in and finding the scene too terrifying to behold is a form of alienation from society and from ourselves. These are part and parcel of our most imaginative literature, and in this anthology stories by Grant Allen, Robert Barr, and Laurence Manning, as well as the excerpt from Frederick Philip Grove's novel, dramatize the pain of dissociation from man and his works.

The fourth characteristic is not so much a theme as an observation — there is a PREVALENCE OF FANTASY OVER SCIENCE FICTION. Canadians prefer the impossible to the possible, and write more fantasy than they do science fiction. There are no stories of technological invention here, and David Ketterer, in his survey of science fiction, connects the low priority Canadians give to research and development and the movement towards deindustrialization with the tenor of our science fiction, which is of the "software" rather than the "hardware" variety. But there is no shortage of hobgoblins and other monsters in our literature, as Margaret Atwood notes in her critical essay. In order to represent the indigenous fantastic dimension of Canadian writing, I have included one of the greatest of all terror tales, Algernon Blackwood's "The Wendigo," as well as moving poems of the weird variety by Archibald Lampman, Bliss Carman, Wilfred Campbell, and others. (The streak of morbidity that runs through Canadian poetry is not often noted.) Phyllis Gotlieb's poems make good use of dissociative devices too. Although I have reprinted much fantasy, I have avoided including animal tales that impart human characteristics to the beasts of the forest and also fantasies that retell the ancient myths in modern garb. Nor is there any supernatural and occult fiction included. The fantasy of contemporary Quebec, which blends supernatural and folkloristic elements, is represented with *contes* by Jacques Ferron and Michel Tremblay, a rich field I could only sample here.

I will leave it to the reader to decide the extent to which these four characteristics—three themes and one observation—are inherent in the genres themselves or are specific Canadian considerations.

Although Canadian SF&F does not rival British or American SF&F in quality or quantity, there has always existed a vigorous readership (as distinct from authorship) for such literature in this country. The only professional magazines to publish SF&F in Canada appeared briefly when American comic books and pulp magazines were embargoed "for the duration" of the Second World War. *Eerie Tales, Uncanny Tales,* and *Les Aventures Futuristes* appeared between 1940 and 1949 to fill the newly bare newsstands, but could not withstand the reappearance of the products from the United States that they so slavishly imitated. In 1948, Toronto was the site of Torcon 1, the first of the World Science Fiction Conventions to be held outside the United States. The guest of honour was Robert Bloch (later of *Psycho* fame) who, by coincidence, was again invited as guest of honour at Torcon 2, held in the same city twenty-five years later.

In the absence of professional magazines, amateur productions (called fanzines) flourished. Three may be singled out for their quality and influence. *Energumen,* published by Michael Glicksohn and Susan Wood in 1970-71, won a Hugo Award for editorial excellence. Currently being published are two critical magazines, *Requiem: Le Fanzine Québecois de la Science-Fiction et du Fantastique,* founded by Norbert Spehner in Montreal in 1974, and *Borealis: A Canadian Magazine of Science Fiction and Fantasy,* founded by John Bell in Halifax in 1978.

Of great importance to Canadian fans of science fiction and fantasy is the Spaced Out Library, founded by Judith Merril in Toronto in 1969. Now part of the Toronto Public Library System, SOL is the world's largest public collection of SF&F. (I have written in more detail about SOL in the later entry on Judith Merril, for I believe the library she set up is of imaginative importance to our country's culture.) Of more interest than importance, perhaps, is another distinction that has come to Canada.

Ours is the only country in the world that can boast a town that was given the name of the hero of a science-fiction novel. (I am excluding from this generalization Tarzana, California.) The hero is Professor Josiah Flintabbaty Flontin, who appears in a dime novel called *The Sunless City* (1905), written by J. E. Preston-Muddock, a British writer of pulp fiction who also used the name Dick Donovan. The town of Flin Flon, in Manitoba, was given the nickname of the Professor, when a tattered copy of the book, now in the Flin Flon Public Library, was found by a prospector on the site of the future town in 1913. In *The Sunless City,* the genial professor visits a "sunless city" which is rich in gold, ruled by women, and located at the center of the earth. Since Flin Flon has extensive gold deposits, the name seemed to fit. In 1962, the city fathers erected a fiberglass figure of the professor, twenty-four feet (seven metres) high, modelled after a drawing supplied by the cartoonist Al Capp, to watch over the town and its gold.

Let me add a personal note to this preface. More than any other anthology I have edited, this one has grown out of my own experience and has provided me with more pleasure and pain than any other. My interest in presenting Canadian materials to a wide public is well known, but when I completed *Colombo's Book of Canada* in 1978, I was in a quandary, for I had pretty well—symbolically at least—anthologized the country's past and present. Casting around for another world to conquer, I thought of the future, then of outer space, then of alternate and parallel pasts and presents. This did not occur by accident, for I have been a contented reader of the literature of the fantastic since my teens. Two important anthologies influenced me when I was a high-school student in Kitchener, Ontario. The first was *Adventures in Time and Space* (1946), which was so well edited by R. J. Healy and J. Francis McComas as to give the reader the thrill of watching an imaginative tradition unfold. The second was *Shot in the Dark* (1950), which happened to be the first collection edited by Judith Merril, and its sure sense of excitement and relevance left me with a taste for the heady wine of modern American science fiction. In those days, briefly at least, I was a fan, for I can boast that I corresponded (once anyway) with Mary Gnaedinger, the editor of *Famous Fantastic Mysteries*. The correspondence column of one issue of that well-loved monthly includes letters from two Canadian writers, Al Purdy and myself. Therefore, my two consuming interests—Canadiana and SF&F—came to coincide in the present collection.

As for the "pleasure and pain" of compiling *Other Canadas*, the pleasures are the thrills I experienced tracing and then revealing this imaginative tradition—a major river's tributary, but our own—and the pains are the decisions, regretfully taken, to exclude so many authors of the past and the present who should be represented, for they too have written stories and poetry that could be enjoyed. Perhaps there will be a successor to the present anthology.

Other Canadas represents the tastes and thoughts of a single person, yet many people have left their marks on the book now in your hands. If Judith Merril had not established the Spaced Out Library in Toronto, it is doubtful that I would ever have attempted this undertaking. (*Other Canadas* is appearing on the tenth anniversary of the founding of the library.) She became a friend and helped me, a fellow anthologist, unstintingly. Doris Mehegan and David Aylward, SOL's two librarians, answered my multitudinous questions with a growing sense of wonder. (At one point, when I knocked off to read novels by Fritz Leiber and Olaf Stapledon, one of them was worried that I would try to argue that they were honorary Canadians.)

Much-needed enthusiasm for the project was supplied by Michael Richardson, a reference librarian with the Bathurst Heights Branch of the North York Library System. He joined with me in the compilation of the first-ever bibliography of Canadian SF&F, which was originally intended as the appendix to the present volume, until it rapidly outgrew those confines and clammered for separate publication. In this endeavour, we were joined by Alexandre L. Amprimoz, now with St. John's College, University of Manitoba, and John Bell of the Archives Division of Dalhousie University. As the annotated checklist—*CDN SF&F: A Bibliography of Canadian Science Fiction and Fantasy* (1979)—grew, *Other Canadas* contracted to fit into one volume. But without the full bibliography, I would have found it impossible to survey Canadian and Canadian-interest material in a systematic way, or to focus on the characteristics of our indigenous imaginative literature.

Other people, too, had a hand in raising the quality of this anthology. David Ketterer of Concordia University in Montreal supplied a critical backup when he wrote his survey article (included in this volume) on Canadian science fiction. Indeed, he kindly shelved plans for his own anthology and helped me with mine. I benefitted from his strong sense of what constitutes science fiction. Chester D. Cuthbert, the noted Winnipeg collector and writer, sent me thoughtful letters full of detailed information. Sam Moskowitz, the American anthologist, drew my attention to those Canadians who had contributed to the pulp magazines in the Thirties. Forrest J. Ackerman helped me with the permissions (and argued in one letter that since H. L. Gold has all these years retained his Canadian citizenship, I should include him in my "Canthology"). Bruce Robbins, a Montreal fan, will be disappointed with the quantity of *Québecois* material in the volume, but he drew my attention to valuable works I would otherwise have missed. Susan Wood of the University of British Columbia made available to me her then-unpublished entry on Canadian SF for *The Encyclopedia of Science Fiction* (1979), edited by Peter Nicholls and John Clute. Other writers, teachers, editors, and publishers who assisted me include: Douglas Barbour, John F. Carr, Chan Davis, Galad Elflandsson, Peter Fitting, Jack Freiburger, Douglas Hill, Monica Hughes, Mel Hurtig, Opal L. Nations, Charles R. Saunders, Darko Suvin, and J. Michael Yates. Let me thank, finally, Dawn Wallace, the McGraw-Hill Ryerson editor, who helped me to prove, by arranging the publication of this anthology, that there *is* a Canadian science fiction and fantasy—and that it is fun to read.

Cyrano de Bergerac
VOYAGE TO NEW FRANCE

Canadian fantastic literature may be said to commence with the crash-landing of an early astronaut in New France in 1657. This unlikely event was related in a burlesque manner by Cyrano de Bergerac (1619-55), the celebrated French author best remembered today as the long-nosed swordsman hero of Edmond Rostand's drama of 1897. Bergerac's Voyages to the Moon and the Sun *appeared anonymously and posthumously in two parts in 1657 and 1662. It was widely read in its day and has been described by the literary historian, Marjorie Hope Nicolson, as "the most brilliant of all seventeenth-century parodies of the cosmic voyage." The opening section is reprinted here in the translation of Richard Aldington, first published in 1923. New France was at its apogee in 1657. The Royal Colony was more than a century and a half old, and it had a century to go before its fall in 1759.*

The moon was full, the sky clear, and the clocks had just struck nine as I was returning with four of my friends from a house near Paris. Our wit must have been sharpened on the cobbles of the road for it thrust home whichever way we turned it; distant as the moon was she could not escape it. The various thoughts provoked in us by the sight of that globe of saffron diverted us on the road and our eyes were filled by this great luminary. Now one of us likened her to a window in Heaven through which the glory of the blessed might be faintly seen; then another, inspired by ancient fables, imagined that Bacchus kept a tavern in Heaven and had hung out the Full Moon for his sign; then another vowed that it was the block where Diana set Apollo's ruffs; another exclaimed that it might well be the Sun himself who, having put off his rays at night, was watching through a hole what the world did when he was not there. For my part, said I, I am desirous to add my fancies to yours and without amusing myself with the witty notions you use to tickle time to make it run the faster, I think that the Moon is a world like this and that our world is their Moon. The company gratified me with a great shout of mirth.

"Perhaps in the same way," said I, "at this moment in the Moon they jest at some one who there maintains that this globe is a world."

But though I showed them that Pythagoras, Epicurus, Democritus and, in our own age, Copernicus and Kepler had been of this opinion, I did but cause them to strain their throats the more heartily.

This thought, whose boldness jumped with my humour, was strengthened by contradiction and sank so deep in me that all the rest of the way I was pregnant with a thousand definitions of the Moon of which I could not be delivered. By supporting this fantastic belief with serious reasoning I grew well-nigh persuaded of it. But hearken, reader, the miracle or accident used by Providence or Fortune to convince me of it:

I returned home and scarcely had I entered my room to rest after the journey when I found on my table an open book which I had not put there. I recognised it as mine, which made me ask my servant why he had taken it out of the book-case. I asked him but perfunctorily, for he was a fat Lorrainer, whose soul admitted of no exercise more noble than those of an oyster. He swore to me that either the Devil or I had put it there. For my own part I was sure I had not handled it for more than a year.

I glanced at it again; it was the works of Cardan; and though I had no idea of reading it I fell, as if directed to it, precisely upon a story told by this philosopher. He says that, reading one evening by candle-light, he perceived two tall old men enter through the closed door of his room and after he had asked them many questions they told him they were inhabitants of the Moon; which said, they disappeared. I remained so amazed to see a book brought there by itself as well as at the time and the leaf at which I found it open that I took this whole train of events to be an inspiration of God urging me to make known to men that the Moon is a world.

"What!" quoth I to myself, "after I have talked of a matter this very day, a book, which is perhaps the only one in a world that treats of this subject, flies down from the shelf on to my table, becomes capable of reason to the extent of opening at the very page of so marvellous an adventure and thereby supplies meditations to my fancy and an object to my resolution. Doubtless," I continued, "the two old men who appeared to that great man are the same who have moved my book and opened it at this page to spare themselves the trouble of making me the harangue they made Cardan. But," I added, "how can I clear up this doubt if I do not go there? And why not?" I answered myself at once, "Prometheus of old went to Heaven to steal fire!"

These feverish outbursts were followed by the hope of making successfully such a voyage.

I shut myself up to achieve my purpose in a rather lonely country-house where, after I had flattered my fancy with several methods which might have borne me up there, I committed myself to the heavens in this manner:

I fastened all about me a number of little bottles filled with dew, and the heat of the Sun drawing them up carried me so high that at last I found myself above the loftiest clouds. But, since this attraction caused me to rise too rapidly and instead of my drawing nearer the Moon, as I desired, she seemed to me further off than when I started, I broke several of my bottles until I felt that my weight overbore the attraction and that I was falling towards the earth. My opinion was not wrong; for I reached ground sometime later when, calculating from the hour at which I had started, it ought to have been midnight. Yet I perceived that the Sun was then at the highest point above the horizon and that it was midday. I leave you to conjecture my surprise; indeed it was so great that not knowing how to explain this miracle I had the insolence to fancy that in compliment to my boldness God had a second time fixed the Sun in Heaven to light so glorious an enterprise. My astonishment increased when I found I did not recognise the country I was in, for it appeared to me that, having risen straight up, I ought to have landed in the place from which I had started. Encumbered as I was I approached a hut where I perceived some smoke and I was barely a pistol-shot from it when I found myself surrounded by a large number of savages. They appeared mightily surprised at meeting me; for I was the first, I think, they had ever seen dressed in bottles. And, to overthrow still more any explanation they might have given of this equipment, they saw that as I walked I scarcely touched the ground. They did not know that at the least movement I gave my body the heat of the midday sun-beams lifted me up with my dew; and if my bottles had been more numerous I should very likely have been carried into the air before their eyes. I tried to converse with them; but, as if terror had changed them into birds, in a twinkling they were lost to sight in the neighbouring woods. Nevertheless I caught one whose legs without doubt betrayed his intention. I asked him with much difficulty (for I was out of breath) how far it was from there to Paris, since when people went naked in France and why they fled from me in such terror. This man to whom I spoke was an old man, yellow as an olive, who cast himself at my knees, joined his hands above his head, opened his mouth and shut his eyes. He muttered for some time but as I could not perceive that he said anything I took his language for the hoarse babble of a dumb man.

Sometime afterwards I saw coming towards me a band of soldiers with drums beating and I noticed that two left the main body to reconnoitre me. When they were near enough to hear I asked them where I was.

"You are in France," replied they, "but who the Devil put you in this condition? How does it happen that we do not know you? Has the fleet arrived? Are you going to warn the Governor of it? Why have you divided your brandy into so many bottles?"

To all this I replied that the Devil had not put me in that condition;

that they did not know me because they could not know all men; that I did not know there were ships on the Seine; that I had no information to give Monsieur de Montbazon and that I was not carrying any brandy.

"Oh! Ho!" said they taking me by the arm, "you are pleased to be merry! The Governor will understand you!"

They carried me towards their main body as they spoke these words and I learned from them that I was indeed in France, but not in Europe, for I was in New France.

I was brought before the Viceroy, Monsieur de Montmagnie. He asked me my country, my name and my rank, and when I had satisfied him by relating the happy success of my voyage, whether he believed it or only feigned to believe it, he had the kindness to allot me a room in his house. I was happy to fall in with a man capable of lofty ideas, who was not scandalised when I said that the earth must have turned while I was above it, seeing that I had begun to rise two leagues from Paris and had fallen by an almost perpendicular line in Canada.

That evening just as I was going to bed he came into my room.

"I should not have interrupted your rest," said he, "had I not believed that a man who travels nine hundred leagues in half a day can easily do so without being weary. But you do not know," added he, "the merry dispute I have just had on your behalf with our Jesuit Fathers? They are convinced that you are a magician and the greatest mercy you can obtain from them is to pass for no more than an impostor. And, after all, this movement you assign to the Earth is surely some neat paradox? The reason I am not of your opinion is that although you may have left Paris yesterday you could still have reached this country to-day without the Earth having turned. For the Sun, which bore you up by means of your bottles, must have drawn you hither since, according to Ptolemy, Tycho Brahe, and modern philosophers it moves in a direction opposite to that in which you say the Earth moves. And then what probability have you for asserting that the Sun is motionless when we see it move, and that the Earth turns about its centre with such rapidity when we feel it firm beneath us?"

"Sir," replied I, "here are the reasons which oblige us to suppose so: First it is a matter of common sense to think that the Sun is placed in the centre of the Universe, since all bodies in Nature need this radical fire, which dwells in the heart of the Kingdom to be in a position to satisfy their necessities promptly; and that the cause of procreation should be placed in the midst of all bodies to act equally upon them: In the same way wise Nature placed the genitals in the centre of man, pips in the centre of apples, kernels in the centre of their fruit; and in the same way the onion shelters within a hundred surrounding skins the precious germ

10

whence ten million others must draw their essence. The apple is a little universe by itself whose core, which is warmer than the other parts, is a Sun spreading about it the preserving heat of its globe; and the germ in the onion is the little Sun of that little world which heats and nourishes the vegetable salt of the mass. Granted this, I say that since the Earth needs the light, the heat and the influence of this great fire, she turns about it to receive equally in every part this strength which conserves her. For it would be as ridiculous to hold that this great luminous body turns about a point of no importance to it as to imagine when we see a roasted lark that it has been cooked by turning the hearth about it. Otherwise, if the Sun were made to perform this labour it would seem that the doctor needs the patient, that the strong must yield to the weak, the great serve the small, and that instead of a ship coasting the shores of a country we must make the country move around the vessel. And if you find it hard to believe that so heavy a mass can move, tell me, I pray you, are the stars and the Heavens that you make so solid any lighter? And it is easy for us who are convinced of the roundness of the earth to deduce its movements from its shape; but why suppose the sky to be round since you cannot know it and since if, of all possible shapes it has not this shape, it certainly cannot move? I do not reproach you with your eccentrics, your concentrics and your epicycles, all of which you can only explain very confusedly and from which my system is free. Let us speak only of the natural causes of this movement. On your side you are compelled to invoke the aid of intelligences to move and direct your globes! But without disturbing the tranquillity of the Sovereign Being, who doubtless created Nature quite perfect and whose wisdom completed it in such a way by fitting it for one thing He has not rendered it unfit for another—I, on my part, find in the Earth herself the power which makes it move. I declare then that the sun-beams, together with the Sun's influence, striking upon the Earth in their motion, make it turn as we turn a globe by striking it with the hand, or that the vapours which continually evaporate from the Earth's bosom on that side where the Sun shines, are repulsed by the cold of the middle regions, rush back on the Earth and, of necessity being able to strike it obliquely, make it dance in this fashion.

"The explanation of the two other movements is still less intricate. Consider I beg of you. . . ."

At these words the Viceroy interrupted me.

"I prefer," he said, "to excuse you from that trouble (I have myself read several books of Gassendi on the subject) provided that you will listen to what I heard one day from one of our Fathers who shared your opinion. 'Truly,' said he, 'I imagine that the Earth turns, not for the reasons alleged by Copernicus but because the fire of Hell (as we learn from Holy

11

Scripture) being enclosed in the centre of the Earth, the damned souls, flying from the heat of the fire to avoid it, clamber upwards and thus make the Earth turn, as a dog makes a wheel turn when he runs round inside it.'"

We praised the good Father's zeal and, having finished the panegyric, the Viceroy said he greatly wondered the system of Ptolemy should be so generally received, considering how little probable it is.

"Sir," I replied, "most men judge only by their senses, are convinced only by their eyes; and just as a man in a ship sailing by the coast thinks himself stationary and the shore moving, so men, turning with the Earth around the sky, believe that the sky itself turns around them. Add to this the intolerable pride of human beings, who are convinced that Nature was made for them alone—as if it were probable that the Sun, a vast body four hundred and thirty-four times greater than the Earth, should have been lighted only to ripen its medlars and to head its cabbages. For my part, far from yielding to their impertinence, I believe that the planets are worlds around the Sun and that the fixed stars are suns too with planets around them, that is to say, worlds, which we cannot see from here because they are too small and because their borrowed light cannot reach us. For, in good faith, how can we suppose that globes so spacious are only huge desert countries and that ours, because we grovel on it before a dozen proud-stomached rogues, should have been made to command them all? What! Because the Sun measures our days and our years, does that mean it was created only to save us from breaking our heads against the wall? No! If this visible God lightens man it is accidental, as the King's torch accidentally lightens a porter passing in the street."

"But," said he, "if, as you assert, the fixed stars are so many suns we may deduce thence that the universe is infinite since it is probable that the people in the worlds about a fixed star, which you take to be a sun, perceive above them other fixed stars which we cannot see from here and that it continues in this manner to infinity."

"Doubt it not," replied I, "as God was able to make the soul immortal so could He make the World infinite, if it be true that Eternity is nothing else than duration without bounds and the infinite, space without limit. And then God Himself would be finite if we believe the world not to be infinite, since He could not be where there is nothing and since He could not increase the size of the World without adding something to His own extent, by beginning to be where He had not been formerly. We must believe then that as we see Saturn and Jupiter from here we should perceive, if we were in one or the other, many worlds we do not perceive from here and that the universe is constructed in this manner to infinity."

12

"Faith!" replied he, "you may well talk but I cannot comprehend infinity."

"Why, tell me," said I, "do you understand better the nothing which is beyond it? Not at all. When you think of this nothing you imagine at least something like wind, something like air, and that is something; but if you do not comprehend infinity as a general idea you may conceive it at least in parts, for it is not difficult to imagine beyond the earth, air and fire that we see, more air and more earth. Infinity is simply a texture without bounds. If you ask me how these worlds were made, seeing that Holy Scripture speaks only of one created by God, I reply that it speaks only of ours because this is the only world God took the trouble to make with His own hand and all the others, whether we see them or do not see them, hanging in the azure of the universe, are dross thrown off by the suns. For how could these great fires continue if they were not united with matter to feed them? Well, just as fire casts off the ashes which choke it, just as gold in the crucible severs itself from the marcasite which lessens its purity, and just as our heart frees itself by vomiting from the indigestible humours which attack it; so the suns disgorge every day and purge themselves of the remnants of that matter which feeds their fire. But when these suns have altogether used up the matter which maintains them, you cannot doubt but that they will spread out on all sides to seek new fuel and will fall upon all the worlds they had thrown off before and particularly upon the nearest ones: Then these great fires again burning up all these bodies will again throw them off pell-mell on all sides as before, and being purified little by little they will begin to act as suns to these little worlds which they engender by casting them out of their spheres; doubtless it was this which made the disciples of Pythagoras predict an universal conflagration. This is not a ridiculous fancy; New France, where we are, produces a very convincing proof. This vast continent of America is one half of the Earth, and though our predecessors had sailed the ocean a thousand times they never discovered it. At that time it did not exist, any more than many islands, peninsulas and mountains which rise on our globe, until the rusts of the Sun being cleaned off and cast far way were condensed into balls heavy enough to be attracted towards the centre of our world, either little by little in small parts or perhaps suddenly in one mass. And this is not so unreasonable but that Saint Augustine would have applauded it had this country been discovered in his time, for this great personage whose genius was enlightened by the Holy Ghost asserts that in his time the Earth was as flat as an oven and that it swam upon the water like half of a cut orange; but if ever I have the honour to see you in France I will prove to you, by means of a very excellent perspective glass I have, that certain obscurities which from here seem to be spots are worlds in process of formation."

My eyes were closing as I said this, which obliged the Viceroy to bid me good-night. The next and following days we had conversations of the like nature; but since some time afterwards the press of business in the Province interrupted our philosophizing I fell back the more eagerly on my plan of reaching the Moon.

As soon as the Moon rose I went off among the woods meditating on the contrivance and issue of my undertaking. At length on Saint John's Eve when those in the fort were debating whether or no they would aid the savages of the country against the Iroquois, I went off by myself behind our house to the summit of a little hill, where I acted as follows.

With a machine I had constructed, which I thought would lift me as much as I wanted, I cast myself into the air from the top of a rock; but because I had taken my measures badly I was tumbled roughly into the valley. Injured as I was I returned to my room without being discouraged. I took beef-marrow and greased all my body with it, for I was bruised from head to foot; and after I had comforted my heart with a bottle of cordial I returned to look for my machine, which I did not find, seeing that certain soldiers who had been sent into the forest to cut wood for the purpose of building a Saint John's fire to be lighted that evening, had come upon it by chance and carried it to the fort. After several hypotheses of what it might be they discovered the device of the spring, when some said they ought to bind around it a number of rockets because their rapid ascent would lift it high in the air, the spring would move its great wings and everyone would take the machine for a fire-dragon.

I sought it for a long time and at last I found it in the middle of the market-place of Quebec just as they were lighting it. The pain of seeing the work of my hands in such peril affected me so much that I rushed forward to grasp the arm of the soldier who was about to fire it. I seized his slow-match and cast myself furiously into the machine to break off the fireworks which surrounded it; but I came too late, for I had scarcely set my two feet in it when I was carried off into the clouds. The fearful horror that dismayed me did not so thoroughly overwhelm the faculties of my soul but that I could recollect afterwards all that happened to me at this moment. You must know then that the flame had no sooner consumed one line of rockets (for they had placed them in sixes by means of a fuse which ran along each half-dozen), when another set caught fire and then another, so that the blazing powder delayed my peril by increasing it. The rockets at length ceased through the exhaustion of material and, while I was thinking I should leave my head on the summit of a mountain, I felt (without my having stirred) my elevation continue; and my machine, taking lease of me, fell towards the Earth. This extraordinary adventure filled me with a joy so uncommon that in

14

my delight at finding myself delivered from certain danger I was impudent enough to philosophize about it. I sought with my eyes and intelligence the reason for this miracle and I perceived that my flesh was still swollen and greasy with the marrow I had rubbed on it for the bruises caused by my fall. I knew that at the time the Moon was waning and that during this quarter she is wont to suck up the marrow of animals; she drank the marrow I had rubbed on myself with the more eagerness in that her globe was nearer me and that her strength was not weakened by any intervening clouds.

When I had traversed, according to the calculation I have since made, more than three-quarters the distance which separates the Earth from the Moon, I suddenly turned a somersault without my having stumbled at all; in fact I should not have perceived it had I not felt my head burdened with the weight of my body. I realised then that I was not falling towards our world, for although I was between two Moons and could see very well that I drew further from the one as I approached the other, I was certain that the larger was our Earth since after a day or two of travelling the distant reflection of the Sun confounded the diversity of bodies and climates and therefore it appeared to me like a large gold platter, similar to the other. From this I supposed I was descending upon the Moon and I was confirmed in this opinion when I remembered that I had only begun to fall when I had passed three-quarters of the distance. For, said I to myself, the Moon's mass being less than ours the sphere of its activity must be less extended and consequently I felt the attraction of its centre more tardily.

After I had been long falling, as I supposed, for the violence of my fall prevented me from observing it, I remember no more than that I found myself under a tree, entangled with three or four rather large branches which I had snapped off in my fall and my face moistened with an apple which had been crushed against it.

As you shall know very soon, this place was happily the Earthly Paradise and the tree I fell on precisely the Tree of Life . . . .

Jules Verne
MOUNT HATTERAS

For centuries the polar north has exerted an almost magnetic attraction on the minds of explorers, adventurers, and artists who have imagined amid the Arctic wastes all manner of wonders. To some, a tropical valley may be found isolated from the rest of the world by walls of ice and mounds of snow. To others, the polar regions conceal the passageway to a world within our world, with its own central sun and fauna and flora. Even Jules Verne (1828-1905), the great French writer of extraordinary voyages and quasi-scientific romances, allowed his imagination full play. His hero, Captain Hatteras, the son of a wealthy London brewer, has a single obsession: to attain the Pole. Just as Captain Nemo explores the South Pole in Twenty Thousand Leagues under the Sea *(1870), Captain Hatteras reaches the North Pole with a loyal crew aboard his Arctic-equipped steam vessel. But disastrous consequences ensue. Among the crew are Dr. Clawbonny (a savant), Altamont (an American), Johnson and Bell (devoted sailors), and Duk (the Captain's faithful dog.)* Les Aventures du Capitaine Hatteras *(1866) is composed of two novels,* Les Anglais au Pôle Nord *(1864) and* Le Désert de Glace *(1866). "Mount Hatteras" is Chapter XXIV of the latter work, reproduced from* Works of Jules Verne *(1911), edited by Charles F. Horne. Verne wrote about faraway places but never visited them. He spent one week in the United States, and on April 19, 1867, he spent sixty minutes on Canadian soil, admiring Niagara Falls.*

After this conversation they all made themselves as comfortable as they could, and lay down to sleep.

All, except Hatteras; and why could this extraordinary man not sleep like the others? Was not the purpose of his life attained now? Had he not realized his most daring project? Why could he not rest? Indeed, might not one have supposed that, after the strain his nervous system had undergone, he would long for rest?

But no, he grew more and more excited, and it was not the thought of returning that so affected him. Was he bent on going further still? Had his passion for travel no limits? Was the world too small for him now he had circumnavigated it?

Whatever might be the cause, he could not sleep; yet this first night at the Pole was clear and calm. The isle was absolutely uninhabited—not a bird was to be seen in this burning atmosphere, not an animal on these scoriae-covered rocks, not a fish in these seething waters.

Next morning, when Altamont and the others awoke, Hatteras was gone. Feeling uneasy at his absence, they hurried out of the grotto in search of him. There he was standing on a rock, gazing fixedly at the top of the mountain. His instruments were in his hand, and he was evidently calculating the exact longitude and latitude.

The Doctor went towards him and spoke, but it was long before he could rouse him from his absorbing contemplations. At last the captain seemed to understand, and Clawbonny said, while he examined him with a keen scrutinizing glance:

"Let us go round the island. Here we are, all ready for our last excursion."

"The last!" repeated Hatteras, as if in a dream. "Yes! the last truly; but," he added, with more animation, "the most wonderful."

He pressed both hands on his brow as he spoke, as if to calm the inward tumult.

Just then Altamont and the others came up, and their appearance seemed to dispel the hallucinations under which he was laboring.

"My friends," he said, in a voice full of emotion, "thanks for your courage, thanks for your perseverance, thanks for your superhuman efforts, through which we are permitted to set our feet on this soil."

"Captain," said Johnson, "we have only obeyed orders; to you alone belongs the honor."

"No, no!" exclaimed Hatteras, with a violent outburst of emotion, "to all of you as much as to me! To Altamont as much as any of us, as much as the Doctor himself! Oh, let my heart break in your hands, it cannot contain its joy and gratitude any longer."

He grasped the hands of his brave companions as he spoke, and paced up and down as if he had lost all self-control.

"We have only done our duty as Englishmen," said Bell.

"And as friends," added Clawbonny.

"Yes; but all did not do it," replied Hatteras; "some gave way. However, we must pardon them—pardon both the traitors and those who were led away by them. Poor fellows! I forgive them. You hear me, Doctor?"

"Yes," replied Clawbonny, beginning to be seriously uneasy at his friend's excitement.

"I have no wish, therefore," continued the captain, "that they should lose the little fortune they came so far to seek. No, the original agreement is to remain unaltered, and they shall be rich—if ever they see England again."

It would have been difficult not to have been touched by the pathetic tone of voice in which Hatteras said this.

"But, captain," interrupted Johnson, trying to joke, "one would think you were making your will!"

"Perhaps I am," said Hatteras gravely.

"And yet you have a long bright career of glory before you!"

"Who knows?" was the reply.

No one answered, and the Doctor did not dare to guess his meaning; but Hatteras soon made them understand it, for presently he said, in a hurried, agitated manner, as if he could scarcely command himself:

"Friends, listen to me. We have done much already, but much yet remains to be done."

His companions heard him with profound astonishment.

"Yes," he resumed, "we are close to the Pole, but we are not on it."

"How do you make that out?" said Altamont.

"Yes," replied Hatteras, with vehemence, "I said an Englishman should plant his foot on the Pole of the world! I said it, and an Englishman shall."

"What!" cried Clawbonny.

"We are still 45″ from the unknown point," resumed Hatteras, with increasing animation, "and to that point I shall go."

"But it is on the summit of the volcano," said the Doctor.

"I shall go."

"It is an inaccessible cone!"

"I shall go."

"But it is a yawning fiery crater!"

"I shall go."

The tone of absolute determination in which Hatteras pronounced these words it is impossible to describe.

His friends were stupefied, and gazed in terror at the blazing mountain.

At last the Doctor recovered himself, and began to urge and entreat Hatteras to renounce his project. He tried every means his heart dictated, from humble supplications to friendly threats; but he could gain nothing —a sort of frenzy had come over the captain, an absolute monomania about the Pole.

Nothing but violent measures would keep him back from destruction, but the Doctor was unwilling to employ these unless driven to extremity.

He trusted, moreover, that physical impossibilities, insuperable obstacles, would bar his further progress, and meantime, finding all protestations were useless, he simply said:

"Very well, since you are bent on it, we'll go too."

"Yes," replied Hatteras, "half-way up the mountain, but not a step beyond. You know you have to carry back to England the duplicate of the document in the cairn————"

"Yes; but————"

"It is settled," said Hatteras, in an imperious tone; "and since the prayers of a friend will not suffice, the captain commands."

The Doctor did not insist longer, and a few minutes after the little band set out, accompanied by Duk.

It was about eight o'clock when they commenced their difficult ascent; the sky was splendid, and the thermometer stood at 52°.

Hatteras and his dog went first, closely followed by the others.

"I am afraid," said Johnson to the Doctor.

"No, no, there's nothing to be afraid of; we are here."

This singular little island appeared to be of recent formation, and was evidently the product of successive volcanic eruptions. The rocks were all lying loose on the top of each other, and it was a marvel how they preserved their equilibrium. Strictly speaking, the mountain was only a heap of stones thrown down from a height, and the mass of rocks which composed the island had evidently come out of the bowels of the earth.

The earth, indeed, may be compared to a vast cauldron of spherical form, in which, under the influence of a central fire, immense quantities of vapors are generated, which would explode the globe but for the safety-valves outside.

These safety-valves are volcanoes; when one closes another opens; and at the Poles, where the crust of the earth is thinner, owing to its being flattened, it is not surprising that a volcano should be suddenly formed by the upheaving of some part of the ocean-bed.

The Doctor, while following Hatteras, was closely following all the peculiarities of the island, and he was further confirmed in his opinion as to its recent formation by the absence of water. Had it existed for centuries, the thermal springs would have flowed from its bosom.

As they got higher, the ascent became more and more difficult, for the flanks of the mountain were almost perpendicular, and it required the utmost care to keep them from falling. Clouds of scoriae and ashes would whirl round them repeatedly, threatening them with asphyxia, or torrents of lava would bar their passage. In parts where these torrents ran horizontally, the outside had become hardened; while underneath was the boiling lava, and every step the travelers took had first to be tested with the iron-tipped staff to avoid being suddenly plunged into the scalding liquid.

At intervals large fragments of red-hot rock were thrown up from the crater, and burst in the air like bomb-shells, scattering the *débris* to enormous distances in all directions.

Hatteras, however, climbed up the steepest ascents with surprising agility, disdaining the help of his staff.

He arrived before long at a circular rock, a sort of plateau about ten feet wide. A river of boiling lava surrounded it except in one part, where it forked away to a higher rock, leaving a narrow passage, through which Hatteras fearlessly passed.

Here he stopped, and his companions managed to rejoin him. He seemed to be measuring with his eye the distance he had yet to get over. Horizontally, he was not more than two hundred yards from the top of the crater, but vertically he had nearly three times that distance to traverse.

The ascent had occupied three hours already. Hatteras showed no signs of fatigue, while the others were almost spent.

The summit of the volcano appeared inaccessible, and the Doctor determined at any price to prevent Hatteras from attempting to proceed. He tried gentle means first, but the captain's excitement was fast becoming delirium. During their ascent, symptoms of insanity had become more and more marked, and no one could be surprised who knew anything of his previous history.

"Hatteras," said the Doctor, "it is enough; we cannot go farther!"

"Stop, then," he replied, in a strangely altered voice; "I am going higher."

"No, it is useless; you are at the Pole already."

"No, no! higher, higher!"

"My friend, do you know who is speaking to you? It is I, Dr. Clawbonny."

"Higher, higher!" repeated the madman.

"Very well, we shall not allow it—that is all."

He had hardly uttered the words before Hatteras, by a superhuman effort, sprang over the boiling lava, and was beyond the reach of his companions.

A cry of horror burst from every lip, for they thought the poor captain must have perished in that fiery gulf; but there he was safe on the other side, accompanied by his faithful Duk, who would not leave him.

He speedily disappeared behind a curtain of smoke, and they heard his voice growing fainter in the distance, shouting:

"To the north! to the north! to the top of Mount Hatteras! Remember Mount Hatteras!"

All pursuit of him was out of the question; it was impossible to leap across the fiery torrent, and equally impossible to get round it. Altamont, indeed, was mad enough to make an attempt, and would certainly have lost his life if the others had not held him back by main force.

"Hatteras! Hatteras!" shouted the Doctor, but no response was heard save the faint bark of Duk.

At intervals, however, a glimpse of him could be caught through the clouds of smoke and showers of ashes. Sometimes his head, sometimes his arm appeared; then he was out of sight again, and a few minutes later was seen higher up clinging to the rocks. His size constantly decreased with the fantastic rapidity of objects rising upwards in the air. In half an hour he was only half his size.

The air was full of the deep rumbling noise of the volcano, and the mountain shook and trembled. From time to time a loud fall was heard behind, and the travelers would see some enormous rock rebounding from the heights to engulf itself in the polar basin below.

Hatteras did not even turn once to look back, but marched straight on, carrying his country's flag attached to his staff. His terrified friends watched every movement, and saw him gradually decrease to microscopic dimensions, while Duk looked no larger than a big rat.

Then came a moment of intense anxiety, for the wind beat down on them an immense sheet of flame, and they could see nothing but the red glare. A cry of agony escaped the Doctor; but an instant afterwards Hatteras reappeared, waving his flag.

For a whole hour this fearful spectacle went on—an hour of battle with unsteady loose rocks and quagmires of ashes, where the foolhardy climber sank up to his waist. Sometimes they saw him hoist himself up by leaning knees and loins against the rocks in narrow, intricate winding paths, and sometimes he would be hanging on by both hands to some sharp crag, swinging to and fro like a withered tuft.

At last he reached the summit of the mountain, the mouth of the crater. Here the Doctor hoped the infatuated man would stop, at any rate, and would, perhaps, recover his senses, and expose himself to no more danger than the descent involved.

Once more he shouted: "Hatteras! Hatteras!"

There was such a pathos of entreaty in his tone that Altamont felt moved to his inmost soul.

"I'll save him yet!" he exclaimed; and before Clawbonny could hinder him, he had cleared with a bound the torrent of fire, and was out of sight among the rocks.

Meantime, Hatteras had mounted a rock which overhung the crater, and stood waving his flag amidst showers of stones which rained down

21

on him. Duk was by his side; but the poor beast was growing dizzy in such close proximity to the abyss.

Hatteras balanced his staff with one hand, and with the other sought to find the precise mathematical point where all the meridians of the globe meet, the point on which it was his sublime purpose to plant his foot.

All at once the rock gave way, and he disappeared. A cry of horror broke from his companions, and rang to the top of the mountain. Clawbonny thought his friend had perished, and lay buried for ever in the depths of the volcano. A second—only a second, though it seemed an age—elapsed, and there was Altamont and the dog holding the ill-fated Hatteras! Man and dog had caught him at the very moment when he disappeared in the abyss.

Hatteras was saved! Saved in spite of himself; and half-an-hour later he lay unconscious in the arms of his despairing companions.

When he came to himself, the Doctor looked at him in speechless anguish, for there was no glance of recognition in his eye. It was the eye of a blind man, who gazes without seeing.

"Good heavens!" exclaimed Johnson, "he is blind!"

"No!" replied Clawbonny, "no! My poor friends, we have only saved the body of Hatteras; his soul is left behind on the top of the volcano. His reason is gone!"

"Insane!" exclaimed Johnson and Altamont, in consternation.

"Insane!" replied the Doctor, and the big tears ran down his cheeks.

James De Mille
THE FINDING OF THE
COPPER CYLINDER

"In the whole of Canadian literature, there is nothing comparable to this remarkable novel, which successfully combines the features of a satirical anti-utopian commentary on contemporary life with a swiftly paced narrative of travel, romance, and fantastic adventure." So wrote the critic, R. E. Watters, in his introduction to the New Canadian Library (1969) reprint of A Strange Manuscript Found in a Copper Cylinder *(1888). The author of this unusual novel was James De Mille (1837- 1880), a professor of English at Dalhousie University. The work was serialized posthumously by* Harper's Weekly *between January 7 and May 12, 1888, and then published in book form. The hero is a sailor named Adam More who, at the South Pole, enters into a world inside this one, where he encounters the strange Kosekins with their inverted value system. He records his experiences in a manuscript which he preserves in a copper cylinder. Rather than reprint one of the later chapters of the book, with its complicated descriptions, I have reproduced the opening chapter of the novel which lays a credible groundwork for the incredible adventures that follow.*

It occurred as far back as February 15, 1850. It happened on that day that the yacht *Falcon* lay becalmed upon the ocean between the Canaries and the Madeira Islands. This yacht *Falcon* was the property of Lord Featherstone, who, being weary of life in England, had taken a few congenial friends for a winter's cruise in these southern latitudes. They had visited the Azores, the Canaries, and the Madeira Islands, and were now on their way to the Mediterranean.

The wind had failed, a deep calm had succeeded, and everywhere, as far as the eye could reach, the water was smooth and glassy. The yacht rose and fell at the impulse of the long ocean undulations, and the creaking of the spars sounded out a lazy accompaniment to the motion of the vessel. All around was a watery horizon, except in one place only, towards the south, where far in the distance the Peak of Teneriffe rose into the air.

The profound calm, the warm atmosphere, the slow pitching of the yacht, and the dull creaking of the spars all combined to lull into a state of indolent repose the people on board. Forward were the crew; some asleep, others smoking, others playing cards. At the stern were Oxenden, the intimate friend of Featherstone, and Dr. Congreve, who had come in the double capacity of friend and medical attendant. These two, like the crew, were in a state of dull and languid repose. Suspended between the two masts, in an Indian hammock, lay Featherstone, with a cigar in his mouth and a novel in his hand, which he was pretending to read. The fourth member of the party, Melick, was seated near the mainmast, folding some papers in a peculiar way. His occupation at length attracted the roving eyes of Featherstone, who poked forth his head from his hammock, and said, in a sleepy voice:

"I say, Melick, you're the most energetic fellah I ever saw. By Jove! you're the only one aboard that's busy. What are you doing?"

"Paper boats," said Melick, in a business-like tone.

"Paper boats! By Jove!" said Featherstone. "What for?"

"I'm going to have a regatta," said Melick. "Anything to kill time, you know."

"By Jove!" exclaimed Featherstone again, raising himself higher in his hammock, "that's not a bad idea. A wegatta! By Jove! glowious! glowious! I say, Oxenden, did you hear that?"

"What do you mean by a regatta?" asked Oxenden, lazily.

"Oh, I mean a race with these paper boats. We can bet on them, you know."

At this Featherstone sat upright, with his legs dangling out of the hammock.

"By Jove!" he exclaimed again. "Betting! So we can. Do you know, Melick, old chap, I think that's a wegular piece of inspiration. A wegatta! and we can bet on the best boat."

"But there isn't any wind," said Oxenden.

"Well, you know, that's the fun of it," said Melick, who went solemnly on as he spoke, folding his paper boats; "that's the fun of it. For you see if there was a wind we should be going on ourselves, and the regatta couldn't come off; but, as it is, the water is just right. You pick out your boat, and lay your bet on her to race to some given point."

"A given point? But how can we find any?"

"Oh, easily enough; something or anything—a bubble 'll do, or we can pitch out a bit of wood."

Upon this Featherstone descended from his perch, and came near to examine the proceedings, while the other two, eager to take advantage of the new excitement, soon joined him. By this time Melick had finished his paper boats. There were four of them, and they were made of different colors, namely, red, green, yellow, and white.

"I'll put these in the water," said Melick, "and then we can lay our bets on them as we choose. But first let us see if there is anything that can be taken as a point of arrival. If there isn't anything, I can pitch out a bit of wood in any direction which may seem best."

Saying this, he went to the side, followed by the others, and all looked out carefully over the water.

"There's a black speck out there," said Oxenden.

"So there is," said Featherstone. "That'll do. I wonder what it is?"

"Oh, a bit of timber," said Melick. "Probably the spar of some ship."

"It don't look like a spar," said the doctor; "it's only a round spot, like the float of some net."

"Oh, it's a spar," said Melick. "It's one end of it, the rest is under water."

The spot thus chosen was a dark, circular object, about a hundred yards away, and certainly did look very much like the extremity of some spar, the rest of which was under water. Whatever it was, however, it served well enough for their present purpose, and no one took any further interest in it, except as the point towards which the paper boats should run in their eventful race.

Melick now let himself down over the side, and placed the paper boats on the water as carefully as possible. After this the four stood watching the little fleet in silence. The water was perfectly still, and there was no perceptible wind, but there were draughts of air caused by the rise and fall of the yacht, and these affected the tiny boats. Gradually they drew apart, the green one drifting astern, the yellow one remaining under the vessel, while the red and the white were carried out in the direction where they were expectd to go, with about a foot of space between them.

"Two to one on the red!" cried Featherstone, betting on the one which had gained the lead.

"Done," said Melick, promptly taking his offer.

Oxenden made the same bet, which was taken by Melick and the doctor.

Other bets were now made as to the direction which they would take, as to the distance by which the red would beat the white, as to the time which would be occupied by the race, and as to fifty other things which need not be mentioned. All took part in this; the excitement rose high and the betting went on merrily. At length it was noticed that the white was overhauling the red. The excitement grew intense; the betting changed its form, but was still kept up, until at last the two paper boats seemed blended together in one dim spot which gradually faded out of sight.

It was now necessary to determine the state of the race, so Featherstone ordered out the boat. The four were soon embarked, and the men rowed out towards the point which had been chosen as the end of the race. On coming near they found the paper boats stuck together, saturated with water, and floating limp on the surface. An animated discussion arose about this. Some of the bets were off, but others remained an open question, and each side insisted upon a different view of the case. In the midst of this Featherstone's attention was drawn to the dark spot already mentioned as the goal of the race.

"That's a queer-looking thing," said he, suddenly. "Pull up, lads, a little; let's see what it is. It doesn't look to me like a spar."

The others, always on the lookout for some new object of interest, were attracted by these words, and looked closely at the thing in question. The men pulled. The boat drew nearer.

"It's some sort of floating vessel," said Oxenden.

"It's not a spar," said Melick, who was at the bow.

And as he said this he reached out and grasped at it. He failed to get it, and did no more than touch it. It moved easily and sank, but soon came up again. A second time he grasped at it, and with both hands. This time he caught it, and then lifted it out of the water into the boat. These proceedings had been watched with the deepest interest; and now, as this curious floating thing made its appearance among them, they all crowded around it in eager excitement.

"It looks like a can of preserved meat," said the doctor.

"It certainly is a can," said Melick, "for it's made of metal; but as to preserved meat, I have my doubts."

The article in question was made of metal, and was cylindrical in shape. It was soldered tight, and evidently contained something. It was about eighteen inches long and eight wide. The nature of the metal was not easily perceptible, for it was coated with slime, and covered over about half its surface with barnacles and sea-weed. It was not heavy, and would have floated higher out of the water had it not been for these encumbrances.

"It's some kind of preserved meat," said the doctor. "Perhaps something good—game, I dare say—yes, Yorkshire game-pie. They pot all sorts of things now."

"If it's game," said Oxenden, "it'll be rather high by this time. Man alive! look at those weeds and shells. It must have been floating for ages."

"It's my belief," said Featherstone, "that it's part of the provisions laid

26

in by Noah for his long voyage in the ark. So come, let's open it, and see what sort of diet the antediluvians had."

"It may be liquor," said Oxenden.

Melick shook his head.

"No," said he; "there's something inside, but whatever it is, it isn't liquor. It's odd, too. The thing is of foreign make, evidently. I never saw anything like it before. It may be Chinese."

"By Jove!" cried Featherstone, "this is getting exciting. Let's go back to the yacht and open it."

The men rowed back to the yacht.

"It's meat of some sort," continued the doctor. "I'm certain of that. It has come in good time. We can have it for dinner."

"You may have my share, then," said Oxenden. "I hereby give and bequeath to you all my right, title, and interest in and to anything in the shape of meat that may be inside."

"Meat cans," said Melick, "are never so large as that."

"Oh, I don't know about that," said the doctor. "They make up pretty large packages of pemmican for the arctic expeditions."

"But they never pack up pemmican in copper cylinders," said Melick, who had been using his knife to scrape off the crust from the vessel.

"Copper!" exclaimed Oxenden. "Is it copper?"

"Look for yourselves," said Melick, quietly.

They all looked, and could see, where the knife had cut into the vessel, that it was as he said. It was copper.

"It's foreign work," said Melick. "In England we make tin cans for everything. It may be something that's drifted out from Mogadore or some port in Morocco."

"In that case," said Oxenden, "it may contain the mangled remains of one of the wives of some Moorish pasha."

By this time they had reached the yacht and hurried aboard. All were eager to satisfy their curiosity. Search was made for a cold-chisel, but to no purpose. Then Featherstone produced a knife which was used to open sardine boxes; but after a faithful trial this proved useless. At length Melick, who had gone off in search of something more effective, made his appearance, armed with an axe. With this he attacked the copper cylinder, and by means of a few dexterous blows succeeded in cutting it open. Then he looked in.

"What do you see?" asked Featherstone.

"Something," said Melick, "but I can't quite make it out."

"If you can't make it out, then shake it out," said Oxenden.

Upon this Melick took the cylinder, turned it upside down, shook it smartly, and then lifted it and pounded it against the deck. This served

27

to loosen the contents, which seemed tightly packed, but came gradually down until at length they could be seen and drawn forth. Melick drew them forth, and the contents of the mysterious copper cylinder resolved themselves into two packages.

The sight of these packages only served to intensify their curiosity. If it had been some species of food it would at once have revealed itself, but these packages suggested something more important. What could they be? Were there treasures inside—jewels, or golden ornaments from some Moorish seraglio, or strange coin from far Cathay?

One of the packages was very much larger than the other. It was enclosed in wrappers made of some coarse kind of felt, bound tight with strong cords. The other was much smaller, and was folded in the same material without being bound. This Melick seized and began to open.

"Wait a minute," said Featherstone. "Let's make a bet on it. Five guineas that it's some sort of jewels!"

"Done," said Oxenden.

Melick opened the package, and it was seen that Featherstone had lost. There were no jewels, but one or two sheets of something that looked like paper. It was not paper, however, but some vegetable product which was used for the same purpose. The surface was smooth, but the color was dingy, and the lines of the vegetable fibres were plainly discernible. These sheets were covered with writing.

"Halloa!" cried Melick. "Why, this is English!"

At this the others crowded around to look on, and Featherstone in his excitement forgot that he had lost his bet. There were three sheets, all covered with writing—one in English, another in French, and a third in German. It was the same message, written in these three different languages. But at that moment they scarcely noticed this. All that they saw was the message itself, with its mysterious meaning.

It was as follows:

"To the finder of this:

"Sir,—I am an Englishman, and have been carried by a series of incredible events to a land from which escape is as impossible as from the grave. I have written this and committed it to the sea, in the hope that the ocean currents may bear it within the reach of civilized man. Oh, unknown friend! whoever you are, I entreat you to let this message be made known in some way to my father, Henry More, Keswick, Cumberland, England, so that he may learn the fate of his son. The MS. accompanying this contains an account of my adventures, which I should like to have forwarded to him. Do this for the sake of that mercy which you may one day wish to have shown to yourself.

"Adam More."

"By Jove!" cried Featherstone, as he read the above, "this is really getting to be something tremendous."

"This other package must be the manuscript," said Oxenden, "and it'll tell all about it."

"Such a manuscript 'll be better than meat," said the doctor, sententiously.

Melick said nothing, but, opening his knife, he cut the cords and unfolded the wrapper. He saw a great collection of leaves, just like those of the letter, of some vegetable substance, smooth as paper, and covered with writing.

"It looks like Egyptian papyrus," said the doctor. "That was the common paper of antiquity."

"Never mind the Egyptian papyrus," said Featherstone, in feverish curiosity. "Let's have the contents of the manuscript. You, Melick, read; you're the most energetic of the lot, and when you're tired the rest of us will take turns."

"Read? Why, it'll take a month to read all this," said Melick.

"All the better," said Featherstone; "this calm will probably last a month, and we shall have nothing to interest us."

Melick made no further objection. He was as excited as the rest, and so he began the reading of the manuscript.

Here Featherstone stopped, yawned, and laid down the manuscript.

"That's enough for to-day," said he; "I'm tired and can't read any more. It's time for supper."

Grant Allen
THE CHILD OF THE PHALANSTERY

So well known in his day was Grant Allen (1848-1899), the author of this story, that H. G. Wells was able to mention him by name in The Time Machine *(1895) and assume readers would catch the reference. His Canadian connection is limited to two considerations. He was born on Wolfe Island, near Kingston, Upper Canada, and lived there for the first thirteen years of his life, leaving with his family for the United States, then France, and finally England. Allen published more than seventy books for a vast Anglo-American reading public. His many journalistic articles and books make use of the insights of the outsider. None of his work is set in Canada. His best-known novel,* The British Barbarians *(1895), is about a time traveller from the twenty-fifth century who visits an English town in Surrey at the turn of the century in order to dissect the social taboos of the day. As Gordon Roper noted in* Literary History of Canada *(second edition, 1976), "It is understandable that Grant Allen, concerned primarily with the discovery and propagation of new truths, found little or nothing in his Canadian past of use in his writings." One of Allen's most gripping science-fiction stories is "The Thames Valley Catastrophe," which Sam Moskowitz reprinted in* Science Fiction by Gaslight *(1968). I have chosen to reprint a lesser-known story, "The Child of the Phalanstery," which originally appeared in* Belgravia *magazine in 1881, from Allen's* Strange Stories *(1884), where he described it as an attempt to present "the moral considerations of a community brought up under a social and ethical environment utterly different from that by which we ourselves are now surrounded."*

Poor little thing," said my strong-minded friend compassionately. "Just look at her! Clubfooted. What a misery to herself and others! In a well-organised state of society, you know, such poor wee cripples as that would be quietly put out of their misery while they were still babies."

"Let me think," said I, "how that would work out in actual practice. I'm not so sure, after all, that we should be altogether the better or the happier for it."

I

They sat together in a corner of the beautiful phalanstery garden, Olive and Clarence, on the marble seat that overhung the mossy dell where the streamlet danced and bickered among its pebbly stickles; they sat there, hand in hand, in lovers' guise, and felt their two bosoms beating and thrilling in some strange, sweet fashion, just like two foolish unregenerate young people of the old antisocial prephalansteric days. Perhaps it was the leaven of their unenlightened ancestors still leavening by heredity the whole lump; perhaps it was the inspiration of the calm soft August evening and the delicate afterglow of the setting sun; perhaps it was the deep heart of man and woman vibrating still as of yore in human sympathy, and stirred to its innermost recesses by the unutterable breath of human emotion. But at any rate there they sat, the beautiful strong man in his shapely chiton, and the dainty fair girl in her long white robe with the dark green embroidered border, looking far into the fathomless depths of one another's eyes, in silence sweeter and more eloquent than many words. It was Olive's tenth day holiday from her share in the maidens' household duty of the community; and Clarence, by arrangement with his friend Germain, had made exchange from his own decade (which fell on Plato) to this quiet Milton evening, that he might wander through the park and gardens with his chosen love, and speak his full mind to her now without reserve.

"If only the phalanstery will give its consent, Clarence," Olive said at last with a little sigh, releasing her hand from his, and gathering up the folds of her stole from the marble flooring of the seat;—"if only the phalanstery will give its consent! but I have my doubts about it. Is it quite right? Have we chosen quite wisely? Will the hierarch and the elder brothers think I am strong enough and fit enough for the duties of the task? It is no light matter, we know, to enter into bonds with one another for the responsibilities of fatherhood and motherhood. I sometimes feel—forgive me, Clarence—but I sometimes feel as if I were allowing my own heart and my own wishes to guide me too exclusively in this solemn question: thinking too much about you and me, about ourselves (which is only an enlarged form of selfishness, after all), and too little about the future good of the community and—and—" blushing a little, for women will be women even in a phalanstery—"and of the precious lives we may be the means of adding to it. You remember, Clarence, what the hierarch said, that we ought to think least and last of our own feelings, first and foremost of the progressive evolution of universal humanity."

"I remember, darling," Clarence answered, leaning over towards her tenderly; "I remember well, and in my own way, so far as a man can (for we men haven't the moral earnestness of you women, I'm afraid, Olive),

I try to act up to it. But, dearest, I think your fears are greater than they need be: you must recollect that humanity requires for its higher development tenderness, and truth, and love, and all the softer qualities, as well as strength and manliness; and if you are a trifle less strong than most of our sisters here, you seem to me at least (and I really believe to the hierarch and to the elder brothers too) to make up for it, and more than make up for it, in your sweet and lovable inner nature. The men of the future mustn't all be cast in one unvarying stereotyped mould; we must have a little of all good types combined, in order to make a perfect phalanstery."

Olive sighed again. "I don't know," she said pensively. "I don't feel sure. I hope I am doing right. In my aspirations every evening I have desired light on this matter, and have earnestly hoped that I was not being misled by my own feelings; for, oh, Clarence, I do love you so dearly, so truly, so absorbingly, that I half fear my love may be taking me unwittingly astray. I try to curb it; I try to think of it all as the hierarch tells us we ought to; but in my own heart I sometimes almost fear that I may be lapsing into the idolatrous love of the old days, when people married and were given in marriage, and thought only of the gratification of their own personal emotions and affections, and nothing of the ultimate good of humanity. Oh, Clarence, don't hate me and despise me for it; don't turn upon me and scold me; but I love you, I love you, I love you; oh, I'm afraid I love you almost idolatrously!"

Clarence lifted her small white hand slowly to his lips, with that natural air of chivalrous respect which came so easily to the young men of the phalanstery, and kissed it twice over fervidly with quiet reverence. "Let us go into the music-room, Olive dearest," he said as he rose; "you are too sad to-night. You shall play me that sweet piece of Marian's that you love so much; and that will quiet you, darling, from thinking too earnestly about this serious matter."

II

Next day, when Clarence had finished his daily spell of work in the fruit-garden (he was third under-gardener to the community), he went up to his own study, and wrote out a little notice in due form to be posted at dinner-time on the refectory door: 'Clarence and Olive ask leave of the phalanstery to enter with one another into free contract of holy matrimony.' His pen trembled a little in his hand as he framed that familiar set form of words (strange that he had read it so often with so little emotion, and wrote it now with so much: we men are so selfish!); but he fixed it boldly with four small brass nails on the regulation notice-board, and waited, not without a certain quiet confidence, for the final result of the communal council.

"Aha!" said the hierarch to himself with a kindly smile, as he passed into the refectory at dinner-time that day, "has it come to that, then? Well, well, I thought as much; I felt sure it would. A good girl, Olive: a true, earnest, lovable girl: and she has chosen wisely, too; for Clarence is the very man to balance her own character as man's and wife's should do. Whether Clarence has done well in selecting her is another matter. For my own part, I had rather hoped she would have joined the celibate sisters, and have taken nurse-duty for the sick and the children. It's her natural function in life, the work she's best fitted for; and I should have liked to see her take to it. But, after all, the business of the phalanstery is not to decide vicariously for its individual members—not to thwart their natural harmless inclinations and wishes; on the contrary, we ought to allow every man and girl the fullest liberty to follow their own personal taste and judgment in every possible matter. Our power of interference as a community, I've always felt and said, should only extend to the prevention of obviously wrong and immoral acts, such as marriage with a person in ill-health, or of inferior mental power, or with a distinctly bad or insubordinate temper. Things of that sort, of course, are as clearly wicked as idling in work-hours, or marriage with a first cousin. Olive's health, however, isn't really bad, nothing more than a very slight feebleness of constitution, as constitutions go with us; and Eustace, who has attended her medically from her babyhood (what a dear crowing little thing she used to be in the nursery, to be sure!), tells me she's perfectly fitted for the duties of her proposed situation. Ah well, ah well; I've no doubt they'll be perfectly happy; and the wishes of the whole phalanstery will go with them in any case, that's certain."

Everybody knew that whatever the hierarch said or thought was pretty sure to be approved by the unanimous voice of the entire community. Not that he was at all a dictatorial or dogmatic old man; quite the contrary; but his gentle kindly way had its full weight with the brothers; and his intimate acquaintance, through the exercise of his spiritual functions, with the inmost thoughts and ideas of every individual member, man or woman, made him a safe guide in all difficult or delicate questions, as to what the decision of the council ought to be. So when, on the first Cosmos, the elder brothers assembled to transact phalansteric business, and the hierarch put in Clarence's request with the simple phrase, "In my opinion, there is no reasonable objection," the community at once gave in its adhesion, and formal notice was posted an hour later on the refectory door, "The phalanstery approves the proposition of Clarence and Olive, and wishes all happiness to them and to humanity from the sacred union they now contemplate." "You see, dearest," Clarence said, kissing her lips for the first time (as unwritten law demanded), now that the seal of the community had been placed upon their choice, "you see, there can't be any harm in our contract, for the elder brothers all approve it."

Olive smiled and sighed from the very bottom of her full heart, and clung to her lover as the ivy clings to a strong supporting oak-tree. "Darling," she murmured in his ear, "if I have you to comfort me, I shall not be afraid, and we will try our best to work together for the advancement and the good of divine humanity."

Four decades later, on a bright Cosmos morning in September, those two stood up beside one another before the altar of humanity, and heard with a thrill the voice of the hierarch uttering that solemn declaration, "In the name of the Past, and of the Present, and of the Future, I hereby admit you, Clarence and Olive, into the holy society of Fathers and Mothers, of the United Avondale Phalanstery, in trust for humanity, whose stewards you are. May you so use and enhance the good gifts you have received from your ancestors that you may hand them on, untarnished and increased, to the bodies and minds of your furthest descendants." And Clarence and Olive answered humbly and reverently, "If grace be given us, we will."

III

Brother Eustace, physiologist to the phalanstery, looked very grave and sad indeed as he passed from the Mothers' Room into the Conversazione in search of the hierarch. "A child is born into the phalanstery," he said gloomily; but his face conveyed at once a far deeper and more pregnant meaning than his mere words could carry to the ear.

The hierarch rose hastily and glanced into his dark keen eyes with an inquiring look. "Not something amiss?" he said eagerly, with an infinite tenderness in his fatherly voice. "Don't tell me that, Eustace. Not . . . oh, not a child that the phalanstery must not for its own sake permit to live! Oh, Eustace, not, I hope, idiotic! And I gave my consent too; I gave my consent for pretty gentle little Olive's sake! Heaven grant I was not too much moved by her prettiness and her delicacy; for I love her, Eustace, I love her like a daughter."

"So we all love the children of the phalanstery, Cyriac, we who are elder brothers," said the physiologist gravely, half smiling to himself nevertheless at this quaint expression of old-world feeling on the part even of the very hierarch, whose bounden duty it was to advise and persuade a higher rule of conduct and thought than such antique phraseology implied. "No, not idiotic; not quite so bad as that, Cyriac; not absolutely a hopeless case, but still, very serious and distressing for all that. The dear little baby has its feet turned inward. She'll be a cripple for life, I fear, and no help for it."

Tears rose unchecked into the hierarch's soft grey eyes. "Its feet turned inward," he muttered sadly, half to himself. "Feet turned inward! Oh, how terrible! This will be a frightful blow to Clarence and to Olive. Poor young things! their first-born, too. Oh, Eustace, what an awful thought that, with all the care and precaution we take to keep all causes of misery away from the precincts of the phalanstery, such trials as this must needs come upon us by the blind workings of the unconscious Cosmos! It is terrible, too terrible!"

"And yet it isn't all loss," the physiologist answered earnestly. "It isn't all loss, Cyriac, heart-rending as the necessity seems to us. I sometimes think that if we hadn't these occasional distressful objects on which to extend our sympathy and our sorrow, we in our happy little communities might grow too smug, and comfortable, and material, and earthly. But things like this bring tears into our eyes, and we are the better for them in the end, depend upon it, we are the better for them. They try our fortitude, our devotion to principle, our obedience to the highest and the hardest law. Every time some poor little waif like this is born into our midst, we feel the strain of old prephalansteric emotions and fallacies of feeling dragging us steadily and cruelly down. Our first impulse is to pity the poor mother, to pity the poor child, and in our mistaken kindness to let an unhappy life go on indefinitely to its own misery and the preventible distress of all around it. We have to make an effort, a struggle, before the higher and more abstract pity conquers the lower and more concrete one. But in the end we are all the better for it: and each such struggle and each such victory, Cyriac, paves the way for that final and truest morality when we shall do right instinctively and naturally, without any impulse on any side to do wrong in any way at all."

"You speak wisely, Eustace," the hierarch answered with a sad shake of his head, "and I wish I could feel like you. I ought to, but I can't. Your functions make you able to look more dispassionately upon these things than I can. I'm afraid there's a great deal of the old Adam lingering wrongfully in me yet. And I'm still more afraid there's a great deal of the old Eve lingering even more strongly in all our mothers. It'll be a long time, I doubt me, before they'll ever consent without a struggle to the painless extinction of necessarily unhappy and imperfect lives. A long time: a very long time. Does Clarence know of this yet?"

"Yes, I have told him. His grief is terrible. You had better go and console him as best you can."

"I will, I will. And poor Olive! Poor Olive! It wrings my heart to think of her. Of course she won't be told of it, if you can help, for the probationary four decades?"

"No, not if we can help it: but I don't know how it can ever be kept from her. She *will* see Clarence, and Clarence will certainly tell her."

The hierarch whistled gently to himself. "It's a sad case," he said ruefully, "a very sad case; and yet I don't see how we can possibly prevent it."

He walked slowly and deliberately into the anteroom where Clarence was seated on a sofa, his head between his hands, rocking himself to and fro in his mute misery, or stopping to groan now and then in a faint feeble inarticulate fashion. Rhoda, one of the elder sisters, held the unconscious baby sleeping in her arms, and the hierarch took it from her like a man accustomed to infants, and looked ruefully at the poor distorted little feet. Yes, Eustace was evidently quite right. There could be no hope of ever putting those wee twisted ankles back straight and firm into their proper place again like other people's.

He sat down beside Clarence on the sofa, and with a commiserating gesture removed the young man's hands from his pale white face. "My dear, dear friend," he said softly, "what comfort or consolation can we try to give you that is not a cruel mockery? None, none, none. We can only sympathise with you and Olive: and perhaps, after all, the truest sympathy is silence."

Clarence answered nothing for a moment, but buried his face once more in his hands and burst into tears. The men of the phalanstery were less careful to conceal their emotions than we old-time folks in these early centuries. "Oh, dear hierarch," he said, after a long sob, "it is too hard a sacrifice, too hard, too terrible! I don't feel it for the baby's sake: for her 'tis better so: she will be freed from a life of misery and dependence; but for my own sake, and oh, above all, for dear Olive's! It will kill her, hierarch; I feel sure it will kill her!"

The elder brother passed his hand with a troubled gesture across his forehead. "But what else can we do, dear Clarence?" he asked pathetically. "What else can we do? Would you have us bring up the dear child to lead a lingering life of misfortune, to distress the eyes of all around her, to feel herself a useless incumbrance in the midst of so many mutually helpful and serviceable and happy people? How keenly she would realise her own isolation in the joyous, busy, labouring community of our phalansteries! How terribly she would brood over her own misfortune when surrounded by such a world of hearty, healthy, sound-limbed, useful persons! Would it not be a wicked and a cruel act to bring her up to an old age of unhappiness and imperfection? You have been in Australia, my boy, when we sent you on that plant-hunting expedition, and you

36

have seen cripples with your own eyes, no doubt, which I have never done—thank Heaven!—I who have never gone beyond the limits of the most highly civilised Euramerican countries. You have seen cripples, in those semi-civilised old colonial societies, which have lagged after us so slowly in the path of progress; and would you like your own daughter to grow up to such a life as that, Clarence? would you like her, I ask you, to grow up to such a life as that?"

Clarence clenched his right hand tightly over his left arm, and answered with a groan, "No, hierarch; not even for Olive's sake could I wish for such an act of irrational injustice. You have trained us up to know the good from the evil, and for no personal gratification of our deepest emotions, I hope and trust, shall we ever betray your teaching or depart from your principles. I know what it is: I saw just such a cripple once, at a great town in the heart of Central Australia—a child of eight years old, limping along lamely on her heels by her mother's side; a sickening sight: to think of it even now turns the blood in one's arteries; and I could never wish Olive's baby to live and grow up to be a thing like that. But, oh, I wish to heaven it might have been otherwise: I wish to heaven this trial might have been spared us both. Oh, hierarch, dear hierarch, the sacrifice is one that no good man or woman would wish selfishly to forgo; yet for all that, our hearts, our hearts are human still; and though we may reason and may act up to our reasoning, the human feeling in us—relic of the idolatrous days, or whatever you like to call it—it will not choose to be so put down and stifled: it will out, hierarch, it will out for all that, in real hot, human tears. Oh, dear, dear kind father and brother, it will kill Olive: I know it will kill her!"

"Olive is a good girl," the hierarch answered slowly. "A good girl, well brought up, and with sound principles. She will not flinch from doing her duty, I know, Clarence; but her emotional nature is a very delicate one, and we have reason indeed to fear the shock to her nervous system. That she will do right bravely, I don't doubt: the only danger is lest the effort to do right should cost her too dear. Whatever can be done to spare her shall be done, Clarence. It is a sad misfortune for the whole phalanstery, such a child being born to us as this: and we all sympathise with you: we sympathise with you more deeply than words can say."

The young man only rocked up and down drearily as before, and murmured to himself, "It will kill her, it will kill her! My Olive, my Olive, I know it will kill her."

They didn't keep the secret of the baby's crippled condition from Olive till the four decades were over, nor anything like it. The moment she saw Clarence, she guessed at once with a woman's instinct that something serious had happened; and she didn't rest till she had found out from him all about it. Rhoda brought her the poor wee mite, carefully wrapped, after the phalansteric fashion, in a long strip of fine flannel, and Olive unrolled the piece until she came at last upon the small crippled feet, that looked so soft and tender and dainty and waxen in their very deformity. The young mother leant over the child a moment in speechless misery. "Spirit of Humanity," she whispered at length feebly, "oh, give me strength to bear this terrible, unutterable trial! It will break my heart. But I will try to bear it."

There was something so touching in her attempted resignation that Rhoda, for the first time in her life, felt almost tempted to wish she had been born in the old wicked prephalansteric days, when they would have let the poor baby grow up to womanhood as a matter of course, and bear its own burden through life as best it might. Presently, Olive raised her head again from the crimson silken pillow. "Clarence," she said, in a trembling voice, pressing the sleeping baby hard against her breast, "when will it be? How long? Is there no hope, no chance of respite?"

"Not for a long time yet, dearest Olive," Clarence answered through his tears. "The phalanstery will be very gentle and patient with us, we know; and brother Eustace will do everything that lies in his power, though he's afraid he can give us very little hope indeed. In any case, Olive darling, the community waits for four decades before deciding anything: it waits to see whether there is any chance for physiological or surgical relief: it decides nothing hastily or thoughtlessly: it waits for every possible improvement, hoping against hope till hope itself is hopeless. And then, if at the end of the quartet, as I fear will be the case—for we must face the worst, darling, we must face the worst—if at the end of the quartet it seems clear to brother Eustace, and the three assessor physiologists from the neighbouring phalansteries, that the dear child would be a cripple for life, we're still allowed four decades more to prepare ourselves in: four whole decades more, Olive, to take our leave of the darling baby. You'll have your baby with you for eighty days. And we must wean ourselves from her in that time, darling. We must try to wean ourselves. But oh Olive, oh Rhoda, it's very hard: very, very, very hard."

Olive answered not a word, but lay silently weeping and pressing the baby against her breast, with her large brown eyes fixed vacantly upon the fretted woodwork of the panelled ceiling.

"You mustn't do like that, Olive dear," sister Rhoda said in a half-frightened voice. "You must cry right out, and sob, and not restrain yourself, darling, or else you'll break your heart with silence and repression. Do cry aloud, there's a dear girl: do cry aloud and relieve yourself. A good cry would be the best thing on earth for you. And think, dear, how much happier it will really be for the sweet baby to sing asleep so peacefully than to live a long life of conscious inferiority and felt imperfection! What a blessing it is to think you were born in a phalansteric land, where the dear child will be happily and painlessly rid of its poor little unconscious existence, before it has reached the age when it might begin to know its own incurable and inevitable misfortune! Oh, Olive, what a blessing that is, and how thankful we ought all to be that we live in a world where the sweet pet will be saved so much humiliation, and mortification, and misery!"

At that moment, Olive, looking within into her own wicked, rebellious heart, was conscious, with a mingled glow, half shame, half indignation, that so far from appreciating the priceless blessings of her own situation, she would gladly have changed places then and there with any barbaric woman of the old semi-civilised prephalansteric days. We can so little appreciate our own mercies. It was very wrong and anti-cosmic, she knew; very wrong indeed, and the hierarch would have told her so at once; but in her own woman's soul she felt she would rather be a miserable naked savage in a wattled hut, like those one saw in old books about Africa before the illumination, if only she could keep that one little angel of a crippled baby, than dwell among all the enlightenment, and knowledge, and art, and perfected social arrangements of phalansteric England without her child—her dear, helpless, beautiful baby. How truly the Founder had said, "Think you there will be no more tragedies and dramas in the world when we have reformed it, nothing but one dreary dead level of monotonous content? Ay, indeed, there will; for that, fear not; while the heart of man remains, there will be tragedy enough on earth and to spare for a hundred poets to take for their saddest epics."

Olive looked up at Rhoda wistfully. "Sister Rhoda," she said in a timid tone, "it may be very wicked—I feel sure it is—but do you know, I've read somewhere in old stories of the unenlightened days that a mother always loved the most afflicted of her children the best. And I can understand it now, sister Rhoda; I can feel it here," and she put her hand upon her poor still heart. "If only I could keep this one dear crippled baby, I could give up all the world beside—except you, Clarence."

"Oh, hush, darling!" Rhoda cried in an awed voice, stooping down half alarmed to kiss her pale forehead. "You mustn't talk like that, Olive dearest. It's wicked; it's undutiful. I know how hard it is not to repine and to rebel; but you mustn't, Olive, you mustn't. We must each strive to bear our own burdens (with the help of the community), and not to put any of them off upon a poor, helpless, crippled little baby."

"But our natures," Clarence said, wiping his eyes dreamily; "our natures are only half attuned as yet to the necessities of the higher social existence. Of course it's very wrong and very sad, but we can't help feeling it, sister Rhoda, though we try our hardest. Remember, it's not so many generations since our fathers would have reared the child without a thought that they were doing anything wicked—nay, rather, would even have held (so powerful is custom) that it was positively wrong to save it by preventive means from a certain life of predestined misery. Our conscience in this matter isn't yet fully formed. We feel that it's right, of course; oh yes, we know the phalanstery has ordered everything for the best; but we can't help grieving over it; the human heart within us is too unregenerate still to acquiesce without a struggle in the dictates of right and reason."

Olive again said nothing, but fixed her eyes silently upon the grave, earnest portrait of the Founder over the carved oak mantelpiece, and let the hot tears stream their own way over her cold, white, pallid, bloodless cheek without reproof for many minutes. Her heart was too full for either speech or comfort.

V

Eight decades passed away slowly in the Avondale Phalanstery; and day after day seemed more and more terrible to poor, weak, disconsolate Olive. The quiet refinement and delicate surroundings of their placid life seemed to make her poignant misery and long anxious term of waiting only the more intense in its sorrow and its awesomeness. Every day the younger sisters turned as of old to their allotted round of pleasant house-work; every day the elder sisters, who had earned their leisure, brought in their dainty embroidery, or their drawing materials, or their other occupations, and tried to console her, or rather to condole with her, in her great sorrow. She couldn't complain of any unkindness; on the contrary, all the brothers and sisters were sympathy itself; while Clarence, though he tried hard not to be *too* idolatrous to her (which is wrong and antisocial, of course), was still overflowing with tenderness and considera-tion for her in their common grief. But all that seemed merely to make things worse. If only somebody would have been cruel to her; if only the hierarch would have scolded her, or the elder sisters have shown any distant coldness, or the other girls have been wanting in sisterly sympathy, she might have got angry or brooded over her wrongs; whereas, now, she could do nothing save cry passively with a vain attempt at resignation. It was nobody's fault; there was nobody to be angry with, there was nothing to blame except the great impersonal laws and circumstances of the Cosmos, which it would be rank impiety and wickedness to question or to gainsay. So she endured in silence, loving only to sit with Clarence's hand in hers, and the dear doomed baby lying peacefully upon the stole

40

in her lap. It was inevitable, and there was no use repining; for so profoundly had the phalanstery schooled the minds and natures of those two unhappy young parents (and all their compeers), that grieve as they might, they never for one moment dreamt of attempting to relax or set aside the fundamental principles of phalansteric society in these matters.

By the kindly rule of the phalanstery, every mother had complete freedom from household duties for two years after the birth of her child; and Clarence, though he would not willingly have given up his own particular work in the grounds and garden, spent all the time he could spare from his short daily task (every one worked five hours every lawful day, and few worked longer, save on special emergencies) by Olive's side. At last, the eight decades passed slowly away, and the fatal day for the removal of little Rosebud arrived. Olive called her Rosebud because, she said, she was a sweet bud that could never be opened into a full-blown rose. All the community felt the solemnity of the painful occasion; and by common consent the day (Darwin, December 20) was held as an intra-phalansteric fast by the whole body of brothers and sisters.

On that terrible morning Olive rose early, and dressed herself carefully in a long white stole with a broad black border of Greek key pattern. But she had not the heart to put any black upon dear little Rosebud; and so she put on her fine flannel wrapper, and decorated it instead with the pretty coloured things that Veronica and Philomela had worked for her, to make her baby as beautiful as possible on this its last day in a world of happiness. The other girls helped her and tried to sustain her, crying all together at the sad event. "She's a sweet little thing," they said to one another as they held her up to see how she looked. "If only it could have been her reception to-day instead of her removal!" But Olive moved through them all with stoical resignation—dry-eyed and parched in the throat, yet saying not a word save for necessary instructions and directions to the nursing sisters. The iron of her creed had entered into her very soul.

After breakfast, brother Eustace and the hierarch came sadly in their official robes into the lesser infirmary. Olive was there already, pale and trembling, with little Rosebud sleeping peacefully in the hollow of her lap. What a picture she looked, the wee dear thing, with the hothouse flowers from the conservatory that Clarence had brought to adorn her fastened neatly on to her fine flannel robe! The physiologist took out a little phial from his pocket, and began to open a sort of inhaler of white muslin. At the same moment, the grave, kind old hierarch stretched out his hands to take the sleeping baby from its mother's arms. Olive shrank back in terror, and clasped the child softly to her heart. "No, no, let me hold her myself, dear hierarch," she said, without flinching. "Grant me

41

this one last favour. Let me hold her myself." It was contrary to all fixed rules; but neither the hierarch nor any one else there present had the heart to refuse that beseeching voice on so supreme and spirit-rending an occasion.

Brother Eustace poured the chloroform solemnly and quietly on to the muslin inhaler. "By resolution of the phalanstery," he said, in a voice husky with emotion, "I release you, Rosebud, from a life for which you are naturally unfitted. In pity for your hard fate, we save you from the misfortune you have never known, and will never now experience." As he spoke he held the inhaler to the baby's face, and watched its breathing grow fainter and fainter, till at last, after a few minutes, it faded gradually and entirely away. The little one had slept from life into death, painlessly and happily, even as they looked.

Clarence, tearful but silent, felt the baby's pulse for a moment, and then, with a burst of tears, shook his head bitterly. "It is all over," he cried with a loud cry. "It is all over; and we hope and trust it is better so."

But Olive still said nothing.

The physiologist turned to her with an anxious gaze. Her eyes were open, but they looked blank and staring into vacant space. He took her hand, and it felt limp and powerless. "Great heaven!" he cried, in evident alarm, "what is this? Olive, Olive, our dear Olive, why don't you speak?"

Clarence sprang up from the ground, where he had knelt to try the dead baby's pulse, and took her unresisting wrist anxiously in his. "Oh, brother Eustace," he cried passionately, "help us, save us; what's the matter with Olive? she's fainting, she's fainting! I can't feel her heart beat, no, not ever so little."

Brother Eustace let the pale white hand drop listlessly from his grasp upon the pale white stole beneath, and answered slowly and distinctly: "She isn't fainting, Clarence; not fainting, my dear brother. The shock and the fumes of chloroform together have been too much for the action of the heart. She's dead too, Clarence; our dear, dear sister; she's dead too."

Clarence flung his arms wildly round Olive's neck, and listened eagerly with his ear against her bosom to hear her heart beat. But no sound came from the folds of the simple black-bordered stole; no sound from anywhere save the suppressed sobs of the frightened women who huddled closely together in the corner, and gazed horror-stricken upon the two warm fresh corpses.

"She was a brave girl," brother Eustace said at last, wiping his eyes and composing her hands reverently. "Olive was a brave girl, and she died doing her duty, without one murmur against the sad necessity that fate had unhappily placed upon her. No sister on earth could wish to die more nobly than by thus sacrificing her own life and her own weak human affections on the altar of humanity for the sake of her child and of the world at large."

"And yet, I sometimes almost fancy," the hierarch murmured, with a violent effort to control his emotions, "when I see a scene like this, that even the unenlightened practices of the old era may not have been quite so bad as we usually think them, for all that. Surely an end such as Olive's is a sad and a terrible end to have forced upon us as the final outcome and natural close of all our modern phalansteric civilisation."

"The ways of the Cosmos are wonderful," said brother Eustace solemnly; "and we, who are no more than atoms and mites upon the surface of its meanest satellite, cannot hope so to order all things after our own fashion that all its minutest turns and chances may approve themselves to us as right in our own eyes."

The sisters all made instinctively the reverential genuflexion. "The Cosmos is infinite," they said together, in the fixed formula of their cherished religion. "The Cosmos is infinite, and man is but a parasite upon the face of the least among its satellite members. May we so act as to further all that is best within us, and to fulfil our own small place in the system of the Cosmos with all becoming reverence and humility! In the name of universal Humanity. So be it."

Robert Barr
THE FEAR OF IT

"An admirable specimen of the man of talent who makes of letters an honest trade" is Arnold Bennett's estimate of Robert Barr (1850-1912). Like Grant Allen, Robert Barr was a popular Anglo-American novelist and short-story writer. Born in Glasgow, Scotland, and brought to Upper Canada at the age of four, Barr grew up in Wallacetown and Windsor. He fought the Fenians, graduated from the Toronto Normal School, taught at the Windsor Central School, and sold humorous sketches under the pseudonym Luke Sharp to Grip and other publications. He joined the Detroit Free Press in 1876, and established its weekly edition in

London in 1881. With the humorist Jerome K. Jerome, he founded The
Idler, *a popular monthly, in 1892. Barr wrote some forty books and much
uncollected fiction and non-fiction, three of which should be noted:* In the
Midst of Alarms *(1894, 1973), about fighting the Fenians;* The Triumphs
of Eugène Valmont *(1906), about a French detective not unlike Hercule
Poirot of later fame; and* The Measure of the Rule *(1906, 1973), about
classes at the Toronto Normal School. "One of the great Canadian
humorists" is how John Parr describes him in* Selected Stories of Robert
Barr *(1977). Sam Moskowitz reprinted "The Doom of London" in*
Science Fiction by Gaslight *(1968). "The Fear of It," which originally
appeared in* The Idler, May, 1893, *is reprinted from* The Face and the
Mask *(1895), a collection of twenty-four stories. Barr's story of the cast-
away who is washed up on the shores of a hitherto unknown island is an
ideal vehicle through which to depict social estrangement, first from the
new society in which he finds himself, then from the old society from
which he has come.*

T he sea was done with him. He had struggled manfully for his life, but
exhaustion came at last, and, realizing the futility of further fighting, he
gave up the battle. The tallest wave, the king of that roaring tumultuous
procession racing from the wreck to the shore, took him in its relentless
grasp, held him towering for a moment against the sky, whirled his heels
in the air, dashed him senseless on the sand, and, finally, rolled him over
and over, a helpless bundle, high up upon the sandy beach.

Human life seems of little account when we think of the trifles that
make toward the extinction or the extension of it. If the wave that bore
Stanford had been a little less tall, he would have been drawn back into
the sea by one that followed. If, as a helpless bundle, he had been turned
over one time more or one less, his mouth would have pressed into the
sand, and he would have died. As it was, he lay on his back with arms
outstretched on either side, and a handful of dissolving sand in one
clinched fist. Succeeding waves sometimes touched him, but he lay there
unmolested by the sea with his white face turned to the sky.

Oblivion has no calendar. A moment or an eternity are the same to it.
When consciousness slowly returned, he neither knew nor cared how
time had fled. He was not quite sure that he was alive, but weakness
rather than fear kept him from opening his eyes to find out whether the
world they would look upon was the world they had last gazed at. His
interest, however, was speedily stimulated by the sound of the English
tongue. He was still too much dazed to wonder at it, and to remember

that he was cast away on some unknown island in the Southern Seas. But the purport of the words startled him.

"Let us be thankful. He is undoubtedly dead." This was said in a tone of infinite satisfaction.

There seemed to be a murmur of pleasure at the announcement from those who were with the speaker. Stanford slowly opened his eyes, wondering what these savages were who rejoiced in the death of an inoffensive stranger cast upon their shores. He saw a group standing around him, but his attention speedily became concentrated on one face. The owner of it, he judged, was not more than nineteen years of age, and the face—at least so it seemed to Stanford at the time—was the most beautiful he had ever beheld. There was an expression of sweet gladness upon it until her eyes met his, then the joy faded from the face, and a look of dismay took its place. The girl seemed to catch her breath in fear, and tears filled her eyes.

"Oh," she cried, "he is going to live."

She covered her face with her hands, and sobbed.

Stanford closed his eyes wearily. "I am evidently insane," he said to himself. Then, losing faith in the reality of things, he lost consciousness as well, and when his senses came to him again he found himself lying on a bed in a clean but scantily furnished room. Through an open window came the roar of the sea, and the thunderous boom of the falling waves brought to his mind the experiences through which he had passed. The wreck and the struggle with the waves he knew to be real, but the episode on the beach he now believed to have been but a vision resulting from his condition.

A door opened noiselessly, and, before he knew of anyone's entrance, a placid-faced nurse stood by his bed and asked him how he was.

"I don't know. I am at least alive."

The nurse sighed, and cast down her eyes. Her lips moved, but she said nothing. Stanford looked at her curiously. A fear crept over him that he was hopelessly crippled for life, and that death was considered preferable to a maimed existence. He felt wearied, though not in pain, but he knew that sometimes the more desperate the hurt, the less the victim feels it at first.

"Are—are any of my—my bones broken, do you know?" he asked.

"No. You are bruised, but not badly hurt. You will soon recover."

"Ah!" said Stanford, with a sigh of relief. "By the way," he added, with sudden interest, "who was that girl who stood near me as I lay on the beach?"

"There were several."

"No, there was but one. I mean the girl with the beautiful eyes and a halo of hair like a glorified golden crown on her head."

"We speak not of our women in words like those," said the nurse, severely; "you mean Ruth, perhaps, whose hair is plentiful and yellow."

Stanford smiled. "Words matter little," he said.

"We must be temperate in speech," replied the nurse.

"We may be temperate without being teetotal. Plentiful and yellow, indeed! I have had a bad dream concerning those who found me. I thought that they—but it does not matter. She at least is not a myth. Do you happen to know if any others were saved?"

"I am thankful to be able to say that every one was drowned."

Stanford started up with horror in his eyes. The demure nurse, with sympathetic tones, bade him not excite himself. He sank back on his pillow.

"Leave the room," he cried, feebly, "Leave me—leave me." He turned his face toward the wall, while the woman left as silently as she had entered.

When she was gone Stanford slid from the bed, intending to make his way to the door and fasten it. He feared that these savages, who wished him dead, would take measures to kill him when they saw he was going to recover. As he leaned against the bed, he noticed that the door had no fastening. There was a rude latch, but neither lock nor bolt. The furniture of the room was of the most meagre description, clumsily made. He staggered to the open window, and looked out. The remnants of the disastrous gale blew in upon him and gave him new life, as it had formerly threatened him with death. He saw that he was in a village of small houses, each cottage standing in its own plot of ground. It was apparently a village of one street, and over the roofs of the houses opposite he saw in the distance the white waves of the sea. What astonished him most was a church with its tapering spire in the end of the street—a wooden church such as he had seen in remote American settlements. The street was deserted, and there were no signs of life in the houses.

"I must have fallen in upon some colony of lunatics," he said to himself. "I wonder to what country these people belong—either to England or the United States, I imagine — yet in all my travels I never heard of such a community."

There was no mirror in the room, and it was impossible for him to know how he looked. His clothes were dry and powdered with salt. He arranged them as well as he could, and slipped out of the house un-noticed. When he reached the outskirts of the village he saw that the inhabitants, both men and women, were working in the fields some distance away. Coming towards the village was a girl with a water-can in either hand. She was singing as blithely as a lark until she saw Stanford, whereupon she paused both in her walk and in her song. Stanford, never a backward man, advanced, and was about to greet her when she forestalled him by saying:

"I am grieved, indeed, to see that you have recovered."

The young man's speech was frozen on his lip, and a frown settled on his brow. Seeing that he was annoyed, though why she could not guess, Ruth hastened to attend matters by adding:

"Believe me, what I say is true. I am indeed sorry."

"Sorry that I live?"

"Most heartily am I."

"It is hard to credit such a statement from one so—from you."

"Do not say so. Miriam has already charged me with being glad that you were not drowned. It would pain me deeply if you also believed as she does."

The girl looked at him with swimming eyes, and the young man knew not what to answer. Finally he said:

"There is some horrible mistake. I cannot make it out. Perhaps our words, though apparently the same, have a different meaning. Sit down, Ruth, I want to ask you some questions."

Ruth cast a timorous glance towards the workers, and murmured something about not having much time to spare, but she placed the water-cans on the ground and sank down on the grass. Stanford throwing himself on the sward at her feet, but, seeing that she shrank back, he drew himself further from her, resting where he might gaze upon her face.

Ruth's eyes were downcast, which was necessary, for she occupied herself in pulling blade after blade of grass, sometimes weaving them together. Stanford had said he wished to question her, but he apparently forgot his intention, for he seemed wholly satisfied with merely looking at her. After the silence had lasted for some time, she lifted her eyes for one brief moment, and then asked the first question herself.

"From what land do you come?"

"From England."

"Ah! that also is an island, is it not?"

He laughed at the "also," and remembered that he had some questions to ask.

"Yes, it is an island—also. The sea dashes wrecks on all four sides of it, but there is no village on its shores so heathenish that if a man is cast upon the beach the inhabitants do not rejoice because he has escaped death."

Ruth looked at him with amazement in her eyes.

"Is there, then, no religion in England?"

"Religion? England is the most religious country on the face of the earth. There are more cathedrals, more churches, more places of worship in England than in any other State that I know of. We send missionaries to all heathenish lands. The Government, itself, supports the Church."

"I imagine, then, I mistook your meaning. I thought from what you said that the people of England feared death, and did not welcome it or rejoice when one of their number died."

"They do not fear death, and they do not rejoice when it comes. Far from it. From the peer to the beggar, everyone fights death as long as he can; the oldest cling to life as eagerly as the youngest. Not a man but will spend his last gold piece to ward off the inevitable even for an hour."

"Gold piece—what is that?"

Stanford plunged his hand into his pocket.

"Ah!" he said, "there are some coins left. Here is a gold piece."

The girl took it, and looked at it with keen interest.

"Isn't it pretty?" she said, holding the yellow coin on her pink palm, and glancing up at him.

"That is the general opinion. To accumulate coins like that, men will lie, and cheat, and steal—yes, and work. Although they will give their last sovereign to prolong their lives, yet will they risk life itself to accumulate gold. Every business in England is formed merely for the gathering together of bits of metal like that in your hand; huge companies of men are formed so that it may be piled up in greater quantities. The man who has most gold has most power, and is generally the most respected; the company which makes most money is the one people are most anxious to belong to."

Ruth listened to him with wonder and dismay in her eyes. As he talked she shuddered, and allowed the yellow coin to slip from her hand to the ground.

"No wonder such a people fears death."

"Do you not fear death?"

"How can we, when we believe in heaven?"

"But would you not be sorry if someone died whom you loved?"

"How could we be so selfish? Would you be sorry if your brother, or someone you loved, became possessed of whatever you value in England —a large quantity of this gold, for instance?"

"Certainly not. But then you see—well, it isn't exactly the same thing. If one you care for dies you are separated from him, and——"

"But only for a short time, and that gives but another reason for welcoming death. It seems impossible that Christian people should fear to enter Heaven. Now I begin to understand why our forefathers left England, and why our teachers will never tell us anything about the people there. I wonder why missionaries are not sent to England to teach them the truth, and try to civilize the people?"

"That would, indeed, be coals to Newcastle. But there comes one of the workers."

"It is my father," cried the girl, rising. "I fear I have been loitering. I never did such a thing before."

The man who approached was stern of countenance.

"Ruth," he said, "the workers are athirst."

The girl, without reply, picked up her pails and departed.

"I have been receiving," said the young man, coloring slightly, "some instruction regarding your belief. I had been puzzled by several remarks I had heard, and wished to make inquiries concerning them."

"It is more fitting," said the man, coldly, "that you should receive instruction from me or from some of the elders than from one of the youngest in the community. When you are so far recovered as to be able to listen to an exposition of our views, I hope to put forth such arguments as will convince you that they are the true views. If it should so happen that my arguments are not convincing, then I must request that you will hold no communication with our younger members. They must not be contaminated by the heresies of the outside world."

Stanford looked at Ruth standing beside the village well.

"Sir," he said, "you underrate the argumentative powers of the younger members. There is a text bearing upon the subject which I need not recall to you. I am already convinced."

Algernon Blackwood
THE WENDIGO

"The Wendigo" may well be the most terrifying tale with a Canadian setting yet written. The Englishman who wrote it, Algernon Blackwood (1869-1951), was "sent" by his parents to Canada at the age of twenty. He lived for two years in the Toronto area, where he worked as an editor on the Canadian Methodist Magazine, *before becoming a dairy farmer and then a hotel-keeper. These experiences are vividly recreated in his auto-biography,* Episodes before Thirty *(1950). Blackwood then returned to*

England and found a large public for his horror fiction. "The Wendigo"
first appeared in The Lost Valley and Other Stories *(1910). Blackwood*
later recalled the conception of this story: "Then the awful Wendigo
comes shouldering up over a hill of memory, a name I remembered
vividly in Hiawatha *('Wendigos and giants' runs the line), yet hardly*
thought of again till a friend, just back from Labrador, told me honest
tales about mysterious evacuations of a whole family from a lonely valley
because the 'Wendigo had come blundering in' and 'scared them stiff'...."
As Northrop Frye has noted, "The feeling for sudden descent or
catastrophe seems to me to have an unusual emphasis in Canada." Dread,
disintegration, and death are in no figure better personified than in the
feared Wendigo, the vampire-like spirit that haunts the Algonkian-
speaking Indians of the northern woods. (See also the poetry section for
George Bowering's poem, "Windigo.")

I

A considerable number of hunting parties were out that year without finding so much as a fresh trail; for the moose were uncommonly shy, and the various Nimrods returned to the bosoms of their respective families with the best excuses the facts or their imaginations could suggest. Dr. Cathcart, among others, came back without a trophy; but he brought instead the memory of an experience which he declares was worth all the bull-moose that had ever been shot. But then Cathcart, of Aberdeen, was interested in other things besides moose—amongst them the vagaries of the human mind. This particular story, however, found no mention in his book on *Collective Hallucination* for the simple reason (so he confided once to a fellow colleague) that he himself played too intimate a part in it to form a competent judgment of the affair as a whole....

Besides himself and his guide, Hank Davis, there was young Simpson, his nephew, a divinity student destined for the "Wee Kirk" (then on his first visit to Canadian backwoods), and the latter's guide, Défago. Joseph Défago was a French "Canuck," who had strayed from his native Province of Quebec years before, and had got caught in Rat Portage when the Canadian Pacific Railway was a-building; a man who, in addition to his unparalleled knowledge of woodcraft and bush-lore, could also sing the old *voyageur* songs and tell a capital hunting yarn into the bargain. He was deeply susceptible, moreover, to that singular spell which the wilderness lays upon certain lonely natures, and he loved the wild solitudes with a kind of romantic passion that amounted almost to an obsession. The life of the backwoods fascinated him—whence, doubtless, his surpassing efficiency in dealing with their mysteries.

50

On this particular expedition he was Hank's choice. Hank knew him and swore by him. He also swore at him, "jest as a pal might," and since he had a vocabulary of picturesque, if utterly meaningless, oaths, the conversation between the two stalwart and hardy woodsmen was often of a rather lively description. This river of expletives, however, Hank agreed to dam a little out of respect for his old "hunting boss," Dr. Cathcart, whom of course he addressed after the fashion of the country as "Doc," and also because he understood that young Simpson was already a "bit of a parson." He had, however, one objection to Défago, and one only—which was, that the French Canadian sometimes exhibited what Hank described as "the output of a cursed and dismal mind," meaning apparently that he sometimes was true to type, Latin type, and suffered fits of a kind of silent moroseness when nothing could induce him to utter speech. Défago, that is to say, was imaginative and melancholy. And, as a rule, it was too long a spell of "civilization" that induced the attacks, for a few days of the wilderness invariably cured them.

This, then, was the party of four that found themselves in camp the last week in October of that "shy moose year" 'way up in the wilderness north of Rat Portage—a forsaken and desolate country. There was also Punk, an Indian, who had accompanied Dr. Cathcart and Hank on their hunting trips in previous years, and who acted as cook. His duty was merely to stay in camp, catch fish, and prepare venison steaks and coffee at a few minutes' notice. He dressed in the worn-out clothes bequeathed to him by former patrons, and except for his coarse black hair and dark skin, he looked in these city garments no more like a real redskin than a stage negro looks like a real African. For all that, however, Punk had in him still the instincts of his dying race; his taciturn silence and his endurance survived; also his superstition.

The party round the blazing fire that night were despondent, for a week had passed without a single sign of recent moose discovering itself. Défago had sung his song and plunged into a story, but Hank, in bad humour, reminded him so often that "he kep' mussing-up the fac's so, that it was 'most all nothin' but a petred-out lie," that the Frenchman had finally subsided into a sulky silence which nothing seemed likely to break. Dr. Cathcart and his nephew were fairly done after an exhausting day. Punk was washing up the dishes, grunting to himself under the lean-to of branches, where he later also slept. No one troubled to stir the slowly dying fire. Overhead the stars were brilliant in a sky quite wintry, and there was so little wind that ice was already forming stealthily along the shores of the still lake behind them. The silence of the vast listening forest stole forward and enveloped them.

Hank broke in suddenly with his nasal voice.

51

"I'm in favour of breaking new ground to-morrow, Doc," he observed with energy, looking across at his employer. "We don't stand a dead Dago's chance about here."

"Agreed," said Cathcart, always a man of few words. "Think the idea's good."

"Sure pop, it's good," Hank resumed with confidence. "S'pose, now, you and I strike west, up Garden Lake way for a change! None of us ain't touched that quiet bit o' land yet—"

"I'm with you."

"And you, Défago, take Mr. Simpson along in the small canoe, skip across the lake, portage over into Fifty Island Water, and take a good squint down that thar southern shore. The moose 'yarded' there like hell last year, and for all we know they may be doin' it agin this year jest to spite us."

Défago, keeping his eyes on the fire, said nothing by way of reply. He was still offended, possibly, about his interrupted story.

"No one's been up that way this year, an' I'll lay my bottom dollar on *that!*" Hank added with emphasis, as though he had a reason for knowing. He looked over at his partner sharply. "Better take the little silk tent and stay away a couple o' nights," he concluded, as though the matter were definitely settled. For Hank was recognized as general organizer of the hunt, and in charge of the party.

It was obvious to any one that Défago did not jump at the plan, but his silence seemed to convey something more than ordinary disapproval, and across his sensitive dark face there passed a curious expression like a flash of firelight—not so quickly, however, that the three men had not time to catch it. "He funked for some reason, *I* thought," Simpson said afterwards in the tent he shared with his uncle. Dr. Cathcart made no immediate reply, although the look had interested him enough at the time for him to make a mental note of it. The expression had caused him a passing uneasiness he could not quite account for at the moment.

But Hank, of course, had been the first to notice it, and the odd thing was that instead of becoming explosive or angry over the other's reluctance, he at once began to humour him a bit.

"But there ain't no *speshul* reason why no one's been up there this year," he said, with a perceptible hush in his tone; "not the reason *you* mean, anyway! Las' year it was the fires that kep' folks out, and this year I guess—I guess it jest happened so, that's all!" His manner was clearly meant to be encouraging.

Joseph Défago raised his eyes a moment, then dropped them again. A breath of wind stole out of the forest and stirred the embers into a passing blaze. Dr. Cathcart again noticed the expression in the guide's face, and again he did not like it. But this time the nature of the look betrayed itself. In those eyes, for an instant, he caught the gleam of a man scared in his very soul. It disquieted him more than he cared to admit.

"Bad Indians up that way?" he asked, with a laugh to ease matters a little, while Simpson, too sleepy to notice this subtle by-play, moved off to bed with a prodigious yawn; "or,—or anything wrong with the country?" he added, when his nephew was out of hearing.

Hank met his eye with something less than his usual frankness.

"He's jest skeered," he replied good-humouredly, "skeered stiff about some ole feery tale! That's all, ain't it, ole pard?" And he gave Défago a friendly kick on the moccasined foot that lay nearest the fire.

Défago looked up quickly, as from an interrupted reverie, a reverie, however, that had not prevented his seeing all that went on about him.

"Skeered—*nuthin'!*" he answered, with a flush of defiance. "There's nuthin' in the Bush that can skeer Joseph Défago, and don't you forget it!" And the natural energy with which he spoke made it impossible to know whether he told the whole truth or only a part of it.

Hank turned towards the doctor. He was just going to add something when he stopped abruptly and looked round. A sound close behind them in the darkness made all three start. It was old Punk, who had moved up from his lean-to while they talked and now stood there just beyond the circle of firelight—listening.

" 'Nother time, Doc!" Hank whispered, with a wink, "when the gallery ain't stepped down into the stalls!" And, springing to his feet, he slapped the Indian on the back and cried noisily, "Come up t' the fire an' warm yer dirty red skin a bit." He dragged him towards the blaze and threw more wood on. "That was a mighty good feed you give us an hour or two back," he continued heartily, as though to set the man's thoughts on another scene, "and it ain't Christian to let you stand there freezin' yer ole soul to hell while we're gettin' all good an' toasted!" Punk moved in and warmed his feet, smiling darkly at the other's volubility which he only half understood, but saying nothing. And presently Dr. Cathcart, seeing that further conversation was impossible, followed his nephew's example and moved off to the tent, leaving the three men smoking over the now blazing fire.

It is not easy to undress in a small tent without waking one's companion, and Cathcart, hardened and warm-blooded as he was in spite of his fifty odd years, did what Hank would have described as "considerable of his twilight" in the open. He noticed, during the process, that Punk had meanwhile gone back to his lean-to, and that Hank and Défago were at it hammer and tongs, or, rather, hammer and anvil, the little French Canadian being the anvil. It was all very like the conventional

53

stage picture of Western melodrama: the fire lighting up their faces with patches of alternate red and black; Défago, in slouch hat and moccasins in the part of the "badlands" villain; Hank, open-faced and hatless, with that reckless fling of his shoulders, the honest and deceived hero; and old Punk, eavesdropping in the background, supplying the atmosphere of mystery. The doctor smiled as he noticed the details; but at the same time something deep within him—he hardly knew what—shrank a little, as though an almost imperceptible breath of warning had touched the surface of his soul and was gone again before he could seize it. Probably it was traceable to that "scared expression" he had seen in the eyes of Défago; "probably"—for this hint of fugitive emotion otherwise escaped his usually so keen analysis. Défago, he was vaguely aware, might cause trouble somehow. . . . He was not as steady a guide as Hank, for instance. . . . Further than that he could not get . . . .

He watched the men a moment longer before diving into the stuffy tent where Simpson already slept soundly. Hank, he saw, was swearing like a mad African in a New York nigger saloon; but it was the swearing of "affection." The ridiculous oaths flew freely now that the cause of their obstruction was asleep. Presently he put his arm almost tenderly upon his comrade's shoulder, and they moved off together into the shadows where their tent stood faintly glimmering. Punk, too, a moment later followed their example and disappeared between his odorous blankets in the opposite direction.

Dr. Cathcart then likewise turned in, weariness and sleep still fighting in his mind with an obscure curiosity to know what it was had scared Défago about the country up Fifty Island Water way,—wondering, too, why Punk's presence had prevented the completion of what Hank had to say. Then sleep overtook him. He would know to-morrow. Hank would tell him the story while they trudged after the elusive moose.

Deep silence fell about the little camp, planted there so audaciously in the jaws of the wilderness. The lake gleamed like a sheet of black glass beneath the stars. The cold air pricked. In the draughts of night that poured their silent tide from the depths of the forest, with messages from distant ridges and from lakes just beginning to freeze, there lay already the faint, bleak odours of coming winter. White men, with their dull scent, might never have divined them; the fragrance of the wood-fire would have concealed from them these almost electrical hints of moss and bark and hardening swamp a hundred miles away. Even Hank and Défago, subtly in league with the soul of the woods as they were, would probably have spread their delicate nostrils in vain. . . .

But an hour later, when all slept like the dead, old Punk crept from his blankets and went down to the shore of the lake like a shadow—

silently, as only Indian blood can move. He raised his head and looked about him. The thick darkness rendered sight of small avail, but, like the animals, he possessed other senses that darkness could not mute. He listened—then sniffed the air. Motionless as a hemlock-stem he stood there. After five minutes again he lifted his head and sniffed, and yet once again. A tingling of the wonderful nerves that betrayed itself by no outer sign, ran through him as he tasted the keen air. Then, merging his figure into the surrounding blackness in a way that only wild men and animals understand, he turned, still moving like a shadow, and went stealthily back to his lean-to and his bed.

And soon after he slept, the change of wind he had divined stirred gently the reflection of the stars within the lake. Rising among the far ridges of the country beyond Fifty Island Water, it came from the direction in which he had stared, and it passed over the sleeping camp with a faint and sighing murmur through the tops of the big tree that was almost too delicate to be audible. With it, down the desert paths of night, though too faint, too high even for the Indian's hair-like nerves, there passed a curious, thin odour, strangely disquieting, an odour of something that seemed unfamiliar—utterly unknown.

The French Canadian and the man of Indian blood each stirred uneasily in his sleep just about this time, though neither of them woke. Then the ghost of that unforgettably strange odour passed away and was lost among the leagues of tenantless forest beyond.

II

In the morning the camp was astir before the sun. There had been a light fall of snow during the night and the air was sharp. Punk had done his duty betimes, for the odours of coffee and fried bacon reached every tent. All were in good spirits.

"Wind's shifted!" cried Hank vigorously, watching Simpson and his guide already loading the small canoe. "It's across the lake—dead right for you fellers. And the snow'll make bully trails! If there's any moose mussing around up thar, they'll not get so much as a tail-end scent of you with the wind as it is. Good luck, Monsieur Défago!" he added, facetiously giving the name its French pronunciation for once, *"bonne chance!"*

Défago returned the good wishes, apparently in the best of spirits, the silent mood gone. Before eight o'clock old Punk had the camp to himself, Cathcart and Hank were far along the trail that led westwards, while the canoe that carried Défago and Simpson, with silk tent and grub for two days, was already a dark speck bobbing on the bosom of the lake, going due east.

The wintry sharpness of the air was tempered now by a sun that topped the wooded ridges and blazed with a luxurious warmth upon the world of lake and forest below; loons flew skimming through the sparkling spray that the wind lifted; divers shook their dripping heads to the sun and popped smartly out of sight again; and as far as eye could reach rose the leagues of endless, crowding Bush, desolate in its lonely sweep and grandeur, untrodden by foot of man, and stretching its mighty and unbroken carpet right up to the frozen shores of Hudson Bay.

Simpson, who saw it all for the first time as he paddled hard in the bows of the dancing canoe, was enchanted by its austere beauty. His heart drank in the sense of freedom and great spaces just as his lungs drank in the cool and perfumed wind. Behind him in the stern seat, singing fragments of his native chanties, Défago steered the craft of birchbark like a thing of life, answering cheerfully all his companion's questions. Both were gay and light-hearted. On such occasions men lose the superficial, worldly distinctions; they become human beings working together for a common end. Simpson, the employer, and Défago, the employed, among these primitive forces, were simply—two men, the "guider," and the "guided." Superior knowledge, of course, assumed control, and the younger man fell without a second thought into the quasi-subordinate position. He never dreamed of objecting when Défago dropped the "Mr.," and addressed him as "Say, Simpson," or "Simpson, boss," which was invariably the case before they reached the farther shore after a stiff paddle of twelve miles against a head wind. He only laughed, and liked it; then ceased to notice it at all.

For this "divinity student" was a young man of parts and character, though as yet, of course, untravelled; and on this trip—the first time he had seen any country but his own and little Switzerland—the huge scale of things somewhat bewildered him. It was one thing, he realized, to hear about primeval forests, but quite another to see them. While to dwell in them and seek acquaintance with their wild life was, again, an initiation that no intelligent man could undergo without a certain shifting of personal values hitherto held for permanent and sacred.

Simpson knew the first faint indication of this emotion when he held the new .303 rifle in his hands and looked along its pair of faultless, gleaming barrels. The three days' journey to their headquarters, by lake and portage, had carried the process a stage farther. And now that he was about to plunge beyond even the fringe of wilderness where they were camped into the virgin heart of uninhabited regions as vast as Europe itself, the true nature of the situation stole upon him with an effect of delight and awe that his imagination was fully capable of appreciating. It was himself and Défago against a multitude—at least, against a Titan!

The bleak splendours of these remote and lonely forests rather overwhelmed him with the sense of his own littleness. That stern quality of the tangled backwoods which can only be described as merciless and terrible, rose out of these far blue woods swimming upon the horizon, and revealed itself. He understood the silent warning. He realized his own utter helplessness. Only Défago, as a symbol of a distant civilization where man was master, stood between him and a pitiless death by exhaustion and starvation.

It was thrilling to him, therefore, to watch Défago turn over the canoe upon the shore, pack the paddles carefully underneath, and then proceed to "blaze" the spruce stems for some distance on either side of an almost invisible trail, with the careless remark thrown in, "Say, Simpson, if anything happens to me, you'll find the canoe all correc' by these marks; —then strike doo west into the sun to hit the home camp agin, see?"

It was the most natural thing in the world to say, and he said it without any noticeable inflexion of the voice, only it happened to express the youth's emotions at the moment with an utterance that was symbolic of the situation and of his own helplessness as a factor in it. He was alone with Défago in a primitive world: that was all. The canoe, another symbol of man's ascendancy, was now to be left behind. Those small yellow patches, made on the trees by the axe, were the only indications of its hiding-place.

Meanwhile, shouldering the packs between them, each man carrying his own rifle, they followed the slender trail over rocks and fallen trunks and across half-frozen swamps; skirting numerous lakes that fairly gemmed the forest, their borders fringed with mist; and towards five o'clock found themselves suddenly on the edge of the woods, looking out across a large sheet of water in front of them, dotted with pine-clad islands of all describable shapes and sizes.

"Fifty Island Water," announced Défago wearily, "and the sun jest goin' to dip his bald old head into it!" he added, with unconscious poetry; and immediately they set about pitching camp for the night.

In a very few minutes, under those skilful hands that never made a movement too much or a movement too little, the silk tent stood taut and cosy, the beds of balsam boughs ready laid, and a brisk cooking-fire burned with the minimum of smoke. While the young Scotchman cleaned the fish they had caught trolling behind the canoe, Défago "guessed" he would "jest as soon" take a turn through the Bush for indications of moose. "*May* come across a trunk where they bin and rubbed horns," he said, as he moved off, "or feedin' on the last of the maple leaves,"—and he was gone.

His small figure melted away like a shadow in the dusk, while Simpson noted with a kind of admiration how easily the forest absorbed him into herself. A few steps, it seemed, and he was no longer visible.

Yet there was little underbrush hereabouts; the trees stood somewhat apart, well spaced; and in the clearings grew silver-birch and maple, spearlike and slender, against the immense stems of spruce and hemlock. But for occasional prostrate monsters, and the boulders of grey rock that thrust uncouth shoulders here and there out of the ground, it might well have been a bit of park in the Old Country. Almost, one might have seen in it the hand of man. A little to the right, however, began the great burnt section, miles in extent, proclaiming its real character—*brulé*, as it is called, where the fires of the previous year had raged for weeks, and the blackened stumps now rose gaunt and ugly, bereft of branches, like gigantic match-heads stuck into the ground, savage and desolate beyond words. The perfume of charcoal and rain-soaked ashes still hung faintly about it.

The dusk rapidly deepened; the glades grew dark; the crackling of the fire and the wash of little waves along the rocky lake shore were the only sounds audible. The wind had dropped with the sun, and in all that vast world of branches nothing stirred. Any moment, it seemed, the woodland gods, who are to be worshipped in silence and loneliness, might sketch their mighty and terrific outlines among the trees. In front, through doorways pillared by huge straight stems, lay the stretch of Fifty Island Water, a crescent-shaped lake some fifteen miles from tip to tip, and perhaps five miles across where they were camped. A sky of rose and saffron, more clear than any atmosphere Simpson had ever known, still dropped its pale streaming fires across the waves, where the islands—a hundred, surely, rather than fifty—floated like the fairy barques of some enchanted fleet. Fringed with pines, whose crests fingered most delicately the sky, they almost seemed to move upwards as the light faded—about to weigh anchor and navigate the pathways of the heavens instead of the currents of their native and desolate lake.

And strips of coloured cloud, like flaunting pennons, signalled their departure to the stars . . .

The beauty of the scene was strangely uplifting. Simpson smoked the fish and burnt his fingers into the bargain in his efforts to enjoy it and at the same time tend the frying-pan and the fire. Yet, ever at the back of his thoughts, lay that other aspect of the wilderness: the indifference to human life, the merciless spirit of desolation which took no note of man. The sense of his utter loneliness, now that even Défago had gone, came close as he looked about him and listened for the sound of his companion's returning footsteps.

There was pleasure in the sensation, yet with it a perfectly comprehensible alarm. And instinctively the thought stirred in him: "What should I—*could* I, do—if anything happened and he did not come back——?"

They enjoyed their well-earned supper, eating untold quantities of fish, and drinking unmilked tea strong enough to kill men who had not covered thirty miles of hard "going," eating little on the way. And when it was over, they smoked and told stories round the blazing fire, laughing, stretching weary limbs, and discussing plans for the morrow. Défago was in excellent spirits, though disappointed at having no signs of moose to report. But it was dark and he had not gone far. The *brulé*, too, was bad. His clothes and hands were smeared with charcoal. Simpson, watching him, realized with renewed vividness their position—alone together in the wilderness.

"Défago," he said presently, "these woods, you know, are a bit too big to feel quite at home in—to feel comfortable in, I mean! . . . Eh?" He merely gave expression to the mood of the moment; he was hardly prepared for the earnestness, the solemnity even, with which the guide took him up.

"You've hit it right, Simpson, boss," he replied, fixing his searching brown eyes on his face, "and that's the truth, sure. There's no end to 'em —no end at all." Then he added in a lowered tone as if to himself, "There's lots found out *that*, and gone plumb to pieces!"

But the man's gravity of manner was not quite to the other's liking; it was a little too suggestive for this scenery and setting; he was sorry he had broached the subject. He remembered suddenly how his uncle had told him that men were sometimes stricken with a strange fever of the wilderness, when the seduction of the uninhabited wastes caught them so fiercely that they went forth, half fascinated, half deluded, to their death. And he had a shrewd idea that his companion held something in sympathy with that queer type. He led the conversation on to other topics, on to Hank and the doctor, for instance, and the natural rivalry as to who should get the first sight of moose.

"If they went doo west," observed Défago carelessly, "there's sixty miles between us now—with ole Punk at halfway house eatin' himself full to bustin' with fish and corfee." They laughed together over the picture. But the casual mention of those sixty miles again made Simpson realize the prodigious scale of this land where they hunted; sixty miles was a mere step; two hundred little more than a step. Stories of lost hunters rose persistently before his memory. The passion and mystery of homeless and wandering men, seduced by the beauty of great forests, swept his soul in a way too vivid to be quite pleasant. He wondered vaguely whether it was the mood of his companion that invited the unwelcome suggestion with such persistence.

"Sing us a song, Défago, if you're not too tired," he asked; "one of those old *voyageur* songs you sang the other night." He handed his tobacco pouch to the guide and then filled his own pipe, while the Canadian, nothing loth, sent his light voice across the lake in one of those plaintive, almost melancholy chanties with which lumbermen and trappers lessen the burden of their labour. There was an appealing and romantic flavour about it, something that recalled the atmosphere of the old pioneer days when Indians and wilderness were leagued together, battles frequent, and the Old Country farther off than it is to-day. The sound travelled pleasantly over the water, but the forest at their backs seemed to swallow it down with a single gulp that permitted neither echo nor resonance.

It was in the middle of the third verse that Simpson noticed something unusual—something that brought his thoughts back with a rush from far-away scenes. A curious change had come into the man's voice. Even before he knew what it was, uneasiness caught him, and looking up quickly, he saw that Défago, though still singing, was peering about him into the Bush, as though he heard or saw something. His voice grew fainter—dropped to a hush—then ceased altogether. The same instant, with a movement amazingly alert, he started to his feet and stood upright—*sniffing the air*. Like a dog scenting game, he drew the air into his nostrils in short, sharp breaths, turning quickly as he did so in all directions, and finally "pointing" down the lake shore, eastwards. It was a performance unpleasantly suggestive and at the same time singularly dramatic. Simpson's heart fluttered disagreeably as he watched it.

"Lord, man! How you made me jump!" he exclaimed, on his feet beside him the same instant, and peering over his shoulder into the sea of darkness. "What's up? Are you frightened——?"

Even before the question was out of his mouth he knew it was foolish, for any man with a pair of eyes in his head could see that the Canadian had turned white down to his very gills. Not even sunburn and the glare of the fire could hide that.

The student felt himself trembling a little, weakish in the knees. "What's up?" he repeated quickly. "D'you smell moose? Or anything queer, anything—wrong?" He lowered his voice instinctively.

The forest pressed round them with its encircling wall; the nearer tree-stems gleamed like bronze in the firelight; beyond that—blackness, and, so far as he could tell, a silence of death. Just behind them a passing puff of wind lifted a single leaf, looked at it, then laid it softly down again without disturbing the rest of the covey. It seemed as if a million invisible causes had combined just to produce that single visible effect. *Other* life pulsed about them—and was gone.

Défago turned abruptly; the livid hue of his face had turned to a dirty grey.

"I never said I heered—or smelt—nuthin'," he said slowly and emphatically, in an oddly altered voice that conveyed somehow a touch of defiance. "I was only—takin' a look round—so to speak. It's always a mistake to be too previous with yer questions." Then he added suddenly with obvious effort, in his more natural voice, "Have you got the matches, Boss Simpson?" and proceeded to light the pipe he had half filled just before he began to sing.

Without speaking another word they sat down again by the fire, Défago changing his side so that he could face the direction the wind came from. For even a tenderfoot could tell that. Défago changed his position in order to hear and smell—all there was to be heard and smelt. And, since he now faced the lake with his back to the trees it was evidently nothing in the forest that had sent so strange and sudden a warning to his marvellously trained nerves.

"Guess now I don't feel like singing any," he explained presently of his own accord. "That song kinder brings back memories that's troublesome to me; I never oughter've begun it. It sets me on t'imagining things, see?"

Clearly the man was still fighting with some profoundly moving emotion. He wished to excuse himself in the eyes of the other. But the explanation, in that it was only a part of the truth, was a lie, and he knew perfectly well that Simpson was not deceived by it. For nothing could explain the livid terror that had dropped over his face while he stood there sniffing the air. And nothing—no amount of blazing fire, or chatting on ordinary subjects—could make that camp exactly as it had been before. The shadow of an unknown horror, naked if unguessed, that had flashed for an instant in the face and gestures of the guide, had also communicated itself, vaguely and therefore more potently, to his companion. The guide's visible efforts to dissemble the truth only made things worse. Moreover, to add to the younger man's uneasiness, was the difficulty, nay, the impossibility he felt of asking questions, and also his complete ignorance as to the cause. . . . Indians, wild animals, forest fires—all these, he knew, were wholly out of the question. His imagination searched vigorously, but in vain. . . .

Yet, somehow or other, after another long spell of smoking, talking and roasting themselves before the great fire, the shadow that had so suddenly invaded their peaceful camp began to lift. Perhaps Défago's efforts, or the return of his quiet and normal attitude accomplished this; perhaps Simpson himself had exaggerated the affair out of all proportion to the truth; or possibly the vigorous air of the wilderness brought its own powers of healing. Whatever the cause, the feeling of immediate horror seemed to have passed away as mysteriously as it had come, for nothing occurred to feed it. Simpson began to feel that he had permitted himself the unreasoning terror of a child. He put it down partly to a certain subconscious excitement that this wild and immense scenery generated in his blood, partly to the spell of solitude, and partly to overfatigue. That pallor in the guide's face was, of course, uncommonly hard to explain, yet it *might* have been due in some way to an effect of firelight, or his own imagination. . . . He gave it the benefit of the doubt; he was Scotch.

When a somewhat unordinary emotion has disappeared, the mind always finds a dozen ways of explaining away its causes. . . . Simpson lit a last pipe and tried to laugh to himself. On getting home to Scotland it would make quite a good story. He did not realize that this laughter was a sign that terror still lurked in the recesses of his soul—that, in fact, it was merely one of the conventional signs by which a man, seriously alarmed, tries to persuade himself that he is *not* so.

Défago, however, heard that low laughter and looked up with surprise on his face. The two men stood, side by side, kicking the embers about before going to bed. It was ten o'clock—a late hour for hunters to be still awake.

"What's ticklin' yer?" he asked in his ordinary tone, yet gravely.

"I—I was thinking of our little toy woods at home, just at that moment," stammered Simpson, coming back to what really dominated his mind, and startled by the question, "and comparing them to—to all this," and he swept his arm round to indicate the Bush.

A pause followed in which neither of them said anything.

"All the same I wouldn't laugh about it, if I was you," Défago added, looking over Simpson's shoulder into the shadows. "There's places in there nobody won't never see into—nobody knows what lives in there either."

"Too big—too far off?" The suggestion in the guide's manner was immense and horrible.

Défago nodded. The expression on his face was dark. He, too, felt uneasy. The younger man understood that in a *hinterland* of this size there might well be depths of wood that would never in the life of the world be known or trodden. The thought was not exactly the sort he welcomed. In a loud voice, cheerfully, he suggested that it was time for bed. But the guide lingered, tinkering with the fire, arranging the stones needlessly, doing a dozen things that did not really need doing. Evidently there was something he wanted to say, yet found it difficult to "get at."

"Say, you, Boss Simpson," he began suddenly, as the last shower of sparks went up into the air, "you don't—smell nothing, do you—nothing pertickler, I mean?" The commonplace question, Simpson realized, veiled a dreadfully serious thought in his mind. A shiver ran down his back.

"Nothing but this burning wood," he replied firmly, kicking again at the embers. The sound of his own foot made him start.

"And all the even' you ain't smelt—nothing?" persisted the guide, peering at him through the gloom; "nothing extrordiny, and different to anything else you ever smelt before?"

"No, no, man; nothing at all!" he replied aggressively, half angrily.

Défago's face cleared. "That's good!" he exclaimed with evident relief. "That's good to hear."

"Have *you?*" asked Simpson sharply, and the same instant regretted the question.

The Canadian came closer in the darkness. He shook his head. "I guess not," he said, though without overwhelming conviction. "It must've been jest that song of mine that did it. It's the song they sing in lumber-camps and god-forsaken places like-that, when they've skeered the Wendigo's somewheres around, doin' a bit of swift travellin'——"

"And what's the Wendigo, pray?" Simpson asked quickly, irritated because again he could not prevent that sudden shiver of the nerves. He knew that he was close upon the man's terror and the cause of it. Yet a rushing passionate curiosity overcame his better judgment, *and* his fear.

Défago turned swiftly and looked at him as though he were suddenly about to shriek. His eyes shone, but his mouth was wide open. Yet all he said, or whispered rather, for his voice sank very low, was——

"It's nuthin'—nuthin' but what those lousy fellers believe when they've bin hittin' the bottle too long—a sort of great animal that lives up yonder," he jerked his head northwards, "quick as lightning in its tracks, an' bigger'n anything else in the Bush, an' ain't supposed to be very good to look at—*that's all!*"

"A backwoods' superstition—" began Simpson, moving hastily towards the tent in order to shake off the hand of the guide that clutched his arm. "Come, come, hurry up for God's sake, and get the lantern going! It's time we were in bed and asleep if we're to be up with the sun to-morrow. . . ."

The guide was close on his heels. "I'm coming," he answered out of the darkness, "I'm coming." And after a slight delay he appeared with the lantern and hung it from a nail in the front pole of the tent. The shadows of a hundred trees shifted their places quickly as he did so, and when he stumbled over the rope, diving swiftly inside, the whole tent trembled as though a gust of wind struck it.

The two men lay down, without undressing, upon their beds of soft balsam boughs, cunningly arranged. Inside, all was warm and cosy, but outside the world of crowding trees pressed close about them, marshalling their million shadows, and smothering the little tent that stood there like a wee white shell facing the ocean of tremendous forest.

Between the two lonely figures within, however, there pressed another shadow that was *not* a shadow from the night. It was the Shadow cast by the strange Fear, never wholly exorcised, that had leaped suddenly upon Défago in the middle of his singing. And Simpson, as he lay there, watching the darkness through the open flap of the tent, ready to plunge into the fragrant abyss of sleep, knew first that unique and profound stillness of a primeval forest when no wind stirs . . . and when the night has weight and substance that enters into the soul to bind a veil about it. . . . Then sleep took him. . . .

III

Thus it seemed to him, at least. Yet it was true that the lap of the water, just beyond the tent door, still beat time with his lessening pulses when he realized that he was lying with his eyes open and that another sound had recently introduced itself with cunning softness between the splash and murmur of the little waves.

And, long before he understood what this sound was, it had stirred in him the centres of pity and alarm. He listened intently, though at first in vain, for the running blood beat all its drums too noisily in his ears. Did it come, he wondered, from the lake, or from the woods? . . .

Then, suddenly, with a rush and a flutter of the heart, he knew that it was close beside him in the tent; and when he turned over for a better hearing, it focussed itself unmistakably not two feet away. It was a sound of weeping; Défago upon his bed of branches was sobbing in the darkness as though his heart would break, the blankets evidently stuffed against his mouth to stifle it.

And his first feeling, before he could think or reflect, was the rush of a poignant and searching tenderness. This intimate, human sound, heard amid the desolation about them, woke pity. It was so incongruous, so pitifully incongruous—and so vain! Tears—in this vast and cruel wilderness: of what avail? He thought of a little child crying in mid-Atlantic. . . . Then, of course, with fuller realization, and the memory of what had gone before, came the descent of the terror upon him, and his blood ran cold.

"Défago," he whispered quickly, "what's the matter?" He tried to make his voice very gentle. "Are you in pain—unhappy——?" There was no reply, but the sounds ceased abruptly. He stretched his hand out and touched him. The body did not stir.

"Are you awake?" for it occurred to him that the man was crying in his sleep. "Are you cold?" He noticed that his feet, which were uncovered, projected beyond the mouth of the tent. He spread an extra fold of his own blankets over them. The guide had slipped down in his bed, and the branches seemed to have been dragged with him. He was afraid to pull the body back again, for fear of waking him.

One or two tentative questions he ventured softly, but though he waited for several minutes there came no reply, nor any sign of movement. Presently he heard his regular and quiet breathing, and putting his hand again gently on the breast, felt the steady rise and fall beneath.

"Let me know if anything's wrong," he whispered, "or if I can do anything. Wake me at once if you feel—queer."

He hardly knew quite what to say. He lay down again, thinking and wondering what it all meant. Défago, of course, had been crying in his sleep. Some dream or other had afflicted him. Yet never in his life would he forget that pitiful sound of sobbing, and the feeling that the whole awful wilderness of woods listened. . . .

His own mind busied itself for a long time with the recent events, of which *this* took its mysterious place as one, and though his reason successfully argued away all unwelcome suggestions, a sensation of uneasiness remained, resisting ejection, very deep-seated—peculiar beyond ordinary.

IV

But sleep, in the long run, proves greater than all emotions. His thoughts soon wandered again; he lay there, warm as toast, exceedingly weary; the night soothed and comforted, blunting the edges of memory and alarm. Half-an-hour later he was oblivious of everything in the outer world about him.

Yet sleep, in this case, was his great enemy, concealing all approaches, smothering the warning of his nerves.

As, sometimes, in a nightmare events crowd upon each others' heels with a conviction of dreadfullest reality, yet some inconsistent detail accuses the whole display of incompleteness and disguise, so the events that now followed, though they actually happened, persuaded the mind somehow that the detail which could explain them had been overlooked in the confusion, and that therefore they were but partly true, the rest delusion. At the back of the sleeper's mind something remains awake, ready to let slip the judgment, "All this is not *quite* real; when you wake up you'll understand."

And thus, in a way, it was with Simpson. The events, not wholly inexplicable or incredible in themselves, yet remain for the man who saw and heard them a sequence of separate acts of cold horror, because the little piece that might have made the puzzle clear lay concealed or overlooked.

So far as he can recall, it was a violent movement, running downwards through the tent towards the door, that first woke him and made him aware that his companion was sitting bolt upright beside him—quivering. Hours must have passed, for it was the pale gleam of the dawn that revealed his outline against the canvas. This time the man was not crying; he was quaking like a leaf; the trembling he felt plainly through the blankets down the entire length of his own body. Défago had huddled down against him for protection, shrinking away from something that apparently concealed itself near the door-flaps of the little tent.

Simpson thereupon called out in a loud voice some question or other —in the first bewilderment of waking he does not remember exactly what—and the man made no reply. The atmosphere and feeling of true nightmare lay horribly about him, making movement and speech both difficult. At first, indeed, he was not sure where he was—whether in one of the earlier camps, or at home in his bed at Aberdeen. The sense of confusion was very troubling.

And next—almost simultaneous with his waking, it seemed—the profound stillness of the dawn outside was shattered by a most uncommon sound. It came without warning, or audible approach; and it was unspeakably dreadful. It was a voice, Simpson declares, possibly a human voice, hoarse yet plaintive—a soft, roaring voice close outside the tent, overhead rather than upon the ground, of immense volume, while in some strange way most penetratingly and seductively sweet. It rang out, too, in three separate and distinct notes, or cries, that bore in some odd fashion a resemblance, far-fetched yet recognizable, to the name of the guide: "*Dé—fa—go!*"

The student admits he is unable to describe it quite intelligently, for it was unlike any sound he had ever heard in his life, and combined a blending of such contrary qualities. "A sort of windy, crying voice," he calls it, "as of something lonely and untamed, wild and of abominable power. . . ."

And, even before it ceased, dropping back into the great gulfs of silence, the guide beside him had sprung to his feet with an answering though unintelligible cry. He blundered against the tent-pole with violence, shaking the whole structure, spreading his arms out frantically for more room, and kicking his legs impetuously free of the clinging blankets. For a second, perhaps two, he stood upright by the door, his outline dark against the pallor of the dawn; then, with a furious, rushing speed, before his companion could move a hand to stop him, he shot with a plunge through the flaps of canvas—and was gone. And as he went—so astonishingly fast that the voice could actually be heard dying in the distance—he called aloud in tones of anguished terror that at the same time held something strangely like the frenzied exultation of delight——

"Oh! oh! My feet of fire! My burning feet of fire! Oh! oh! This height and fiery speed!"

And then the distance quickly buried it, and the deep silence of very early morning descended upon the forest as before.

It had all come about with such rapidity that, but for the evidence of the empty bed beside him, Simpson could almost have believed it to have been the memory of a nightmare carried over from sleep. He still felt the warm pressure of that vanished body against his side; there lay the twisted blankets in a heap; the very tent yet trembled with the vehemence of the impetuous departure. The strange words rang in his ears, as though he still heard them in the distance—wild language of a suddenly stricken mind. Moreover, it was not only the senses of sight and hearing that reported uncommon things to his brain, for even while the man cried and ran, he had become aware that a strange perfume, faint yet pungent, pervaded the interior of the tent. And it was at this point, it seems, brought to himself by the consciousness that his nostrils were taking this distressing odour down into his throat, that he found his courage, sprang quickly to his feet—and went out.

The grey light of dawn that dropped, cold and glimmering, between the trees revealed the scene tolerably well. There stood the tent behind him, soaked with dew; the dark ashes of the fire, still warm; the lake, white beneath a coating of mist, the islands rising darkly out of it like objects packed in wool; and patches of snow beyond among the clearer spaces of the Bush—everything cold, still, waiting for the sun. But nowhere a sign of the vanished guide—still, doubtless, flying at frantic speed through the frozen woods. There was not even the sound of disappearing footsteps, nor the echoes of the dying voice. He had gone—utterly.

There was nothing; nothing but the sense of his recent presence, so strongly left behind about the camp; and—this penetrating, all-pervading odour.

And even this was now rapidly disappearing in its turn. In spite of his exceeding mental perturbation, Simpson struggled hard to detect its nature, and define it, but the ascertaining of an elusive scent, not recognized subconsciously and at once, is a very subtle operation of the mind. And he failed. It was gone before he could properly seize or name it. Approximate description, even, seems to have been difficult, for it was unlike any smell he knew. Acrid rather, not unlike the odour of a lion, he thinks, yet softer and not wholly unpleasing, with something almost sweet in it that reminded him of the scent of decaying garden leaves, earth, and the myriad, nameless perfumes that make up the odour of a big forest. Yet the "odour of lions" is the phrase with which he usually sums it all up.

Then—it was wholly gone, and he found himself standing by the ashes of the fire in a state of amazement and stupid terror that left him the helpless prey of anything that chose to happen. Had a musk-rat poked its pointed muzzle over a rock, or a squirrel scuttled in that instant down the bark of a tree, he would most likely have collapsed without more ado and fainted. For he felt about the whole affair the touch somewhere of a great Outer Horror . . . and his scattered powers had not as yet had time to collect themselves into a definite attitude of fighting self-control.

Nothing did happen, however. A great kiss of wind ran softly through the awakening forest, and a few maple leaves here and there rustled tremblingly to earth. The sky seemed to grow suddenly much lighter. Simpson felt the cool air upon his cheek and uncovered head; realized that he was shivering with the cold; and, making a great effort, realized next that he was alone in the Bush—*and* that he was called upon to take immediate steps to find and succour his vanished companion.

Make an effort, accordingly, he did, though an ill-calculated and futile one. With that wilderness of trees about him, the sheer of water cutting him off behind, and the horror of that wild cry in his blood, he did what any other inexperienced man would have done in similar bewilderment: he ran about, without any sense of direction, like a frantic child, and called loudly without ceasing the name of the guide——

"Défago! Défago! Défago!" he yelled, and the trees gave him back the name as often as he shouted, only a little softened—"Défago! Défago! Défago!"

He followed the trail that lay for a short distance across the patches of snow, and then lost it again where the trees grew too thickly for snow to lie. He shouted till he was hoarse, and till the sound of his own voice in all the unanswering and listening world began to frighten him. His confusion increased in direct ratio to the violence of his efforts. His distress became formidably acute, till at length his exertions defeated their own object, and from sheer exhaustion he headed back to the camp again. It remains a wonder that he ever found his way. It was with great difficulty, and only after numberless false clues, that he at last saw the white tent between the trees, and so reached safety.

Exhaustion then applied its own remedy, and he grew calmer. He made the fire and breakfasted. Hot coffee and bacon put a little sense and judgment into him again, and he realized that he had been behaving like a boy. He now made another, and more successful attempt to face the situation collectedly, and, a nature naturally plucky coming to his assistance, he decided that he must first make as thorough a search as possible, failing success in which, he must find his way to the home camp as best he could and bring help.

And this was what he did. Taking food, matches and rifle with him, and a small axe to blaze the trees against his return journey, he set forth. It was eight o'clock when he started, the sun shining over the tops of the trees in a sky without clouds. Pinned to a stake by the fire he left a note in case Défago returned while he was away.

This time, according to a careful plan, he took a new direction, intending to make a wide sweep that must sooner or later cut into indications of the guide's trail and, before he had gone a quarter of a mile he came across the tracks of a large animal in the snow, and beside it the light and smaller tracks of what were beyond question human feet—the feet of Défago. The relief he at once experienced was natural, though brief; for at first sight he saw in these tracks a simple explanation of the whole matter: these big marks had surely been left by a bull moose that, wind against it, had blundered upon the camp, and uttered its singular cry of warning and alarm the moment its mistake was apparent. Défago, in whom the hunting instinct was developed to the point of uncanny perfection, had scented the brute coming down the wind hours before. His excitement and disappearance were due, of course, to—to his——

Then the impossible explanation at which he grasped faded, as common sense showed him mercilessly that none of this was true. No guide, much less a guide like Défago, could have acted in so irrational a way, going off even without his rifle . . . ! The whole affair demanded a far more complicated elucidation, when he remembered the details of it all—the cry of terror, the amazing language, the grey face of horror when his nostrils first caught the new odour; that muffled sobbing in the darkness, and—for this, too, now came back to him dimly—the man's original aversion for this particular bit of country. . . .

Besides, now that he examined them closer, these were not the tracks of a moose at all! Hank had explained to him the outline of a bull's hoofs, of a cow's or calf's, too, for that matter; he had drawn them clearly on a strip of birch bark. And these were wholly different. They were big, round, ample, and with no pointed outline as of sharp hoofs. He wondered for a moment whether bear-tracks were like that. There was no other animal he could think of, for caribou did not come so far south at this season, and, even if they did, would leave hoof-marks.

They were ominous signs—these mysterious writings left in the snow by the unknown creature that had lured a human being away from safety—and when he coupled them in his imagination with that haunting sound that broke the stillness of the dawn, a momentary dizziness shook his mind, distressing him again beyond belief. He felt the *threatening* aspect of it all. And, stooping down to examine the marks more closely, he caught a faint whiff of that sweet yet pungent odour that made him instantly straighten up again, fighting a sensation almost of nausea.

Then his memory played him another evil trick. He suddenly recalled those uncovered feet projecting beyond the edge of the tent, and the body's appearance of having been dragged towards the opening; the man's shrinking from something by the door when he woke later. The details now beat against his trembling mind with concerted attack. They seemed to gather in those deep spaces of the silent forest about him, where the host of trees stood waiting, listening, watching to see what he would do. The woods were closing round him.

With the persistence of true pluck, however, Simpson went forward, following the tracks as best he could, smothering these ugly emotions that sought to weaken his will. He blazed innumerable trees as he went, ever fearful of being unable to find the way back, and calling aloud at intervals of a few seconds the name of the guide. The dull tapping of the axe upon the massive trunks, and the unnatural accents of his own voice became at length sounds that he even dreaded to make, dreaded to hear. For they drew attention without ceasing to his presence and something was hunting himself down in the same way that he was hunting down another——

With a strong effort, he crushed the thought out the instant it rose. It was the beginning, he realized, of a bewilderment utterly diabolical in kind that would speedily destroy him.

Although the snow was not continuous, lying merely in shallow flurries over the more open spaces, he found no difficulty in following the tracks for the first few miles. They went straight as a ruled line wherever the trees permitted. The stride soon began to increase in length, till it finally assumed proportions that seemed absolutely impossible for any ordinary animal to have made. Like huge flying leaps they became. One of these he measured, and though he knew that "stretch" of eighteen feet must be somehow wrong, he was at a complete loss to understand why he found no signs on the snow between the extreme points. But what perplexed him even more, making him feel his vision had gone utterly awry, was that Défago's stride increased in the same manner, and finally covered the same incredible distances. It looked as if the great beast had lifted him with it and carried him across these astonishing intervals.

Simpson, who was much longer in the limb, found that he could not compass even half the stretch by taking a running jump.

And the sight of these huge tracks, running side by side, silent evidence of a dreadful journey in which terror or madness had urged to impossible results, was profoundly moving. It shocked him in the secret depths of his soul. It was the most horrible thing his eyes had ever looked upon. He began to follow them mechanically, absent-mindedly almost, ever peering over his shoulder to see if he, too, were being followed by something with a gigantic tread. . . . And soon it came about that he no longer quite realized what it was they signified—these impressions left upon the snow by something nameless and untamed, always accompanied by the footmarks of the little French Canadian, his guide, his comrade, the man who had shared his tent a few hours before, chatting, laughing, even singing by his side. . . .

V

For a man of his years and inexperience, only a canny Scot, perhaps, grounded in common sense and established in logic, could have preserved even that measure of balance that this youth somehow or other did manage to preserve through the whole adventure. Otherwise, two things, he presently noticed, while forging pluckily ahead, must have sent him headlong back to the comparative safety of his tent, instead of only making his hands close more tightly upon the rifle-stock, while his heart, trained for the Wee Kirk, sent a wordless prayer winging its way to heaven. Both tracks, he saw, had undergone a change, and this change, so far as it concerned the footsteps of the man, was in some undecipherable manner—appalling.

It was in the bigger tracks he first noticed this, and for a long time he could not quite believe his eyes. Was it the blown leaves that produced odd effects of light and shade, or that the dry snow, drafting like finely-grounded rice about the edges, cast shadows and high lights? Or was it actually the fact that the great marks had become faintly coloured? For round about the deep, plunging holes of the animal there now appeared a mysterious, reddish tinge that was more like an effect of light than of anything that dyed the substance of the snow itself. Every mark had it, and had it increasingly—this indistinct fiery tinge that painted a new touch of ghastliness into the picture.

But when, wholly unable to explain or credit it, he turned his attention to the other tracks to discover if they, too, bore similar witness, he noticed that these had meanwhile undergone a change that was infinitely worse, and charged with far more horrible suggestion. For, in the last hundred yards or so, he saw that they had grown gradually into the semblance of the parent tread. Imperceptibly the change had come about, yet unmistakably. It was hard to see where the change first began. The result, however, was beyond question. Smaller, neater, more cleanly modelled, they formed now an exact and careful duplicate of the larger tracks beside them. The feet that produced them had, therefore, also changed. And something in his mind reared up with loathing and with terror as he saw it.

Simpson, for the first time, hesitated; then, ashamed of his alarm and indecision, took a few hurried steps ahead; the next instant stopped dead in his tracks. Immediately in front of him all signs of the trail ceased; both tracks came to an abrupt end. On all sides, for a hundred yards and more, he searched in vain for the least indication of their continuance. There was—nothing.

The trees were very thick just there, big trees all of them, spruce, cedar, hemlock; there was no underbrush. He stood, looking about him, all distraught; bereft of any power of judgment. Then he set to work to search again, and again, and yet again, but always with the same result: *nothing.* The feet that printed the surface of the snow thus far had now, apparently, left the ground!

And it was in that moment of distress and confusion that the whip of terror laid its most nicely calculated lash about his heart. It dropped with deadly effect upon the sorest spot of all, completely unnerving him. He had been secretly dreading all the time that it would come—and come it did.

Far overhead, muted by great height and distance, strangely thinned and wailing, he heard the crying voice of Défago, the guide.

The sound dropped upon him out of that still, wintry sky with an effect of dismay and terror unsurpassed. The rifle fell to his feet. He stood motionless an instant, listening as it were with his whole body, then staggered back against the nearest tree for support, disorganized hopelessly in mind and spirit. To him, in that moment, it seemed the most shattering and dislocating experience he had even known, so that his heart emptied itself of all feeling whatsoever as by a sudden draught.

"Oh! oh! This fiery height! Oh, my feet of fire! My burning feet of fire . . . !" ran in far, beseeching accents of indescribable appeal this voice of anguish down the sky. Once it called—then silence through all the listening wilderness of trees.

And Simpson, scarcely knowing what he did, presently found himself running wildly to and fro, searching, calling, tripping over roots and boulders, and flinging himself in a frenzy of undirected pursuit after the Caller. Behind the screen of memory and emotion with which experience veils events, he plunged, distracted and half-deranged, picking up false lights like a ship at sea, terror in his eyes and heart and soul. For the Panic of the Wilderness had called to him in that far voice—the Power of untamed Distance—the Enticement of the Desolation that destroys. He knew in that moment all the pains of some one hopelessly and irretrievably lost, suffering the lust and travail of a soul in the final Loneliness. A vision of Défago, eternally hunted, driven and pursued across the skiey vastness of those ancient forests, fled like a flame across the dark ruin of his thoughts. . . .

It seemed ages before he could find anything in the chaos of his disorganized sensations to which he could anchor himself steady for a moment, and think. . . .

The cry was not repeated; his own hoarse calling brought no response; the inscrutable forces of the Wild had summoned their victim beyond recall—and held him fast.

Yet he searched and called, it seems, for hours afterwards, for it was late in the afternoon when at length he decided to abandon a useless pursuit and return to his camp on the shores of Fifty Island Water. Even then he went with reluctance, that crying voice still echoing in his ears. With difficulty he found his rifle and the homeward trail. The concentration necessary to follow the badly blazed trees, and a biting hunger that gnawed, helped to keep his mind steady. Otherwise, he admits, the temporary aberration he had suffered might have been prolonged to the point of positive disaster. Gradually the ballast shifted back again, and he regained something that approached his normal equilibrium.

But for all that the journey through the gathering dusk was miserably haunted. He heard innumerable following footsteps; voices that laughed and whispered; and saw figures crouching behind trees and boulders, making signs to one another for a concerted attack the moment he had passed. The creeping murmur of the wind made him start and listen. He went stealthily, trying to hide where possible, and making as little sound as he could. The shadows of the woods, hitherto protective or covering merely, had now become menacing, challenging; and the pageantry in his frightened mind masked a host of possibilities that were all the more ominous for being obscure. The presentiment of a nameless doom lurked ill-concealed behind every detail of what had happened.

It was really admirable how he emerged victor in the end; men of riper powers and experience might have come through the ordeal with less success. He had himself tolerably well in hand, all things considered, and his plan of action proves it. Sleep being absolutely out of the question, and travelling an unknown trail in the darkness equally impracticable, he sat up the whole of that night, rifle in hand, before a fire he never for a single moment allowed to die down. The severity of the haunted vigil marked his soul for life; but it was successfully accomplished; and with the very first signs of dawn he set forth upon the long return journey to the home-camp to get help. As before, he left a written note to explain his absence, and to indicate where he had left a plentiful *cache* of food and matches—though he had no expectation that any human hands would find them!

How Simpson found his way alone by lake and forest might well make a story in itself, for to hear him tell it is to *know* the passionate loneliness of soul that a man can feel when the Wilderness holds him in the hollow of its illimitable hand—and laughs. It is also to admire his indomitable pluck.

He claims no skill, declaring that he followed the almost invisible trail mechanically, and without thinking. And this, doubtless, is the truth. He relied upon the unconscious mind, which is instinct. Perhaps, too, some sense of orientation, known to animals and primitive men, may have helped as well, for through all that tangled region he succeeded in reaching the exact spot where Défago had hidden the canoe nearly three days before with the remark, "Strike doo west across the lake into the sun to find the camp."

There was not much sun left to guide him, but he used his compass to the best of his ability, embarking in the frail craft for the last twelve miles of his journey, with a sensation of immense relief that the forest was at last behind him. And, fortunately, the water was calm; he took his line across the centre of the lake instead of coasting round the shores for another twenty miles. Fortunately, too, the other hunters were back. The light of their fires furnished a steering-point without which he might have searched all night long for the actual position of the camp.

It was close upon midnight all the same when his canoe grated on the sandy cove, and Hank, Punk and his uncle, disturbed in their sleep by his cries, ran quickly down and helped a very exhausted and broken specimen of Scotch humanity over the rocks towards a dying fire.

VI

The sudden entrance of his prosaic uncle into this world of wizardry and horror that had haunted him without interruption now for two days and two nights, had the immediate effect of giving to the affair an entirely new aspect. The sound of that crisp "Hulloa, my boy! And what's up *now*?" and the grasp of that dry and vigorous hand introduced another standard of judgment. A revulsion of feeling washed through him. He realized that he had let himself "go" rather badly. He even felt vaguely ashamed of himself. The native hard-headedness of his race reclaimed him.

74

And this doubtless explains why he found it so hard to tell that group round the fire—everything. He told enough, however, for the immediate decision to be arrived at that a relief party must start at the earliest possible moment, and that Simpson, in order to guide it capably, must first have food and, above all, sleep. Dr. Cathcart observing the lad's condition more shrewdly than his patient knew, gave him a very slight injection of morphine. For six hours he slept like the dead.

From the description carefully written out afterwards by this student of divinity, it appears that the account he gave to the astonished group omitted sundry vital and important details. He declares that, with his uncle's wholesome, matter-of-fact countenance staring him in the face, he simply had not the courage to mention them. Thus, all the search-party gathered, it would seem, was that Défago had suffered in the night an acute and inexplicable attack of mania, had imagined himself "called" by some one or something, and had plunged into the bush after it without food or rifle, where he must die a horrible and lingering death by cold and starvation unless he could be found and rescued in time. "In time," moreover, meant "at once."

In the course of the following day, however—they were off by seven, leaving Punk in charge with instructions to have food and fire always ready—Simpson found it possible to tell his uncle a good deal more of the story's true inwardness, without divining that it was drawn out of him as a matter of fact by a very subtle form of cross-examination. By the time they reached the beginning of the trail, where the canoe was laid up against the return journey, he had mentioned how Défago spoke vaguely of "something he called a 'Wendigo'"; how he cried in his sleep; how he imagined an unusual scent about the camp; and had betrayed other symptoms of mental excitement. He also admitted the bewildering effect of "that extraordinary" odour upon himself, "pungent and acrid like the odour of lions." And by the time they were within an easy hour of Fifty Island Water he had let slip the further fact—a foolish avowal of his own hysterical condition, as he felt afterwards—that he had heard the vanished guide call "for help." He omitted the singular phrases used, for he simply could not bring himself to repeat the preposterous language. Also, while describing how the man's footsteps in the snow had gradually assumed an exact miniature likeness of the animal's plunging tracks, he left out the fact that they measured a *wholly* incredible distance. It seemed a question, nicely balanced between individual pride and honesty, what he should reveal and what suppress. He mentioned the fiery tinge in the snow, for instance, yet shrank from telling that body and bed had been partly dragged out of the tent. . . .

With the net result that Dr. Cathcart, adroit psychologist that he fancied himself to be, had assured him clearly enough exactly where his mind, influenced by loneliness, bewilderment and terror, had yielded to the strain and invited delusion. While praising his conduct, he managed at the same time to point out where, when, and how his mind had gone astray. He made his nephew think himself finer than he was by judicious praise, yet more foolish than he was by minimizing the value of his evidence. Like many another materialist, that is, he lied cleverly on the basis of insufficient knowledge, *because* the knowledge supplied seemed to his own particular intelligence inadmissible.

"The spell of these terrible solitudes," he said, "cannot leave any mind untouched, any mind, that is, possessed of the higher imaginative qualities. It has worked upon yours exactly as it worked upon my own when I was your age. The animal that haunted your little camp was undoubtedly a moose, for the 'belling' of a moose may have, sometimes, a very peculiar quality of sound. The coloured appearance of the big tracks was obviously a defect of vision in your own eyes produced by excitement. The size and stretch of the tracks we shall prove when we come to them. But the hallucination of an audible voice, of course, is one of the commonest forms of delusion due to mental excitement—an excitement, my dear boy, perfectly excusable, and, let me add, wonderfully controlled by you under the circumstances. For the rest, I am bound to say, you have acted with a spendid courage, for the terror of feeling oneself lost in this wilderness is nothing short of awful, and, had I been in your place, I don't for a moment believe I could have behaved with one quarter of your wisdom and decision. The only thing I find it uncommonly difficult to explain is—that—damned odour."

"It made me feel sick, I assure you," declared his nephew, "positively dizzy!" His uncle's attitude of calm omniscience, merely because he knew more psychological formulæ, made him slightly defiant. It was so easy to be wise in the explanation of an experience one has not personally witnessed. "A kind of desolate and terrible odour is the only way I can describe it," he concluded, glancing at the features of the quiet, unemotional man beside him.

"I can only marvel," was the reply, "that under the circumstances it did not seem to you even worse." The dry words, Simpson knew, hovered between the truth, and his uncle's interpretation of "the truth."

And so at last they came to the little camp and found the tent still standing, the remains of the fire, and the piece of paper pinned to a stake beside it—untouched. The *cache*, poorly contrived by inexperienced hands, however, had been discovered and opened—by musk rats, mink and squirrel. The matches lay scattered about the opening, but the food had been taken to the last crumb.

"Well, fellers, he ain't here," exclaimed Hank loudly after his fashion, "And that's as sartain as the coal supply down below! But whar he's got to by this time is 'bout as onsartain as the trade in crowns in t'other place." The presence of a divinity student was no barrier to his language at such a time, though for the reader's sake it may be severely edited. "I propose," he added, "that we start out at once an' hunt for'm like hell!"

The gloom of Défago's probable fate oppressed the whole party with a sense of dreadful gravity the moment they saw the familiar signs of recent occupancy. Especially the tent, with the bed of balsam branches still smoothed and flattened by the pressure of his body, seemed to bring his presence near to them. Simpson, feeling vaguely as if his word were somehow at stake, went about explaining particulars in a hushed tone. He was much calmer now, though overwearied with the strain of his many journeys. His uncle's method of explaining—"explaining away," rather—the details still fresh in his haunted memory helped, too, to put ice upon his emotions.

"And that's the direction he ran off in," he said to his two companions, pointing in the direction where the guide had vanished that morning in the grey dawn. "Straight down there he ran like a deer, in between the birch and the hemlock. . . ."

Hank and Dr. Cathcart exchanged glances.

"And it was about two miles down there, in a straight line," continued the other, speaking with something of the former terror in his voice, "that I followed his trail to the place where—it stopped—dead!"

"And where you heered him callin' an' caught the stench, an' all the rest of the wicked entertainment," cried Hank, with a volubility that betrayed his keen distress.

"And where your excitement overcame you to the point of producing illusions," added Dr. Cathcart under his breath, yet not so low that his nephew did not hear it.

It was early in the afternoon, for they had travelled quickly, and there were still a good two hours of daylight left. Dr. Cathcart and Hank lost no time in beginning the search, but Simpson was too exhausted to accompany them. They would follow the blazed marks on the trees, and where possible, his footsteps. Meanwhile the best thing he could do was to keep a good fire going, and rest.

But after something like three hours' search, the darkness already down, the two men returned to camp with nothing to report. Fresh snow had covered all signs, and though they had followed the blazed trees to the spot where Simpson had turned back, they had not discovered the smallest indications of a human being—or for that matter, of an animal. There were no fresh tracks of any kind; the snow lay undisturbed.

It was difficult to know what was best to do, though in reality there was nothing more they *could* do. They might stay and search for weeks without much chance of success. The fresh snow destroyed their only hope, and they gathered round the fire for supper, a gloomy and despondent party. The facts, indeed, were sad enough, for Défago had a wife at Rat Portage, and his earnings were the family's sole means of support.

Now that the whole truth in all its ugliness was out, it seemed useless to deal in further disguise or pretence. They talked openly of the facts and probabilities. It was not the first time, even in the experience of Dr. Cathcart, that a man had yielded to the singular seduction of the Solitudes and gone out of his mind; Défago, moreover, was predisposed to something of the sort, for he already had the touch of melancholia in his blood, and his fibre was weakened by bouts of drinking that often lasted for weeks at a time. Something on this trip—one might never know precisely what—had sufficed to push him over the line, that was all. And he had gone, gone off into the great wilderness of trees and lakes to die by starvation and exhaustion. The chances against his finding camp again were overwhelming; the delirium that was upon him would also doubtless have increased, and it was quite likely he might do violence to himself and so hasten his cruel fate. Even while they talked, indeed, the end had probably come. On the suggestion of Hank, his old pal, however, they proposed to wait a little longer and devote the whole of the following day, from dawn to darkness, to the most systematic search they could devise. They would divide the territory between them. They discussed their plan in great detail. All that men could do they would do.

And, meanwhile, they talked about the particular form in which the singular Panic of the Wilderness had made its attack upon the mind of the unfortunate guide. Hank, though familiar with the legend in its general outline, obviously did not welcome the turn the conversation had taken. He contributed little, though that little was illuminating. For he admitted that a story ran over all this section of country to the effect that several Indians had "seen the Wendigo" along the shores of Fifty Island Water in the "fall" of last year, and that this was the true reason of Défago's disinclination to hunt there. Hank doubtless felt that he had in a sense helped his old pal to death by over-persuading him. "When an Indian goes crazy," he explained, talking to himself more than to the others, it seemed, "it's always put that he's 'seen the Wendigo.' An' pore old Défaygo was superstitious down to his very heels. . . !"

And then Simpson, feeling the atmosphere more sympathetic, told over again the full story of his astonishing tale; he left out no details this time; he mentioned his own sensations and gripping fears. He only omitted the strange language used.

"But Défago surely had already told you all these details of the Wendigo legend, my dear fellow," insisted the doctor. "I mean, he had talked about it, and thus put into your mind the ideas which your own excitement afterwards developed?"

Whereupon Simpson again repeated the facts. Défago, he declared, had barely mentioned the beast. He, Simpson, knew nothing of the story, and, so far as he remembered, had never even read about it. Even the word was unfamiliar.

Of course he was telling the truth, and Dr. Cathcart was reluctantly compelled to admit the singular character of the whole affair. He did not do this in words so much as in manner, however. He kept his back against a good, stout tree; he poked the fire into a blaze the moment it showed signs of dying down; he was quicker than any of them to notice the least sound in the night about them—a fish jumping in the lake, a twig snapping in the bush, the dropping of occasional fragments of frozen snow from the branches overhead where the heat loosened them. His voice, too, changed a little in quality, becoming a shade less confident, lower also in tone. Fear, to put it plainly, hovered close about that little camp, and though all three would have been glad to speak of other matters, the only thing they seemed able to discuss was this—the source of their fear. They tried other subjects in vain; there was nothing to say about them. Hank was the most honest of the group; he said next to nothing. He never once, however, turned his back to the darkness. His face was always to the forest, and when wood was needed he didn't go farther than was necessary to get it.

VII

A wall of silence wrapped them in, for the snow, though not thick, was sufficient to deaden any noise, and the frost held things pretty tight besides. No sound but their voices and the soft roar of the flames made itself heard. Only, from time to time, something soft as the flutter of a pine-moth's wings went past them through the air. No one seemed anxious to go to bed. The hours slipped towards midnight.

"The legend is picturesque enough," observed the doctor after one of the longer pauses, speaking to break it rather than because he had anything to say, "for the Wendigo is simply the Call of the Wild personified, which some natures hear to their own destruction."

"That's about it," Hank said presently. "An' there's no misunderstandin' when you hear it. It calls you by name right 'nough."

Another pause followed. Then Dr. Cathcart came back to the forbidden subject with a rush that made the others jump.

"The allegory *is* significant," he remarked, looking about him into the darkness, "for the Voice, they say, resembles all the minor sounds of the Bush—wind, falling water, cries of animals, and so forth. And, once the victim hears *that*—he's off for good, of course! His most vulnerable points, moreover, are said to be the feet and the eyes; the feet, you see, for the lust of wandering, and the eyes for the lust of beauty. The poor beggar goes at such a dreadful speed that he bleeds beneath the eyes, and his feet burn."

Dr. Cathcart, as he spoke, continued to peer uneasily into the surrounding gloom. His voice sank to a hushed tone.

"The Wendigo," he added, "is said to burn his feet—owing to the friction, apparently caused by its tremendous velocity—till they drop off, and new ones form exactly like its own."

Simpson listened in horrified amazement; but it was the pallor on Hank's face that fascinated him most. He would willingly have stopped his ears and closed his eyes, had he dared.

"It don't always keep to the ground neither," came in Hank's slow, heavy drawl, "for it goes so high that he thinks the stars have set him all a-fire. An' it'll take great thumpin' jumps sometimes, an' run along the tops of the trees, carrying its partner with it, an' then droppin' him jest as a fish-hawk 'll drop a pickerel to kill it before eatin'. An' its food, of all the muck in the whole Bush is—moss!" And he laughed, a short, unnatural laugh. "It's a moss-eater, is the Wendigo," he added, looking up excitedly into the faces of his companions. "Moss-eater" he repeated, with a string of the most out-landish oaths he could invent.

But Simpson now understood the true purpose of all this talk. What these two men, each strong and "experienced" in his own way, dreaded more than anything else was—silence. They were talking against time. They were also talking against darkness, against the invasion of panic, against the admission reflection might bring that they were in an enemy's country—against anything, in fact, rather than allow their inmost thoughts to assume control. He himself, already initiated by the awful vigil with terror, was beyond both of them in this respect. He had reached the stage where he was immune. But these two, the scoffing, analytical doctor, and the honest, dogged backwoodsman, each sat trembling in the depths of his being.

Thus the hours passed; and thus, with lowered voices and a kind of taut inner resistance of spirit, this little group of humanity sat in the jaws of the wilderness and talked foolishly of the terrible and haunting legend. It was an unequal contest, all things considered, for the wilderness had already the advantage of first attack—and of a hostage. The fate of their comrade hung over them with a steadily increasing weight of oppression that finally became insupportable.

It was Hank, after a pause longer than the preceding ones that no one seemed able to break, who first let loose all this pent-up emotion in very unexpected fashion, by springing suddenly to his feet and letting out the most ear-shattering yell imaginable into the night. He could not contain himself any longer, it seemed. To make it carry even beyond an ordinary cry he interrupted its rhythm by shaking the palm of his hand before his mouth.

"That's for Défago," he said, looking down at the other two with a queer, defiant laugh, "for it's my belief"—the sandwiched oaths may be omitted—"that my ole partner's not far from us at this very minute."

There was a vehemence and recklessness about his performance that made Simpson, too, start to his feet in amazement, and betrayed even the doctor into letting the pipe slip from between his lips. Hank's face was ghastly, but Cathcart's showed a sudden weakness—a loosening of all his faculties, as it were. Then a momentary anger blazed into his eyes, and he too, though with deliberation born of habitual self-control, got upon his feet and faced the excited guide. For this was unpermissible, foolish, dangerous, and he meant to stop it in the bud.

What might have happened in the next minute or two one may speculate about, yet never definitely know, for in the instant of profound silence that followed Hank's roaring voice, and as though in answer to it, something went past through the darkness of the sky overhead at terrific speed—something of necessity very large, for it displaced much air, while down between the trees there fell a faint and windy cry of a human voice, calling in tones of indescribable anguish and appeal——

"Oh, oh! This fiery height! Oh, oh! My feet of fire! My burning feet of fire!"

White to the very edge of his shirt, Hank looked stupidly about him like a child. Dr. Cathcart uttered some kind of unintelligible cry, turning as he did so with an instinctive movement of blind terror towards the protection of the tent, then halting in the act as though frozen. Simpson, alone of the three, retained his presence of mind a little. His own horror was too deep to allow of any immediate reaction. He had heard that cry before.

Turning to his stricken companions, he said almost calmly——

"That's exactly the cry I heard—the very words he used!"

Then, lifting his face to the sky, he cried aloud, "Défago, Défago! Come down here to us! Come down——!"

And before there was time for anybody to take definite action one way or another, there came the sound of something dropping heavily between the trees, striking the branches on the way down, and landing with a dreadful thud upon the frozen earth below. The crash and thunder of it was really terrific.

"That's him, s'help me the good Gawd!" came from Hank in a whispering cry half choked, his hand going automatically towards the hunting-knife in his belt. "And he's coming! He's coming!" he added, with an irrational laugh of terror, as the sounds of heavy footsteps crunching over the snow became distinctly audible, approaching through the blackness towards the circle of light.

And while the steps, with their stumbling motion, moved nearer and nearer upon them, the three men stood round that fire, motionless and dumb. Dr. Cathcart had the appearance as of a man suddenly withered; even his eyes did not move. Hank, suffering shockingly, seemed on the verge again of violent action; yet did nothing. He, too, was hewn of stone. Like stricken children they seemed. The picture was hideous. And, meanwhile, their owner still invisible, the footsteps came closer, crunching the frozen snow. It was endless—too prolonged to be quite real—this measured and pitiless approach. It was accursed.

VIII

Then at length the darkness, having thus laboriously conceived, brought forth—a figure. It drew forward into the zone of uncertain light where fire and shadows mingled, not ten feet away; then halted, staring at them fixedly. The same instant it started forward again with the spasmodic motion as of a thing moved by wires, and coming up closer to them, full into the glare of the fire, they perceived then that—it was a man; and apparently that this man was—Défago.

Something like a skin of horror almost perceptibly drew down in that moment over every face, and three pairs of eyes shone through it as though they saw across the frontiers of normal vision into the Unknown.

Défago advanced, his tread faltering and uncertain; he made his way straight up to them as a group first, then turned sharply and peered close into the face of Simpson. The sound of a voice issued from his lips——

"Here I am, Boss Simpson. I heered some one calling me." It was a faint, dried-up voice, made wheezy and breathless as by immense exertion. "I'm havin' a reg'lar hell-fire kind of a trip, I am." And he laughed, thrusting his head forward into the other's face.

But that laugh started the machinery of the group of wax-work figures with the wax-white skins. Hank immediately sprang forward with a stream of oaths so far-fetched that Simpson did not recognize them as English at all, but thought he had lapsed into Indian or some other lingo. He only realized that Hank's presence, thrust thus between them, was welcome—uncommonly welcome. Dr. Cathcart, though more calmly and leisurely, advanced behind him, heavily stumbling.

Simpson seems hazy as to what was actually said and done in those next few seconds, for the eyes of that detestable and blasted visage peering at such close quarters into his own utterly bewildered his senses at first. He merely stood still. He said nothing. He had not the trained will of the older men that forced them into action in defiance of all emotional stress. He watched them moving as behind a glass, that half destroyed their reality: it was dreamlike; perverted. Yet, through the torrent of Hank's meaningless phrases, he remembers hearing his uncle's tone of authority—hard and forced—saying several things about food and warmth, blankets, whisky and the rest; . . . and, further, that whiffs of that penetrating, unaccustomed odour, vile, yet sweetly bewildering, assailed his nostrils during all that followed.

It was no less a person than himself, however—less experienced and adroit than the others though he was—who gave indistinctive utterance to the sentence that brought a measure of relief into the ghastly situation by expressing the doubt and thought in each one's heart.

"It *is*—YOU, isn't it, Défago?" he asked under his breath, horror breaking his speech.

And at once Cathcart burst out with the loud answer before the other had time to move his lips. "Of course it is! Of course it is! Only—can't you see—he's nearly dead with exhaustion, cold and terror? Isn't *that* enough to change a man beyond all recognition?" It was said in order to convince himself as much as to convince the others. And continually, while he spoke and acted, he held a handkerchief to his nose. That odour pervaded the whole camp.

For the "Défago" who sat huddled by the big fire, wrapped in blankets, drinking hot whisky and holding food in wasted hands, was no more like the guide they had last seen alive than the picture of a man of sixty is like the daguerreotype of his early youth in the costume of another generation. Nothing really can describe that ghastly caricature, that parody, masquerading there in the firelight as Défago. From the ruins of the dark and awful memories he still retains, Simpson declares that the face was more animal than human, the features drawn about into wrong proportions, the skin loose and hanging, as though he had been subjected to extraordinary pressures and tensions. It made him think vaguely of those bladder-faces blown up by the hawkers on Ludgate Hill, that change their expression as they swell, and as they collapse emit a faint and wailing imitation of a voice. Both face and voice suggested some such abominable resemblance. But Cathcart long afterwards, seeking to describe the indescribable, asserts that thus might have looked a face and body that had been in air so rarefied that, the weight of atmosphere being removed, the entire structure threatened to fly asunder and become —*incoherent....*

It was Hank, though all distraught and shaking with a tearing volume of emotion he could neither handle nor understand, who brought things to a head without more ado. He went off to a little distance from the fire, apparently so that the light should not dazzle him too much, and shading his eyes for a moment with both hands, shouted in a loud voice that held anger and affection dreadfully mingled—

"You ain't Défaygo! You ain't Défaygo at all! I don't give a—damn, but that ain't you, my ole pal of twenty years!" He glared upon the huddled figure as though he would destroy him with his eyes. "An' if it is I'll swab the floor of hell with a wad of cotton-wool on a toothpick, s'help me the good Gawd!" he added, with a violent fling of horror and disgust.

It was impossible to silence him. He stood there shouting like one possessed, horrible to see, horrible to hear—*because it was the truth*. He repeated himself in fifty different ways, each more outlandish than the last. The woods rang with echoes. At one time it looked as if he meant to fling himself upon "the intruder," for his hand continually jerked towards the long hunting-knife in his belt.

But in the end he did nothing, and the whole tempest completed itself very nearly with tears. Hank's voice suddenly broke, he collapsed on the ground, and Cathcart somehow or other persuaded him at last to go into the tent and lie quiet. The remainder of the affair, indeed, was witnessed by him from behind the canvas, his white and terrified face peeping through the crack of the tent door-flap.

Then Dr. Cathcart, closely followed by his nephew who so far had kept his courage better than all of them, went up with a determined air and stood opposite to the figure of Défago huddled over the fire. He looked him squarely in the face and spoke. At first his voice was firm.

"Défago, tell us what's happened—just a little, so that we can know how best to help you?" he asked in a tone of authority, almost of command. And at that point, it *was* command. At once afterwards, however, it changed in quality, for the figure turned up to him a face so piteous, so terrible and so little like humanity, that the doctor shrank back from him as from something spiritually unclean. Simpson, watching close behind him, says he got the impression of a mask that was on the verge of dropping off, and that underneath they would discover something black and diabolical, revealed in utter nakedness. "Out with it, man, out with it!" Cathcart cried, terror running neck and neck with entreaty.

"None of us can stand this much longer . . . !" It was the cry of instinct over reason.

And then "Défago," smiling *whitely,* answered in that thin and fading voice that already seemed passing over into a sound of quite another character—

"I seen that great Wendigo thing," he whispered, sniffing the air about him exactly like an animal. "I been with it too——"

Whether the poor devil would have said more, or whether Dr. Cathcart would have continued the impossible cross-examination cannot be known, for at that moment the voice of Hank was heard yelling at the top of his voice from behind the canvas that concealed all but his terrified eyes. Such a howling was never heard.

"His feet! Oh, Gawd, his feet! Look at his great changed—feet!"

Défago, shuffling where he sat, had moved in such a way that for the first time his legs were in full light and his feet were visible. Yet Simpson had no time, himself, to see properly what Hank had seen. And Hank has never seen fit to tell. That same instant, with a leap like that of a frightened tiger, Cathcart was upon him, bundling the folds of blanket about his legs with such speed that the young student caught little more than a passing glimpse of something dark and oddly massed where moccasined feet ought to have been, and saw even that but with uncertain vision.

Then, before the doctor had time to do more, or Simpson time to even think a question, much less ask it, Défago was standing upright in front of them, balancing with pain and difficulty, and upon his shapeless and twisted visage an expression so dark and so malicious that it was, in the true sense, monstrous.

"Now *you* seen it too," he wheezed, "you seen my fiery, burning feet! And now—that is, unless you kin save me an' prevent—it's 'bout time for——"

His piteous and beseeching voice was interrupted by a sound that was like the roar of wind coming across the lake. The trees overhead shook their tangled branches. The blazing fire bent its flames as before a blast. And something swept with a terrific, rushing noise about the little camp and seemed to surround it entirely in a single moment of time. Défago shook the clinging blankets from his body, turned towards the woods behind, and with the same stumbling motion that had brought him—was gone: gone, before any one could move muscle to prevent him, gone with an amazing, blundering swiftness that left no time to act. The darkness positively swallowed him; and less than a dozen seconds later, above the roar of the swaying trees and the shout of the sudden wind, all three men, watching and listening with stricken hearts, heard a cry that seemed

85

to drop down upon them from a great height of sky and distance——

"Oh, oh! This fiery height! Oh, oh! My feet of fire! My burning feet of fire . . . !" then died away, into untold space and silence.

Dr. Cathcart—suddenly master of himself, and therefore of the others—was just able to seize Hank violently by the arm as he tried to dash headlong into the Bush.

"But I want ter know,——you!" shrieked the guide. "I want ter see! That ain't him at all, but some——devil that's shunted into his place . . . !"

Somehow or other—he admits he never quite knew how he accomplished it—he managed to keep him in the tent and pacify him. The doctor, apparently, had reached the stage where reaction had set in and allowed his own innate force to conquer. Certainly he "managed" Hank admirably. It was his nephew, however, hitherto so wonderfully controlled, who gave him most cause for anxiety, for the cumulative strain had now produced a condition of lachrymose hysteria which made it necessary to isolate him upon a bed of boughs and blankets as far removed from Hank as was possible under the circumstance.

And there he lay, as the watches of that haunted night passed over the lonely camp, crying startled sentences, and fragments of sentences, into the folds of his blankets. A quantity of gibberish about speed and height and fire mingled oddly with biblical memories of the class-room. "People with broken faces all on fire are coming at a most awful, awful, pace towards the camp!" he would moan one minute; and the next would sit up and stare into the woods, intently listening, and whisper, "How terrible in the wilderness are—are the feet of them that——" until his uncle came across to change the direction of his thoughts and comfort him.

The hysteria, fortunately, proved but temporary. Sleep cured him, just as it cured Hank.

Till the first signs of daylight came, soon after five o'clock, Dr. Cathcart kept his vigil. His face was the colour of chalk, and there were strange flushes beneath the eyes. An appalling terror of the soul battled with his will all through those silent hours. These were some of the outer signs. . . .

At dawn he lit the fire himself, made breakfast, and woke the others, and by seven they were well on their way back to the home camp—three perplexed and afflicted men, but each in his own way having reduced his inner turmoil to a condition of more or less systematized order again.

IX

They talked little, and then only of the most wholesome and common things, for their minds were charged with painful thoughts that clamoured for explanation, though no one dared refer to them. Hank, being nearest to primitive conditions, was the first to find himself, for he was also less complex. In Dr. Cathcart "civilization" championed his forces against an attack singular enough. To this day, perhaps, he is not *quite* sure of certain things. Anyhow, he took longer to "find himself."

Simpson, the student of divinity, it was who arranged his conclusions probably with the best, though not most scientific, appearance of order. Out there, in the heart of unreclaimed wilderness, they had surely witnessed something crudely and essentially primitive. Something that had survived somehow the advance of humanity had emerged terrifically, betraying a scale of life still monstrous and immature. He envisaged it rather as a glimpse into prehistoric ages, when superstitions, gigantic and uncouth, still oppressed the hearts of men; when the forces of nature were still untamed, the Powers that may have haunted a primeval universe not yet withdrawn. To this day he thinks of what he termed years later in a sermon "savage and formidable Potencies lurking behind the souls of men, not evil perhaps in themselves, yet instinctively hostile to humanity as it exists."

With his uncle he never discussed the matter in detail, for the barrier between the two types of mind made it difficult. Only once, years later, something led them to the frontier of the subject—of a single detail of the subject, rather——

"Can't you even tell me what—*they* were like?" he asked; and the reply, though conceived in wisdom, was not encouraging, "It is far better you should not try to know, or to find out."

"Well—that odour . . . ?" persisted the nephew. "What do you make of that?"

Dr. Cathcart looked at him and raised his eyebrows.

"Odours," he replied, "are not so easy as sounds and sights of telepathic communication. I make as much, or as little, probably, as you do yourself."

He was not quite so glib as usual with his explanations. That was all.

At the fall of day, cold, exhausted, famished, the party came to the end of the long portage and dragged themselves into a camp that at first glimpse seemed empty. Fire there was none, and no Punk came forward to welcome them. The emotional capacity of all three was too over-spent to recognize either surprise or annoyance; but the cry of spontaneous affection that burst from the lips of Hank, as he rushed ahead of them towards the fireplace, came probably as a warning that the end of the amazing affair was not quite yet. And both Cathcart and his nephew confessed afterwards that when they saw him kneel down in his excitement and embrace something that reclined, gently moving, beside the extinguished ashes, they felt in their very bones that this "something" would prove to be Défago—the true Défago, returned.

And so, indeed, it was.

It is soon told. Exhausted to the point of emaciation, the French Canadian—what was left of him, that is—fumbled among the ashes, trying to make a fire. His body crouched there, the weak fingers obeying feebly the instinctive habit of a lifetime with twigs and matches. But there was no longer any mind to direct the simple operation. The mind had fled beyond recall. And with it, too, had fled memory. Not only recent events, but all previous life was a blank.

This time it was the real man, though incredibly and horribly shrunken. On his face was no expression of any kind whatever—fear, welcome, or recognition. He did not seem to know who it was that embraced him, or who it was that fed, warmed and spoke to him the words of comfort and relief. Forlorn and broken beyond all reach of human aid, the little man did meekly as he was bidden. The "something" that had constituted him "individual" had vanished for ever.

In some ways it was more terribly moving than anything they had yet seen—that idiot smile as he drew wads of coarse moss from his swollen cheeks and told them that he was "a damned moss eater"; the continued vomiting of even the simplest food; and, worst of all, the piteous and childish voice of complaint in which he told them that his feet pained him—"burn like fire"—which was natural enough when Dr. Cathcart examined them and found that both were dreadfully frozen. Beneath the eyes there were faint indications of recent bleeding.

The details of how he survived the prolonged exposure, of where he had been, or of how he covered the great distance from one camp to the other, including an immense detour of the lake on foot since he had no canoe—all this remains unknown. His memory had vanished completely. And before the end of the winter whose beginning witnessed this strange occurrence, Défago, bereft of mind, memory and soul, had gone with it. He lingered only a few weeks.

And what Punk was able to contribute to the story throws no further light upon it. He was cleaning fish by the lake shore about five o'clock in the evening—an hour, that is, before the search party returned—when he saw this shadow of the guide picking its way weakly into camp. In advance of him, he declares, came the faint whiff of a certain singular odour.

That same instant old Punk started for home. He covered the entire journey of three days as only Indian blood could have covered it. The terror of a whole race drove him. He knew what it all meant. Défago had "seen the Wendigo."

Frederick Philip Grove
CONSIDER HER WAYS

An apogee of fantastic writing has to be the "Ant-Book," which served for decades as the working title of Consider Her Ways *(1947). This amazing, three-hundred-page novel was written by Frederick Philip Grove (1879-1948), who claimed he was born of Swedish parents in Russia but whom scholars now believe was born Felix Paul Greve in Radomno on the Polish-Prussian border. Greve translated books by H. G. Wells and Oscar Wilde into German and then disappeared from the annals of German literature. Grove immigrated to North America in 1892 and began teaching in Manitoba in 1912. He was a chronicler of prairie life second to none in such works as* Over Prairie Trails *(1922) and* A Search for America *(1927). Less widely read is* Consider Her Ways, *which represents an ant's eye view of human civilization. It takes the form of an ant's first-person account of a scientific expedition of ten thousand worker ants which, over a period of eight years, treks from the rain forests of Venezuela, across the Panama Canal and the Great American Plains, to New York, before returning (by train) to Venezuela. The plan for this work "reaches back to 1892 or 1893," Grove explained in his correspondence, but the novel was actually written in 1919-20. "The Ant-Book has one great advantage: it is startling," Grove wrote to the editor Lorne Pierce.* Consider Her Ways *was added to the New Canadian Library in 1977. In the excerpt that follows, the expedition has been reduced to three ants. Wawa-Quee (the narrator and commander), Bissatee (the zoologist), and Azte-ca (the signaller) have taken refuge in the New York Public Library. Here Wawa-Quee explains why "our own race stands at the very apex of creation as far as that creation is completed today."*

W hen I recovered my consciousness, I was alone, surrounded by twilight, though, throughout the outer reaches of the structure in which I was, broad daylight flooded the air. I had some trouble in remembering; too much had happened. But as my memory returned, I saw myself, or rather the three of us, struggling again through snow and sleet and rain, the human road roaring with noise and traffic; and I felt sorry for myself.

I tried to move but could not. Where was I? Though I recalled that I must be in that great hominary where the humans of this city kept their records, I had not the slightest idea of what was immediately surrounding me. To the right, a rough earthen wall rose to a dizzy height; to the left, there were peculiar columnar structures fifteen antlengths high, terminating in an uneven line above; these exhaled the smell of paper made of wood and of cotton fabrics mixed with that of fish glue and oil—a mixture I had never smelt before.

There was no light near me; but as my glance followed the right-hand wall upward, it lost itself in a sea of sunlight above, barred with black lines of shadow. Again I tried to move and failed in the attempt. My wounds, which I now remembered again, did not smart while I lay still; but at every motion a pain as of tightening ligatures encircled my thorax, so intense that I winced and henceforth was content to remain motionless. Thus I lay for hours.

Then, to my infinite joy, I scented Bissa-tee approaching along the broken upper edge of the columnar structures to my left. I even saw her peering down at me. But she did not yet come. In my weakened and helpless state, this precipitated me into the depths of despair. I feared I was completely abandoned; I was left there to die alone; for, unless I was surrounded by the care of helpful friends, I could see nothing ahead of me but a miserable end.

However, presently Bissa-tee returned.

I must here express my profound and sincere sorrow at Bissa-tee's untimely death of which we shall hear in due course; not only because by that death she was deprived of the full harvest of renown and glory which was her due on account of her great discoveries and achievements in zoology; but also because the example of her unrivalled tact as a medical ant was lost to ant-kind. Her surgical and medicinal knowledge and skill, I have no doubt, can be equalled by others, remarkable though they were; but the subtle gradations of her bedside manner were unique. It was her theory that a patient must above all heal herself; and that a doctor could help most by putting her into the humour which was appropriate to her condition. Thus when rest and relaxation were indicated, she could be so tenderly and sorrowfully sympathetic that her patient simply surrendered herself to her ministrations, just as a callow surrenders herself to her nurse-ant; and when a cheerful fighting spirit was needed, she would beat her thorax and rumble along in a loud, boisterous way which made you laugh and desire to get up at once in order to have a playful bout with her. Between these two extremes she had an infinite number of gradations so subtly adapted to the condition of the patient that I am inclined to assert her mere occasional presence had a curative effect even on my wounds, however slight or serious they may have been.

On the present occasion she was all soothing drowsiness. In sweet, soporific scents she assured me that I was doing famously; but I must not yet try to satisfy my curiosity; I must lie quite still; with proper treatment and nourishing food I should, in a very few days, be exploring again for myself.

At the scent of "nourishing food" I realized with something like a pang just how hungry I was; for I had not eaten since, led by our tiny friends, we had left our station in the middle-west of the continent. So, when Bissa-tee gently raised my head and regurgitated food for me, it seemed the most natural thing for her to do—as though the mere fact of her having anything to regurgitate were not an almost miraculous circumstance. And what she had was fungi; it is true they were not the species cultivated at home; in fact, as I found out, they were properly moulds and not fungi at all; but Bissa-tee administered them with such a matter-of-course air that I swallowed them readily, in spite of a slightly bitter taste which I ascribed to medicinal ingredients. Meanwhile she kept up a constant, murmuring stream of scents, conveying to me the information that, for the time being, all our troubles were at an end: man was providing for us, not only shelter and heat, but excellent food as well.

If it was her purpose to put me quietly to sleep again, she succeeded completely; as, after having partaken of this food, I became drowsy, her manner changed to one of absolute somnolence; as though, like some goddess of sleep, she were pouring hypnotics into my antennæ.

I believe I slept for many days; for, when I awoke at last, my wounds were nearly healed; and Bissa-tee had completely changed her behaviour. This time she was present at the moment of my awaking; and she was engaged in dissolving those tight bands about my thorax by applying saliva to them. No sooner did she notice that I was emerging from my long sleep than she began to scent to me in the most inspiriting way that, as soon as she had finished removing my bandages, I might go and find out where I was.

Only then did it strike me as curious that, while I had a subconscious memory of the frequent visits of Bissa-tee during my long illness, I had not once, in all that time, been visited by Azte-ca. I promptly enquired after her; and Bissa-tee shook with laughter. It took her quite a while to recover from her mirth; but when she did, she told me that Azte-ca was indeed lost to the world: she had succeeded in deciphering the human records and had now no time for anything else. She was positively reckless, Bissa-tee added; she was transscenting some of her more amazing discoveries at a point to which she, Bissa-tee, could lead me if I so desired. Her recklessness consisted in pursuing her studies day and night, often under the very noses and eyes of man; and she devoted no more than an indispensable minimum of time to rest and sleep. She frankly admitted, Bissa-tee added, that she exposed herself to constant danger; but she had gone insane with her curiosity; and she averred that, since her discoveries were scented on the wall of the building, her death did not matter, so long as she could pursue her studies, as she called them, to the end.

My impatience became such that I could hardly wait till Bissa-tee had finished her task before I asked her to show me these scent-fields—for such she called them—of Azte-ca's. Accordingly, as soon as we could, we set out for the place which was excellently chosen, for to the left, there being a gap in the obscuring columnar structures, a warm current of air ascended along the wall. These walls curved upwards from all sides to a circular opening which was crowned by a vaulted dome admitting a flood of light from above. As far as I could survey it, the whole chamber resembled, on a gigantic scale, those which we build for our fungus-gardens. No doubt some man had seen the latter and brought home the art; for man is the most imitative of all animals.

Incidentally, I discovered on this first trip of exploration the source of the food which Bissa-tee had administered to me. I must, however, not forget to mention that she had also informed me of the nature of the columnar structures which I had noticed to my left. They were what, in a scent new to me, she called books or human records; and in describing them as a collective unit she used another scent unknown to me—a scent which I will render by our own scent literature. Now all this human literature was mouldy; and, as I walked along behind my physician and nurse, I could not refrain here and there from nibbling at these moulds which had the exact taste of Bissa-tee's regurgitation. When, on the present occasion, she saw me, she laughed. "Bitter?" she asked; and when I agreed, she added, "Queer stuff; no doubt the bitterness is imparted by the contents. It's wholesome food; but, if I'm any judge, it must be poison for man. You won't see many healthy and normal specimens here, such as we've seen in the fields and the streets; those that come here, somehow look like worms to me; if it were not flattering them, I'd call them bookworms. I hope no real bookworm will scent me, though." And again she laughed in her boisterous way, shaking from head to gaster as she went on, "They'd have made good food for our lamented friend Assa-ree and her hordes."

I thought her almost frivolous; it had been tacitly understood between us that Assa-ree was not to be mentioned.

But to come to our records. I was soon absorbed in what Azte-ca had recorded: it formed amazing scenting.

First of all, in an introduction of her own, she explained the physical nature of human records. Man had a limited number of visual symbols standing for sounds. These sound-symbols were arranged in groups called words; and words were arranged in lines; and groups of lines in pages. These pages were imprinted on sheets of paper made by chewing wood—a manufacture familiar to us from certain tribes of our own kind as well as from wasps. These sheets of paper, both sides of which were used, were then fastened together in bunches of from one to three hundred and formed a book. The only way in which an ant, even when she had deciphered this cumbersome system of symbols, could read human records was to run along line after line and to look at symbol after symbol, carefully fitting them together into an auditional perception; and, next, to fit the auditional perceptions together into a conceptual context. By way of an admiring foot-note, Azte-ca added that man had taken great pains to guard against these records being used by the uninitiated; for, she explained, the same symbol or group of symbols is often used for very different sounds; and many symbols are carefully imprinted between others without having any sound-value whatever: a perversity which, to me, seemed to render the whole system worthless. I was inclined to think that Azte-ca was simply mistaken in her assumptions; I convinced myself later on that she was right; but I did not agree with her in admiring man for having found a way of making access to his records intellectually very difficult to his fellow-men. Still later I found, from man's own records, that it takes his callows, according to the degree of initiation required, from six to sixteen years to acquire the art of deciphering such records as they may need in the station of life which they wish to occupy. On the other hand, it took me, once I had grasped the complicated principles involved, exactly one hour to learn to read any record of his.

But to continue. When such a book is opened, two consecutive pages are accessible; to make the next two available, a leaf has to be turned. And this, Azte-ca stated, she had learned to do. One considerable difficulty, which I discovered later, Azte-ca failed to mention, namely, that the order in which the primary sound-symbols are printed runs invariably from left to right, instead of alternating from line to line, which means that we, after having run along one line, had to return to our starting-point idle. The labour involved was thereby doubled.

In order to finish this topic before I proceed, I will anticipate here. Azte-ca was indefatigable in her labours and soon became so infatuated with man's perverse ways that she devoured this literature of his seemingly for no other purpose than to transscent it on the walls of the building. Whatever books she found open on the reading tables provided for humans she went through indiscriminately. Bissa-tee, on the other hand, though she learned the art of deciphering, never indulged in its exercise beyond a measure which she prescribed for herself for the purpose of reducing or "slimming" as she called it; like our lamented Anna-zee, she was rapidly becoming obese.

I myself used more discrimination in the choice of books which I read. I soon found that Azte-ca was wasting her time on an enormous amount of what the humans call fiction, i.e., books written on entirely imaginary things; she actually used to get excited about them, especially when they dealt with crime and its detection. It did not take me long to find out that, whenever she came to a record of human science or history, she promptly left it; I only needed to watch her in order to have the very thing which I wanted; it was invariably what she disdained. As for her omnivorous and injudicious reading, I will give one or two figures. During the seventeen moons which we spent in this hominary, she read no less than 6,321 books; which feat involved travelling, afoot and at top speed, a total distance of 1,769,880,000 antlengths or about 13,696 human miles. In all which she had no other aim than to satisfy a vulgar curiosity. I myself, on the other hand, aimed at understanding man's social organization which would decide his position in the phylogenetic scale of evolution.

It goes without saying that in this brief record I cannot even summarize the information gathered. The curious are referred to scent-trees 346 to 389 and 733 to 813 for such a summary. At present I must be content to relate events rather than give the results of investigation and research.

During our stay in this *library* we had, naturally, to adjust our own day to that of the humans. Or perhaps it would be more correct to state that I had to do so; for Bissa-tee stood apart from our labours, learning to decipher the records of man more from a motive of vanity than from that of a thirst for knowledge which is the fountain head of all intellectual achievement; and Azte-ca, in spite of repeated warnings, took such risks as no ant should take.

To speak of her first, I might say that she pursued her reading at almost any time of the day or night. Usually the library began to fill with human readers quite early in the morning; and Azte-ca soon knew a good many of them. That is to say, she knew their tastes in literature and the places where they preferred to sit. There was accommodation for eight hundred human readers. I will briefly tell of the circumstances which first induced her to disregard all danger. On the counter near the door where at night nearly all books that had been used and were required again must be deposited, she had become acquainted with a record which, from what she reported about it, dealt with a peculiarly intricate murder story; and she had just reached the most exciting part of it (for in all this branch of literature man aims chiefly at excitement) when, next morning, the human officers of the library arrived; so far she had always taken that for a signal to retire; and she did so on this occasion. She watched, however, for she was trembling with excitement; and soon she saw a human female appear and take up this record which she carried to a certain favourite seat of hers. This was exactly what Azte-ca had expected. But within an hour the human female finished her reading and returned the book to the counter where she was supplied with another. Azte-ca had, in the meantime, on one of the shelves where the books were kept, run the whole round of the hall, getting herself quite out of breath with hurry. She hated to lose sight of that precious record. To her disgust, a human attendant promptly picked it up and replaced it on one of the shelves. Again Azte-ca ran a race with this man and, helpless to prevent it, saw what he did. There it was to stand henceforth, much regretted by Azte-ca, tightly wedged in between other records. I believe that, had she lived a thousand years, she would still have been impatient whenever anyone alluded to that book; for although she read meanwhile thousands upon thousands of other books, she could never forget her being disappointed of this one. She asserted, of course, that her curiosity was solely concerned with the question whether man's resolution of the mystery agreed with her own which she pronounced to be highly ingenious. We often teased her about it. But from that day on she began to take undue risks. Whenever, henceforth, she had been unable to finish a book, she made it a point to linger about the counter where she could not turn the pages without being detected; and when the human reader returned for the book, she jumped on to his flowing outer integuments and climbed up on shoulder or head of this reader. When he sat down, she remained and read with him. This was an art which she acquired by infinite practice: I never did; my eye-sight was no longer good enough. For man does not run along the lines when he reads; he merely follows them with his eyes; and Azte-ca who, as I have repeatedly said, was a genius in her way, soon learned from him. Many and many a time she was seen, of course, and ruthlessly brushed to the ground by a human fore-foot; but she was not to be discouraged by such slight reverses, not even after she had lost a middle leg by a fall. Ultimately, as we shall see, Azte-ca brought disaster upon herself and came near bringing it upon Bissa-tee and me as well.

I myself read chiefly at night and rested in day-time. The sort of books I read—science, history, philosophy, and the like—were mostly used by privileged human readers of a more or less advanced age who had the

95

right to leave them, piled together, on the tables where they had their seats; and there these books were left undisturbed when at night their readers went home. Such records, which were often of considerable bulk, presented, however, one considerable difficulty, namely, that they were exceedingly hard to open. Almost every night I had to enlist the help of both my associates in order to achieve that feat; and though I did manage to turn the often large and stiff pages by myself, that task, too, required the exertion of every ounce of my strength. I pursued my studies invariably till the first human readers appeared which was an hour or two after the attendants had arrived at the counter.

As for Bissa-tee, I have already said that she took no interest whatever in our pursuits; for two or three hours every morning she indulged in what she called gymnastics, in order to keep her ever growing bulk within manageable limits; after that she undid whatever effect these exercises might have had by roaming all over this hominary in search of the choicest moulds; she asserted that these varied considerably according to the kind of literature they grew on, being bitter and tasting of medicinal substances when growing on philosophic works; sweet and ethereal, when growing on poetry written by females; and having an outright intoxicating effect when growing on works of so-called theology. Personally, I never could taste the difference.

For a long while—in fact, for over a year—life thus went on placidly enough. The moulds growing on this human literature furnished an inexhaustible and nourishing though, to me, slightly unpalatable food; the temperature was almost as equable as in our brood-chambers; and we seemed to be perfectly safe.

Then I had the first terrifying intimation of the fact that our presence had not remained unnoticed. What I am about to relate forms one of the most harassing memories of this period; and it is with some hesitation that I set it down; only a strict regard for truth forces me not to suppress a single feature of the adventure.

I had by this time completely mastered the art of understanding human speech. For this purpose I had my ear-drums coated, just as in the past I had coated those of Azte-ca; but we now used a different substance for the purpose, namely, a liquid which, on exposure to the air, hardened quickly and which we found in large glasses on the counter by the door; man calls it *mucilage*. These coatings which Bissa-tee applied for me, so deadened the thunder of the human voice that it reached my delicate auditory nerves as from a great distance, resembling the pleasant murmur of a brook.

One night, then—I believe it was in the fourteenth moon of our stay in the library—I had run across a book dealing with ourselves. My students will hardly credit the fact, which is nevertheless quite true: this book was written by our old friend or enemy, the Wheeler. It seems only natural that I should have been sufficiently absorbed to lose track of the passage of time; and suddenly I became aware that I had read on, still turning the pages, till it was broad daylight. Already there were numbers of human readers scattered throughout the great chamber and engaged in their studies. Now the human which had frequented this particular reading platform, in a remote corner of the hall, was a young female which did not, as a rule, make its appearance much before noon. So, glancing about and finding that I was in fair privacy, I made up my mind that it was safe to go on for another hour or so; for I had just reached an account, from the human point of view, of the Attas.

To my dismay, however, the human female appeared shortly, and at the very moment when I was laboriously turning a page. She was a bold sort of callow, not over forty years old; and humans, I suppose, would have called her handsome. Her head was covered by a sort of smooth clypeus; and her neck rolled up in a thick fur resembling that of a fox (I shall have more to say about these singular human integuments in the next section). She was tall, slender, and athletic; and her face showed several coatings of a wax-like substance of two colours, white and red. This coating, Bissa-tee conjectured, was applied by the tongues of males; one day, she asserted, she had, in a recess of the library, distinctly seen a male applying its mouth to the cheek of a female; and, investigating at once, she had, beyond the possibility of a doubt, ascertained the fact that the same substance, also red and white, was coating the lips of the male which promptly protruded its tongue to lick it back into its mouth.

Now I must explain that, from the very moment on when Azte-ca had first deciphered human speech and records, I had cherished the hope of establishing communication with man. This could not be done orally; for man's auditory nerves are far too coarse to perceive the fine and delicate sounds we produce by stridulation. It could be done only by way of his records, and I had already conceived a practicable method.

When, therefore, the human female appeared on this fateful morning, I made up my mind to attempt this great task then and there. Here, I said to myself, is a human being which, by the very nature of its reading, shows that it is interested in ants. What better opportunity could I expect to find?

I dropped the leaf I was on the point of turning and began running along the lines of the page; and whenever I found one of the symbols I needed, I carefully deposited a drop of my black anal secretion below it. I could not believe that she would fail to see it.

Imagine, therefore, my surprise when this female, at sight of me, uttered a low scream and instinctively, at least so it seemed, swept me to the ground by a terrible swoop of her fore-foot. Yet even then I could not conceive of a young female's soul being so devoid of all finer stirrings as to make it instinctively bent on murder. Had she watched for just a minute, she could not have failed to grasp my intention. But what did she do? She ran after me and, raising her hind-foot, tried to bring it down on me, just as the man had done in the street some fourteen moons ago.

It was my good fortune that I did not for a moment lose my presence of mind. Seeing what this human female was about, I remembered an anatomical peculiarity of the female foot as compared with that of the male. The fore-part of the foot consists, on its under side, of a huge, flat expanse which, towards the rear, curves up into a vault behind which there is a columnar heel; this heel is, in the female, much higher than in the male. I have sometimes thought that it would be possible to classify human beings by their heels: the higher it is, the larger the share of the female characteristics, even in males; and the lower it is, the larger the share of the male characteristics, even in females. I believe this would furnish a perfectly sound basis for division. But to return to my story.

Remembering this peculiarity of the foot of the female, I turned on my back when I saw the foot descending upon me. At the exactly right moment I propelled myself upward with an extreme exertion, first raising abdomen and head and then bringing them down with a thump on the smooth stone of the floor, imparting a spring to my whole body. I had to calculate that jump to a nicety; for had I reached sole or heel instead of the arch of the foot, it would have meant certain death. To my relief, however, I found myself, a moment later, securely clinging to the vaulted roof of that arch; and then the foot, with a terrific impact, came down on the floor, nearly dislodging me.

Apparently the human female was half exhausted by the effort; for she dropped into a sitting posture in what humans call an arm-chair. This sitting position was of a kind peculiar to humans which must ever seem offensive to the modesty of ants. My students can imagine the state of mind I was in. The moment the tension resolved itself into the feeling of relief, I simply shook with indignation: a clumsy human female had nearly annihilated me, the depositary of the most advanced science of ants!

In relating the remainder of this adventure, however, I cannot but confess to a certain degree of shame. I, a votary of science, having just, by a special dispensation, escaped from imminent danger, should not have allowed myself to be carried away by unreasoning anger. Yet, had I not been so carried away, we should not have had the warning to which I have referred. Let the student remember that even science leaves us, in our lesser moments, mere formicarian beings subject to passion. For my own justification I can say that I struggled against the lower impulse which, however, proved stronger than my more elevated thought.

Slowly and stealthily I left the cave of my refuge and swung up on top of that foot. There, too, it was partly covered with the same coriaceous integument as the sole. I proceeded upward along the tibial reach of the leg, covered, up to and slightly beyond the genicular joint, by a different, fibrous integument. Over this I ran carefuly and swiftly, feeling comparatively safe, for I was here hidden from the female's eye by a series of outer, long, curtain-like coverings. More than once, however, the human female made sudden rubbing movements, leg against leg, as if to brush me off, just as we should try to brush off a particle of dust irritating our legs. Whenever she did so, I stopped, keeping out of the way.

And then I reached a large, bare expanse of soft white skin and stopped. I was standing on the very edge of the fibrous integument covering her tibia. While pausing, I collected in my poison glands as large a quantity of formic acid as I could muster; and, taking hold, with my jaws, of the soft flesh, I injected, in a sudden giddy burst of passion quite unworthy of myself, an enormous dose of the poison.

A scream resounded such as I never hope to hear again. The sound loosened my joints. It was followed by a most violent motion. The human female had, with one single bound, sought the privacy of a niche behind a book-rack; and before I was aware of what was happening, she there lifted up her outer, loose integuments. She must actually have seen me in the act of withdrawing my sting. Fortunately her scream had attracted the attention of a number of males who came running; and as they appeared, the young female for one reason or other dropped those fringe-like integuments. I took a leap, reached the rear edge of these fringes, and jumped to safety on a book-shelf.

Thence I watched and listened. The young female turned to one of the males who seemed to be a man in authority and said, her eyes flashing, "The whole place swarms with ants!" "Yes," replied the male. "We have had complaints before. I shall see to it shortly."

That was our warning; and I did not fail to communicate it to my associates. The incident has been given in such detail chiefly because I suspect it led directly to the catastrophe which was to terminate our stay in the library. But, strange to say, this catastrophe was delayed for several moons, perhaps because we, having had a warning, became much more cautious; till, early in the spring of the second year, the seventh of our absence from home, we became just a little careless again and thereby precipitated the vengeance of man.

One morning there appeared a whole squad of old human females of a type which we had, so far, seen only singly. They were the charwomen who looked after the cleaning of the floors. Bissa-tee was, at the time, absorbed in her gymnastic exercises which she now performed religiously every morning in order to keep her ever growing corpulency down: she was at the back of that row of books behind which, a year and a half ago, I had regained consciousness. Azte-ca was on the counter near the open door, reading a detective story and, therefore, lost to the world. I was sunning myself on a shelf along the eastern wall. It was a most beautiful day of the early spring.

The moment I saw that squad of old women with their pails, carrying long-handled, loose, fringy things called mops, I felt invaded by a sense of coming disaster. They looked so sinister and determined. Only then did it strike me that no human readers had yet appeared although it was quite late in the day. For a moment I thought this must be one of those periodically recurring days on which the library remained closed. But I also knew that these days came in a regular succession and that none was due. I felt it my duty to investigate at once.

One of the women emptied the fluid in her pail on the floor; and promptly all of them began to swish it about with their mops. By this time I had gained a vantage-point on a window-ledge directly above them.

There I felt suddenly assailed by sickening fumes rising from that liquid which they were mopping about. For the fraction of a second I remained inactive; for the fumes seemed to deprive me of the power of motion; in fact, I came very near to falling off the ledge.

Then, with the sense of a coming disaster intensifying, I made a super-formicarian effort and hastened away, towards the place where Bissa-tee was performing her exercises. I was still under the illusion that Azte-ca was on the counter near the door. Unfortunately I chose the outside of the shelf for my hurried run. Had I been on the inside, between books and wall, I could not but have passed the very place where, at that moment, Azte-ca was engaged in recording the contents of her latest story on the wall. Only when I arrived opposite the spot where, an hour or so ago, I had left Bissa-tee, I swung up on the cliff formed by the books; and, a moment later, I espied Bissa-tee who had interrupted her exercises and was now standing rigid, waving her antennæ in a first realization of the coming danger; for the fumes were already faintly perceptible even here. When she saw me, she scented the single word,

"Chlorine," and stared at me. I told her what I had observed; and she turned at once, scenting, "Come," and began to scale the wall. This wall consisted of a rough-cast of aluminious clay. I soon passed Bissa-tee who, by reason of her recently-acquired obesity, was no longer quite as quick as she might have been. But when she reached the dizzy height of the next tier of windows, her scent overtook me, signalling "Stop!" We were here above the fumes; but I feared that, owing to the diffusing power of gases, they would soon reach us. I waited for Bissa-tee who was laboriously following in my wake. She turned at right angles to our previous line of ascent; and, going north, we reached a window-shelf, I being first again; but when Bissa-tee caught me up, she, to my infinite relief, pointed out a small round opening between frame and sash of the window—an opening through which a strong current of fresh air was entering from the outside. This opening was large enough for us to crawl through, a feat which Bissa-tee promptly proposed to perform. It was a feat indeed, for the air pressure against which we should have had to work was enormous. At the very moment, however, at which Bissa-tee was ins rting her head into this tunnel, I thought of Azte-ca and held her back.

Having communicated to her my misgivings with regard to our associate, I took a flying leap down to the topmost book-shelf where I intended to wait for Bissa-tee. But when she did not come, I looked up and saw her on the very edge of the ledge where she stood, waving to me in great distress that, owing to a fatty degeneration of her heart, she dared not to take the leap. I signalled back to her to wait and hurriedly ran south, in the direction of the counter near the door. Azte-ca was not there. I became frantic with alarm.

I quickly descended to the lower shelf on which we had our quarters. Here, the fumes were now much thicker; but disregarding all danger I dashed forward at a speed of which I should not have thought myself capable. I had barely reached our abandoned station when I caught sight of Azte-ca on the wall where she had only just become aware of the fumes.

I noticed that these fumes had here already taken sufficient effect to shrivel up the delicate moulds on which we had lived so long. But I did not delay over that; I was bent only on attracting Azte-ca's attention; and I cannot believe that the powerful scents I emitted should have failed to reach her; yet she paid no attention to them.

For a long while Azte-ca had shown symptoms of a peculiar mental aberration. It had become a mania with her to imagine herself in the part of a human being engaged in detecting crime. She had even elaborately constructed methods of committing such crime in a way which would make its detection impossible or at least exceedingly difficult. I am sorry to say that both Bissa-tee and myself had, in the beginning, encouraged her in this pernicious activity. We took an unreasonable pride in the fact that an ant should prove herself superior in ingenuity to man, a thing we should have treated as a matter of course. For our justification I can only aver that we ceased doing this as soon as we became aware of the effect this preoccupation had upon Azte-ca's practical sense.

This utter lack of practical sense, a consequence of the submersion of her mind in human folly, showed itself disastrously at the present moment. Already half overcome by the fumes, Azte-ca, instead of obeying my summons, precipitated herself from the dizzy height at which she was to the floor beneath. She was alive when she landed; but in her panic she made a dash in a direction exactly opposite to that which she should have taken. A moment later she lay, expiring, in the swirling flood whence our danger arose. It was my sad destiny to see her perish there. One of the old women said in a voice full of unspeakable disgust, "The nahsty crayture!" and squarely planted her foot on the dying ant. Thus perished Azte-ca, one of the most ingenious signallers the world had ever seen. She was crushed to a pulp. To such senseless accidents are we ants exposed on this earth!

I could not help her; I was by that time half overcome myself; and I sought safety in flight.

When I rejoined Bissa-tee, the news I brought almost prostrated her; and if I had not kept my head and propelled her towards the tunnel, she would have stayed behind and perished like Azte-ca. There was not a moment to lose.

The narrowness of the passage came near frustrating our escape. More than once Bissa-tee found her abdomen tightly jammed between its walls. Fortunately I was behind her; and so, after much squeezing and pushing, we arrived outside. When we did, we were so exhausted that we resolved to anchor ourselves as best we could and to stay where we were till we had regained a measure of our strength. During the interval of waiting we vowed to each other that under no circumstances would we allow ourselves to be separated after we had descended to earth. There was much speculation with regard to the direction to follow; for neither of us had paid much attention to this matter when we had arrived a year and a half ago: at that time we had simply followed the lead of our lamented Azte-ca.

We left our eyrie with the fall of night; and when the steep descent was accomplished, we struck east. There was no lack of light and scarcely a diminution of the traffic usual on these human roads; and we found this so harassing that, after a few hours, we were glad, on catching sight of another huge hominary, to be able to escape from it. This hominary which we thus entered by a mere chance turned out to be a sort of aphis-shed or stable for those enormous beasts that pull the human space-machines over the bands of steel provided for their progress.

We remained there for many days, watching and studying; Bissa-tee regained a measure of her former agility and enterprise and spent many hours exploring by herself. Ultimately she brought the news that she had found out when and whence a certain space-machine was going to start for the south-west.

That this south-west of the continent must be our destination was tacitly understood between us. With only the two of us left, we were bound to strike for home at last; and such is the power of hope which dwells forever in the breast of ants, that from now on we began to live mentally once more in the great and glorious formicary in the valley of the Orinoco River. I, for one, needed only to close my eyes in order to see myself stretched out luxuriously while half a dozen mediæ groomed my long-neglected body—a luxury which I had foregone for so many years. Bissa-tee, too, avowed that when she slept she dreamt of home; and henceforth, when we were awake, we both struggled and fought in order to get there. Already the sufferings and incessant labours which lay behind us counted for nothing; ahead of us lay the happy return.

A matter of six or seven days later we arrived, in a human space-machine, in a city near the mouth of that very river which we had crossed so long ago by way of the metal-threads of that mysterious spider which we had never seen after all. The river we crossed by an enormous bridge built on the same principle of which we make use in spanning smaller waters; and after various vicissitudes of which there is no need to speak in detail, we were launched on our last great march to the south and west. The difficulties and privations we had to cope with were worthy to inspire our minstrels and to be preserved for the memory of posterity as an inspiration to future generations.

Stephen Leacock
A FRAGMENT FROM UTOPIA

There is hardly a subject, including the future, that Stephen Leacock (1869-1944) did not lampoon somewhere in his voluminous writings. In Afternoons in Utopia: Tales of the New Time *(1932), which includes "A Fragment from Utopia: The Fifty-Fifty Sexes," he burlesques social-ism, communism and futurology. He specifically parodies Edward Bel-lamy's utopian novel* Looking Backward *(1887). As Ralph L. Curry noted in* Stephen Leacock: Humorist and Humanist *(1959): "Leacock did not bother with the garrulous style of* Looking Backward; *that was not the big fault. He made a logical extension of Bellamy's socialist Utopia until it became so perfect and dull that its citizens wanted to die." The excerpt printed here deals with feminism in a comical way.*

Note:
In this third decade of the twentieth century, it is already clear that the two sexes are moving towards a complete equality. Political equality came first, a thing practically everywhere achieved and now taken for granted. Economic equality is rapidly following, and social and domestic equality will ensue as an obvious consequence. Only one element, per-haps, was very generally left out of consideration in this process of social change. The two sexes necessarily react upon one another. Equalization will therefore be brought about not solely by modifying the character and status of the women, but also by altering that of the men. As Utopia approaches, men will be found more and more endowed with the grac-iousness and charm of the other sex, while losing nothing of the virtues of their own. Without an appreciation of this fact, a person of today would be perplexed and mystified in reading any account of social life in Utopia. As witness of the fact, let us take the following pages, a fragment of a Utopian novel, to which this antecedent note supplies the key:

Edward Evenshade had no sooner unfolded his newspaper on his way downtown that morning, than he saw that it contained news of the gravest importance, indeed news of an ominous significance. His eye had only half scanned the list of the foreign despatches when a tele-graphic item arrested his attention. It read:

"Current advices from Paris seem to make it certain that this season the waistline will be brought down low, and will even be kept close to the hip-bones."

All the way to his office, Edward could think of little else than this newest revolutionary dictate of fashion. If he had only known it, the news items of the year 1932, long before he was born, had contained exactly such an item. The waist-line had been shoved down to the hip-bones and held there. But in that remote day such an item referred only to women. In Edward Evenshade's time, men also had learned to take that anxious thought for a pleasing appearance which had previously been the sole prerogative of women. In Edward's day, if the waistline were moved by a decree of fashion to the hip-bone, no business man could hope to carry on his business without conforming to it. In fact, his clients and customers would expect it.

Evenshade threw the paper on his office desk.

"Have you seen it, Undertone?" he asked of his partner.

"I have," said Undertone, with evident indisposition, "and it's no use asking me. I *can't*. Mine won't stay there."

"Of course," said Edward, "if you will read a little further you'll have to admit that they modify it just a little. You see, it says you can define it with a narrow suède belt, if it is preferred."

"Can I do that?" asked Undertone. "Let me see it. Yes, that's right, 'can be defined if it is preferred by a narrow suède or fabric belt.' That might not look so bad, eh—a suède belt. Does it say anything about the colour?"

"Not here, but I've read elsewhere that the colours allowed this season will be principally puce or beige or, in the evening, navy blue and carnation pink."

"Is that so?" said Undertone. He seemed to fall into a sort of reverie. "Is that so?" he muttered again. Then, looking up from his fit of abstraction, "Did you say pink carnation or dull red carnation?" he asked.

"Pink," answered Edward.

"Well, say, I don't think pink would look so bad, eh? I've been trying it before the mirror here. Pink wouldn't be too young for me, would it?"

Edward Evenshade was still thinking of this ominous news item when he went over to his bank where he had to meet two or three of the directors in the board room. As he came in, they were leaning across the table reading one of these same despatches.

"I call it ridiculous," said the vice-president, the senior of the men present. "It is not only ridiculous but it is practically tyranny. Have you seen this, Evenshade?" he asked, turning to Edward as he entered.

"Yes," Edward said, "I saw it. It is outrageous, isn't it, to think that a set of men over in Paris—heaven knows who they are—should dictate to us men over here what we are to wear and how we are to wear it."

"Listen to this," said the vice-president. "'Coats are to be loose or belted and to achieve a straight simplicity by intricate smooth goring.' What this 'goring' is, I don't know, but it seems to me that a man won't be allowed to wear buttons on his coat."

"That's what it means," said Edward, "because it tells you elsewhere that smooth surfaces will be stressed, eliminating buttons almost entirely."

"What about pants?" asked the vice-president, "any buttons to them?"

"It doesn't seem to mention them," answered Edward.

The vice-president looked at the newspaper and ran his eye further down the column. "Listen to this—'Wide shoulders will be broadened by tricky cuts rather than by big sleeves, and narrow hips will be simulated by tailored fabric belts giving the impression of a high waistline.' "

"What's that?" interposed the general manager, a stout man, who hadn't yet spoken. "Let me see that about the wide shoulders—there seems some sense in that, eh? I don't know that I would object to that. When do we wear that, is that for the office or what?"

"Yes," said the vice-president, "that's for the day-time. It says that for the evening you wear a waist-length velvet evening jacket with a huge fur collar, often in skunk, and perhaps with cartridge-pleated velvet collar and cuffs."

"That sounds pretty nifty, doesn't it?" said the general manager.

"It does," said the vice-president. "I admit there's something in that. I've often thought, you know, that you'd get quite an effect with a really fine bit of fur like that—I mean for the evening when you want to wear something worth while. Does it say anything as to what kind of stuff or what coloured stuff you wear with it?"

They were all quite animated now, bending over the newspaper, their indignation apparently evaporated. "Here it is," said Edward Evenshade. "The best things seem to be a smooth printed Shantung or a pink organdie, with pastels as a distinct feature."

"I wonder how those would look?" said the vice-president.

"What is organdie, anyway?" asked the general manager.

"I don't know," said the third director, "but let's send out and get some." He rang the bell. "Young man," he said "kindly go down the street and get some Shantung and organdie."

"Yes, sir," said the young man, "already mixed or in two bottles?"

"No, no, it's a fabric. Get—oh, get about ten pounds of each."

106

"And while you're there, ask them if they have any skunk fur and a case of cartridges."

"Directly, sir," said the young man.

"You know," said the vice-president, stepping over to the large mirror at one side of the room and trimming his coat tight in to his waist, "I've often thought that in a way our clothes are all wrong. You take that line now—there—see what I mean, John—"

"I know," said the general manager, "or even drawn in a little more smartly—allow me—so, like that, eh?"

"You're right," said the vice-president. "I see how it means. The paper says, doesn't it, that the general effect aimed at is that of Egyptian silhouette? Something like this, eh?"

Edward realized that it was no use for him to try to do business with his fellow directors in their present preoccupation. He left, promising to come back later in the day. They were so absorbed that they hardly saw him go.

From the bank, as his business of the day demanded, Evenshade went to the office of the president of one of the great railways.

"Can I see the president?" he asked of the secretary in the outer office. The president and Edward Evenshade were old personal friends, and Edward was never denied an access to the private office of the magnate.

"I'm afraid not," said the young man.

"Is he busy with a conference?"

"No," said the secretary somewhat reluctantly, "not exactly that. His milliner is with him."

"His milliner?" said Edward.

"Yes. To tell the truth, it arose out of something in the morning's paper about the new change in the waistline—wait a minute—I have it here—'It is generally understood in Paris that the contemplated revolution in the waistline will react at once upon the hat. It is claimed that hats will be drawn lower in the brim than ever and set a little sideways with a suggestion of espièglerie, or even diablerie calculated to intrigue.' Yes, that was it; he was talking about it with the traffic manager and they sent out for some. I think they're trying them on."

"Perhaps I might wait," said Edward.

"I hardly think so," said the secretary, "they've been half an hour already."

At this moment a smart-looking messenger boy burst his way in. He had in each hand a huge round cardboard hat-box. "Hats for the president," he said. "I don't think—" began the secretary. "It's all right," said the boy. "He telephoned for them."

Edward realized that the ominous news from Paris had utterly upset the commercial world for the day. It was impossible to transact business in an atmosphere so tense with apprehension.

In fact, for the rest of the day he made no attempt to carry on the usual work of the office, merely sitting with Undertone discussing the outlook for a modified waistline and exchanging with his friends, over the telephone, comments on the extent to which a man might hold out against the decree.

It was a great relief to Edward when the wearisome business day was at last over, and he was able to set his face homewards. The pleasure was all the greater in that Edward had before him the anticipation of a dinner party which would at any rate give him a chance to wear some of his pretty things so soon to be discarded at the inexorable bidding of fashion.

That evening at about seven o'clock Edward Evenshade was seated on a low stool in front of a long mirror, engaged in dressing for dinner. Several new people were expected and naturally Edward wished to look his best.

But a choice is difficult. The litter of frills and laces on the floor beside him showed the vacillation of his mind. He had already almost decided on an evening dress shirt of soft white foulard with ruchings up to the throat, when he rejected it in favour of a dainty clinging slip-over of passementerie worn over a low brasserie. Then again he wondered whether burnt umber was really his colour. He picked up the dainty little dinner jacket and turned it in his hands. It was sweet, there was no doubt of it. On the other hand, not everybody can wear burnt umber. Would he look better in terra cotta or potash? But then again, the evening candle light at dinner is not like sunlight. But if he didn't wear the burnt umber then a jacket with a higher collar would mean doing his hair all over again, or at least clipping it close round his ears. Or would that show the shape of his head too much? He knew that the shape of his head, though he hated to admit it, was not his best point. It was shaped too much like a nut.

So sat Edward Evenshade in perplexity till the slamming of the front door and the sound of hurried steps on the stairs told him that Clara had come home.

"I'm late as hell, Eddie!" she called from the landing, "but it will be all right. I've still time to chuck on my clothes for dinner."

"No, come in here," called Edward from his dressing-room. "I want you to help me pick something to wear."

Clara strode into Edward's dressing-room.

"Why, Eddie," she exclaimed, "you're only half ready."

"I know, Clara. I just couldn't decide about the colours. Look! how do you like that?"

As he spoke, Edward held the little burnt umber dinner jacket up against his cheeks.

"Why, you look perfectly sweet," Clara said.

"No, but is the colour too strong for me?"

"I don't think so, dear, not in evening light. But if you think it is, why not put on something else? But I must skip. I've simply got to get ready. They'll be here in ten minutes."

"No, it's all right. They're invited for eight; there's lots of time. Before you go, what about money for Bridge tonight? Have you got any, or do you want any? And where do we stand today? You know, Clara, if we don't do up accounts each night it gets so complicated, doesn't it?"

"I know, Eddie," answered Clara, "but I write it down always. I've got it here in my little book. Yes, here it is. You paid me up to the day before yesterday, Tuesday—No, I'm wrong, we were square till last night. There's only today."

"All right, what are the items?"

Edward and Clara, like all other reasonable husbands and wives in Utopia, knew nothing of that economic dependence of the wife upon the husband which is the blot of our present situation. Although, in their case, Edward was the outside breadwinner and Clara lived at home, it was recognized that her functions in life and her work were just as much an economic contribution to their welfare as the money which Edward earned in his office. Their accounts were kept in accordance with this principle.

"What are the items?" asked Edward.

"Well," said Clara, "first, I took baby out of his cradle and washed him—two dollars is right, isn't it?"

"Quite right," said Edward. "If you sent him to the laundry they'd charge that."

"Then I rocked his cradle for an hour—"

"Two dollars," said Edward.

"But I sang to him," said Clara.

Edward looked doubtful. "I don't think that's extra," he said.

"All right, Eddie," said Clara good-naturedly, "let it go at that. Here are the other things, at the rates we've generally set for them—"

"Ordering the food over the telephone, fifty cents."

"Right!"

"Directions to maid about how not to cook the food for the dinner party, fifty cents."

"Right!"

"Having lunch with your mother at her house, five dollars."

"I suppose so," said Edward.

"Visit from the Reverend Canon Jaw and refusing a subscription to build a new chancel. What's that worth, Eddie, be fair? That saved a lot of money. And think of it! he was here an hour."

"I admit," said Edward, "that's tough; go on though, and we'll lump it together. What else?"

"Well, really nothing much," said Clara, looking at her notes. "Taking baby up, putting baby down, singing to baby, talking to Mrs. Woundup over the 'phone—but let that go. And then I went to golf at four and I'm just back."

"Well, call it for the whole of it, fifteen dollars, will that be all right?"

"Oh, quite right, Eddie, perfectly fair."

"As a matter of fact," said Edward, as he felt in his pocket for the money, "it's more than I made myself today downtown. Hardly any of us did much."

"Why?" asked Clara.

"Oh, this blasted news from Paris."

"I didn't see it. What news? Is it another market smash?"

"No, no, not that. This infernal fall of the waistline to the hips. But I suppose if we've got to do it, we must make up our minds to it like men. But skip, Clara, and get ready."

"Give me a kiss first," said Clara.

"Who pays?" asked Eddie.

"Fifty-fifty," she said.

A. E. van Vogt
BLACK DESTROYER

The initial letters "A. E." in this author's name stand for Alfred Elton, but according to that fan of fans, Forrest J. Ackerman, they should stand for "Amazing" and "Extraordinary." Of Dutch extraction, A. E. van Vogt was born in Winnipeg in 1912, and raised in Neville and Swift Current, Saskatchewan, and in Morden and Winnipeg, Manitoba. At fourteen he bought a copy of Amazing Stories *and became a devoted reader and then an inspired writer of SF&F. His first science-fiction story to appear in print, "Black Destroyer," was accepted by John W. Campbell, Jr., and published in the July 1939 issue of* Astounding Science Fiction. *That same year he married E. Mayne Hull, a Winnipeg-born writer, and the couple moved to Ottawa where van Vogt (exempt from military service because of poor eyesight) worked for the Department of National Defence. During this period he wrote the magazine versions of* Slan *(in 1940) and* The Weapon Makers *(in 1943).* Slan *was inspired by a reading of Ernest Thompson Seton's* The Biography of a Grizzly *(1900). After a brief stay in Toronto, where he became a member of the Canadian Authors Association, van Vogt and his wife moved to Los Angeles in 1944, and eventually became American citizens. He is the author of more than forty very popular novels and collections of stories.* Slan *(1946, revised 1951), the classic novel about the persecuted mutant, and* The Weapon Makers *(1947), a libertarian novel about the right to resist a tyrannical government, may be considered his "Canadian novels." Much of the above information appears in* Reflections of A. E. van Vogt *(1975). Elsewhere, Joanna Russ, the writer, has called van Vogt's writing "dream literature." Van Vogt himself stresses the heroic quality of his work: "Science fiction, as I personally try to write it, glorifies man and his future." The story reprinted here is hard to beat for energy and excitement. Van Vogt enters into the consciousness of this brilliant beast and shows how, through reason and technology, brute force may be overcome.*

O n and on Coeurl prowled! The black, moonless, almost starless night yielded reluctantly before a grim reddish dawn that crept up from his left. A vague, dull light it was, that gave no sense of approaching warmth, no comfort, nothing but a cold, diffuse lightness, slowly revealing a nightmare landscape.

Black, jagged rock and black, unliving plain took form around him, as a pale-red sun peered at last above the grotesque horizon. It was then Coeurl recognized suddenly that he was on familiar ground.

He stopped short. Tenseness flamed along his nerves. His muscles pressed with sudden, unrelenting strength against his bones. His great forelegs—twice as long as his hindlegs—twitched with a shuddering movement that arched every razor-sharp claw. The thick tentacles that sprouted from his shoulders ceased their weaving undulation, and grew taut with anxious alertness.

Utterly appalled, he twisted his great cat head from side to side, while the little hairlike tendrils that formed each ear vibrated frantically, testing every vagrant breeze, every throb in the ether.

But there was no response, no swift tingling along his intricate nervous system, not the faintest suggestion anywhere of the presence of the all-necessary id. Hopelessly, Coeurl crouched, an enormous catlike figure silhouetted against the dim reddish skyline, like a distorted etching of a black tiger resting on a black rock in a shadow world.

He had known this day would come. Through all the centuries of restless search, this day had loomed ever nearer, blacker, more frightening —this inevitable hour when he must return to the point where he began his systematic hunt in a world almost depleted of id-creatures.

The truth struck in waves like an endless, rhythmic ache at the seat of his ego. When he had started, there had been a few id-creatures in every hundred square miles, to be mercilessly rooted out. Only too well Coeurl knew in this ultimate hour that he had missed none. There were no id-creatures left to eat. In all the hundreds of thousands of square miles that he had made his own by right of ruthless conquest—until no neighboring coeurl dared to question his sovereignty—there was no id to feed the otherwise immortal engine that was his body.

Square foot by square foot he had gone over it. And now—he recognized the knoll of rock just ahead, and the black rock bridge that formed a queer, curling tunnel to his right. It was in that tunnel he had lain for days, waiting for the simple-minded, snakelike id-creature to come forth from its hole in the rock to bask in the sun—his first kill after he had realized the absolute necessity of organized extermination.

He licked his lips in brief gloating memory of the moment his slavering jaws tore the victim into precious toothsome bits. But the dark fear of an idless universe swept the sweet remembrance from his consciousness, leaving only certainty of death.

He snarled audibly, a defiant, devilish sound that quavered on the air, echoed and re-echoed among the rocks, and shuddered back along his nerves—instinctive and hellish expression of his will to live.

And then—abruptly—it came.

He saw it emerge out of the distance on a long downward slant, a tiny glowing spot that grew enormously into a metal ball. The great shining globe hissed by above Coeurl, slowing visibly in quick deceleration. It sped over a black line of hills to the right, hovered almost motionless for a second, then sank down out of sight.

Coeurl exploded from his startled immobility. With tiger speed, he flowed down among the rocks. His round, black eyes burned with the horrible desire that was an agony within him. His ear tendrils vibrated a message of id in such tremendous quantities that his body felt sick with the pangs of his abnormal hunger.

The little red sun was a crimson ball in the purple-black heavens when he crept up from behind a mass of rock and gazed from its shadows at the crumbling, gigantic ruins of the city that sprawled below him. The silvery globe, in spite of its great size, looked strangely inconspicuous against that vast, fairylike reach of ruins. Yet about it was a leashed aliveness, a dynamic quiescence that, after a moment, made it stand out, dominating the foreground. A massive, rock-crushing thing of metal, it rested on a cradle made by its own weight in the harsh, resisting plain which began abruptly at the outskirts of the dead metropolis.

Coeurl gazed at the strange, two-legged creatures who stood in little groups near the brilliantly lighted opening that yawned at the base of the ship. His throat thickened with the immediacy of his need; and his brain grew dark with the first wild impulse to burst forth in furious charge and smash these flimsy, helpless-looking creatures whose bodies emitted the id-vibrations.

Mists of memory stopped that mad rush when it was still only electricity surging through his muscles. Memory that brought fear in an acid stream of weakness, pouring along his nerves, poisoning the reservoirs of his strength. He had time to see that the creatures wore things over their real bodies, shimmering transparent material that glittered in strange, burning flashes in the rays of the sun.

Other memories came suddenly. Of dim days when the city that spread below was the living, breathing heart of an age of glory that dissolved in a single century before flaming guns whose wielders knew only that for the survivors there would be an ever-narrowing supply of id.

It was the remembrance of those guns that held him there, cringing in a wave of terror that blurred his reason. He saw himself smashed by balls of metal and burned by searing flame.

Came cunning—understanding of the presence of these creatures. This, Coeurl reasoned for the first time, was a scientific expedition from another star. In the olden days, the coeurls had thought of space travel, but disaster came too swiftly for it ever to be more than a thought.

Scientists meant investigation, not destruction. Scientists in their way were fools. Bold with his knowledge, he emerged into the open. He saw the creatures become aware of him. They turned and stared. One, the smallest of the group, detached a shining metal rod from a sheath, and held it casually in one hand. Coeurl loped on, shaken to his core by the action; but it was too late to turn back.

Commander Hal Morton heard little Gregory Kent, the chemist, laugh with the embarrassed half gurgle with which he invariably announced inner uncertainty. He saw Kent fingering the spindly metalite weapon.

Kent said: "I'll take no chances with anything as big as that."

Commander Morton allowed his own deep chuckle to echo along the

113

communicators. "That," he grunted finally, "is one of the reasons why you're on this expedition, Kent—because you never leave anything to chance."

His chuckle trailed off into silence. Instinctively, as he watched the monster approach them across that black rock plain, he moved forward until he stood a little in advance of the others, his huge form bulking the transparent metalite suit. The comments of the men pattered through the radio communicator into his ears:

"I'd hate to meet that baby on a dark night in an alley."

"Don't be silly. This is obviously an intelligent creature. Probably a member of the ruling race."

"It looks like nothing else than a big cat, if you forget those tentacles sticking out from its shoulders, and make allowances for those monster forelegs."

"Its physical development," said a voice, which Morton recognized as that of Siedel, the psychologist, "presupposes an animal-like adaptation to surroundings, not an intellectual one. On the other hand, its coming to us like this is not the act of an animal but of a creature possessing a mental awareness of our possible identity. You will notice that its movements are stiff, denoting caution, which suggests fear and consciousness of our weapons. I'd like to get a good look at the end of its tentacles. If they taper into handlike appendages that can really grip objects, then the conclusion would be inescapable that it is a descendant of the inhabitants of this city. It would be a great help if we could establish communication with it, even though appearances indicate that it has degenerated into a historyless primitive."

Coeurl stopped when he was still ten feet from the foremost creature. The sense of id was so overwhelming that his brain drifted to the ultimate verge of chaos. He felt as if his limbs were bathed in molten liquid; his very vision was not quite clear, as the sheer sensuality of his desire thundered through his being.

The men—all except the little one with the shining metal rod in his fingers—came closer. Coeurl saw that they were frankly and curiously examining him. Their lips were moving, and their voices beat in a monotonous, meaningless rhythm on his ear tendrils. At the same time he had the sense of waves of a much higher frequency—his own communication level—only it was a machinelike clicking that jarred his brain. With a distinct effort to appear friendly, he broadcast his name from his ear tendrils, at the same time pointing at himself with one curving tentacle.

Gourlay, chief of communications, drawled: "I got a sort of static in my radio when he wiggled those hairs, Morton. Do you think—"

"Looks very much like it," the leader answered the unfinished question. "That means a job for you, Gourlay. If it speaks by means of radio waves, it might not be altogether impossible that you can create some sort of television picture of its vibrations, or teach him the Morse code."

"Ah," said Siedel. "I was right. The tentacles each develop into seven strong fingers. Provided the nervous system is complicated enough, those fingers could, with training, operate any machine."

Morton said: "I think we'd better go in and have some lunch. Afterward, we've got to get busy. The material men can set up their machines and start gathering data on the planet's metal possibilities, and so on. The others can do a little careful exploring. I'd like some notes on architecture and on the scientific development of this race, and particularly what happened to wreck the civilization. On earth civilization after civilization crumbled, but always a new one sprang up in its dust. Why didn't that happen here? Any questions?"

"Yes. What about pussy? Look, he wants to come in with us."

Commander Morton frowned, an action that emphasized the deep-space pallor of his face. "I wish there was some way we could take it in with us, without forcibly capturing it. Kent, what do you think?"

"I think we should first decide whether it's an it or a him, and call it one or the other. I'm in favor of him. As for taking him in with us—" The little chemist shook his head decisively. "Impossible. This atmosphere is twenty-eight per cent chlorine. Our oxygen would be pure dynamite to his lungs."

The commander chuckled. "He doesn't believe that, apparently." He watched the catlike monster follow the first two men through the great door. The men kept an anxious distance from him, then glanced at Morton questioningly. Morton waved his hand. "O. K. Open the second lock and let him get a whiff of the oxygen. That'll cure him."

A moment later, he cursed his amazement. "By Heaven, he doesn't even notice the difference! That means he hasn't any lungs, or else the chlorine is not what his lungs use. Let him in! You bet he can go in! Smith, here's a treasure house for a biologist—harmless enough if we're careful. We can always handle him. But what a metabolism!"

Smith, a tall, thin, bony chap with a long, mournful face, said in an oddly forceful voice: "In all our travels, we've found only two higher forms of life. Those dependent on chlorine, and those who need oxygen—the two elements that support combustion. I'm prepared to stake my reputation that no complicated organism could ever adapt itself to both gases in a natural way. At first thought I should say here is an extremely advanced form of life. This race long ago discovered truths of biology that we are just beginning to suspect. Morton, we mustn't let this creature get away if we can help it."

"If his anxiety to get inside is any criterion," Commander Morton laughed, "then our difficulty will be to get rid of him."

He moved into the lock with Coeurl and the two men. The automatic machinery hummed; and in a few minutes they were standing at the bottom of a series of elevators that led up to the living quarters.

"Does that go up?" One of the men flicked a thumb in the direction of the monster.

"Better send him up alone, if he'll go in."

Coeurl offered no objection, until he heard the door slam behind him; and the closed cage shot upward. He whirled with a savage snarl, his reason swirling into chaos. With one leap, he pounced at the door. The metal bent under his plunge, and the desperate pain maddened him. Now, he was all trapped animal. He smashed at the metal with his paws, bending it like so much tin. He tore great bars loose with his thick tentacles. The machinery screeched; there were horrible jerks as the limitless power pulled the cage along in spite of projecting pieces of metal that scraped the outside walls. And then the cage stopped, and he snatched off the rest of the door and hurtled into the corridor.

He waited there until Morton and the men came up with drawn weapons. "We're fools," Morton said. "We should have shown him how it works. He thought we'd double-crossed him."

He motioned to the monster, and saw the savage glow fade from the coal-black eyes as he opened and closed the door with elaborate gestures to show the operation.

Coeurl ended the lesson by trotting into the large room to his right. He lay down on the rugged floor, and fought down the electric tautness of his nerves and muscles. A very fury of rage against himself for his fright consumed him. It seemed to his burning brain that he had lost the advantage of appearing a mild and harmless creature. His strength must have startled and dismayed them.

It meant greater danger in the task which he now knew he must accomplish: To kill everything in the ship, and take the machine back to their world in search of unlimited id.

With unwinking eyes, Coeurl lay and watched the two men clearing away the loose rubble from the metal doorway of the huge old building. His whole body ached with the hunger of his cells for id. The craving tore through his palpitant muscles, and throbbed like a living thing in his brain. His every nerve quivered to be off after the men who had wandered into the city. One of them, he knew, had gone—alone.

The dragging minutes fled; and still he restrained himself, still he lay there watching, aware that the men knew he watched. They floated a metal machine from the ship to the rock mass that blocked the great half-open door, under the direction of a third man. No flicker of their fingers escaped his fierce stare, and slowly, as the simplicity of the machinery became apparent to him, contempt grew upon him.

He knew what to expect finally, when the flame flared in incandescent violence and ate ravenously at the hard rock beneath. But in spite of his preknowledge, he deliberately jumped and snarled as if in fear, as that white heat burst forth. His ear tendrils caught the laughter of the men, their curious pleasure at his simulated dismay.

The door was released, and Morton came over and went inside with the third man. The latter shook his head.

"It's a shambles. You can catch the drift of the stuff. Obviously, they used atomic energy, but . . . but it's in wheel form. That's a peculiar development. In our science, atomic energy brought in the nonwheel machine. It's possible that here they've progressed further to a new type of wheel mechanics. I hope their libraries are better preserved than this, or we'll never know. What could have happened to a civilization to make it vanish like this?"

A third voice broke through the communicators: "This is Siedel. I heard your question, Pennons. Psychologically and sociologically speaking, the only reason why a territory becomes uninhabited is lack of food."

"But they're so advanced scientifically, why didn't they develop space flying and go elsewhere for their food?"

"Ask Gunlie Lester," interjected Morton. "I heard him expounding some theory even before we landed."

The astronomer answered the first call. "I've got to verify all my facts, but this desolate world is the only planet revolving around that miserable red sun. There's nothing else. No moon, not even a planetoid. And the nearest star system is *nine hundred light-years away.*

"So tremendous would have been the problem of the ruling race of this world, that in one jump they would not only have had to solve interplanetary but interstellar space traveling. When you consider how slow our own development was—first the moon, then Venus—each success leading to the next, and after centuries to the nearest stars; and last of all to the anti-accelerators that permitted galactic travel—considering all this, I maintain it would be impossible for any race to create such machines without practical experience. And, with the nearest star so far away, they had no incentive for the space adventuring that makes for experience."

Coeurl was trotting briskly over to another group. But now, in the driving appetite that consumed him, and in the frenzy of his high scorn, he paid no attention to what they were doing. Memories of past knowledge, jarred into activity by what he had seen, flowed into his consciousness in an ever developing and more vivid stream.

From group to group he sped, a nervous dynamo—jumpy, sick with his awful hunger. A little car rolled up, stopping in front of him, and a formidable camera whirred as it took a picture of him. Over on a mound of rock, a gigantic telescope was rearing up toward the sky. Nearby, a disintegrating machine drilled its searing fire into an ever-deepening hole, down and down, straight down.

Coeurl's mind became a blur of things he watched with half attention. And ever more imminent grew the moment when he knew he could no longer carry on the torture of acting. His brain strained with an irresistible impatience; his body burned with the fury of his eagerness to be off after the man who had gone alone into the city.

He could stand it no longer. A green foam misted his mouth, maddening him. He saw that, for the bare moment, nobody was looking.

Like a shot from a gun, he was off. He floated along in great, gliding leaps, a shadow among the shadows of the rocks. In a minute, the harsh terrain hid the spaceship and the two-legged beings.

Coeurl forgot the ship, forgot everything but his purpose, as if his brain had been wiped clear by a magic, memory-erasing brush. He circled widely, then raced into the city, along deserted streets, taking short cuts with the ease of familiarity, through gaping holes in time-weakened walls, through long corridors of moldering buildings. He slowed to a crouching lope as his ear tendrils caught the id vibrations.

Suddenly, he stopped and peered from a scatter of fallen rock. The man was standing at what must once have been a window, sending the glaring rays of his flashlight into the gloomy interior. The flash-light clicked off. The man, a heavy-set, powerful fellow, walked off with quick, alert steps. Coeurl didn't like that alertness. It presaged trouble; it meant lightning reaction to danger.

Coeurl waited till the human being had vanished around a corner, then he padded into the open. He was running now, tremendously faster than a man could walk, because his plan was clear in his brain. Like a wraith, he slipped down the next street, past a long block of buildings. He turned the first corner at top speed; and then, with dragging belly, crept into the half-darkness between the building and a huge chunk of débris. The street ahead was barred by a solid line of loose rubble that made it like a valley, ending in a narrow, bottlelike neck. The neck had its outlet just below Coeurl.

His ear tendrils caught the low-frequency waves of whistling. The sound throbbed through his being; and suddenly terror caught with icy

A. E. van Vogt

fingers at his brain. The man would have a gun. Suppose he leveled one burst of atomic energy—*one burst*—before his own muscles could whip out in murder fury.

A little shower of rocks streamed past. And then the man was beneath him. Coeurl reached out and struck a single crushing blow at the shimmering transparent headpiece of the spacesuit. There was a tearing sound of metal and a gushing of blood. The man doubled up as if part of him had been telescoped. For a moment, his bones and legs and muscles combined miraculously to keep him standing. Then he crumpled with a metallic clank of his space armor.

Fear completely evaporated, Coeurl leaped out of hiding. With ravenous speed, he smashed the metal and the body within it to bits. Great chunks of metal, torn piecemeal from the suit, sprayed the ground. Bones cracked. Flesh crunched.

It was simple to tune in on the vibrations of the id, and to create the violent chemical disorganization that freed it from the crushed bone. The id was, Coeurl discovered, mostly in the bone.

He felt revived, almost reborn. Here was more food than he had had in the whole past year.

Three minutes, and it was over, and Coeurl was off like a thing fleeing dire danger. Cautiously, he approached the glistening globe from the opposite side to that by which he had left. The men were all busy at their tasks. Gliding noiselessly, Coeurl slipped unnoticed up to a group of men.

Morton stared down at the horror of tattered flesh, metal and blood on the rock at his feet, and felt a tightening in his throat that prevented speech. He heard Kent say:

"He *would* go alone, damn him!" The little chemist's voice held a sob imprisoned; and Morton remembered that Kent and Jarvey had chummed together for years in the way only two men can.

"The worst part of it is," shuddered one of the men, "it looks like a senseless murder. His body is spread out like little lumps of flattened jelly, but it seems to be all there. I'd almost wager that if we weighed everything here, there'd still be one hundred and seventy-five pounds by earth gravity. That'd be about one hundred and seventy pounds here."

Smith broke in, his mournful face lined with gloom: "The killer attacked Jarvey, and then discovered his flesh was alien—uneatable. Just like our big cat. Wouldn't eat anything we set before him—" His words died out in sudden, queer silence. Then he said slowly: "Say, what about that creature? He's big enough and strong enough to have done this with his own little paws."

119

Morton frowned. "It's a thought. After all, he's the only living thing we've seen. We can't just execute him on suspicion, of course—"

"Besides," said one of the men, "he was never out of my sight."

Before Morton could speak, Siedel, the psychologist, snapped, "Positive about that?"

The man hesitated. "Maybe he was for a few minutes. He was wandering around so much, looking at everything."

"Exactly," said Siedel with satisfaction. He turned to Morton. "You see, commander, I, too, had the impression that he was always around; and yet, thinking back over it, I find gaps. There were moments—probably long minutes—when he was completely out of sight."

Morton's face was dark with thought, as Kent broke in fiercely: "I say, take no chances. Kill the brute on suspicion before he does any more damage."

Morton said slowly: "Korita, you've been wandering around with Cranessy and Van Horne. Do you think pussy is a descendant of the ruling class of this planet?"

The tall Japanese archeologist stared at the sky as if collecting his mind. "Commander Morton," he said finally, respectfully, "there is a mystery here. Take a look, all of you, at that majestic skyline. Notice the almost Gothic outline of the architecture. In spite of the megalopolis which they created, these people were close to the soil. The buildings are not simply ornamented. They are ornamental in themselves. Here is the equivalent of the Doric column, the Egyptian pyramid, the Gothic cathedral, growing out of the ground, earnest, big with destiny. If this lonely, desolate world can be regarded as a mother earth, then the land had a warm, a spiritual place in the hearts of the race.

"The effect is emphasized by the winding streets. Their machines prove they were mathematicians, but they were artists first; and so they did not create the geometrically designed cities of the ultra-sophisticated world metropolis. There is a genuine artistic abandon, a deep joyous emotion written in the curving and unmathematical arrangements of houses, buildings and avenues; a sense of intensity, of divine belief in an inner certainty. This is not a decadent, hoary-with-age civilization, but a young and vigorous culture, confident, strong with purpose.

"There it ended. Abruptly, as if at this point culture had its Battle of Tours, and began to collapse like the ancient Mohammedan civilization. Or as if in one leap it spanned the centuries and entered the period of contending states. In the Chinese civilization that period occupied 480-230 B.C., at the end of which the State of Tsin saw the beginning of the Chinese Empire. This phase Egypt experienced between 1780-1580 B.C., of which the last century was the 'Hyksos'—unmentionable—time. The

120

classical experienced it from Chæronea—338—and, at the pitch of horror, from the Gracchi—133—to Actium—31 B.C. The West European Americans were devastated by it in the nineteenth and twentieth centuries, and modern historians agree that, nominally, we entered the same phase fifty years ago; though, of course, we have solved the problem.

"You may ask, commander, what has all this to do with your question? My answer is: there is no record of a culture entering abruptly into the period of contending states. It is always a slow development; and the first step is a merciless questioning of all that was once held sacred. Inner certainties cease to exist, are dissolved before the ruthless probings of scientific and analytic minds. The skeptic becomes the highest type of being.

"I say that this culture ended abruptly in its most flourishing age. The sociological effects of such a catastrophe would be a sudden vanishing of morals, a reversion to almost bestial criminality, unleavened by any sense of ideal, a callous indifference to death. If this . . . this pussy is a descendant of such a race, then he will be a cunning creature, a thief in the night, a cold-blooded murderer, who would cut his own brother's throat for gain."

"That's enough!" It was Kent's clipped voice. "Commander, I'm willing to act the role of executioner."

Smith interrupted sharply: "Listen, Morton, you're not going to kill that cat yet, even if he is guilty. He's a biological treasure house."

Kent and Smith were glaring angrily at each other. Morton frowned at them thoughtfully, then said: "Korita, I'm inclined to accept your theory as a working basis. But one question: Pussy comes from a period earlier than our own? That is, we are entering the highly civilized era of our culture, while he became suddenly historyless in the most vigorous period of his. *But* it is possible that his culture is a later one on this planet than ours is in the galactic-wide system we have civilized?"

"Exactly. His may be the middle of the tenth civilization of his world; while ours is the end of the eighth spung from earth, each of the ten, of course, having been builded on the ruins of the one before it."

"In that case, pussy would not know anything about the skepticism that made it possible for us to find him out so positively as a criminal and murderer?"

"No; it would be literally magic to him."

Morton was smiling grimly. "Then I think you'll get your wish, Smith. We'll let pussy live; and if there are any fatalities, now that we know him, it will be due to rank carelessness. There's just the chance, of course, that we're wrong. Like Siedel, I also have the impression that he was

121

always around. But now—we can't leave poor Jarvey here like this. We'll put him in a coffin and bury him."

"No, we won't!" Kent barked. He flushed. "I beg your pardon, commander. I didn't mean it that way. I maintain pussy wanted something from that body. It looks to be all there, but something must be missing. I'm going to find out what, and pin this murder on him so that you'll have to believe it beyond the shadow of a doubt."

It was late night when Morton looked up from a book and saw Kent emerge through the door that led from the laboratories below.

Kent carried a large, flat bowl in his hands; his tired eyes flashed across at Morton, and he said in a weary, yet harsh, voice: "Now watch!"

He started toward Coeurl, who lay sprawled on the great rug, pretending to be asleep.

Morton stopped him. "Wait a minute, Kent. Any other time, I wouldn't question your actions, but you look ill; you're overwrought. What have you got there?"

Kent turned, and Morton saw that his first impression had been but a flashing glimpse of the truth. There were dark pouches under the little chemist's gray eyes—eyes that gazed feverishly from sunken cheeks in an ascetic face.

"I've found the missing element," Kent said. "It's phosphorus. There wasn't so much as a square millimeter of phosphorus left in Jarvey's bones. Every bit of it had been drained out—by what super-chemistry I don't know. There are ways of getting phosphorus out of the human body. For instance, a quick way was what happened to the workman who helped build this ship. Remember, he fell into fifteen tons of molten metalite—at least, so his relatives claimed—but the company wouldn't pay compensation until the metalite, on analysis, was found to contain a high percentage of phosphorus—"

"What about the bowl of food?" somebody interrupted. Men were putting away magazines and books, looking up with interest.

"It's got organic phosphorus in it. He'll get the scent, or whatever it is that he uses instead of scent—"

"I think he gets the vibrations of things," Gourlay interjected lazily. "Sometimes, when he wiggles those tendrils, I get a distinct static on the radio. And then, again, there's no reaction, just as if he's moved higher or lower on the wave scale. He seems to control the vibrations at will."

Kent waited with obvious impatience until Gourlay's last word, then abruptly went on: "All right, then, when he gets the vibration of the phosphorus and reacts to it like an animal, then—well, we can decide what we've proved by his reaction. May I go ahead, Morton?"

"There are three things wrong with your plan," Morton said. "In the first place, you seem to assume that he is only animal; you seem to have forgotten he may not be hungry after Jarvey; you seem to think that he will not be suspicious. But set the bowl down. His reaction may tell us something."

Coeurl stared with unblinking black eyes as the man set the bowl before him. His ear tendrils instantly caught the id-vibrations from the contents of the bowl—and he gave it not even a second glance.

He recognized this two-legged being as the one who had held the weapon that morning. Danger! With a snarl, he floated to his feet. He caught the bowl with the fingerlike appendages at the end of one looping tentacle, and emptied its content into the face of Kent, who shrank back with a yell.

Explosively, Coeurl flung the bowl aside and snapped a hawser-thick tentacle around the cursing man's waist. He didn't bother with the gun that hung from Kent's belt. It was only a vibration gun, he sensed—atomic powered, but not an atomic disintegrator. He tossed the kicking Kent onto the nearest couch—and realized with a hiss of dismay that he should have disarmed the man.

Not that the gun was dangerous—but, as the man furiously wiped the gruel from his face with one hand, he reached with the other for his weapon. Coeurl crouched back as the gun was raised slowly and a white beam of flame was discharged at his massive head.

His ear tendrils hummed as they canceled the efforts of the vibration gun. His round, black eyes narrowed as he caught the movement of men reaching for their metalite guns. Morton's voice lashed across the silence.

"Stop!"

Kent clicked off his weapon; and Coeurl crouched down, quivering with fury at this man who had forced him to reveal something of his power.

"Kent," said Morton coldly, "you're not the type to lose your head. You deliberately tried to kill pussy, knowing that the majority of us are in favor of keeping him alive. You know what our rule is: If anyone objects to my decisions, he must say so at the time. If the majority object, my decisions are overruled. In this case, no one but you objected, and, therefore, your action in taking the law into your own hands is most reprehensible, and automatically debars you from voting for a year."

Kent stared grimly at the circle of faces. "Korita was right when he said ours was a highly civilized age. It's decadent." Passion flamed harshly in his voice. "My God, isn't there a man here who can see the horror of the situation? Jarvey dead only a few hours, and this creature, whom we all know to be guilty, lying there unchained, planning his next murder; and the victim is right here in this room. What kind of men are we—fools, cynics, ghouls—or is it that our civilization is so steeped in reason that we can contemplate a murderer sympathetically?"

He fixed brooding eyes on Coeurl. "You were right, Morton, that's no animal. That's a devil from the deepest hell of this forgotten planet, whirling its solitary way around a dying sun."

"Don't go melodramatic on us," Morton said. "Your analysis is all wrong, so far as I am concerned. We're not ghouls or cynics; we're simply scientists, and pussy here is going to be studied. Now that we suspect him, we doubt his ability to trap any of us. One against a hundred hasn't a chance." He glanced around. "Do I speak for all of us?"

"Not for me, commander!" It was Smith who spoke, and, as Morton stared in amazement, he continued: "In the excitement and momentary confusion, no one seems to have noticed that when Kent fired his vibration gun, the beam hit this creature squarely on his cat head—and didn't hurt him."

Morton's amazed glance went from Smith to Coeurl, and back to Smith again. "Are you certain it hit him? As you say, it all happened so swiftly —when pussy wasn't hurt I simply assumed that Kent had missed him."

"He hit him in the face," Smith said positively. "A vibration gun, of course, can't even kill a man right away—but it can injure him. There's no sign of injury on pussy, though, not even a singed hair."

"Perhaps his skin is a good insulation against heat of any kind."

"Perhaps. But in view of our uncertainty, I think we should lock him up in the cage."

While Morton frowned darkly in thought, Kent spoke up. "Now you're talking sense, Smith."

Morton asked: "Then you would be satisfied, Kent, if we put him in the cage?"

Kent considered, finally: "Yes. If four inches of micro-steel can't hold him, we'd better give him the ship."

Coeurl followed the men as they went out into the corridor. He trotted docilely along as Morton unmistakably motioned him through a door he had not hitherto seen. He found himself in a square, solid metal room. The door clanged metallically behind him; he felt the flow of power as the electric lock clicked home.

His lips parted in a grimace of hate, as he realized the trap, but he gave no other outward reaction. It occurred to him that he had progressed a long way from the sunk-into-primitiveness creature who, a few hours before, had gone incoherent with fear in an elevator cage. Now, a thousand memories of his powers were reawakened in his brain; ten thousand cunnings were, after ages of disuse, once again part of his very being.

He sat quite still for a moment on the short, heavy haunches into which his body tapered, his ear tendrils examining his surroundings. Finally, he lay down, his eyes glowing with contemptuous fire. The fools! The poor fools!

It was about an hour later when he heard the man—Smith—fumbling overhead. Vibrations poured upon him, and for just an instant he was startled. He leaped to his feet in pure terror—and then realized that the vibrations were vibrations, not atomic explosions. Somebody was taking pictures of the inside of his body.

He crouched down again, but his ear tendrils vibrated, and he thought contemptuously: the silly fool would be surprised when he tried to develop those pictures.

After a while the man went away, and for a long time there were noises of men doing things far away. That, too, died away slowly.

Coeurl lay waiting, as he felt the silence creep over the ship. In the long ago, before the dawn of immortality, the coeurls, too, had slept at night; and the memory of it had been revived the day before when he saw some of the men dozing. At last, the vibration of two pairs of feet, pacing, pacing endlessly, was the only human-made frequency that throbbed on his ear tendrils.

Tensely, he listened to the two watchmen. The first one walked slowly past the cage door. Then about thirty feet behind him came the second. Coeurl sensed the alertness of these men; knew that he could never surprise either while they walked separately. It meant—he must be doubly careful!

Fifteen minutes, and they came again. The moment they were past, he switched his senses from their vibrations to a vastly higher range. The pulsating violence of the atomic engines stammered its soft story to his brain. The electric dynamos hummed their muffled song of pure power. He felt the whisper of that flow through the wires in the walls of his cage, and through the electric lock of his door. He forced his quivering body into straining immobility, his senses seeking, searching, to tune in on the sibilant tempest of energy. Suddenly, his ear tendrils vibrated in harmony—he caught the surging change into shrillness of that rippling force wave.

There was a sharp click of metal on metal. With a gentle touch of one tentacle, Coeurl pushed open the door, and glided out into the dully gleaming corridor. For just a moment he felt contempt, a glow of superiority, as he thought of the stupid creatures who dared to match their wit against a coeurl. And in that moment, he suddenly thought of other coeurls. A queer, exultant sense of race pounded through his being; the

125

driving hate of centuries of ruthless competition yielded reluctantly before pride of kinship with the future rulers of all space.

Suddenly, he felt weighed down by his limitations, his need for other coeurls, his aloneness—one against a hundred, with the stake all eternity; the starry universe itself beckoned his rapacious, vaulting ambition. If he failed, there would never be a second chance—no time to revive long-rotted machinery, and attempt to solve the secret of space travel.

He padded along on tensed paws—through the salon—into the next corridor—and came to the first bedroom door. It stood half open. One swift flow of synchronized muscles, one swiftly lashing tentacle that caught the unresisting throat of the sleeping man, crushing it; and the lifeless head rolled crazily, the body twitched once.

Seven bedrooms; seven dead men. It was the seventh taste of murder that brought a sudden return of lust, a pure, unbounded desire to kill, return of a millennium-old habit of destroying everything containing the precious id.

As the twelfth man slipped convulsively into death, Coeurl emerged abruptly from the sensuous joy of the kill to the sound of footsteps.

They were not near—that was what brought wave after wave of fright swirling into the chaos that suddenly became his brain.

The watchmen were coming slowly along the corridor toward the door of the cage where he had been imprisoned. In a moment, the first man would see the open door—and sound the alarm.

Coeurl caught at the vanishing remnants of his reason. With frantic speed, careless now of accidental sounds, he raced—along the corridor with its bedroom doors—through the salon. He emerged into the next corridor, cringing in awful anticipation of the atomic flame he expected would stab into his face.

The two men were together, standing side by side. For one single instant, Coeurl could scarcely believe his tremendous good luck. Like a fool the second had come running when he saw the other stop before the open door. They looked up, paralyzed, before the nightmare of claws and tentacles, the ferocious cat head and hate-filled eyes.

The first man went for his gun, but the second, physically frozen before the doom he saw, uttered a shriek, a shrill cry of horror that floated along the corridors—and ended in a curious gurgle, as Coeurl flung the two corpses with one irresistible motion the full length of the corridor. He didn't want the dead bodies found near the cage. That was his one hope.

Shaking in every nerve and muscle, conscious of the terrible error he actuated the cage audioscope and looked in. A few moments now, and the other bodies would be discovered.

"Siedel gone!" Morton said numbly. "What are we going to do without Siedel? And Breckenridge! And Coulter and—Horrible!"

He covered his face with his hands, but only for an instant. He looked up grimly, his heavy chin outthrust as he stared into the stern faces that surrounded him. "If anybody's got so much as a germ of an idea, bring it out."

"Space madness!"

"I've thought of that. But there hasn't been a case of a man going mad for fifty years. Dr. Eggert will test everybody, of course, and right now he's looking at the bodies with that possibility in mind."

As he finished, he saw the doctor coming through the door. Men crowded aside to make way for him.

"I heard you, commander," Dr. Eggert said, "and I think I can say right now that the space-madness theory is out. The throats of these men have been squeezed to a jelly. No human being could have exerted such enormous strength without using a machine."

Morton saw that the doctor's eyes kept looking down the corridor, and he shook his head and groaned:

"It's no use suspecting pussy, doctor. He's in his cage, pacing up and down. Obviously heard the racket and—Man alive! You can't suspect him. That cage was built to hold literally *anything*—four inches of micro-steel—and there's not a scratch on the door. Kent, even you won't say, 'Kill him on suspicion,' because there can't be any suspicion, unless there's a new science here, beyond anything we can imagine—"

"On the contrary," said Smith flatly, "we have all the evidence we need. I used the telefluor on him—you know the arrangement we have on top of the cage—and tried to take some pictures. They just blurred. Pussy jumped when the telefluor was turned on, as if he felt the vibrations.

"You all know what Gourlay said before? This beast can apparently receive and send vibrations of any lengths. The way he dominated the power of Kent's gun is final proof of his special ability to interfere with energy."

"What in the name of all the hells have we got here?" One of the men groaned. "Why, if he can control that power, and send it out in any vibrations, there's nothing to stop him killing all of us."

"Which proves," snapped Morton, "that he isn't invincible, or he would have done it long ago."

Very deliberately, he walked over to the mechanism that controlled the prison cage.

"You're not going to open the door!" Kent gasped, reaching for his gun.

"No, but if I pull this switch, electricity will flow through the floor, and electrocute whatever's inside. We've never had to use this before, so you had probably forgotten about it."

He jerked the switch hard over. Blue fire flashed from the metal, and a bank of fuses above his head exploded with a single bang.

Morton frowned. "That's funny. Those fuses shouldn't have blown! Well, we can't even look in, now. That wrecked the audios, too."

Smith said: "If he could interfere with the electric lock, enough to open the door, then he probably probed every possible danger and was ready to interfere when you threw that switch."

"At least, it proves he's vulnerable to our energies!" Morton smiled grimly. "Because he rendered them harmless. The important thing is, we've got him behind four inches of the toughest of metal. At the worst we can open the door and ray him to death. But first, I think we'll try to use the telefluor power cable—"

A commotion from inside the cage interrupted his words. A heavy body crashed against a wall, followed by a dull thump.

"He knows what we were trying to do!" Smith grunted to Morton. "And I'll bet it's a very sick pussy in there. What a fool he was to go back into that cage and does he realize it!"

The tension was relaxing; men were smiling nervously, and there was even a ripple of humorless laughter at the picture Smith drew of the monster's discomfiture.

"What I'd like to know," said Pennons, the engineer, "is, why did the telefluor meter dial jump and waver at full power when pussy made that noise? It's right under my nose here, and the dial jumped like a house afire!"

There was silence both without and within the cage, then Morton said: "It may mean he's coming out. Back, everybody, and keep your guns ready. Pussy was a fool to think he could conquer a hundred men, but he's by far the most formidable creature in the galactic system. He may come out of that door, rather than die like a rat in a trap. And he's just tough enough to take some of us with him—if we're not careful."

The men backed slowly in a solid body; and somebody said: "That's funny, I thought I heard the elevator."

"Elevator!" Morton echoed. "Are you sure, man?"

"Just for a moment I was!" The man, a member of the crew, hesitated. "We were all shuffling our feet—"

"Take somebody with you, and go look. Bring whoever dared to run off back here—"

There was a jar, a horrible jerk, as the whole gigantic body of the ship careened under them. Morton was flung to the floor with a violence that stunned him. He fought back to consciousness, aware of the other men lying all around him. He shouted: "Who the devil started those engines!"

The agonizing acceleration continued; his feet dragged with awful exertion, as he fumbled with the nearest audioscope, and punched the engine-room number. The picture that flooded onto the screen brought a deep bellow to his lips:

"It's pussy! He's in the engine room—and we're heading straight out into space."

The screen went black even as he spoke, and he could see no more.

It was Morton who first staggered across the salon floor to the supply room where the spacesuits were kept. After fumbling almost blindly into his own suit, he cut the effects of the body-torturing acceleration, and brought suits to the semiconscious men on the floor. In a few moments, other men were assisting him; and then it was only a matter of minutes before everybody was clad in metalite, with anti-acceleration motors running at half power.

It was Morton then who, after first looking into the cage, opened the door and stood, silent as the others crowded about him, to stare at the gaping hole in the rear wall. The hole was a frightful thing of jagged edges and horribly bent metal, and it opened upon another corridor.

"I'll swear," whispered Pennons, "that it's impossible. The ten-ton hammer in the machine shops couldn't more than dent four inches of micro with one blow—and we only heard one. It would take at least a minute for an atomic disintegrator to do the job. Morton, this is a super-being."

Morton saw that Smith was examining the break in the wall. The biologist looked up. "If only Breckinridge weren't dead! We need a metallurgist to explain this. Look!"

He touched the broken edge of the metal. A piece crumbled in his finger and slithered away in a fine shower of dust to the floor. Morton noticed for the first time that there was a little pile of metallic debris and dust.

"You've hit it." Morton nodded. "No miracle of strength here. The monster merely used his special powers to interfere with the electronic tensions holding the metal together. That would account, too, for the drain on the telefluor power cable that Pennons noticed. The thing used the power with his body as a transforming medium, smashed through the wall, ran down the corridor to the elevator shaft, and so down to the engine room."

129

"In the meantime, commander," Kent said quietly, "we are faced with a super-being in control of the ship, completely dominating the engine room and its almost unlimited power, and in possession of the best part of the machine shops."

Morton felt the silence, while the men pondered the chemist's words. Their anxiety was a tangible thing that lay heavily upon their faces; in every expression was the growing realization that here was the ultimate situation in their lives; their very existence was at stake and perhaps much more. Morton voiced the thought in everybody's mind:

"Suppose he wins. He's utterly ruthless, and he probably sees galactic power within his grasp."

"Kent is wrong," barked the chief navigator. "The thing doesn't dominate the engine room. We've still got the control room, and that gives us *first* control of all the machines. You fellows may not know the mechanical set-up we have; but, though he can eventually disconnect us, we can cut off all the switches in the engine room now. Commander, why didn't you just shut off the power instead of putting us into space-suits? At the very least you could have adjusted the ship to the acceleration."

"For two reasons," Morton answered. "Individually, we're safer within the force fields of our spacesuits. And we can't afford to give up our advantages in panicky moves."

"Advantages! What other advantages have we got?"

"We know things about him," Morton replied. "And right now, we're going to make a test. Pennons, detail five men to each of the four approaches to the engine room. Take atomic disintegrators to blast through the big doors. They're all shut, I noticed. He's locked himself in.

"Selenski, you go up to the control room and shut off everything except the drive engines. Gear them to the master switch, and shut them off all at once. One thing, though—leave the acceleration on full blast. No anti-acceleration must be applied to the ship. Understand?"

"Aye, sir!" The pilot saluted.

"And report to me through the communicators if any of the machines start to run again." He faced the men. "I'm going to lead the main approach. Kent, you take No. 2; Smith, No. 3, and Pennons, No. 4. We're going to find out right now if we're dealing with unlimited science, or a creature limited like the rest of us. I'll bet on the second possibility."

Morton had an empty sense of walking endlessly, as he moved, a giant of a man in his transparent space armour, along the glistening metal tube that was the main corridor of the engine-room floor. Reason told him the creature had already shown feet of clay, yet the feeling that here was an invincible being persisted.

He spoke into the communicator: "It's no use trying to sneak up on him. He can probably hear a pin drop. So just wheel up your units. He hasn't been in that engine room long enough to do anything.

"As I've said, this is largely a test attack. In the first place, we could never forgive ourselves if we didn't try to conquer him now, before he's had time to prepare against us. But, aside from the possibility that we can destroy him immediately, I have a theory.

"The idea goes something like this: Those doors are built to withstand accidental atomic explosions, and it will take fifteen minutes for the atomic disintegrators to smash them. During that period the monster will have no power. True, the drive will be on, but that's straight atomic explosion. My theory is, he can't touch stuff like that; and in a few minutes you'll see what I mean—I hope."

His voice was suddenly crisp: "Ready, Selenski?"

"Aye, ready."

"Then cut the master switch."

The corridor—the whole ship, Morton knew—was abruptly plunged into darkness. Morton clicked on the dazzling light of his spacesuit; the other men did the same, their faces pale and drawn.

"Blast!" Morton barked into his communicator.

The mobile units throbbed; and then pure atomic flame ravened out and poured upon the hard metal of the door. The first molten droplet rolled reluctantly, not down, but up the door. The second was more normal. It followed a shaky downward course. The third rolled sideways—for this was pure force, not subject to gravitation. Other drops followed until a dozen streams trickled sedately yet unevenly in every direction—streams of hellish, sparkling fire, bright as fairy gems, alive with the coruscating fury of atoms suddenly tortured, and running blindly, crazy with pain.

The minutes ate at time like a slow acid. At last Morton asked huskily: "Selenski?"

"Nothing yet, commander."

Morton half whispered: "But he must be doing something. He can't be just waiting in there like a cornered rat. Selenski?"

"Nothing, commander."

Seven minutes, eight minutes, then twelve.

"Commander!" It was Selenski's voice, taut. "He's got the electric dynamo running."

Morton drew a deep breath, and heard one of his men say:

"That's funny. We can't get any deeper. Boss, take a look at this."

131

Morton looked. The little scintillating streams had frozen rigid. The ferocity of the disintegrators vented in vain against metal grown suddenly invulnerable.

Morton sighed. "Our test is over. Leave two men guarding every corridor. The others come up to the control room."

He seated himself a few minutes later before the massive control keyboard. "So far as I'm concerned the test was a success. We know that of all the machines in the engine room, the most important to the monster was the electric dynamo. He must have worked in a frenzy of terror while we were at the doors."

"Of course, it's easy to see what he did," Pennons said. "Once he had the power he increased the electronic tensions of the door to their ultimate."

"The main thing is this," Smith chimed in. "He works with vibrations only so far as his special powers are concerned, and the energy must come from outside himself. Atomic energy in its pure form, not being vibration, he can't handle any differently than we can."

Kent said glumly: "The main point in my opinion is that he stopped us cold. What's the good of knowing that his control over vibrations did it? If we can't break through those doors with our atomic disintegrators, we're finished."

Morton shook his head. "Not finished—but we'll have to do some planning. First, though, I'll start these engines. It'll be harder for him to get control of them when they're running."

He pulled the master switch back into place with a jerk. There was a hum, as scores of machines leaped into violent life in the engine room a hundred feet below. The noises sank to a steady vibration of throbbing power.

Three hours later, Morton paced up and down before the men gathered in the salon. His dark hair was uncombed; the space pallor of his strong face emphasized rather than detracted from the outthrust aggressiveness of his jaw. When he spoke, his deep voice was crisp to the point of sharpness:

"To make sure that our plans are fully co-ordinated, I'm going to ask each expert in turn to outline his part in the overpowering of this creature. Pennons first!"

Pennons stood up briskly. He was not a big man, Morton thought, yet he looked big, perhaps because of his air of authority. This man knew engines, and the history of engines. Morton had heard him trace a machine through its evolution from a simple toy to the highly complicated modern instrument. He had studied machine development on a hundred planets; and there was literally nothing fundamental that he didn't know about mechanics. It was almost weird to hear Pennons, who could have spoken for a thousand hours and still only have touched upon his subject, say with absurd brevity:

"We've set up a relay in the control room to start and stop every engine rhythmically. The trip lever will work a hundred times a second, and the effect will be to create vibrations of every description. There is just a possibility that one or more of the machines will burst, on the principle of soldiers crossing a bridge in step—you've heard that old story, no doubt —but in my opinion there is no real danger of a break of that tough metal. The main purpose is simply to interfere with the interference of the creature, and smash through the doors."

"Gourlay next!" barked Morton.

Gourlay climbed lazily to his feet. He looked sleepy, as if he was somewhat bored by the whole proceedings, yet Morton knew he loved people to think him lazy, a good-for-nothing slouch, who spent his days in slumber and his nights catching forty winks. His title was chief communication engineer, but his knowledge extended to every vibration field; and he was probably, with the possible exception of Kent, the fastest thinker on the ship. His voice drawled out, and—Morton noted—the very deliberate assurance of it had a soothing effect on the men—anxious faces relaxed, bodies leaned back more restfully:

"Once inside," Gourlay said, "we've rigged up vibration screens of pure force that should stop nearly everything he's got on the ball. They work on the principle of reflection, so that everything he sends will be reflected back to him. In addition, we've got plenty of spare electric energy that we'll just feed him from mobile copper cups. There must be a limit to his capacity for handling power with those insulated nerves of his."

"Selenski!" called Morton.

The chief pilot was already standing, as if he had anticipated Morton's call. And that, Morton reflected, was the man. His nerves had that rock-like steadiness which is the first requirement of the master controller of a great ship's movements; yet that very steadiness seemed to rest on dynamite ready to explode at its owner's volition. He was not a man of great learning, but he "reacted" to stimuli so fast that he always seemed to be anticipating.

"The impression I've received of the plan is that it must be cumulative. Just when the creature thinks that he can't stand any more, another thing happens to add to his trouble and confusion. When the uproar's at its height, I'm supposed to cut in the anti-accelerators. The commander thinks with Gunlie Lester that these creatures will know nothing about anti-acceleration. It's a development, pure and simple, of the science of interstellar flight, and couldn't have been developed in any other way. We think when the creature feels the first effects of the anti-acceleration—you all remember the caved-in feeling you had the first month—it won't know what to think or do."

"Korita next."

"I can only offer you encouragement," said the archeologist, "on the basis of my theory that the monster has all the characteristics of a criminal of the early ages of any civilization, complicated by an apparent reversion to primitiveness. The suggestion has been made by Smith that his knowledge of science is puzzling, and could only mean that we are dealing with an actual inhabitant, not a descendant of the inhabitants of the dead city we visited. This would ascribe a virtual immortality to our enemy, a possibility which is borne out by his ability to breathe both oxygen and chlorine—or neither—but even that makes no difference. He comes from a certain age in his civilization; and he has sunk so low that his ideas are mostly memories of that age.

"In spite of all the powers of his body, he lost his head in the elevator the first morning, until he remembered. He placed himself in such a position that he was forced to reveal his special powers against vibrations. He bungled the mass murders a few hours ago. In fact, his whole record is one of the low cunning of the primitive, egotistical mind which has little or no conception of the vast organization with which it is confronted.

"He is like the ancient German soldier who felt superior to the elderly Roman scholar, yet the latter was part of a mighty civilization of which the Germans of that day stood in awe.

"You may suggest that the sack of Rome by the Germans in later years defeats my argument; however, modern historians agree that the 'sack' was an historical accident, and not history in the true sense of the word. The movement of the 'Sea-peoples' which set in against the Egyptian civilization, from 1400 B.C. succeeded only as regards the Cretan island-realm—their mighty expeditions against the Libyan and Phoenician coasts, with the accompaniment of viking fleets, failed as those of the Huns failed against the Chinese Empire. Rome would have been abandoned in any event. Ancient, glorious Samarra was desolate by the tenth century; Pataliputra, Asoka's great capital, was an immense and completely uninhabited waste of houses when the Chinese traveler Hsinan-tang visited it about A.D. 635.

"We have, then, a primitive, and that primitive is now far out in space, completely outside of his natural habitat. I say, let's go in and win."

One of the men grumbled, as Korita finished: "You can talk about the sack of Rome being an accident, and about this fellow being a primitive,

134

but the facts are facts. It looks to me as if Rome is about to fall again; and it won't be no primitive that did it, either. This guy's got plenty of what it takes."

Morton smiled grimly at the man, a member of the crew. "We'll see about that—right now!"

In the blazing brilliance of the gigantic machine shop, Coeurl slaved. The forty-foot, cigar-shaped spaceship was nearly finished. With a grunt of effort, he completed the laborious installation of the drive engines, and paused to survey his craft.

Its interior, visible through the one aperture in the outer wall, was pitifully small. There was literally room for nothing but the engines—and a narrow space for himself.

He plunged frantically back to work as he heard the approach of the men, and the sudden change in the tempest-like thunder of the engines— a rhythmical off-and-on hum, shriller in tone, sharper, more nerve-racking than the deep-throated, steady throb that had preceded it. Suddenly, there were the atomic disintegrators again at the massive outer doors.

He fought them off, but never wavered from his task. Every mighty muscle of his powerful body strained as he carried great loads of tools, machines and instruments, and dumped them into the bottom of his makeshift ship. There was no time to fit anything into place, no time for anything—no time—no time.

The thought pounded at his reason. He felt strangely weary for the first time in his long and vigorous existence. With a last, tortured heave, he jerked the gigantic sheet of metal into the gaping aperture of the ship —and stood there for a terrible minute, balancing it precariously.

He knew the doors were going down. Half a dozen disintegrators concentrating on one point were irresistibly, though slowly, eating away the remaining inches. With a gasp, he released his mind from the doors and concentrated every ounce of his mind on the yard-thick outer wall, toward which the blunt nose of his ship was pointing.

His body cringed from the surging power that flowed from the electric dynamo through his ear tendrils into that resisting wall. The whole inside of him felt on fire, and he knew that he was dangerously close to carrying his ultimate load.

And still he stood there, shuddering with the awful pain, holding the unfastened metal plate with hard-clenched tentacles. His massive head pointed as in dread fascination at that bitterly hard wall.

He heard one of the engine-room doors crash inward. Men shouted; disintegrators rolled forward, their raging power unchecked. Coeurl heard the floor of the engine room hiss in protest, as those beams of atomic energy tore everything in their path to bits. The machines rolled closer; cautious footsteps sounded behind them. In a minute they would be at the flimsy doors separating the engine room from the machine shop.

Suddenly, Coeurl was satisfied. With a snarl of hate, a vindictive glow of feral eyes, he ducked into his little craft, and pulled the metal plate down into place as if it was a hatchway.

His ear tendrils hummed, as he softened the edges of the surrounding metal. In an instant, the plate was more than welded—it was part of his ship, a seamless, rivetless part of a whole that was solid opaque metal except for two transparent areas, one in the front, one in the rear.

His tentacle embraced the power drive with almost sensuous tenderness. There was a forward surge of his fragile machine, straight at the great outer wall of the machine shops. The nose of the forty-foot craft touched —and the wall dissolved in a glittering shower of dust.

Coeurl felt the barest retarding movement; and then he kicked the nose of the machine out into the cold of space, twisted it about, and headed back in the direction from which the big ship had been coming all these hours.

Men in space armor stood in the jagged hole that yawned in the lower reaches of the gigantic globe. The men and the great ship grew smaller. Then the men were gone; and there was only the ship with its blaze of a thousand blurring portholes. The ball shrank incredibly, too small now for individual portholes to be visible.

Almost straight ahead, Coeurl saw a tiny, dim, reddish ball—his own sun, he realized. He headed toward it at full speed. There were caves where he could hide and with other coeurls build secretly a spaceship in which they could reach other planets safely—now that he knew how.

His body ached from the agony of acceleration, yet he dared not let up for a single instant. He glanced back, half in terror. The globe was still there, a tiny dot of light in the immense blackness of space. Suddenly it twinkled and was gone.

For a brief moment, he had the empty, frightened impression that just before it disappeared, it moved. But he could see nothing. He could not escape the belief that they had shut off all their lights, and were sneaking up on him in the darkness. Worried and uncertain, he looked through the forward transparent plate.

A tremor of dismay shot through him. The dim red sun toward which he was heading was not growing larger. It was becoming smaller by the instant, and it grew visibly tinier during the next five minutes, became a pale-red dot in the sky—and vanished like the ship.

Fear came then, a blinding surge of it, that swept through his being and left him chilled with the sense of the unknown. For minutes, he stared frantically into the space ahead, searching for some landmark. But only the remote stars glimmered there, unwinking points against a velvet background of unfathomable distance.

Wait! One of the points was growing larger. With every muscle and nerve tensed, Coeurl watched the point becoming a dot, a round ball of light—red light. Bigger, bigger, it grew. Suddenly, the red light shimmered and turned white—and there, before him, was the great globe of the spaceship, lights glaring from every porthole, the very ship which a few minutes before he had watched vanish behind him.

Something happened to Coeurl in that moment. His brain was spinning like a flywheel, faster, faster, more incoherently. Suddenly, the wheel flew apart into a million aching fragments. His eyes almost started from their sockets as, like a maddened animal, he raged in his small quarters.

His tentacles clutched at precious instruments and flung them insensately; his paws smashed in fury at the very walls of his ship. Finally, in a brief flash of sanity, he knew that he couldn't face the inevitable fire of atomic disintegrators.

It was a simple thing to create the violent disorganization that freed every drop of id from his vital organs.

They found him lying dead in a little pool of phosphorus.

"Poor pussy," said Morton. "I wonder what he thought when he saw us appear ahead of him, after his own sun disappeared. Knowing nothing of anti-accelerators, he couldn't know that we could stop short in space, whereas it would take him more than three hours to decelerate; and in the meantime he'd be drawing farther and farther away from where he wanted to go. He couldn't know that by stopping, we flashed past him at millions of miles a second. Of course, he didn't have a chance once he left our ship. The whole world must have seemed topsy-turvy."

"Never mind the sympathy," he heard Kent say behind him. "We've got a job—to kill every cat in that miserable world."

Korita murmured softly: "That should be simple. They are but primitives; and we have merely to sit down, and they will come to us, cunningly expecting to delude us."

Smith snapped: "You fellows make me sick! Pussy was the toughest nut we ever had to crack. He had everything he needed to defeat us—"

Morton smiled as Korita interrupted blandly: "Exactly, my dear Smith, except that he reacted according to the biological impulses of his type. His defeat was already foreshadowed when we unerringly analyzed him as a criminal from a certain era of his civilization.

"It was history, honorable Mr. Smith, our knowledge of history that defeated him," said the Japanese archeologist, reverting to the ancient politeness of his race.

Laurence Manning
GOOD-BYE, ILHA!

Laurence Manning (1899-1972) has been called "one of the best writers of early science fiction." Born in Saint John, New Brunswick, and educated at King's College, Halifax, Nova Scotia, Manning flew with the RCAF during the Second World War. He settled in the United States, wrote a very popular manual on gardening, and became a founder of the American Rocket Society as well as editor of its publication, Astronautics. As Isaac Asimov noted in Before the Golden Age: A Science Fiction Anthology of the 1930s *(1974), "Manning, like many science-fiction writers, went through a spurt of production and stopped. There were fifteen stories between 1932 and 1935 and then nothing." Asimov reprinted in his anthology "The Man Who Awoke" from* Wonder Stories, *the opening section of Manning's serial of ecological and philosophical interest finally published as* The Man Who Awoke *by Ballantine Books in 1975. "Good-bye, Ilha!" was first published by Judith Merril in her anthology,* Beyond Human Ken *(1952), where she noted: "This, too, is a story about some BEMs [Bug-Eyed Monsters]. But it's hard to say who they are; this time the humans are the alien invaders."*

You are so punctual, Ilha, I know you will be here exactly one hour after dawn, as we arranged yesterday. I am leaving this letter to explain why I cannot meet you. You must report to World Resource headquarters. Be quick. Roll to the place we left the skid-plane; fly with throttle wide open; you should arrive before noon.

Claim emergency; get an immediate interview with the Director.

Before the afternoon is over he is to blanket the whole area, quad 73:61 on the map, with infrared heat. Not to kill, tell him. Raise the absolute temperature only about 10 percent, just enough to make it thoroughly uncomfortable. These visitors endanger our whole civilization, but I think that will drive them away. However, it may not, so at noon the *next* day push the power up to full killing temperatures for a few minutes.

He will object, but what if a few miles of sand are fused? You know the area. It was so thoroughly blasted during the Age of Wars that no more damage is possible, and anyway, it will be centuries before the

138

reclamation engineers touch this part of our planet. You can—you *must* persuade him, Ilha!

It is rude, I know, to begin with such urgency, omitting the traditional greeting phrases, writing without Limik calmness or philosophy. But you may as well get used to it, for the creatures I write about are totally un-Limik—utterly out of this world!

I found them yesterday about where the disturbance showed on the magnetic map, near the center of the quad. Their rocket ship is much like the ancient ones in the museum at Prr, but larger and made of magnesium. I hid behind a sand dune until dark, when I could examine it safely. Light streamed from two round windows and also from a tall, narrow, opening—a door in spite of its fantastic shape (twice as high as it was broad)—opening from a small vestibule. There were two inner doors, one open and one closed. From the closed one came loud roarings and barkings as of wild animals, but modulated by a variety of smacks, gargles and splutterings. I soon realized these sounds were signals—a regular code language, like our own writing. I could sense the thought associated with each sound; but evidently the animals behind the door, though all present together, could not. They had to make these sound signals to understand each other. Curious and primitive, isn't it?

These were three voices, one much stronger than the other two. I caught thought phrases like "I am hungry," "Is not that drink cold yet?" and "When do we eat?" There were thoughts I sensed, which made no meaning to me. There were also sounds, many of them, that had no thought behind them at all: "WEL-IL-BEDAM" was one, "OG-O-AWN" was another, commonest of all was a sort of barking, "HAW-HAW-HAW." All meaning dissolved when they barked, their minds seemed pleased with themselves in a strange, bubbling, thought-free sort of way. "HAW HAW HAW" would go the biggest voice and the other two (no, not its mates; I still know nothing of their reproductive customs except that the wrappings on their bodies have something to do with it) would join "HAW HAW HAW" like so many flepas barking at the moon. Only flepas think sad hungry thoughts when they bark; these creatures stopped thinking altogether.

I stood there outside the door delighted with it. I suppose it doesn't sound attractive—though I ask you, can any Limik stop thinking—ever? But it is more than not thinking. It is the feeling that goes with it—a lifting of the spirits, refreshing, youthful. . . . Oh well, I'll continue.

The open door showed a small empty room, its walls fitted with shelves and cabinets. I tip-probed in, hoping to learn something about this unknown species from its environment. A repulsive odor came from a bowl on the long shelf and I climbed up—burning myself, incidentally, for all that part of the shelf was hot. What do you suppose was in that bowl? Pieces torn from the bodies of living vegetables and animals, all stewing together in a revolting mixture. Their food! Our savage ancestors might have enjoyed it; I was filled with horror and retreated along the shelf to the other end of the room. Here stood a smaller metal bowl, icy cold, smelling like our own poggle fruit. You know me and poggles! I think the brightest page in Limik history is our treaty with the poggle-people— we enjoy the fruit, they have their seeds better distributed. The odor from this bowl was irresistible, contrasted with the gruesome stench from the other end of the room. I dipped in my courtesy probe and drank.

It was not poggle juice, but some strange poison!

I wooshed, too late. My probe tip began to swell and throb; my fore-eye rolled so dizzily I had to somersault tail-over-feeler, putting my crippled probe in tail position. Even then I could not stand up, but fell several times. I thought I was going to die.

I know our literature demands that I pause here to detail the stream of consciousness and the philosophy. I cannot do more than outline. How invalid our pretty refinements are! If I had been brought up in a lower-class nest such social distinctions as courtesy, tail and feeler would not even exist—one probe would be no different from another. I had no time to elaborate these ideas. While I tumbled about on that shelf I knocked over a pile of plates. They fell to the floor with an enormous crash, and an instant later the closed door burst open and three amazing monsters thundered into the room.

They were about six probes high, scarcely one wide—weird, attenuated and huge. They had five probes. Two were feelers, or perhaps tails, kept covered (they call them "LAIGS"). Two were courtesy probes ("HANS") uncovered at the tips, which have no openings (I suppose the passages have atrophied) but are each slit into five small tentacles. The fifth probe was short, stubby, and has no counterpart in Limik anatomy. It ends in a great bristle of hairs; two of the monsters had brown hairs, one red. All had one huge opening set with even, white pieces of bone—a little like a grinding machine. Two eyes were in each of these probes (migrated here from the body? I don't know. Our old bio professor would be interested. There may be residual eyes left on the body, too. They keep them tightly wrapped so there is no way to find out).

They strode with enormous steps—*sideways,* not probe after probe like our amble—and swayed awkwardly as they came. I remember thinking that our own wheel-like rolling would out-distance them, if I could ever get a free start. But they stood between me and the door. I was caught. The whole room rolled and turned before my eyes.

They began to roar at each other sounds with no thought except surprise. "LOOKOOSERE, WEL-IL-BEDAM," they shouted. I expected to be seized and thrown into that boiling bowl and shrank back in despair. The only hope that occurred to me in this dreadful situation was that perhaps they would not kill me—at least not at once—if I could show them I was intelligent. But how show that? They could not read thoughts, remember. Well, Ilha, you know how baby Limikles bubble and gargle the soft flap in their probe passages, and snort by half-closing the tips? That infantile exercise saved my life. I imitated their sounds.

"LOOKOOSERE WEL-IL-BEDAM," I managed. Then I grew so dizzy I fell once again and wooshed all over the shelf.

There was an instant of portentous silence. Then they began barking like mad things.

"The little fellow's been at our coktal, HAW HAW HAW," Big-voice roared and pointed to the bowl. They all burst out barking with him— LAFF is their word for it. Deafened and desperate, I raised my probe and LAFF-ed, too.

"HAW HAW" I gasped. That set them off louder than ever. Curiously, I felt better. Laff-ing spreads from mind to mind like fire in a pile of sticks.

Red-head came close and held out his "HANS," but Big-voice said "Look out. Even if he can't bite, he may sting!"

The third monster said, "AGO-AWN he's a gentle old fellow—aren't you? Just a little poisoned (their word is TITE) that's all." He picked me up to nestle on his courtesy probe, squeezed against his great body.

I was terrified. My eyes rolled up dizzily; but I managed to splutter "AGO-AWN HAW HAW HAW," and tried to add "gentle old fellow," but was nauseated again, so that unfortunately it came out "Shentle ol WOOSH!"

My captor set me hastily back on the shelf. He did it gently though, and I felt safer anyway, for his "HANS" were not too certain a support and it was easily a three-probe fall to the floor.

They all went off into a wild storm of roaring, stamping about the room, striking each other on the back, gasping for breath—quite insane. Then they began crying, "Pour out the drinks," and all three drank some of the poison, but were not ill; only a little redder and louder.

I had another bad moment when they dished out the food and began eating—suppose they found there was not quite enough to satisfy their hunger? I need not have worried. One of them even put a little dish of it in front of me. I drew back quickly, but the odor was too strong for my control. I was nauseated again.

"Try him with a little water, BILL," said Big-voice.

My captor, "Bill," brought a container and I drank eagerly and felt better at last. I was sure now that they did not intend to eat me. I leaned against the wall, watching them. The meal ended with boiling water and brown powder called "CUP-ACAWFEE"—another unpleasant odor. Bill brought from a shelf a small bowl filled with white grains which Big-voice called "PASSASHUGA" and they spooned a little of this into their hot brown drink. A few grains spilled on the shelf and I investigated. To my delight it was sugar. Sugar, Ilha! The basic food of nature from which all living tissue is derived, the synthesis of which has made possible our Limik way of life, but used by them as a *condiment!*

I was hungry. Greatly daring, I imitated their signal as well as I could: "PASSASHUGA." And it worked. They HAW-HAW-ed, but in a surprised and kindly way, and Bill put a little heap of it on the shelf so that I actually shared in their amazing meal after all, and enjoyed it too. I did not eat much, but of course I had to have exercise at once to restore my energy balance. I began to roll tail-over-courtesy all down the shelf and back.

Big-voice did not LAFF, though the others did. He looked suddenly thoughtful, said, "He can go fast, can't he," and reached out to shut the door. "We don't want to lose this fellow. Get down the cage, Bill."

Bill brought out a huge cage—a very room made of wires. He said, "The door's too small; we'll have to take off the bottom to get him in. It hasn't been cleaned since the (something) died, has it?" He washed it and lifted me in. It was just about big enough to turn around in, but I didn't care, for I had gone into my digestive stupor by then and drowsed while they carried me, cage and all, into the other room.

Here they sprawled themselves out on cushioned frames, leaning their bodies against back supports. It looked uncomfortable—halfway between standing and lying down. Then they put little white tubes into their mouths and set them on fire, blowing narcotic smoke about the room. They talked and I listened.

Bill said, "Maybe this planet isn't all desert. We haven't seen it all."

Big-voice said, "That fellow in the cage could tell us if he wanted to."

Red-head blew smoke, then said, "I thought we had agreed to leave here tomorrow and try the other planet in this system?"

"Not if this one will do," put in Big-voice. "We wouldn't think much of our own world if we landed in one of the deserts."

"This desert is bigger than any on earth," objected Bill. "We saw enough to know that much. It covers half the planet, anyway. Still, the other half would be big enough, at that—but how do we know this little chap isn't a desert animal?"

Big-voice said, "Maybe we can get him to talk tomorrow."

Laurence Manning

All the time their thoughts ran swiftly under the slow pace of their sound-signals—and I could read the thoughts. I suddenly realized that these three were scouts. When they had found a good world they would guide a horde of other "HEW-MEN" to it. All they had come for was to find a planet worth the trouble of taking over; if ours proved desirable they would calmly kill its present inhabitants! I caught mental glimpses of the way they imagined other forms of life. There were only two kinds in their thoughts: those that could be eaten and those that should be destroyed as inedible nuisances!

It was a pretty grim moment, Ilha.

I had got over my first fright and had actually begun to enjoy being with them before this awful conviction was forced upon me. After that I knew I had to escape and warn our world.

They talked a long time. Every so often they would burst into a chorus of HAW HAW's without apparent reason. There is a contagious sort of charm in this LAFF-ing of theirs. Oh, not the sound—that is mere cacophony—but the soft dissolving of all serious thought that goes with it. I became very sad, lying there, thinking how unfortunate it was that such pleasant creatures had to be destroyed.

Then came a new thing. Red-head said, "I feel like MEWSIK," and went to a corner of the room to turn on a machine of some kind. Oh Ilha! Such a burst of overpoweringly sweet sound came from it that my probe tips quivered in ecstasy. They are masters of sound, these HEW-MEN. Not in my life have I imagined such an art. There was a mathematically regulated change of pitch, recurring with an urgent feeling of logic; there was a blending of tones in infinite variety; there was a measured rhythm. But none of these will give you the slightest idea of the effect on me, when all were put together. We Limiks have nothing in the slightest like it. Oh well, the rhythm, perhaps. Limikles in their nest being taught numbers by beating sticks in 3-4-5 pattern do a little suggest that phase of this MEW-SIK—but only as a shadow suggests the solid.

When it stopped I was desperately unhappy. If these monsters were killed, I would never again hear this miracle. And yet they would certainly kill us if they stayed here.

Then my great idea was born—the Blue Planet!

The ghoulish and savage Gryptrrs, unless they have greatly changed since our last expedition there, deserve consideration from no Limik. Why could I not persuade these HEW-MEN to go there and settle? Certainly, if they once saw those lush landscapes they would far prefer it to ours. Would they not, cruel and selfish as they are, make far better neighbors than the untamable Gryptrrs? Moreover, they were half per-

143

suaded already. I had only to convince them that our world was even more unsuitable than it appeared.

I knew how to do that. Don't you see, Ilha? Remember in literature class that story of Vraaltr's—"The un-Limik Letter," I think it was called? To write one thing and think another is stupid among ourselves, because the true thought is revealed when next writer and reader come together. But these HEW-MEN cannot see thoughts at all. All they understand is the agreed meaning of arbitrary sounds. They even have a word ("FOOLME") for such spoken untruths. Their minds grope constantly in search of each other's meaning.

Well, tomorrow I shall talk their language. Not too freely; not enough to make them fear Limiks as dangerously intelligent; certainly I shall not tell them I can read their thoughts. I shall speak just as well enough to answer the questions they are certain to ask. And I shall answer them: Oh, we have the most dreadful heatwaves on this desert world, lasting weeks at a time; our lives are a struggle for bare existence with water our most valuable possession! (These things are untrue. What of it? They won't know that.)

So that's why I want the infrared heat—a foretaste of one of those "heatwaves" of ours. Please, Ilha, make it hot enough to discourage any lingering. I think this rocket ship will take off for the Blue Planet not later than tomorrow night, if you do your part.

Speaking of night, these monsters fall into a stupor then. Apparently they think of it as a regular thing, every night of their lives. Their stupor lasts all the dark hours. Last night their lights blazed a few hours, then they began to blink their eyes and gape—as we do after each meal. They said "GOOD NITE" to each other and went into another room, putting out all lights in the ship. That is when I escaped.

Nothing could have been simpler. I merely unfastened the cage and lifted it off me. The door of the room was closed, but I could just reach its fastening when I stood on probe-tip. I was out on the desert sand!

I am not much of an athlete, but I rolled here in an hour. Of course, the desert is fairly smooth and the air cool at night. I shall have time to return more sedately, for it is still three hours before dawn and I have almost finished writing.

Oh yes, I am going back. Frankly, it is not just because my plan requires me to talk to them. It may be hard for you to understand, Ilha, but I *want* to return. I like them.

I suppose from my description they must seem horrible to you. In many ways they are horrible. I like them in spite of that. They are not always evenly balanced in their emotions, not always reasonable like a Limik. They leap from love to hate and back again twenty times an hour over unimportant matters. We regard every form of life with unvarying benignance; they do not. Either they bear a highly prejudiced affection toward others, or else they hold them in utter contempt. True, they kill remorselessly; but also true, they risk their own lives freely for those they happen to like—at least so I read Red-head's unspoken thoughts toward Bill. No Limik, of course, could ever be capable of either extreme. On the whole, the average between their vices and virtues is not really very far from our own unchanging reasonableness; but if they happen to regard you as friendly, they are far more pleasant—to *you*—than any group of Limiks would be.

I am regarded as a friend—certainly by Bill and Red-head, though Big-voice is not quite sure yet. I could sense his thoughts, anticipating the trouble of feeding me, and caring for me if I were ill, resenting all that prospective effort and yet suspecting that I might be worth it. Why? Because I look harmless and LAFF-able! Even with a far better reason, no Limik would go to so much trouble for me—would you, Ilha?

I am back once again to their LAFF-ing. I wish I could explain the sort of thing it is, but I do not even know exactly what starts it. It might be something ridiculous, or clever, or even obviously untrue. I have noted a few examples, but they would not help you; it is utterly un-Limik and unreasonable. But it is contagious. I don't suppose I could LAFF by myself—oh, I could bark HAW HAW but that isn't it—I could not give myself that odd sparkling freedom of mind. It is the most refreshing experience I have ever had, for I have experienced it, or very nearly, when I was in the same room with these HEW-MEN. It warms me like a fire inside my cold consciousness. The mere chance that I may finally learn to LAFF as freely as they do is alone worth the risk of my life—worth it many times over. It is like being made young again for a few minutes.

Our sober, worrying, serious ways are no doubt admirable—certainly reasonable. But tell me this: how many of us ever die a natural death from old age? You know as well as I that every Limik, sooner or later, is driven by our racial melancholy to end his own life. Not me, though— not now! Yet I have been melancholy of late. Life has never seemed the same since my mate Wkap died. She was different from the other two. Mind you, they are splendid breeding partners, none better; but I won't miss them nor they me. Each has her two other consorts; they will find a third to take my place before next twining-time.

So I am going back to these likable monsters. More than that, I am going to help them in every way I can—I intend to be a small but very loyal member of their crew. I may even learn to eat some of their food— after all, some forms of life on their world may be so low in the scale of

145

evolution they cannot even think, perhaps not even feel. Just because no such life exists here does not mean it cannot elsewhere.

I am X-SITED—which means, I think, less than no calmness at all, if you can imagine such a state of mind. It has no equivalent in Limik writing, but then I am almost no longer Limik.

I hope I can persuade them to leave this planet before noon tomorrow. But you must not risk our entire civilization merely because I have taken a liking to these monsters—and it is a real risk, for they are truly dangerous. Killing heat tomorrow noon, remember. All I ask is that you make the heat *really* killing; I have no wish to fry slowly!

For if they stay I shall stay (and die) with them. So, either way it is . . . Good-bye, Ilha.

Gordon R. Dickson
OF THE PEOPLE

"Because he was born in Canada and has spent most of his adult life in Minneapolis, he often uses Canadian and Midwestern settings to good effect," wrote the critic, Sandra Miesel, of Gordon R. Dickson. This popular and prolific author, born the son of a mining engineer in Edmonton in 1923, is the younger brother of Lovat Dickson, the Anglo-Canadian biographer. The family moved to the midwestern United States when Gordon R. Dickson was thirteen. He remained there, graduating from the University of Minnesota and setting up shop in Minneapolis in 1950, as a writer of science fiction and fantasy, including juveniles and "space operas." Dickson is neither a Canadian writer nor an American writer but very much a North American writer. He has kept alive his Canadian connections and even at one point contemplated editing a collection of Canadian science fiction. The Dorsal Irregulars is the name of a Toronto-based fan club devoted to his work. (The club takes its name from a race of mercenary warriors of the future, described in his "Childe Cycle" series of novels.) A bibliography of his work appears in Gordon R. Dickson's SF Best (1978), edited by James R. Frenkel, with an introduction by Spider Robinson. I have represented the author with a short work of fantasy which first appeared in Fantasy and Science

Fiction, *December 1955, and was subsequently collected in* Mutants: A
Science Fiction Adventure *(1970). "Of the People" is vintage Dickson
but not completely representative of the author's work, which is inclined
to be lengthy and detailed and set in the far future. "Of the People" is a
fantasy, almost a fable, about a man who may be facing a mid-life crisis,
or a saviour who may have forgotten his divine mission, or none of
the above.*

But you know, I could sense it coming a long time off. It was a little
extra time taken in drinking a cup of coffee, it was lingering over the
magazines in a drugstore as I picked out a handful. It was a girl I looked
at twice as I ran out and down the steps of a library.

And it wasn't any good and I knew it. But it kept coming and it kept
coming, and one night I stayed working at the design of a power cruiser
until it was finished, before I finally knocked off for supper. Then, after
I'd eaten, I looked ahead down twelve dark hours to daylight, and I
knew I'd had it.

So I got up and I walked out of the apartment. I left my glass half full
and the record player I had built playing the music I had written to the
pictures I had painted. Left the organ and the typewriter, left the dark-
room and the lab. Left the jammed-full filing cabinets. Took the elevator
and told the elevator boy to head for the ground floor. Walked out into
the deep snow.

"You going out in January without an overcoat, Mr. Crossman?" asked
the doorman.

"Don't need a coat," I told him. "Never no more, no coats."

"Don't you want me to phone the garage for your car, then?"

"Don't need a car."

I left him and I set out walking. After a while it began to snow, but
not on me. And after a little more while people started to stare, so I
flagged down a cab.

"Get out and give me the keys," I told the driver.

"You drunk?" he said.

"It's all right, son," I said. "I own the company. But you'll get out
nonetheless and give me the keys." He got out and gave me the keys and
I left him standing there.

I got in the cab and drove it off through the night-lit downtown streets,
and I kissed the city good-by as I went. I blew a kiss to the grain exchange
and a kiss to the stockyards. And a kiss to every one of the fourteen offices
in the city that knew me each under a different title as head of a different

business. You've got to get along without me now, city and people, I said, because I'm not coming back, no more, no more.

I drove out of downtown and out past Longview Acres and past Manor Acres and past Sherman Hills and I blew them all a kiss, too. Enjoy your homes, you people, I told them, because they're good homes—not the best I could have done you by a damn sight, but better than you'll see elsewhere in a long time, and your money's worth. Enjoy your homes and don't remember me.

I drove out to the airport and there I left the cab. It was a good airport. I'd laid it out myself and I knew. It was a good airport and I got eighteen days of good hard work out of the job. I got myself so lovely and tired doing it I was able to go out to the bars and sit there having half a dozen drinks—before the urge to talk to the people around me became unbearable and I had to get up and go home.

There were planes on the field. A good handful of them. I went in and talked to one of the clerks.

"Mr. Crossman!" he said, when he saw me.

"Get me a plane," I said. "Get me a plane headed east and then forget I was in tonight."

He did; and I went. I flew to New York and changed planes and flew to London; and changed again and came in by jet to Bombay.

By the time I reached Bombay, my mind was made up for good, and I went through the city as if it were a dream of buildings and people and no more. I went through the town and out of the town and I hit the road north, walking. And as I walked, I took off my coat and my tie. And I opened my collar to the open air and I started my trek.

I was six weeks walking it. I remember little bits and pieces of things along the way—mainly faces, and mainly the faces of the children, for they aren't afraid when they're young. They'd come up to me and run alongside, trying to match the strides I'd take, and after a while they'd get tired and drop back—but there were always others along the way. And there were adults, too, men and women, but when they got close they'd take one look at my face and go away again. There was only one who spoke to me in all this trip, and that was a tall, dark brown man in some kind of uniform. He spoke to me in English and I answered him in dialect. He was scared to the marrow of his bones, for after he spoke I could hear the little grinding of his teeth in the silence as he tried to keep them from chattering. But I answered him kindly, and told him I had business in the north that was nobody's business but my own. And when he still would not move—he was well over six feet and nearly as tall as I —I opened my right hand beneath his nose and showed him himself, small and weak as a caterpillar in the palm of it. And he fell out of my path as if his legs had all the strength gone out of them, and I went on.

I was six weeks walking it. And when I came to the hills, my beard was grown out and my pants and my shirt were in tatters. Also, by this time, the word had gone ahead of me. Not the official word, but the little words of little people, running from mouth to mouth. They knew I was coming and they knew where I was headed—to see the old man up beyond Mutteeanee Pass, the white-bearded, holy man of the village between two peaks.

He was sitting on his rock out on the hillside, with his blind eyes following the sun and the beard running white and old between his thin knees and down to the brown earth.

I sat down on a smaller rock before him and caught my breath.

"Well, Erik," I said. "I've come."

"I'm aware you have, Sam."

"By foot," I said. "By car and plane, too, but mostly by foot, as time goes. All the way from the lowlands by foot, Erik. And that's the last I do for any of them."

"For them, Sam?"

"For me, then."

"Not for you, either, Sam," he said. And then he sighed. "Go back, Sam," he said.

"Go back!" I echoed. "Go back to hell again? No thank you, Erik."

"You faltered," he said. "You weakened. You began to slow down, to look around. There was no need to, Sam. If you hadn't started to slacken off, you would have been all right."

"All right? Do you call the kind of life I lead, that? What do you use for a heart, Erik?"

"A heart?" And with that he lowered his blind old eyes from the sun and turned them right on me. "Do you accuse me, Sam?"

"With you it's choice," I said. "You can go."

"No," he shook his head. "I'm bound by choice, just as you are bound by the greater strength in me. Go back, Sam."

"Why?" I cried. And I pounded my chest like a crazy man. "Why me? Why can others go and I have to stay? There's no end to the universe. I don't ask for company. I'll find some lost hole somewhere and bury myself. Anywhere, just so I'm away."

"Would you, Sam?" he asked. And at that, there was pity in his voice. When I did not answer, he went on, gently. "You see, Sam, that's exactly why I can't let you go. You're capable of deluding yourself, of telling yourself that you'll do what we both know you will not, cannot do. So you must stay."

"No," I said. "All right." I got up and turned to go. "I came to you first and gave you your chance. But now I'll go on my own, and I'll get off somehow."

"Sam, come back," he said. And abruptly, my legs were mine no longer.

"Sit down again," he said. "And listen for a minute."

My traitorous legs took me back, and I sat.

"Sam," he said, "you know the old story. Now and then, at rare intervals, one like us will be born. Nearly always, when they are grown, they leave. Only a few stay. But only once in thousands of years does one like yourself appear who must be chained against his will to our world."

"Erik," I said, between my teeth. "Don't sympathize."

"I'm not sympathizing, Sam," he said. "As you said yourself, there is no end to the universe, but I have seen it all and there is no place in it for you. For the others that have gone out, there are places that are no places. They sup at alien tables, Sam, but always and forever as a guest. They left themselves behind when they went and they don't belong any longer to our Earth."

He stopped for a moment, and I knew what was coming.

"But you, Sam," he said, and I heard his voice with my head bowed, staring at the brown dirt. He spoke tenderly. "Poor Sam. You'd never be able to leave the Earth behind. You're one of us, but the living cord binds you to the others. Never a man speaks to you, but your hands yearn towards him in friendship. Never a woman smiles your way, but love warms that frozen heart of yours. You can't leave them, Sam. If you went out now, you'd come back, in time, and try to take them with you. You'd hurry them on before they are ripe. And there's no place out there in the universe for them—yet."

I tried to move, but could not. Tried to lift my face to his, but I could not.

"Poor Sam," he said, "trapped by a common heart that chains the lightning of his brain. Go back, Sam. Go back to your cities and your people. Go back to a thousand little jobs, and the work that is no greater than theirs, but many times as much so that it drives you without a pause twenty, twenty-two hours a day. Go back, Sam, to your designing and your painting, to your music and your business, to your engineering and your landscaping, and all the other things. Go back and keep busy, so busy your brain fogs and you sleep without dreaming. And wait. Wait for the necessary years to pass until they grow and change and at last come to their destiny.

"When that time comes, Sam, they will go out. And you will go with them, blood of their blood, flesh of their flesh, kin and comrade to them all. You will be happier than any of us have ever been, when that time

150

comes. But the years have still to pass, and now you must go back. Go back, Sam. Go back, go back, go back."

And so I have come back. O people that I hate and love!

Hugh Hood
AFTER THE SIRENS

Nowhere have the effects of a nuclear attack on a small family living in the suburb of a large city been more grippingly presented than in "After the Sirens" by Hugh Hood. The novelist and story writer, born in Toronto in 1928, has lived in Montreal since 1961. Hood's chef d'oeuvre is a series of twelve linked novels which will document and dramatize the social history of Ontario from 1925 to the year 2000. "After the Sirens" is Hood's single foray into science fiction, although the element of fantasy is everpresent in stories found in The Fruit Man, the Meat Man, and the Manager *(1971) and* Dark Glasses *(1976). "After the Sirens," first published in* Esquire, *August 1960, is reprinted from* Flying a Red Kite *(1962).*

They heard the sirens first about four forty-five in the morning. It was still dark and cold outside and they were sound asleep. They heard the noise first in their dreams and, waking, understood it to be real.

"What is it?" she asked him sleepily, rolling over in their warm bed. "Is there a fire?"

"I don't know," he said. The sirens were very loud. "I've never heard anything like that before."

"It's some kind of siren," she said, "downtown. It woke me up."

"Go back to sleep!" he said. "It can't be anything."

"No," she said, "I'm frightened. I wonder what it is. I wonder if the baby has enough covers." The wailing was still going on. "It couldn't be an air-raid warning, could it?"

"Of course not," he said reassuringly, but she could hear the indecision in his voice.

151

"Why don't you turn on the radio," she said, "just to see? Just to make sure. I'll go and see if the baby's covered up." They walked down the hall in their pajamas. He went into the kitchen, turned on the radio and waited for it to warm up. There was nothing but static and hum.

"What's that station?" he called to her. "Conrad, or something like that."

"That's 640 on the dial," she said, from the baby's room. He twisted the dial and suddenly the radio screamed at him, frightening him badly.

"This is not an exercise. This is not an exercise. This is not an exercise," the radio blared. *"This is an air-raid warning. This is an air-raid warning. We will be attacked in fifteen minutes. We will be attacked in fifteen minutes. This is not an exercise."* He recognized the voice of a local announcer who did an hour of breakfast music daily. He had never heard the man talk like that before. He ran into the baby's room while the radio shrieked behind him: *"We will be attacked in fifteen minutes. Correction. Correction. In fourteen minutes. In fourteen minutes. We will be attacked in fourteen minutes. This is not an exercise."*

"Look," he said, "don't ask me any questions, please, just do exactly what I tell you and don't waste any time." She stared at him with her mouth open. "Listen," he said, "and do exactly as I say. They say this is an air-raid and we'd better believe them." She looked frightened nearly out of her wits. "I'll look after you," he said; "just get dressed as fast as you can. Put on as many layers of wool as you can. Got that?"

She nodded speechlessly.

"Put on your woollen topcoat and your fur coat over that. Get as many scarves as you can find. We'll wrap our faces and hands. When you're dressed, dress the baby the same way. We have a chance, if you do as I say without wasting time." She ran off up the hall to the coat closet and he could hear her pulling things about.

"This will be an attack with nuclear weapons. You have thirteen minutes to take cover," screamed the radio. He looked at his watch and hurried to the kitchen and pulled a cardboard carton from under the sink. He threw two can openers into it and all the canned goods he could see. There were three loaves of bread in the breadbox and he crammed them into the carton. He took everything that was wrapped and solid in the refrigerator and crushed it in. When the carton was full he took a bucket which usually held a garbage bag, rinsed it hastily, and filled it with water. There was a plastic bottle in the refrigerator. He poured the tomato juice out of it and rinsed it and filled it with water.

"This will be a nuclear attack." The disc jockey's voice was cracking with hysteria. *"You have nine minutes, nine minutes, to take cover. Nine*

minutes." He ran into the dark hall and bumped into his wife who was swaddled like a bear.

"Go and dress the baby," he said. "We're going to make it, we've just got time. I'll go and get dressed." She was crying, but there was no time for comfort. In the bedroom he forced himself into his trousers, a second pair of trousers, two shirts and two sweaters. He put on the heaviest, loosest jacket he owned, a topcoat, and finally his overcoat. This took him just under five minutes. When he rejoined his wife in the living room, she had the baby swaddled in her arms, still asleep.

"Go to the back room in the cellar, where your steamer trunk is," he said, "and take this." He gave her a flashlight which they kept in their bedroom. When she hesitated he said roughly, "Go on, get going."

"Aren't you coming?"

"Of course I'm coming," he said. He turned the radio up as far as it would go and noted carefully what the man said. *"This will be a nuclear attack. The target will probably be the aircraft company. You have three minutes to take cover."* He picked up the carton and balanced the bottle of water on it. With the other hand he carried the bucket. Leaving the kitchen door wide open, he went to the cellar, passed through the dark furnace room, and joined his wife.

"Put out the flashlight," he said. "We'll have to save it. We have a minute or two, so listen to me." They could hear the radio upstairs. *"Two minutes,"* it screamed.

"Lie down in the corner of the west and north walls," he said quickly. "The blast should come from the north if they hit the target, and the house will blow down and fall to the south. Lie on top of the baby and I'll lie on top of you!"

She cuddled the sleeping infant in her arms. "We're going to die right now," she said, as she held the baby closer to her.

"No, we aren't," he said, "we have a chance. Wrap the scarves around your face and the baby's, and lie down." She handed him a plaid woollen scarf and he tied it around his face so that only his eyes showed. He placed the water and food in a corner and then lay down on top of his wife, spreading his arms and legs as much as possible, to cover and protect her.

"Twenty seconds," shrieked the radio. *"Eighteen seconds. Fifteen."*

He looked at his watch as he fell. "Ten seconds," he said aloud. "It's five o'clock. They won't waste a megaton bomb on us. They'll save it for New York." They heard the radio crackle into silence and they hung onto each other, keeping their eyes closed tightly.

Instantaneously the cellar room lit up with a kind of glow they had never seen before, the earthen floor began to rock and heave, and the absolutely unearthly sound began. There was no way of telling how far off it was, the explosion. The sound seemed to be inside them, in their bowels; the very air itself was shattered and blown away in the dreadful sound that went on and on and on.

They held their heads down, hers pushed into the dirt, shielding the baby's scalp, his face crushed into her hair, nothing of their skin exposed to the glow, and the sound went on and on, pulsing curiously, louder than anything they had ever imagined, louder than deafening, quaking in their eardrums, louder and louder until it seemed that what had exploded was there in the room on top of them in a blend of smashed, torn air, cries of the instantly dead, fall of steel, timber, and brick, crash of masonry and glass—they couldn't sort any of it out—all were there, all imaginable noises of destruction synthesized. It was like absolutely nothing they had ever heard before and it so filled their skulls, pushing outward from the brainpan, that they could not divide it into its parts. All that they could understand, if they understood anything, was that this was the ultimate catastrophe, and that they were still recording it, expecting any second to be crushed into blackness, but as long as they were recording it they were still living. They felt, but did not think, this. They only understood it instinctively and held on tighter to each other, waiting for the smash, the crush, the black.

But it became lighter and lighter, the glow in the cellar room, waxing and intensifying itself. It had no color that they recognized through their tightly-shut eyelids. It might have been called green, but it was not green, nor any neighbor of green. Like the noise, it was a dreadful compound of ultimately destructive fire, blast, terrible energy released from a bursting sun, like the birth of the solar system. Incandescence beyond an infinite number of lights swirled around them.

The worst was the nauseous rocking to and fro of the very earth beneath them, worse than an earthquake, which might have seemed reducible to human dimensions, those of some disaster witnessed in the movies or on television. But this was no gaping, opening seam in the earth, but a threatened total destruction of the earth itself, right to its core, a pulverization of the world. They tried like animals to scrabble closer and closer in under the north cellar wall even as they expected it to fall on them. They kept their heads down, waiting for death to take them as it had taken their friends, neighbors, fellow workers, policemen, firemen, soldiers; and the dreadful time passed and still they did not die in the catastrophe. And they began to sense obscurely that the longer they were left uncrushed, the better grew their chances of survival. And pitifully slowly their feelings began to resume their customary segmented play amongst themselves, while the event was still unfolding. They could not help doing the characteristic, the human thing, the beginning to think and struggle to live.

Through their shut eyelids the light began to seem less incandescent, more recognizably a color familiar to human beings and less terrifying because it might be called a hue of green instead of no-color-at-all. It became green, still glowing and illuminating the cellar like daylight, but anyway green, nameable as such and therefore familiar and less dreadful. The light grew more and more darkly green in an insane harmony with the rocking and the sound.

As the rocking slowed, as they huddled closer and closer in under the north foundation, a split in the cellar wall showed itself almost in front of their hidden faces, and yet the wall stood and did not come in on top of them. It held and, holding, gave them more chance for survival although they didn't know it. The earth's upheaval slowed and sank back and no gaps appeared in the earth under them, no crevasse to swallow them up under the alteration of the earth's crust. And in time the rocking stopped and the floor of their world was still, but they would not move, afraid to move a limb for fear of being caught in the earth's mouth.

The noise continued, but began to distinguish itself in parts, and the worst basic element attenuated itself; that terrible crash apart of the atmosphere under the bomb had stopped by now, the atmosphere had parted to admit the ball of radioactivity, had been blown hundreds of miles in every direction and had rushed back to regain its place, disputing that place with the ball of radioactivity, so that there grew up a thousand-mile vortex of cyclonic winds around the hub of the displacement. The cyclone was almost comforting, sounding, whistling, in whatever stood upright, not trees certainly, but tangled steel beams and odd bits of masonry. The sound of these winds came to them in the cellar. Soon they were able to name sounds, and distinguish them from others which they heard, mainly sounds of fire—no sounds of the dying, no human cries at all, no sounds of life. Only the fires and cyclonic winds.

Now they could feel, and hear enough to shout to each other over the fire and wind.

The man tried to stir, to ease his wife's position. He could move his torso so far as the waist or perhaps the hips. Below that, although he was in no pain and not paralyzed, he was immobilized by a heavy weight. He could feel his legs and feet; they were sound and unhurt, but he could not move them. He waited, lying there trying to sort things out, until some sort of ordered thought and some communication was possible, when the noise should lessen sufficiently. He could hear his wife shouting something into the dirt in front of her face and he tried to make it out.

155

"She slept through it," he heard, "she slept through it," and he couldn't believe it, although it was true. The baby lived and recollected none of the horror.

"She slept through it," screamed the wife idiotically, "she's still asleep." It couldn't be true, he thought, it was impossible, but there was no way to check her statement until they could move about. The baby must have been three feet below the blast and the glow, shielded by a two-and-a-half foot wall of flesh, his and his wife's, and the additional thickness of layers of woollen clothing. She should certainly have survived, if they had, but how could she have slept through the noise, the awful light, and the rocking? He listened and waited, keeping his head down and his face covered.

Supposing that they had survived the initial blast, as seemed to be the case; there was still the fallout to consider. The likelihood, he thought (he was beginning to be able to think) was that they were already being eaten up by radiation and would soon die of monstrous cancers, or plain, simple leukemia, or rottenness of the cortex. It was miraculous that they had lived through the first shock; they could hardly hope that their luck would hold through the later dangers. He thought that the baby might not have been infected so far, shielded as she was, as he began to wonder how she might be helped to evade death from radiation in the next few days. Let her live a week, he thought, and she may go on living into the next generation, if there is one.

Nothing would be the same in the next generation; there would be few people and fewer laws, the national boundaries would have perished—there would be a new world to invent. Somehow the child must be preserved for that, even if their own lives were to be forfeited immediately. He felt perfectly healthy so far, untouched by any creeping sickness as he lay there, forcing himself and the lives beneath him deeper into their burrow. He began to make plans; there was nothing else for him to do just then.

The noise of the winds had become regular now and the green glow had subsided; the earth was still and they were still together and in the same place, in their cellar, in their home. He thought of his books, his checkbook, his phonograph records, his wife's household appliances. They were gone, of course, which didn't matter. What mattered was that the way they had lived was gone, the whole texture of their habits. The city would be totally uninhabitable. If they were to survive longer, they must get out of the city at once. They would have to decide immediately when they should try to leave the city, and they must keep themselves alive until that time.

"What time is it?" gasped his wife from below him in a tone pitched in

156

almost her normal voice. He was relieved to hear her speak in the commonplace, familiar tone; he had been afraid that hysteria and shock would destroy their personalities all at once. So far they had held together. Later on, when the loss of their whole world sank in, when they appreciated the full extent of their losses, they would run the risk of insanity or, at least, extreme neurotic disturbance. But right now they could converse, calculate, and wait for the threat of madness to appear days, or years, later.

He looked at his watch. "Eight-thirty," he said. Everything had ended in three-and-a-half hours. "Are you all right?" he asked.

"I think so," she said, "I don't feel any pain and the baby's fine. She's warm and she doesn't seem frightened."

He tried to move his legs and was relieved to see that they answered the nervous impulse. He lifted his head fearfully and twisted it around to see behind him. His legs were buried under a pile of loose brick and rubble which grew smaller toward his thighs; his torso was quite uncovered. "I'm all right," he said, beginning to work his legs free; they were undoubtedly badly bruised, but they didn't seem to be crushed or broken; at the worst he might have torn muscles or a bad sprain. He had to be very careful, he reasoned, as he worked at his legs. He might dislodge something and bring the remnant of the house down around them. Very, very slowly he lifted his torso by doing a push-up with his arms. His wife slid out from underneath, pushing the baby in front of her. When she was free she laid the child gently to one side, whispering to her and promising her food. She crawled around to her husband's side and began to push the bricks off his legs.

"Be careful," he whispered. "Take them as they come. Don't be in too much of a hurry."

She nodded, picking out the bricks gingerly, but as fast as she could. Soon he was able to roll over on his back and sit up. By a quarter to ten he was free and they took time to eat and drink. The three of them sat together in a cramped, narrow space under the cellar beams, perhaps six feet high and six or seven feet square. They were getting air from somewhere although it might be deadly air, and there was no smell of gas. He had been afraid that they might be suffocated in their shelter.

"Do you suppose the food's contaminated?" she asked.

"What if it is?" he said. "So are we, just as much as the food. There's nothing to do but risk it. Only be careful what you give the baby."

"How can I tell?"

"I don't know," he said. "Say a prayer and trust in God." He found the flashlight, which had rolled into a corner, and tried it. It worked very well.

"What are we going to do? We can't stay here."

"I don't even know for sure that we can get out," he said, "but we'll try. There should be a window just above us that leads to a crawl-space under the patio. That's one of the reasons why I told you to come here. In any case we'd be wise to stay here for a few hours until the very worst of the fallout is down."

"What'll we do when we get out?"

"Try to get out of town. Get our outer clothes off, get them all off for that matter, and scrub ourselves with water. Maybe we can get to the river."

"Why don't you try the window right now so we can tell whether we can get out?"

"I will as soon as I've finished eating and had a rest. My legs are very sore."

He could hear her voice soften. "Take your time," she said.

When he felt rested, he stood up. He could almost stand erect and with the flashlight was able to find the window quickly. It was level with his face. He piled loose bricks against the wall below it and climbed up on them until the window was level with his chest. Knocking out the screen with the butt of the flashlight, he put his head through and then flashed the light around; there were no obstructions that he could see, and he couldn't smell anything noxious. The patio, being a flat, level space, had evidently been swept clean by the blast without being flattened. They could crawl out of the cellar under the patio, he realized, and then kick a hole in the lath and stucco which skirted it.

He stepped down from the pile of brick and told his wife that they would be able to get out whenever they wished, that the crawl space was clear.

"What time is it?"

"Half-past twelve."

"Should we try it now?"

"I think so," he said. "At first I thought we ought to stay here for a day or two, but now I think we ought to try and get out from under the fallout. We may have to walk a couple of hundred miles."

"We can do it," she said and he felt glad. She had always been able to look unpleasant issues in the face.

He helped her through the cellar window and handed up the baby, who clucked and chuckled when he spoke to her. He pushed the carton of food and the bucket of water after them. Then he climbed up and they inched forward under the patio.

"I hear a motor," said his wife suddenly.

He listened and heard it too.

158

"Looking for survivors," he said eagerly. "Probably the Army or Civil Defense. Come on."

He swung himself around on his hips and back and kicked out with both feet at the lath and stucco. Three or four kicks did it. His wife went first, inching the baby through the hole. He crawled after her into the daylight; it looked like any other day except that the city was leveled. The sky and the light were the same; everything else was gone. They sat up, muddy, scratched, nervously exhausted, in a ruined flower bed. Not fifty feet away stood an olive-drab truck, the motor running loudly. Men shouted to them.

"Come on, you!" shouted the men in the truck. "Get going!" They stood and ran raggedly to the cab, she holding the child and he their remaining food and water. In the cab was a canvas-sheeted, goggled driver, peering at them through huge eyes. "Get in the back," he ordered. "We've got to get out right away. Too hot." They climbed into the truck and it began to move instantly.

"Army Survival Unit," said a goggled and hooded man in the back of the truck. "Throw away that food and water; it's dangerous. Get your outer clothing off quickly. Throw it out!" They obeyed him without thinking, stripping off their loose outer clothes and dropping them out of the truck.

"You're the only ones we've found in a hundred city blocks," said the soldier. "Did you know the war's over? There's a truce."

"Who won?"

"Over in half an hour," he said, "and nobody won."

"What are you going to do with us?"

"Drop you at a check-out point forty miles from here. Give you the scrub-down treatment, wash off the fallout. Medical check for radiation sickness. Clean clothes. Then we send you on your way to a refugee station."

"How many died?"

"Everybody in the area. Almost no exception. You're a statistic, that's what you are. Must have been a fluke of the blast."

"Will we live?"

"Sure you will. You're living now, aren't you?"

"I guess so," he said.

"Sure you'll live! Maybe not too long. But everybody else is dead! And you'll be taken care of." He fell silent.

They looked at each other, determined to live as long as they could. The wife cuddled the child close against her thin silk blouse. For a long time they jolted along over rocks and broken pavement without speaking. When the pavement smoothed out the husband knew that they must be

out of the disaster area. In a few more minutes they were out of immediate danger; they had reached the checkout point. It was a quarter to
three in the afternoon.

"Out you get," said the soldier. "We've got to go back." They climbed
out of the truck and he handed down the baby. "You're all right now,"
he said. "Good luck."

"Good-bye," they said.

The truck turned about and drove away and they turned silently, hand
in hand, and walked toward the medical tents. They were the seventh,
eighth, and ninth living persons to be brought there after the sirens.

Margaret Laurence
A QUEEN IN THEBES

*"A Queen in Thebes" is what science-fiction writers call a post-holocaust
story. The story does not describe the actual destruction of a society or a
world, but the consequences and aftermath of that destruction, a far more
human subject than how radioactive fallout destroyed hundreds of thousands or untold millions of people. This look at the human heart, and
how civilization has to begin anew, was written by Margaret Laurence,
the distinguished novelist who was born in 1926 in Neepawa, Manitoba,
and has written such novels as* The Stone Angel *(1964) and* The Diviners
(1975). Fantastic descriptions play an important role in Long Drums and
Cannons *(1971), her study of contemporary Nigerian literature, and in*
Jason's Quest *(1970), her children's book. "A Queen in Thebes" first
appeared in* The Tamarack Review, *Summer 1964 and is reprinted from*
The Canadian Century: English-Canadian Writing Since Confederation
(1973), edited by A. J. M. Smith.

Fear of a war was not what had taken them to the cottage in the
mountains. Everyone had feared war for so long that it seemed it might

never happen after all. Nerves cannot be kept on edge year in and year out without a boredom taking hold of the tension, calcifying it, ultimately making the possibility of devastation seem impossible in the face of the continuing realities—the newspapers delivered each day to the door, the passing of seasons, the favourite TV serials which would, everyone somehow felt, continue in spite of the fires of hell or the Day of Judgement. No, they had simply gone to the mountains because it would be good to get the baby out of the stifling city for the summer, into the cooler air and the quiet. It was a long way for her husband to drive for the weekends, but he said he did not mind, and later in the summer he would be getting his two weeks' holiday. Her husband had built the cottage the year they were married. It was only a shack, really, and it was not close to any settlement or town. They had to bring in all their supplies, and they decided to have the tinned goods sent in all at once, by truck, enough to last the summer, so her husband would not have to bother with much shopping when he came up on the weekends. Although it was isolated, it was a place they both loved. The lake was nearby, azure, and alive with fishes, and the pine and tamarack brushed their low-sweeping boughs against the windows as the night wind stirred them. Her husband spent a day in getting enough firewood for a week, making certain everything was all right.

"You don't mind being alone here with Rex?" he said. "If anything happens, you can always walk down the hill to Benson's Garage, and phone me."

She was afraid, but she did not say so. He went back to the city then. The day after he left, the sky turned to fire, as though the sun had exploded.

The city was a long way off, down on the plains, too far for the death to reach here, but she saw it like the disintegrating sun, the light like no other light, a dark illumination and not the health which we associate with light. Then the dust cloud formed like the shape of a giant and poisonous toadstool, and she knew the thing had come which everyone had feared. She herself had feared it until it no longer seemed real, and now it had come. She did not scream or cry, after the first unbelieving cry. She hid her eyes, lest the sight damage them. She ran into the cottage and sat quite still. It grew dark, and the baby was crying. She fed him, picking him up with small stiff movements of her hands. Then she put him into his bed and he went to sleep. She did not think at all of the cloud or the light or the death, or of how it would be this moment in what had been the city. She was waiting for her husband to arrive.

In the morning, she looked out and saw the sun rising. The fire of it glowed red and quiet in the sky. For an instant she gazed at it in panic.

161

Then she drew the curtains across the windows so the light would not infect her or the baby. Everything was all right, she calmed herself. It was only that she had never been away from people before, although she was twenty years old. Either her family or her husband had always been with her. He will soon come, she told herself. She fed the baby. Then she took out her purse mirror and combed her hair, so she would look nice when her husband arrived.

She lived this way for some days, going outside the shack only at night. Then one morning she knew the sun did not threaten her. She walked out in the daylight, although she still could not look directly at the sun. When she looked beyond the forest, in the direction of the far-off city, she remembered the death. She ran back to the shack and took the baby in her arms. She rocked him there, and for the first time she cried and could not stop. She mourned wordlessly, and when her tears were done and the violence of the pain had momentarily spent itself, she thought of herself and the baby. She set out, carrying the child, to find people.

When she reached the foot of the mountain, she found no-one at Benson's Garage. The place had been deserted. The money was gone from the till, but otherwise everything had been left as it was. The people must have felt that they were not far enough away, thinking of the dust that could enter them in the air they breathed, rotting the blood and bone. They must have fled to some more distant and uncontaminated place. She wondered dully if they had found such a place, or if they had only run into other deaths, other polluted places, other cities shattered and lying like hulked shadows on the earth. She became afraid of the air now herself, and because she felt safer on the mountain, she wanted to start back. But she thought of the telephone, and an unreasoning hope possessed her. She was certain her husband was still somewhere and that she would be granted the miracle of his voice. She lifted the receiver and dialled. There was no response. She tried again and again, but there was no sound. She replaced the phone carefully, as though it mattered. Then she took the baby and began walking up the hill.

She knew she had to find people. In the days that followed, she walked long distances through the forest, marking her way so she would not get lost. She walked down the hill on every side, through the heavy bracken and the snarled bushes, until her legs and arms were bleeding with the small incisions of thorns and branches, and her arms ached with the fatigue of carrying the child, for she would not leave him alone in the shack. But in all her treks she found no-one. At night she did not cry. She lay sleepless, her eyes open, listening to owls and wind, trying to believe what had happened.

162

The leaves of the poplar were turning a clear yellow, and she knew it was autumn. She looked with sudden terror at the tins of food on the shelves, and saw they were almost gone. She picked berries and cooked them on the wood stove, wondering how long they would keep. She had fished only to provide her daily needs, but now she caught as many fish as she could. She slit and cleaned them, and laid them out in the sun to dry. One afternoon she found a black bear from the forest, feeding on the outspread fish. She had no gun. At that moment she was not afraid of the animal. She could think only of the sun-dried fish, hers, the food she had caught. She seized a stick and flew at the bear. The creature, taken by surprise, looked at her with shaggy menace. Then it lumbered off into the green ferns and the underbrush.

Each evening now, when the child was asleep, she lighted one of the remaining candles for only a few minutes and looked at herself in the mirror. She saw her long brownish blond hair and her thin tanned face and eyes she hardly knew as hers. Sometimes she wondered if her husband would recognize her when he arrived. Then she would remember, and would pick up the child and hold him tightly, and speak his name.

"Rex—it's all right. We're going to be all right."

The baby, wakened by her tears, would be frightened, and then she would be sufficiently occupied in quieting him. Sometimes, after she had looked in the mirror, she would not recall what had happened. She would go to bed comforted by the thoughts of her husband's arrival and would sleep without dreaming of the human shadows which she had long ago heard were etched on stone, their grotesque immortality.

Only when the first snow fell did she really believe that her husband was dead. She wanted and needed to die then, too, but she could not bring herself to kill her son and she could not leave him alone, so she was condemned to life.

The winter went on and on, and she thought they would not live until spring. The snow was banked high around the shack, and in the forest the hollows were filled with white, a trap to her unsure feet. She stumbled and fell, gathering firewood, and her axe severed the leather of the old boots which had been her husband's, cutting deeply into her ankle. She bound the wound clumsily, not expecting it to heal. It did heal, but the muscle had been affected and she walked with difficulty for a long time. She and the child were always cold and usually hungry. The thought uppermost in her mind was that she had to keep the fire going. She became obsessed with the gathering of wood, and would go out and drag the spruce branches back, even when the pile of boughs outside the shack was still high.

She prayed for help to come, but none came. Gradually she stopped

163

praying. She did not curse God, nor feel she had been deserted by Him. She simply forgot, God seemed related to what had once been and was no more. The room in her mind where the prayers had dwelt became vacant and uninhabited.

The thing she loved was the sound of the child's voice. What she missed most now was not her husband's protective presence, nor his warmth, but the sound of human voices. The child was learning to talk, and soon they would be able to speak together, as people do. This thought heartened her.

When she looked in the mirror now, she saw how bony and drawn her face had become, but the wide eyes were harder than before, and an alertness lurked in them. Her hearing was becoming keener. She could hear the deer that approached the cabin at night, and she would look out at them, but although she tried making traps, she caught only an occasional jack-rabbit. Once, seeing the deer, their bodies heavy with meat, she took the axe and went out, ready to attempt them. But they were too quick and they vanished into the night forest where she dared not follow.

The dried fish were almost gone. She lived in a semi-conscious state, drugged by exhaustion and hunger. Even her despair had lost its edge and was only a dulled apprehension of hopelessness. One day she threw the bones of a rabbit out into the snow, and for a moment sank down beside them, summoning strength to walk back into the cabin. A flock of sparrows landed on the snow beside her and began to explore the gnawed bones. She remembered dimly having once put out bread crumbs for the birds in winter. Delicately, hardly realizing she was doing it, her hands moved with a swiftness she had not known she possessed. She reached out and seized. When she drew back her hands, she had a live sparrow in each. She throttled them between thumb and forefinger, and began to tear off the feathers even before the small wings had stopped palpitating. Stolidly, feeling nothing, she cooked the birds and ate them. Then she vomited, and frightened the child with the way she cried afterwards. But the next time, when she caught birds and felt the life ebbing away between her fingers, she did not vomit or cry.

When the days began to lengthen, and spring came, she did not know whether it mattered that she and Rex were still alive. She moved only between one sunrise and the next. She could not think ahead. When the pain took possession of her heart, she still believed that she did not care whether they lived or died. Yet every day she gathered the firewood and foraged for some kind of food, and nothing was loathsome to her now, if her teeth and stomach could turn it into one more day of life.

She had kept only an approximate accounting of seasons, but one day she realized that Rex must be nearly six years old. She was much stronger than she had been—how weak and stupid she had been in the early days, after the Change—but now the boy was almost as strong as she. He was better at trapping rabbits and birds, and when he went to the lake, he never came back without fish. He would lie for hours on the shore, watching where the fish surfaced and which reedy places in the shallows were most likely to contain them. His eyes were better than hers, and his ears, and he had discovered for himself how to walk through the forest noiselessly, without allowing the ferns and bracken to snap under his feet.

At first she had tried to teach him things from that other world—how to read and how to pray. But he only laughed, and after a while she laughed, too, seeing how little use it was to them. She taught him instead what she had learned here—always to keep the fire going, always to gather wood, how to uproot dandelions and how to find the giant slugs where they concealed themselves on the underside of fallen logs. Then, gradually and imperceptibly, the boy began to teach her.

He was standing in the doorway now, and across his shoulders was a young deer with its throat slit.

"Rex—where? How?" They did not speak together tenderly and at length, as she once had imagined they would. Their days were too driven by the immediate matters of food, and in the evenings they wanted only to sleep. They spoke briefly, abruptly, exchanging only what was necessary.

The boy grinned. "I ran after it, and then I used my knife. You never tried. Why?"

"I tried," she said. She turned away. The boy was laughing softly to himself as he took the animal outside and began to skin it. She looked out the doorway at him as he squatted beside the deer, his face frowning in concentration as he tried to decide how to do something he had not done before. He took the skin off badly, and grew furious, and hacked at the slain animal with his knife. They ate meat that night, though, and that was what counted. But for the first time she felt a fear not of the many things there were to fear outside, but of something inside the dwelling, something unknown. When the boy was sleeping, she took out her mirror and looked. *I am strong*, she thought. *We can live. I have made this possible.* But her own eyes seemed unfamiliar to her, and she looked at the image in the glass as though it were separate from herself.

The years were not longer years but seasons—the season of warmth and growth, when the green forest provided deer and the lake swarmed with fish; the season of coolness and ripening, when the berries reddened on the bushes; the season of snow and penetrating chill, when the greatest fear was that the fire might die. But when, after all the seasons of care, the fire did die, it happened in spring, when the melting snow drenched into the shack one night through the weakening timbers of the roof. She had left the iron lid off the old stove so it would draw better, for the wood was not quite dry. It was her fault that the fire died, and both of them knew it. Rex was almost as tall as she was, now, and he grasped her wrist in his intensely strong hand and led her to see.

"You have killed the fire. Now what will we do? You are stupid, stupid, stupid!"

She looked at his other hand, which was clenched, and wondered if she dared draw away from his grip. Then some deep pride straightened her. She pried at the noose-like fingers which held her wrist, and she used her fingernails like talons. He let go and gazed his rage at her. Then he dropped his eyes. He was not yet full grown.

"What will we do?" he repeated.

She saw then that he was waiting for her to tell him, and she laughed —but silently, for she could not risk his hearing. She put her hands gently on his shoulders and stroked the pliant sun-browned skin until he turned to her and put his head against her in a gesture of need and surrender. Then, quickly, he jerked away and stood facing her, his eyes bold and self-contained once more.

"I have tried to strike fire from stone," she said. "We must try again."

They did try, but the sparks were too light and fleeting, and the shreds of birch bark never caught fire. They ate their meat raw that summer, and when the evenings lengthened into the cool of autumn, they shivered under the deer hides that were their blankets.

Rex became ill on meat that had spoiled. They had both been sick before, many times, but never as badly as this. He vomited until his stomach was empty, and still he could not stop retching. She gave him water and sat beside him. There was nothing else she could do. The cabin was almost a wreck now, for although they had tried to repair it, they lacked sufficient tools, and Rex was not old enough yet to invent new and untried ways of building. They hardly moved outside for many days, and in this period the shack's mustiness and disrepair came to her consciousness as never before, and she looked with fear at the feeble timbers and the buckling walls, thinking of the winter. One night, when Rex's fever was at its height, and he lay silently, contracted with pain, she tried to think back to the distant times before the Change. She had forgotten her husband. But she remembered that some words used to be spoken, something powerful when everything else had failed.

"I should—pray," she said.

He opened his eyes. "Pray?"

She felt then, in some remote and dusty room of her mind, that she had not imparted to him something which was his due. There was always too much to do. She was too tired to talk much in the evenings.

"We used to speak of God," she said. "All life comes from God. Something great and powerful, greater than we are. When many people lived, they used to say these things."

The boy looked at her vacantly, not comprehending. Later, however, he asked her again, and she attempted once more to tell him.

"All life comes from God——" but she no longer understood this very well herself and could not express it.

Gradually the illness left, and Rex grew strong again. One day he came back to the shack and told her he had found a cave in the side of a cliff.

"It will be better for the winter," he said.

She knew he was right. They moved everything they had, the knives and axe, the worn utensils, the tattered blankets, the deer hides. When she left the shack she cried, and the boy looked at her in astonishment.

Late that summer there was a severe storm, and the lightning descended to earth all around them, gashes of white light streaking the sky and tearing apart the darkness. She crouched on the cave floor and hid her eyes, as she always did in the presence of a sudden violence of light. Her fear was mingled with a sorrow whose roots she could no longer clearly trace. The boy knelt beside her and put his hands on her hair, and spoke to her, not roughly but quietly. He was afraid of the lightning, too, for he had learned her fear. But he was less afraid than she. He had no memory, not even her dim and confused ones, of any other life.

When the storm was over, they saw that the lightning had set the forest ablaze, a long way off, on the crest of the hill beyond their territory. The boy went off by himself. He was away for several days and nights, but when he returned he was carrying a smouldering pine torch. Their fire came to life again, and as it flared up in the circle of stones on the floor of the dark cave, the boy made an involuntary movement, as though compelled by something beyond his own decision. He raised his hands and bowed his head. Then, as though feeling that this was not enough, he knelt on the rock of the cave floor. He looked up and saw her standing immobile beside him, and his eyes became angry. With a sharp downward motion of his hand, he signalled what she was to do.

Slowly, doubtfully, and then as she stared at him at last unresisting, she went down onto her knees beside the circle of stones that contained the living fire. Together they knelt before the god.

One day she looked at Rex and saw he was much taller than she. He killed deer now mainly with his spear, and unless it was an exceptionally dry summer when the deer moved away in search of grazing, they were always well supplied with meat. The boy's hair grew down around his shoulders, but he lopped it off with his knife when it grew too long, for it got in his way when he was hunting. The hair was growing now on his face, but he did not bother to cut this. Age had no meaning for them, but she tried to count, as they counted the dried fish and strips of dried venison for the winter. The boy would be fifteen, perhaps, or sixteen.

She told him, without knowing in advance that she was going to say it, that the time had come for them to try once more to find the people. They thought of them as *The People,* those who perhaps lived somewhere beyond the mountain. She believed in their existence, but Rex believed only occasionally.

"There are no people," he said now.

"Yes," she said. "We must try."

"Why?" he asked.

She did not reply. She could only repeat the same words, over and over. "We must try." Rex shrugged.

"You go, then."

So she went alone, walking through the forest, descending into gullies where the loose shale slid under her feet, drinking face down from mountain streams, trapping squirrel and rabbit when she could. For many days and nights she travelled, but she did not find the people. Once she came to some dwellings, a few houses with weeds grown into the doorways, but they were deserted except for the mice and rats which eyed her, unblinking, from the corners of the dusty floors. Finally she knew she could not travel far enough. She was not any longer certain, herself, that people really existed. She turned and started back.

When she reached the mountain once more, and entered the cave, Rex looked different, or else her time away from him had enabled her to see him differently.

"You are back," he said, with neither gladness nor regret.

But that evening in front of the fire, she saw he really had changed. He knelt as before, but more hastily, more casually, as though it were not quite so important as it had been. He saw her questioning eyes.

"I was wrong," he explained.

"Wrong?" she was bewildered.

He indicated the fire. "This one is small. There is—something else."

He did not say anything more. He turned away and went to sleep. He wakened her at dawn and told her to come outside the cave. He pointed to the sun, which was appearing now over the lake, a red globe in the pale sky of morning.

"Our fire comes from there. The voices told me when you were not here. I was alone, and I could hear them. They were waiting for you to go away. You do not hear the voices. Only I can hear them, when I am alone."

He spoke almost pityingly, and with a certainty she had not heard before. She wanted to cry out against what he said, but she did not know why, nor what she could say to him.

"Look——" he said. "You look."

He knew she could not look directly at the sun. She feared, always, that the sight would damage her. The man grinned and turned his face to the sky.

"I can look," he said. "I can look at God. The fire comes from there. He does as He wishes. If He is pleased, then all things will go well. If He is angry, then we will suffer."

He went into the cave and brought forth the liver and heart of the deer he had killed the evening before. He laid these on a raised slab of stone. He brought a pine brand and made a fire underneath the entrails. Then he knelt, not as he had inside the cave, but prostrating himself, forehead to the earth in obeisance.

"Shall I kneel?" she asked him.

"Yes," he said. "But you are not to touch this stone and this fire and this meat. That is for me to do."

She obeyed. There was nothing else she could do. When he had gone to the lake to fish, she went to the corner of the cave where the cooking pots were piled. She had dug a niche into the rock, and here her secret possession lay. She took out the bundle of dried leaves, unfolded them carefully, and held the mirror in her hands. She looked into it for a long time. It calmed her, as though it were a focus for the scattered fragments of herself. Dream and daylight hovered in uncertain balance within her, always. Only when she looked in the mirror did she momentarily know she really existed.

"What is that?" The man's voice was harsh. She glanced up and quickly tried to conceal what she held in her hands. She had never allowed him to see her looking at herself. He had never seen a mirror. He had seen his own image in the quivering lakewater, but never the sharp, painful, and yet oddly reassuring picture she had of her own cruel and gentle eyes.

"It is nothing," she told him.

He took hold of her hand and forced it open. He looked at the shining object. His face was puzzled, but only for an instant. He glanced out the cave entrance to the sky and the mid-morning sun. Then he hurled the mirror from his hand, and it shattered against the rock of the cave walls. After that, he hit her, again and again and again.

"You are unclean!" he cried.

She knew then he was afraid of her, too. They were afraid of each other.

The seasons went by, and she kept no account of time. Generally she was content. She sat crosslegged now on the wide ledge ouside the cave entrance. She was scraping a deer hide with the bone blade Rex had made. He had discovered, on one of his longer trips, a place where the people used to live and where pieces of iron lay rusting, and he had brought some back and fashioned spearheads and knives and an axe. But these were kept for his use, for he needed them more in hunting than she did in scraping the hides and making them into clothes. It was slow work, this, but she did not mind. The sun of late spring warmed her, and the raw trilling of frogs from the lake made her feel glad, for this was a good time of year, with hunger gone. The fish and game were plentiful, and the roots and leaves of the dandelions were succulent and tender.

The pointed shadow of the altar stone on the rock ledge told her that he would soon be back from the forest. She must prepare food, for he would be hungry when he returned. He did not like to be kept waiting. That was as it should be. A man was hungry after hunting.

But still she sat in the sunshine, drowsing over her work. Then the insinuating voice began, humming its tune inside her, and she blinked and shook her head as though to shake the whispered song away, for when it came to her she felt threatened and unsafe and she did not want to listen. Rex said the voices came only to him. But she heard this voice occasionally, unknown to him, in the deep quietness of the morning, when the birds were suddenly still, or in the wind that brushed through the forest at night. She did not recall when the voice had begun. She did not have a name for herself, as Rex did, and although it was enough to be what she was, in some way the voice was connected with the name she had once held, the name which had been shattered somewhere, some time, like lake-water when a stone is thrown into it. She never understood what the voice was saying to her, with its jingling music, a monotonous chanting from a long way off and yet close as her blood. The words, familiar in form but totally unfamiliar in meaning, were like the dry and twisted shells she found on the shore of the lake, objects that had once contained live creatures, but very long ago, so that no trace of flesh remained. The voice echoed again now, hurting and frightening her.

Lavender's blue, dilly dilly, lavender's green,
When you are king, dilly dilly, I shall be queen.

She half shut her eyes, and listened intently, but still she could not

170

understand and could only feel troubled by something untouchable, some mystery that remained just beyond her grasp.

Then, inside the cave, one of the children began crying, and she went to give comfort.

Yves Thériault
AKUA NUTEN

"Thériault himself has claimed to be more of a storyteller than a novelist. He seems more at ease in exploring his own imaginary world, in creating characters and situations bordering on the epic, than in following the conventions of the novel." So wrote the critic L. W. Keffer in Supplement to The Oxford Companion to Canadian History and Literature *(1973), edited by William Toye. Whether storyteller or novelist, Yves Thériault, who was born in Quebec City, in 1915, of Montagnais Indian background, may well be Quebec's most prolific writer. He is best known in English Canada for such novels of native life as* Agaguk *(1967),* N'Tusk *(1968),* Ashini *(1972), and* Agoak *(1979), all available in English translation. Thériault's work is represented here with "Akua Nuten (The South Wind)," originally published in* Si la Bombe M'Etait Contée *(1962), translated by Howard Roiter in* Stories from Québec *(1974), edited by Philip Stratford.*

Kakatso, the Montagnais Indian, felt the gentle flow of the air and noticed that the wind came from the south. Then he touched the moving water in the stream to determine the temperature in the highlands. Since everything pointed to nice June weather, with mild sunshine and light winds, he decided to go to the highest peak of the reserve, as he had been planning to do for the past week. There the Montagnais lands bordered those of the Waswanipis.

There was no urgent reason for the trip. Nothing really pulled him there except the fact that he hadn't been for a long time; and he liked steep mountains and frothy, roaring streams.

171

Three days before he had explained his plan to his son, the thin Grand-Louis, who was well known to the white men of the North Shore. His son had guided many white in the regions surrounding the Manicouagan and Bersimis rivers.

He had told him: "I plan to go way out, near the limits of the reserve." This was clear enough, and Grand-Louis had simply nodded his head. Now he wouldn't worry, even if Kakatso disappeared for two months. He would know that his father was high in the hills, breathing the clean air and soaking up beautiful scenes to remember in future days.

Just past the main branch of the Manicouagan there is an enormous rock crowned by two pines and a fir tree which stand side by side like the fingers of a hand, the smallest on the left and the others reaching higher.

This point, which Kakatso could never forget, served as his sign-post for every trail in the area; and other points would guide him north, west, or in any other direction. Kakatso, until his final breath, would easily find his way about there, guided only by the memory of a certain tree, the silhouette of the mountain outlined against the clear skies, the twisting of a river bed, or the slope of a hill.

In strange territory Kakatso would spend entire days precisely organizing his memories so that if he ever returned no trail there would be unknown to him.

Thus, knowing every winding path and every animal's accustomed lair, he could set out on his journey carrying only some salt, tea, and shells for his rifle. He could live by finding his subsistence in the earth itself and in nature's plenty.

Kakatso knew well what a man needed for total independence: a fishhook wrapped in paper, a length of supple cord, a strong knife, waterproof boots, and a well-oiled rifle. With these things a man could know the great joy of not having to depend on anyone but himself, of wandering as he pleased one day after another, proud and superior, the owner of eternal lands that stretched beyond the horizon.

(To despise the reserve and those who belonged there. Not to have any allegiance except a respect for the water, the sky, and the winds. To be a man, but a man according to the Indian image and not that of the whites. The Indian image of a real man was ageless and changeless, a true image of man in the bosom of a wild and immense nature.)

Kakatso had a wife and a house and grown-up children whom he rarely saw. He really knew little about them. One daughter was a nurse in a white man's city, another had married a turncoat Montagnais who lived in Baie-Comeau and worked in the factories. A son studied far away, in Montreal, and Kakatso would probably never see him again. A son who would repudiate everything, would forget the proud Montagnais language and change his name to be accepted by the whites in spite of his dark skin and slitty eyes.

The other son, Grand-Louis . . . but this one was an exception. He had inherited Montagnais instincts. He often came down to the coast, at Godbout or Sept-Iles, or sometimes at Natashquan, because he was ambitious and wanted to earn money. But this did not cause him to scorn or detest the forest. He found a good life there. For Kakatso, it was enough that this child, unlike so many others, did not turn into a phony white man.

As for Kakatso's wife, she was still at home, receiving Kakatso on his many returns without emotion or gratitude. She had a roof over her head, warmth, and food. With skilled fingers she made caribou skin jackets for the white man avid for the exotic. The small sideline liberated Kakatso from other obligations towards her. Soon after returning home, Kakatso always wanted to get away again. He was uncomfortable in these white men's houses that were too high, too solid, and too neatly organized for his taste.

So Kakatso lived his life in direct contact with the forest, and he nurtured life itself from the forest's plenty. Ten months of the year he roamed the forest trails, ten months he earned his subsistence from hunting, trapping, fishing, and smoking the caribou meat that he placed in caches for later use. With the fur pelts he met his own needs and those of the house on the reserve near the forest, although these needs were minimal because his wife was a good earner.

He climbed, then, towards the northern limits of the Montagnais lands on this June day, which was to bring calamity of which he was completely unaware.

Kakatso had heard of the terrible bomb. For twenty years he had heard talk of it, and the very existence of these horrendous machines was not unknown to him. But how was he to know the complex fabric of events happening in the world just then? He never read the newspapers and never really listened to the radio when he happened to spend some hours in a warm house. How could be conceive of total annihilation threatening the whole world? How could he feel all the world's people trembling?

In the forest's vast peace, Kakatso, knowing nature's strength, could easily believe that nothing and nobody could prevail against the mountains, the rivers, and the forest itself stretching out all across the land. Nothing could prevail against the earth, the unchangeable soil that regenerated itself year after year.

He travelled for five days. On the fifth evening it took Kakatso longer to fall asleep. Something was wrong. A silent anguish he did not understand was disturbing him.

He had lit his evening fire on a bluff covered with soft moss, one hundred feet above the lake. He slept there, rolled in his blanket in a deeply dark country interrupted only by the rays of the new moon.

Sleep was slow and when it came it did not bring peace. A jumble of snarling creatures and swarming, roaring masses invaded Kakatso's sleep. He turned over time and again, groaning restlessly. Suddenly he awoke and was surprised to see that the moon had gone down and the night's blackness was lit only by stars. Here, on the bluff, there was a bleak reflection from the sky, but that long valley and the lake remained dark. Exhausted by his throbbing dreams, Kakatso got up, stretched his legs and lit his pipe. On those rare occasions when his sleep was bad he had always managed to recover his tranquillity by smoking a bit, motionless in the night, listening to the forest sounds.

Suddenly the light came. For a single moment the southern and western horizons were illuminated by this immense bluish gleam that loomed up, lingered a moment, and then went out. The dark became even blacker and Kakatso muttered to himself. He wasn't afraid because fear had always been totally foreign to him. But what did this strange event mean? Was it the anger of some old mountain spirit?

All at once the gleam reappeared, this time even more westerly. Weaker this time and less evident. Then the shadows again enveloped the land.

Kakatso no longer tried to sleep that night. He squatted, smoking his pipe and trying to find some explanation for these bluish gleams with his simple ideas, his straightforward logic and vivid memory.

When the dawn came the old Montagnais, the last of his people, the great Abenakis, carefully prepared his fire and boiled some water for his tea.

For some hours he didn't feel like moving. He no longer heard the inner voices calling him to the higher lands. He felt stuck there, incapable of going further until the tumult within him died down. What was there that he didn't know about his skies, he who had spent his whole life wandering in the woods and sleeping under the stars? The sky over his head was as familiar to him as the soil of the underbrush, the animal trails and the games of the trout in their streams. But never before had he seen such gleams and they disturbed him.

At eight o'clock the sun was slowly climbing into the sky, and Kakatso was still there.

At ten he moved to the shore to look at the water in the lake. He saw a minnow run and concluded that the lake had many fish. He then attached his fire cord to the hook tied with partridge feathers he had found in the branches of a wild hawthorn bush. He cast the fly with a deliberate, almost solemn movement and it jumped on the smooth water. After Kakatso cast three more times a fat trout swallowed the hook and he pulled him in gently, quite slowly, letting him fight as much as he wanted. The midday meal was in hand. The Montagnais, still in no great hurry to continue his trip, began to prepare his fish.

He was finishing when the far-away buzz of a plane shook him out of his reveries. Down there, over the mountains around the end of the lake, a plane was moving through the sky. This was a familiar sight to Kakatso because all this far country was visited only by planes that landed on the lakes. In this way the Indian had come to know the white man. This was the most frequent place of contact between the two: a large body of quiet water where a plane would land, where the whites would ask for help and finding nothing better than an Indian to help them.

Even from a distance Kakatso recognized the type of plane. It was a single-engine, deluxe Bonanza, a type often used by the Americans who came to fish for their salmon in our rivers.

The plane circled the lake and flew over the bluff where Kakatso's fire was still burning. Then it landed gently, almost tenderly. The still waters were only lightly ruffled and quickly returned to their mirror smoothness. The plan slowed down, the motor coughed once or twice, then the craft made a complete turn and headed for the beach.

Kakatso, with one hand shading his eyes, watched the landing, motionless.

When the plane was finally still and the tips of its pontoons were pulled up on the sandy beach, two men, a young woman, and a twelve-year-old boy got out.

One of the men was massive. He towered a head over Kakatso although the Montagnais himself was rather tall.

"Are you an Indian?" the man asked suddenly.

Kakatso nodded slowly and blinked his eyes once.

"Good, I'm glad, you can save us," said the man.

"Save you?" said Kakatso. "Save you from what?"

"Never mind," said the woman, "that's our business."

Standing some distance away, she gestured to the big man who had first spoken to Kakatso.

"If you're trying to escape the police," said Kakatso, "I can't do anything for you."

"It has nothing to do with the police," said the other man who had not spoken previously.

He moved towards Kakatso and proffered a handshake. Now that he was close the Montagnais recognized a veteran bush pilot. His experience could be seen in his eyes, in the squint of his eyelids, and in the way he treated an Indian as an equal.

"I am Bob Ledoux," the man said. "I am a pilot. Do you know what nuclear war is?"

"Yes," answered Kakatso, "I know."

"All the cities in the south have been destroyed," said Ledoux. "We were able to escape."

"Is that a real one?" asked the boy, who had been closely scrutinizing Kakatso. "Eh, Mom, is it really one of those savages?"

"Yes," answered the woman, "certainly." And to Kakatso she said, "Please excuse him. He has never been on the North Shore."

Naturally Kakatso did not like to be considered a savage. But he didn't show anything and he swallowed his bitterness.

"So," said the pilot, "here we are without resources."

"I have money," said the man.

"This is Mr. Perron," said the pilot, "Mrs. Perron, and their son. . . ."

"My name is Roger," said the boy. "I know how to swim."

The Montagnais was still undecided. He did not trust intruders. He preferred, in his simple soul, to choose his own objectives and decide his day's activities. And here were outsiders who had fallen from the sky, almost demanding his help . . . but what help?

"I can't do much for you," he said after a while.

"I have money," the man repeated.

Kakatso shrugged. Money? Why money? What would it buy up here?

Without flinching he had heard how all the southern cities had been destroyed. Now he understood the meaning of those sudden gleams that lit the horizon during the night. And because this event had been the work of whites, Kakatso completely lost interest in it.

So his problem remained these four people he considered spoilers.

"Without you," said the woman, "we are going to perish."

And because Kakatso looked at her in surprise, she added, in a somewhat different tone: "We have no supplies at all and we are almost out of fuel."

"That's true," said the pilot.

"So," continued the woman, "if you don't help us find food, we will die."

Kakatso, with a sweeping gesture, indicated the forests and the lake: "There is wild game there and fish in the waters. . . ."

"I don't have a gun or fishhooks," said the pilot. "And it's been a very long time since I came so far north."

He said this with a slightly abashed air and Kakatso saw clearly that the man's hands were too white; the skin had become too soft and smooth.

"I'll pay you whatever is necessary," said Mr. Perron.

"Can't you see," said his wife, "that money doesn't interest him?"

Kakatso stood there, looking at them with his shining impassive eyes, his face unsmiling and his arms dangling at his sides.

"Say something," cried the woman. "Will you agree to help us?"

"We got away as best we could," said the pilot. "We gathered the attack on Montreal was coming and we were already at the airport when the warning sirens went off. But I couldn't take on enough fuel. There were other planes leaving too. I can't even take off again from this lake. Do you know if there is a supply cache near here?"

Throughout the northern forests pilots left emergency fuel caches for use when necessary. But if Kakatso knew of several such places he wasn't letting on in front of the intruders.

"I don't know," he said.

There was silence.

The whites looked at the Indian and desperately sought words to persuade him. But Kakatso did not move and said nothing. He had always fled the society of whites and dealt with them only when it was unavoidable. Why should he treat those who surfaced here now any differently? They were without food; the forest nourishes those who know how to take their share. This knowledge was such an instinctive part of an Indian's being that he couldn't realize how some people could lack it. He was sure that these people wanted to impose their needs on him and enslave him. All his Montagnais pride revolted against this thought. And yet, he could help them. Less than one hour away there was one of those meat caches of a thousand pounds of smoked moose, enough to see them through a winter. And the fish in the lake could be caught without much effort. Weaving a simple net of fine branches would do it, or a trap of bulrushes.

But he didn't move a muscle.

Only a single fixed thought possessed Kakatso, and it fascinated him. Down there, in the south, the white had been destroyed. Never again would they reign over these forests. In killing each other, they had rid the land of their kind. Would the Indians be free again? All the Indians, even those on the reserves? Free to retake the forests?

And these four whites: could they be the last survivors?

Brothers, thought Kakatso, all my brothers: it is up to me to protect your new freedom.

"The cities," he finally said, "they have really been destroyed?"

"Yes," said the pilot.

"Nothing is left any more," said the woman. "Nothing at all. We saw the explosion from the plane. It was terrible. And the wind pushed up for a quarter of an hour. I thought we were going to crash."

"Nothing left," said the boy, "nobody left. Boom! One bomb did it."

He was delighted to feel himself the hero—a safe and sound hero—of such an adventure. He didn't seem able to imagine the destruction and death, only the spectacular explosion.

But the man called Perron had understood it well. He had been able to estimate the real power of the bomb.

"The whole city is destroyed," he said. "A little earlier, on the radio, we heard of the destruction of New York, then Toronto and Ottawa. . . ."

"Many other cities too," added the pilot. "As far as I'm concerned, nothing is left of Canada, except perhaps the North Shore. . . ."

"And it won't be for long," said Perron. "If we could get further up, further north. If we only had food and gasoline."

This time he took a roll of money out of his pocket and unfolded five bills, a sum Kakatso had never handled at one time. Perron offered them to the Indian.

"Here. The only thing we ask you for is a little food and gas if you can get some. Then we could leave."

"When such a bomb explodes," said Kakatso without taking the bills, "does it kill all the whites?"

"Yes," said the pilot. "In any case, nearly all."

"One fell on Ottawa?"

"Yes."

"Everybody is dead there?"

"Yes. The city is small and the bomb was a big one. The reports indicate there were no survivors."

Kakatso nodded his head two or three times approvingly. Then he turned away and took his rifle which had been leaning on a rock. Slowly, aiming at the whites, he began to retreat into the forest.

"Where are you going?" cried the woman.

"Here," said the man. "Here's all my money. Come back!"

Only the pilot remained silent. With his sharp eyes he watched Kakatso.

When the Indian reached the edge of the forest it was the boy's turn. He began to sob pitifully, and the woman also began to cry.

"Don't leave," she cried. "Please, help us. . . ."

For all of my people who cried, thought Kakatso, all who begged, who wanted to defend their rights for the past two hundred years: I take revenge for them all.

But he didn't utter another word.

And when the two men wanted to run after him to stop him, he put his rifle to his shoulder. The bullet nicked the pilot's ear. Then the men understood that it would be futile to insist, and Kakatso disappeared into the forest which enclosed him. Bent low, he skimmed the ground, using every bush for cover, losing himself in the undergrowth, melting into the forest where he belonged.

Later, having circled the lake, he rested on a promontory hidden behind many spreading cedars. He saw that the pilot was trying to take off to find food elsewhere.

But the tanks were nearly empty and when the plane reached an altitude of a thousand feet the motor sputtered a bit, backfired and stopped.

The plane went into a nosedive.

When it hit the trees it caught fire.

In the morning Kakatso continued his trip towards the highlands.

He felt his first nausea the next day and vomited blood two days later. He vomited once at first, then twice, then a third time, and finally one last time.

The wind kept on blowing from the south, warm and mild.

Michel Tremblay
MR. BLINK

Michel Tremblay, who was born in Montreal in 1942, is a talented and productive playwright whose plays, like Les Belles-Soeurs *(1968), and* Hosanna *(1974), present a serio-comic satire on contemporary Quebec life. They have been successfully staged in French and English Canada. But Tremblay is also an accomplished fantasist. Twenty-five of his weird tales appear in* Contes pour Buveurs Attardés *(1966), translated by Michael Bullock as* Stories for Late Night Drinkers *(1977). "Mr. Blink" comes from that collection, and it catches the verve and vigour of Trem-*

blay's style and vision of a contemporary Everyman caught in social movements he could not contain even if he wished to. Tremblay is also the author of La Cité dans l'Oeuf *(1969), which tells of the discovery and the destruction of a fantasy world enclosed in a glass egg.*

Mr. Blink was dumbfounded. What kind of a joke was this? Who had dared. . . . In front of him, on the wooden wall flanking Cedar Street, someone had pasted a huge poster and from the centre of this poster Mr. Blink himself was smiling at him. Above his photograph, in huge, bright red capital letters, was printed a staggering sentence, a sentence that made Mr. Blink's heart stand still: "Vote for Mr. Blink, the candidate of the future."

Mr. Blink took off his glasses, wiped them nervously, put them back on his nose and looked at the poster again.

He was seized with fear. He began to run and plunged into the first bus that came along. "No, it's impossible," Mr. Blink said to himself. "I was dreaming. I must have been dreaming. Me, a candidate?"

For weeks people had been talking about these famous elections. They said these elections would surely be the most important elections of the century. The country's two major parties were about to engage in a fight to the death, that was certain.

Mr. Blink trembled. He tried to read his paper, but he couldn't concentrate on the little black characters, which seemed to be delirious flies rather than letters.

For weeks people had been talking about these famous elections. "Oh, I must have misread it." The most important elections of the century. Surely the most important elections of the century. "It was a joke."

The most important elections. . . . He cried out. On the centre page the largest advertisement he had ever seen in a newspaper, on the centre page, occupying the whole page, there he was. There was Mr. Blink smiling at him. "Vote for Mr. Blink, the candidate of the future." He closed his paper and threw it out of the window.

Just in front of him, a small boy leaned over to his mother and said: "Look Mummy, that's the man on the poster." When she recognized Mr. Blink the little boy's mother rose and threw herself on the poor man, who thought he would die of fear. "Mr. Blink," cried the lady, seizing his hands, "Mr. Blink, our saviour!" She kissed the hands of Mr. Blink, who seemed on the verge of a nervous breakdown. "Come, come, madam," he finally murmured, "I'm not your saviour." But the woman cried out, as though she were insane: "Long live Mr. Blink, our saviour! Long live Mr. Blink, the candidate of the future." Everyone in the bus repeated in chorus: "Long live Mr. Blink."

At a drugstore near his home, Mr. Blink bought a bottle of aspirin tablets. "Well, well," said the druggist, "so you're going in for politics now?" In his buttonhole he wore a blue ribbon bearing in red the words . . . .

His caretaker stopped him. "Mr. Blink," she said, "could you by any chance give me a ticket for your big meeting this evening?" Mr. Blink nearly tumbled down the few steps he had just come up. A meeting? What meeting? No one had ever said anything to him about a meeting! "What a secretive fellow you are. Still waters run deep. I should have guessed that important things were going on inside that head of yours. You've certainly given my husband and me a big surprise."

That evening Mr. Blink did not dine. Even if he had wanted to, he wouldn't have had a chance. The telephone rang incessantly. Admirers wanting to know at what time he would be arriving at the big meeting. Mr. Blink thought he was going mad. He took off the receiver, put out all the lights in his apartment, put on his pyjamas and went to bed.

The crowd was shouting for its saviour. They even threatened to break down the door if he didn't answer in ten minutes. Then the caretaker said something terrible, something that almost produced a riot. "Perhaps Mr. Blink is ill," she said to a journalist. Ten second later Mr. Blink's door was forced and the crowd carried off its saviour in his pyjamas. People thought his costume very original. How good his publicity was! Some men even went home and put on pyjamas. Women in nightdresses came out into the street and followed the procession singing hymns. Flabbergasted, Mr. Blink dared not move, seated as he was on the shoulders of two of the country's leading journalists.

The meeting was a triumph. Mr. Blink did not speak.

The new party, the people's party, Mr. Blink's party, burst into the country's political life like a bomb. People booed the old parties and cried that slavery was at an end, thanks to Mr. Blink. B-L-I-N-K. Blink! Blink! Blink! Hurray! No more income tax increases, Mr. Blink would fix everything. No more political squabbling, Mr. Blink would fix everything. No further rise in the cost of living. . . . Blink! Blink! Blink!

Once only did Mr. Blink try to rise to his feet and speak. But the crowd cheered him so loudly and so long that he was afraid of upsetting them and sat down again.

His followers poured champagne into him and in the end Mr. Blink himself thought he was a great hero. As a souvenir of that memorable evening, Mr. Blink took home with him an enormous streamer bearing in letters two feet high. . . .

Next day, Mr. Blink was elected Prime Minister of his country.

Jacques Ferron
THE ARCHANGEL
OF THE SUBURB

"He is a conteur *in his own right—the last, as he says, of an oral tradition, the first of the written one." So wrote Betty Bednarski of Jacques Ferron, who was born in 1921, in Louisville, Quebec. As well as being a prolific writer, Ferron practises medicine in Ville Jacques-Cartier, a working-class suburb of Montreal. Fantasy enlightens all his writings—stories, tales, novels, plays. The tales found in* Contes du Pays Incertain *(1962), and* Contes Anglais et Autres *(1964), mix fantasy with humour and folklore. Betty Bednarski translated eighteen of these as* Tales from the Uncertain Country *(1972). "The Archangel of the Suburb," in which an archangel finds himself stranded on earth in rural Quebec, is from that book. As the translator explains: "Ferron in a sense picks up where the folktale left off. He transforms it from a spoken into a written art and broadens its relevance and its appeal. His are tales for the present, providing at the same time continuity with the past. Fantasy spreads from the country into the urban environment."*

The archangel Zag was not in Heaven at the time of the famous battle between Lucifer and Saint Michael; he was on Earth. When word of it reached him, he concluded that he had been most inspired to make this trip and decided to extend his stay. So it was that until quite recently he still dwelt among us, in a shack along Chambly Road, near the marsh which then served as boundary and garbage dump for the parishes of Saint-Hubert and Saint-Antoine-de-Longueuil. To the profane he was an old anarchist, a retired vagabond, one of those likeable outlaws who are the very charm of the suburbs. As for the clerics, they did not even suspect he was there. Zag avoided them, was distrustful of them as of the devil. With the exception of one, Brother Benoit of the Coteau-Rouge Franciscans, who often came to see him and whom he received with pleasure. Brother Benoit would bring holy pictures and religious trinkets, which Zag, out of regard for him and also as a precaution against the police, who can always make things difficult for a tramp, used to decorate his hut. But that was as far as he would go. He had said to Brother Benoit: "Why do you try to convert me? I don't try to make an angel out of you." He would not tolerate the mention of good or evil, of Heaven or Hell; to him these distinctions were distasteful. So Brother Benoit had ceased to preach at him, continuing nevertheless to visit him, out of pure loving-kindness, good Franciscan that he was.

Now Zag, who in spite of everything was no earthling, set out one morning bright and early along Chambly Road in the direction of Longueuil. At the first crossroads he turned left and found himself on the Coteau-Rouge road, heading for Saint-Josaphat. In actual fact he was not too sure where he was going. He zigzagged along as if drunk; at times his feet would leave the ground; he continued in this fashion for quite some distance. Apart from his flying, he looked for all the world like a wino. Meanwhile it was getting later, the suburb was waking up, three or four clandestine cocks crowed in defiance of the municipal regulations, and people began to gather at the street corners to wait for the yellow bus of their misfortune, people still exhausted from the previous day's work. And that same rattle-trap bus was now heading straight for Zag, who leapt up into the air and clear over it. The driver, flabbergasted, drove right past the next stop, cursed by those he had forgotten and whose protests brought the archangel back to his senses. He felt ashamed of himself, and returned to his shack in low spirits. But the next morning he was again excited, light-headed as a bird on the eve of migration. This time he went off across the fields, and following the marsh, soon found himself near the Franciscan monastery. It was warm and pleasant. He stretched out on the grass. In the distance he could see the pink and grey haze of the city, the arches of the bridge and the summit of Mount Royal. However, a bush was blocking his view. Zag said to it: "Cast off thy leaves." The bush obeyed so promptly that a hen, perched among the foliage, was stripped of her feathers at the same time. This hen stared at Zag in dumb amazement, and he, equally surprised, stared back at the naked fowl. They finally came to their senses, the hen protesting, the archangel laughing; and the louder the one laughed the angrier the other became. When Zag had laughed his fill, he said: "Don't fret, old dear, I'll soon fix that. Only I can't promise to put your feathers back exactly where you had them; I might make a mistake and put one of the tail-feathers on the wing or one from the neck on the tail." But the hen demanded to be feathered as before.

"In that case," said Zag, "go fetch me some dry chips of wood." The hen brought them to him.

"Now an iron rod." She brought that too.

"And last of all," said Zag, "go into the monastery kitchen; there you'll find some matches."

The hen went into the monastery kitchen, found the matches and brought them. Then Zag grabbed hold of her, skewered her, lit a fire and roasted her. Brother Benoit, who happened to be in the monastery kitchen, meditating on a pot of chick-peas and herring, for it was a Friday, had had his appetite whetted and had followed the naked fowl.

"Ah! Brother Benoit," cried Zag, "You couldn't have come at a better moment! I have a theological problem to put to you."

Brother Benoit stretched out on the grass.

"What advice would you give to an archangel in exile on Earth, who was beginning to lose his sense of gravity and jump in the air like a harum scarum?" asked Zag.

Brother Benoit answered, "There is only one thing for him to do: go back to Heaven."

"That's all very well," said Zag, "but it so happens that this archangel was absent at the time of the Lucifer-Saint Michael match; how can he be sure he would have been on the latter's side?"

Brother Benoit asked, "While this archangel was on Earth, did he seek out the company of the proud and the mighty, of aldermen and other potentates?"

"No," replied Zag. And as he spoke he handed Brother Benoit a chicken leg. The fasting Franciscan took a bite and found it to his liking. In his satisfaction he declared: "Let him go to Heaven!"

"Then farewell, my friend," said the archangel Zag. And the beggar's garment, the wino's rags fell among the leaves of the bush and the feathers of the late hen. Brother Benoit ran to the monastery and to his Father Superior he related the wondrous story.

"What is that?" asked the Father Superior.

"A chicken bone."

"And what day of the week is it, Brother?"

"Friday," poor Benoit had to admit.

And thus it was that a great miracle ended in a confession. An angel, even an archangel, cannot spend time on Earth without falling into some mischief.

Phyllis Gotlieb
THE MILITARY HOSPITAL

"Phyllis Gotlieb, on the basis of the quality and quantity of her output and as a native-born Canadian actually living in Canada, must be considered the central figure in Canadian science fiction. Indeed, it might be argued that Ms. Gotlieb is Canadian science fiction." Such is the opinion of the SF critic, David Ketterer. The author was born in Toronto in 1926, and was influenced quite early by the pulp magazines of the Thirties. More than a dozen of her stories have appeared in such magazines as Galaxy, If, *and* Fantasy and Science Fiction; *she has also published two novels,* Sunburst *(1964), and* O Master Caliban! *(1975). She is a fine poet as well, and three of her highly imaginative poems appear elsewhere in this anthology. I have represented her fiction with "The Military Hospital" which originally appeared in* Fourteen Stories High *(1971), edited by David Helwig and Tom Marshall. The story, told with deft precision, presents an unusual view of the future from the vantagepoint of the wards of a hospital, and questions the nature of human beings and of human experience.*

The helicopter moved through the city in the airlane between sky scrapers. It was on autopilot, preset course, and there was no-one to squint down the canyons of the streets where the life-mass seethed. Children looked up at it with dull eyes; if it had come lower they would have stoned or shot at it. The armoured cars that burrowed among them were scratched and pocked from their attacks.

Fresh and smooth, dressed in crisp white, DeLazzari came into the Control Room at the top of the Hospital. He had had a week off, he was on for three; he ran the Hospital, supervised nurse-patient relationships, directed the sweepers in the maintenance of sterility, and monitored the pile. He took over this function wherever he was told to go, but he particularly liked the Military Hospital because it was clean, roomy, and had very few patients. He was a stocky man with thick black hair, broad wings of moustache, and skin the colour of baked earth; he had the blood of all nations in him. "The bad blood of all nations," he would add with a laugh if he felt like impressing one of the trots Mama Rakosy sent up to the apartment, though it was rare he felt like impressing anyone. He was sworn to forego women, drugs and liquor for three weeks, so he switched on the big external screen and dumped out of his bag the cigars, candy and gum that would sustain him, while he watched the course of the helicopter over the city.

A trasher's bomb went off in one of the buildings; daggers of glass blew out singing, and sliced at the scalps and shoulders of a knot of demonstrators clumped at its base; a fragment of concrete hurled outward and grazed the helicoper, then fell to dent a fibreglass helmet and concuss the bike-rider who fell from his machine and lay unconscious under the bruising feet; the wounded demonstrators scattered or crawled, leaving their placards, and others took their places, raising neon-coloured cold-light standards of complicated symbols; they camped in the table-sized space, oblivious to bloody glass, hardhats with crossbows, skinheads with slingshots, longhairs, freaks, mohicans, children, and above all the whoop and howl of police sirens coming up.

The helicopter moved north and away; the armoured cars butted their way through, into less crowded streets where merchants did business across wickets in iron cages in which one touch of a floor button dropped steel shutters and made a place impregnable fast enough to cut a slice off anyone who got in the way. Farther north the City Hospital and the Central Police Depot formed two wings of a great moth-shaped complex webbed about by stalled paddy-wagons and ambulances.

DeLazzari grinned. In City Hospital twelve Directors manned the Control Room, endlessly profane and harried. Shop was always depleted: the sweepers rusted and ground down from lack of parts and the nurses were obsolete and inefficient. Only the Doctors moved at great speed and in Olympian calm.

He switched on his own O.R. screen. Doctors were already closing round the operating table, waiting. They were silver, slab-shaped, feature-less. They drew power from a remote source, and nobody he knew had any idea where it was. They had orders and carried them out—or perhaps they simply did what they chose. He had never been in their physical presence, nor wanted to be.

The helicopter was passing between blank-walled buildings where the dead were stored in very small vaults, tier upon tier upon tier; at street level the niches reserved for floral tributes were empty except for wire frames to which a few dried leaves and petals clung trembling in the down draft from the rotors. North beyond that in the concrete plaza the racers were heating up for the evening, a horde endlessly circling.

But the city had to end in the north at the great circle enclosing the Military Hospital. It had no wall, no road, no entrance at ground level.

What it had was a force-field the helicopter had to rise steeply to sur-
mount. Within, for a wall it had a thicket of greenery half a mile deep
going all the way round; outside the field there was a circuit of tumbled
masonry pieces, stones, burnt sticks, as if many ragged armies had tried
to storm it and retreated, disgusted and weary.

Inside there was no great mystery. The Military Hospital healed broken
soldiers from distant and ancient wars; the big circular building had
taken no architectural prizes, and on its rolling greens two or three
stumbling patients were being supported on their rounds by nurses. Like
all Directors DeLazzari tended to make himself out a minor Dracula;
like all the rest his power lay in the modicum of choice he had among the
buttons he pushed.

The helicopter landed on its field and discharged its cell, a Life Unit
in which a dying soldier lay enmeshed; it took on another cell, containing
another soldier who had been pronounced cured and would be discharged
germ-free into his theatre of war; it was also boarded by the previous
Director, pocket full of credits and head full of plans for a good week.

The Hospital doors opened, the cell rolled through them down a hall
into an ante-room where it split, a wagon emerged from it carrying the
patient and his humming, flickering life-system, the ante-room sealed
itself, flooded with aseptic sprays and drained, washing away blood-traces;
the O.R. sweeper removed the wet packs from the ruined flesh and
dropped them on the floor, which dissolved them. In the operating room
the TV system was pumping, the monitors pulsed, the Doctors activated
their autoclaves in one incandescent flash and then extruded a hundred
tentacles, probes, knives, sensors, and flexed them; their glitter and flash
was almost blinding in the harsh light. DeLazzari was obliged to watch
them; he hated it, and they needed no light. It was provided on demand
of the Supervisors' and Directors' Union, though if machines chose to go
renegade there was very little the Supervisors and Directors could say
or do.

Doctors had never gone renegade. Neither had sweepers or nurses; it
was a delicious myth citizens loved to terrify themselves with, perhaps
because they resented the fact that madness should be reserved for people.
DeLazzari thought that was pretty funny and he was scared too.

The O.R. sweeper sprayed himself (De Lazzari thought of it as delous-
ing), the doors opened, the sweeper pushed in the body, still housing its
low flicker of life, removed the attachments and set it on the table. The
Doctors reattached what was needed; the sweeper backed into a corner
and turned his own power down. DeLazzari flicked a glance at the
indicator and found it correct.

One Doctor swabbed the body with a personal nozzle and began to remove steel fragments from belly and groin, another slit the chest and reached in to remove bone slivers from the left lung, a third trimmed the stump of the right forefinger and fitted a new one from the Parts Bank, a fourth tied off and removed torn veins from the thighs, all without bumping head shoulders or elbows because they had none, a fifth kept the throat clear, a sixth gave heart massage, the first opened the belly and cut out a gangrened bowel section, the third sewed and sealed the new right forefinger and as an afterthought trimmed the nail, the fifth, still watching every breath, peeled back sections of the scalp and drilled holes in the skull. All in silence except for the soft clash and ringing of sensors, knives and probes. Blood splashed; their body surfaces repelled it in a mist of droplets and the floor washed it away.

The sweeper turned his power up on some silent order and fetched a strange small cage of silver wires. The fifth Doctor took it, placed it over the soldier's head, and studied its nodes as co-ordinates in relation to the skull. Then he spoke at last. "Awaken," he said.

DeLazzari gave a hoarse nervous laugh and whispered, *Let there be light*. The boy's eyelids flickered and opened. The eyes were deep blue; the enlarged pupils contracted promptly and at an equal rate. DeLazzari wondered, as always, if he were conscious enough to be afraid he was lying in an old cemetery among the gravestones. Silver graves.

"Are you awake?" The voice was deep, God-the-Father-All-Powerful. The Doctor checked the nose tube and cleared the throat. "Max, are you awake?"

"Yes . . . yes . . . yes. . . ."

"Can you answer questions?"

"Yes."

"Recording for psychiatric report." He extruded a fine probe and inserted it into the brain. "What do you see? Tell me what you see."

"I see . . . from the top of the ferris wheel I can see all the boats in the harbour, and when I come down in a swoop all the people looking up . . . ."

The probe withdrew and re-entered. "What do you see now, Max?"

"My father says they're not sweet peas but a wildflower, like a wild cousin of the sweet pea, toadflax, some people call them butter-and-eggs . . . . 'Scrophulariaceae Linaria vulgaris is the big name for them, Max, and that *vulgaris* means common, but they're not so common any more . . . .' "

Probe.

". . . something like the fireworks I used to watch when I was a kid,

188

but they're not fireworks, they're the real thing, and they turn the sky on fire . . . ."

"Area established."

Probe.

"One eye a black hole and the kid lying across her with its skull, with its skull, with its skull, I said Chrissake, Yvon, why'd you have to? Yvon? why'd you have to? why? he said ohmigod Max how was I to know whether they were? Max? how was I to know whether?"

The probe tip burned, briefly.

"Yes, Max? He said: how was I to know whether what?"

"Know what? Who's he? I don't know what you're talking about."

DeLazzari watched the probes insinuate the cortex and withdraw. The Doctors pulled at the associations, unravelling a tangled skein; they didn't try to undo all the knots, only the most complicated and disturbing. Was the act, he wondered, a healing beneficence or a removal of guilt associated with killing?

After four or five burns the cage was removed and the scalp repaired. Surprised, DeLazzari punched O.R. Procedures, Psych Division, and typed:

WHY SURGEONS OMIT DEEP MIL. INDOCTRINATION?

NEW RULING ONE WEEK PREVIOUS, the computer said.

WHOSE AUTHORITY?

BOARD OF SUPERVISORS.

And who ordered them around? He switched off and turned back to the Doctors.

After their duties had been completed they followed some mysteriously-developed ritual that looked like a laying on of hands. All probes and sensors extended, they would go over a body like a fine-tooth comb, slicing off a wart, excising a precancerous mole, straightening a twisted septum. DeLazzari switched off and lit a cigar. There were no emergencies to be expected in the next ten minutes. He blinked idly at a small screen recording the flat encephalogram of a dead brain whose body was being maintained for Parts.

The Doctors had other customs that both annoyed and amused him by their irrationality. Tonight they had been quiet, but sometimes one of them, sectioning a bowel, might start a running blue streak of chatter like a Las Vegas comic while another, probing the forebrain, would burst out in a mighty organ baritone, "Nearer My God To Thee." On the rare but inevitable occasions when an irreparable patient died with finality they acted as one to shut down the life system and retract their instruments; then stood for five minutes in a guardian circle of quietness, like the great

189

slabs of Stonehenge, around the body before they would allow the sweeper to take it away.

The big external screen was still on and DeLazzari looked down into the city, where a torchlight procession was pushing its flaming way up the avenue and the walls to either side wavered with unearthly shadows. He shut off and called Shop. He peered at the fax sheet on Max Vingo clipped to his notice-board and typed:

YOU GOT A CAUCASIAN TYPE NURSE APPROX FIVE-SEVEN FAIR HAIR QUIET VOICE NOT PUSHY MILD-TO-WARM AND FIRST RATE?

2482 BEST QUALITY CHECKED OUT LIGHT BROWN WE CAN MAKE IT FAIR HAIR. LIGHT BROWN OK HEALING UNIT 35.

He yawned. Nothing more for the moment. He dialled supper, surveyed the sleeping-alcove and bathroom, all his own, with satisfaction, checked the pill dispenser which allowed him two headache tablets on request, one sleeping pill at 11 p.m. and one laxative at 7.30 a.m. if required. He was perfectly content.

All nurses looked about twenty-five years old, unutterably competent but not intimidating unless some little-boy type needed a mother. 2482 was there when Max Vingo first opened his eyes and stirred weakly in his mummy-wrappings.

"Hello," she said quietly.

He swallowed; his throat was still sore from the respirator. "I'm alive."

"Yes, you are, and we're glad we have you."

"This is a hospital."

"It is, and I'm your nurse, 2482."

He stared at her. "You're a—a mechanical—I've heard about you—you're a mechanical—"

"I'm a Robonurse," she said.

"Huh . . . it sounds like some kind of a tank."

"That's a joke, baby—God help us," said DeLazzari, and turned her dial up half a point.

She smiled. "I'm not at all like a tank."

"No." He gave it a small interval of thought. "No, not at all."

It was the third day. DeLazzari never bothered to shave or wash on duty where he didn't see another human being; his face was covered with grey-flecked stubble. Outside he was vain, but here he never glanced into a mirror. The place was quiet; no new patients had come in, no alarms had sounded, the walking wounded were walking by themselves. Besides 2482 there were only two other nurses on duty, one with a nephritis and another tending the body soon to be frozen for Parts. Still, he did have 2482 to control and he watched with weary amusement as she warmed up under the turn of his dial.

"You're getting better already." She touched Max Vingo's forehead, a non-medical gesture since the thermocouple already registered his temperature. Her fingers were as warm as his skin. "You need more rest. Sleep now." Narcotic opened into his bloodstream from an embedded tube, and he slept.

On the fifth day the people of the city rose up against their government and it fell before them. Officers elected themselves, curfews were established, the torchlight parades and demonstrations stopped; occasionally a stray bomb exploded in a callbox. Packs of dogs swarmed up the avenue, pausing to sniff at places where the blood had lain in puddles; sometimes they met a congregation of cats and there were snarling yelping skirmishes. DeLazzari eyed them on his screen, devoutly thankful that he was not stationed in City Hospital. He filled City's requests for blood, plasma and parts as far as regulations required and didn't try to contact their Control Room.

At the Military Hospital the nephritis got up and walked out whole, the deadhead was cut up and frozen in Parts, an interesting new malaria mutation came in and was assigned a doctor to himself in Isolation. 2482 peeled away the bandages from Max Vingo's head and hand.

He asked for a mirror and when she held it before him he examined the scars visible on his forehead and scalp and said, "I feel like I'm made up of spare parts." He lifted his hand and flexed it. "That's not so funny." The forefinger was his own now, but it had once belonged to a black man and though most of the pigment had been chemically removed it still had an odd bluish tinge. "I guess it's better than being without one."

"You'll soon be your old handsome self."

"I bet you say that to all the formerly handsome guys."

"Of course. How would you get well otherwise?"

He laughed, and while she was wiping his face with a soft cloth he said, "2482, haven't you ever had a name?"

"I've never needed one."

"I guess if I get really familiar I can call you 2 for short."

"Hoo boy, this is a humourist." DeLazzari checked the dial and indicator and left them steady on for the while. The malaria case went into convulsions without notice and he turned his attention elsewhere.

191

She rubbed his scalp with a cream to quicken regrowth of hair.

"What does that do for a bald guy?"

"Nothing. His follicles no longer function."

He flexed his new finger again and rubbed the strange skin with the fingertips of his other hand. "I hope mine haven't died on me."

By day 7 DeLazzari was beginning to look like a debauched beachcomber. His hospital whites were grimy and his moustache ragged. However, he kept a clean desk, his sweeper cleared away the cigar stubs and the ventilators cleaned the air. Two badly-scarred cases of yaws came in from a tropical battleground and two Doctors called for skin grafts and whetted their knives. In the city a curfew violator was shot and killed, and next morning the first of the new demonstrators appeared. One of the Doctors took the chance of visiting Max for the first time when he was awake.

The soldier wasn't dismayed; he answered questions readily enough, showed off his growing hair, and demonstrated his attempts to use the grafted finger, but he kept looking from the Doctor to 2482 and back in an unsettling way, and DeLazzari turned up the nurse's dial a point.

When the Doctor was gone she said, "Did he disturb you?"

"No." But his eyes were fixed on her.

She took his hand. "Does that feel good?"

"Yes," he said. "That feels good." And he put his other hand on top of hers.

DeLazzari ate and slept and monitored the screens and supervised the duties of nurses and sweepers. Sometimes he wiped his oily face with a tissue and briefly considered rationing his cigars, which he had been smoking excessively because of boredom. Then three cases of cholera came in from the east; one was dead on arrival and immediately incinerated, the other two occupied him. But he still had time to watch the cure of Max Vingo and by turns of the dial nourish his relationship with 2482. He thought they were a pretty couple.

Max got unhooked from his TV, ate solid food with a good appetite and got up and walked stiffly on his scarred legs, now freed of their bandages. His hair grew in, black as DeLazzari's but finer, and the marks on his skin were almost invisible. He played chess sometimes with 2482 and didn't make any comments when she let him win. But there was an odd sadness about him, more than DeLazzari might have guessed from his Psych report. Although the ugliest of his memories had been burned away the constellations of emotion attached to them had remained and the Doctors would never be able to do anything about those during the short time he stayed in the Hospital.

192

So that often at night, even sometimes when he fell into a light doze, he had sourceless nightmares he couldn't describe, and when he flailed his arms in terrified frustration 2482 took his hands and held them in her own until he slept at peace.

DeLazzari watched the TV news, followed the courses of battles over the world and on Moonbase and Marsport, and made book with himself on where his next casualties would be coming from. Not from the planets, which had their own Hospitals, or from the usual Military Base establishments. His own Hospital (he liked to think of it as his own because he was so fond of its conveniences and so full of respect for its equipment) was one of the rare few that dealt with the unusual, the interesting and the hopeless. Down in the city the fire marchers were out and the bombs were exploding again. He knew that soon once more the people of the city would rise against their government and it would fall before them, and he kept check of blood and parts and ordered repairs on old scuppered nurses.

Max Vingo dressed himself now and saw the scars fade on his newly-exposed torso. Because he was so far away from it he didn't think of the battle he might be going into. It was when he had stood for a long time at the window looking out at the rain, at how much greener it made the grass, that 2482 said to him, "Max, is there something you're afraid of?"

"I don't know."

"Is it the fighting?"

"I don't even remember much of that."

"The Doctors took those memories away from you."

"Hey!" DeLazzari growled, hand poised over the control. "Who said you could say a thing like that?"

"I don't mind that," Max said.

DeLazzari relaxed.

"Don't you want to know why?"

"If you want to tell me."

"I'm not sure . . . but I think it was because the Doctors knew you were a gentle and loving man, and they didn't want for you to be changed."

He turned and faced her. "I'm the same. But I'm still a man who has to dress up like a soldier—and I don't know when that will ever change. Maybe that's why I'm frightened."

DeLazzari wondered for a moment what it would be like to be sick and helpless and taken care of by a loving machine in the shape of a beautiful woman. Then he laughed his hoarse derisive crow and went back to work. He had never been sick.

On the eighteenth day five poison cases came in from a bloodless coup in a banana republic; DeLazzari sent a dozen nurses with them into the Shock Room and watched every move. He was hot and itchy, red-eyed and out of cigars, and thinking he might as well have been in City Hospital. They were having their troubles over there, and once again he sent out the supplies. By the time he had leisure for a good look at Max Vingo, 2482's dial was all the way up and Max was cured and would be going out next day: day 21, his own discharge date. He listened to their conversation for a while and whistled through his teeth. "End of a beautiful interlude," he said.

That evening Max ate little and was listless and depressed. 2482 didn't press him to eat or speak, nor did DeLazzari worry. The behaviour pattern was normal for situation and temperament.

Max went to sleep early but woke about eleven and lay in the darkness without calling or crying out, only stared toward the ceiling; sometimes for a moment he had a fit of trembling.

2482 came into the room softly, without turning on the light. "Max, you're disturbed."

"How do you know?" he said in an expressionless voice.

"I watch your heartbeat and your brainwaves. Are you feeling ill?"

"No."

"Then what is the matter? Do you have terrible thoughts?"

"It's the thoughts I can't think that bother me, what's behind everything that got burned away. Maybe they shouldn't have done that, maybe they should have let me become another person, maybe if I knew, really knew, really knew what it was like to hurt and kill and be hurt and be killed and live in filth for a lifetime and another lifetime, ten times over, I'd get to laugh at it and like it and say it was the way to be, the only way to be and the way I should have been . . . ."

"Oh no, Max. No, Max. I don't believe so."

Suddenly he folded his arms over his face and burst out weeping, in ugly tearing sobs.

"Don't, Max." She sat down beside him and pulled his arms away. "No, Max. Please don't." She pulled apart the fastenings of her blouse and clasped his head between her tender, pulsing and unfleshly breasts.

DeLazzari grinned lasciviously and watched them on the infrared scanner, chin propped on his hand. "Lovely, lovely, lovely," he whispered. Then he preset 2482's dial to move down three points during the next four hours, popped his pill and went to bed.

The alarm woke him at four. "Now what in hell is that?" He staggered groggily over to the console to find the source. He switched on lights. The red warning signal was on over 2482's dial. Neither the dial nor the indicator had moved from UP position. He turned on Max Vingo's screen. She had lain down on the bed beside him and he was sleeping peacefully in her arms. DeLazzari snarled. "Circuit failure." The emergency panel checked out red in her number. He dialled Shop.

REROUTE CONTROL ON 2482.

CONTROL REROUTED, the machine typed back.

WHY DID YOU NOT REROUTE ON AUTO WHEN FAILURE REGISTERED?

REGULATION STATES DIRECTOR AUTONOMOUS IN ALL ASPECTS NURSE-PATIENT RELATIONSHIP NOW ALSO INCLUDING ALTERNATE CIRCUITS.

WHY WAS I NOT TOLD THAT BEFORE?

THAT IS NEW REGULATION. WHY DO YOU NOT REQUEST LIST OF NEW REGULATIONS DAILY UPDATED AND READILY AVAILABLE ALL TIMES?

"At four o'clock in the morning?" DeLazzari punched off. He noted that the indicator was falling now, and on the screen he could see 2482 moving herself away from Max and smoothing the covers neatly over him.

DeLazzari woke early on the last day and checked out the cholera, the yaws and the poison. The choleras were nearly well; one of the yaws needed further work on palate deformity; one of the poisons had died irrevocably, he sent it to Autopsy; another was being maintained in Shock, the rest recovering.

While he ate breakfast he watched the news of battle and outrage; growing from his harshly uprooted childhood faith a tendril of thought suggested that Satan was plunging poisoned knives in the sores of the world. "DeLazzari the Metaphysician!" He laughed. "Go on, you bastards, fight! I need the work." The city seemed to be doing his will, because it was as it had been.

Max Vingo was bathing himself, depilating his own face, dressing himself in a new uniform. A sweeper brought him breakfast. DeLazzari, recording his Director's Report, noted that he seemed calm and rested, and permitted himself a small glow of satisfaction at a good job nearly finished.

When the breakfast tray was removed, Max stood up and looked around the room as if there was something he might take with him, but he had no possessions. 2482 came in and stood by the door.

"I was waiting for you," he said.

"I've been occupied."

"I understand. It's time to go, I guess."

"Good luck."

"I've had that already." He picked up his cap and looked at it. "2482 —Nurse, may I kiss you?"

DeLazzari gave her the last downturn of the dial.

She stared at him and said firmly, "I'm a machine, sir. You wouldn't want to kiss a machine." She opened the top of her blouse, placed her hands on her chest at the base of her neck and pulled them apart, her skin opened like a seam. Inside she was the gold and silver gleam of a hundred metals threaded in loops, wound on spindles, flickering in minute gears and casings; her workings were almost fearsomely beautiful, but she was not a woman.

"Gets 'em every time." DeLazzari yawned and waited for the hurt shock, the outrage, the film of hardness coming down over the eyes like a third eyelid.

Max Vingo stood looking at her in her frozen posture of display. His eyelids twitched once, then he smiled. "I would have been very pleased and grateful to kiss a machine," he said and touched her arm lightly. "Goodbye, Nurse." He went out and down the hall toward his transportation cell.

DeLazzari's brows rose. "At least that's a change." 2482 was still standing there with her innards hanging out. "Close it up, woman. That's indecent." For a wild moment he wondered if there might be an expression trapped behind her eyes, and shook his head. He called down Shop and sent her for post-patient diagnostic with special attention to control system.

He cleaned up for the new man. That is, he evened up the pile of tape reels and ate the last piece of candy. Then he filched an ID plate belonging to one of the poison cases, put everything on AUTO, went down a couple of floors and used the ID to get into Patients' Autobath. For this experience of hot lather, stinging spray, perfume and powder he had been saving himself like a virgin.

When he came out in half an hour he was smooth, sweet-smelling and crisply clothed. As the door locked behind him five Doctors rounded a corner and came down the corridor in single file. DeLazzari stood very still. Instead of passing him they turned with a soft whirr of their lucite castors and came near. He breathed faster. They formed a semicircle around him; they were featureless and silver, and smelt faintly of warm metal. He coughed.

"What do you want?"

They were silent.

"What do you want, hey? Why don't you say something?"

They came nearer and he shrank against the door, but there were more machines on the other side.

"Get away from me! I'm not one of your stinking zombies!"

The central Doctor extruded a sensor, a slender shining limb with a small bright bulb on the end. It was harmless, he had seen it used thousands of times from the Control Room, but he went rigid and broke out into a sweat. The bulb touched him very lightly on the forehead, lingered a moment, and retracted. The Doctors, having been answered whatever question they had asked themselves, backed away, resumed their file formation, and went on down the hall. DeLazzari burst into hoarse laughter and scrubbed with his balled fist at the place the thing had touched. He choked on his own spit, sobered after a minute, and walked away very quickly in the opposite direction, even though it was a long way around to where he wanted to go. Much later he realized that they had simply been curious and perplexed in the presence of an unfamiliar heartbeat.

He went out in the same helicopter as Max Vingo, though the soldier in his sterile perimeter didn't know that. In the Control Room the new Director, setting out his tooth-cleaner, depilatory and changes of underwear, watched them on the monitor. Two incoming helicopters passed them on the way; the city teemed with fires and shouting and the children kicked at the slow-moving cars. In the operating theatre the silver Doctors moved forward under the lights, among the machines, and stood motionless around the narrow tables.

Michael G. Coney
SPARKLEBUGS, HOLLY AND LOVE

The most prolific writer of science fiction and fantasy in the country is undoubtedly Michael G. Coney. Born in 1932 in Birmingham, England, and qualified to practise as a chartered accountant, he ran a pub in Devon and managed a hotel in Antigua before arriving in Canada in 1972. Coney lives with his wife and family in Victoria where he works as a management specialist with the British Columbia Forestry Service. Among his more than a dozen novels are Friends Come in Boxes *(1973),* Winter's Children *(1974), and* The Ultimate Jungle *(1978). Nine short stories appear in* Monitor Found in Orbit *(1974). He is represented here with a story about an extraordinary woman and some strange insects found in an exotic place known as The Peninsula. It first appeared in* The Magazine of Fantasy and Science Fiction, *December 1977.*

There is a shock which comes slowly, when the mind will not accept the message from the eyes.

And there is an innocence about a clear blue sky, a thing so tranquil and free from the machineries of civilization that it plays a lullaby to that same mind.

Put these two things together. Imagine a crowd of people—around five hundred people—standing on a warm windless day and watching that sky and seeing something happen slowly and terribly, so that they don't believe it until that sky delivers its message to them personally, in little pieces, such as a Halloween mask, such as a child's doll, such as a severed arm.

The anatomy of a human disaster. We watched the shuttle descending at Sentry Down spaceport, and we—all of us—refused to believe that it was coming down too fast. That the antigrav mechanisms had failed and that still-far-off blob was hurtling towards us out of control. We might have been mistaken, and we didn't want to start screaming too soon. Beside me a woman was saying too brightly, too casually:

"I haven't seen Steve for eight years, can you believe that?"

Far off, a hooter sounded. Blocky red vehicles sidled out of sheds.

Now someone screamed. The woman beside me said, "Oh, my God.

Oh, my God," over and over. She wasn't praying. She was acknowledging the purport of that scream. A communal babbling arose.

The shuttles had been coming and going for hours in their eerie silence, ferrying passengers and freight between this hot platform of concrete and the starship *Hetherington Venturer,* which orbited out there, a secret of the blue sky.

But the tumbling triangular shape was no secret. It seemed to be dropping vertically towards the public observation enclosure, and now people were beginning to run aimlessly in all directions. A man thumped into me, and I took my gaze away from the sky, but he was gone, mumbling something mindless. A number of people seemed to be fighting, but in retrospect I think they had simply collided and were unwilling to change course; panic does funny things to people. I didn't panic but this is no credit to me; I was too numbed for quick action. I looked back at the sky.

It was empty.

At the same instant the earth erupted nearby as the shuttle, a thing of hugeness and complexity with a payload of nine hundred people and countless items of freight, smashed into the concrete landing pad after a free fall of one kilometer.

Afterwards, the images of such events became fragmented by shock. I remember the fire engines moving in, then waiting, purposelessly, because there was no fire. Ambulances stood still because there were no living. The center of impact was a quarter kilometer away, but the wreckage extended to within fifty meters of the enclosure gates. The wreckage consisted of small items which I am trying to forget. I remember afterwards drinking in the spaceport bar with a middle-aged woman who was not crying and who kept telling me that Bart was coming on a later shuttle. She said this over and over, while the speaker system recited an endless passenger list, and one of the names made her eyes go dead.

And, outside, the shuttles continued to land and take off—but from an alternative pad, as though the authorities had always planned for this eventuality.

Maybe the most horrible—I remember the Barrelorgans. The big truck from the Organ Pool rolled up, and the rear doors opened, and overalled men came running down the ramp wheeling the machines before them. They scuttled across the concrete like scavenging crabs, stopping beside inert pieces of humanity and loaded them quickly into the drum-shaped containers. Every minute counted. When each Barrelorgan was full, they dogged the lid down and pressed a button, and we heard the hiss as air was evacuated and the contents were quick-frozen. Then the man would come running back to the truck, load the full Barrelorgan on board and emerge with another empty one. In a way it was not very efficient, but an accident of this magnitude doesn't happen often. The men rushed to and fro, saving human remains for future use as organ transplants, limb grafts. The Barrelorgans were bright red drums mounted on wheeled boxes. From a distance they looked like childs' toys.

Much later I remembered my own mission. I picked up the small parcel of Sparklebugs from the freight office and felt guilty that I had not suffered loss in any way whatsoever.

Then I caught the hoverferry home.

Some gregarious alien races do not distinguish between loneliness and solitude in their vocabulary. To them, the two are synonymous, equally unpleasant. For me however, solitude is a very necessary thing, a time in which to stop working and fighting and hating, a time to realize the stupidity of expending all that effort, a time to meditate and think about peace and love—and then, refreshed, to get back to the fighting again. For some reason it is impossible to think about peace and love in the company of others—or even in the company of a bottle, because then the meditation becomes jerky and scrambled—so I catch myself sober and alone and think it all out.

There is a beach on the east coast of the Peninsula, long and sandy and all littered with ancient silver logs, and at twilight when the tourists have gone it's a good place.

The sun had dropped below the treetops inland so that the beach was in shadow, but the dying rays still picked out the offshore islands and occasionally glittered starlike from a rising shuttle at Sentry Down, thirty kilometers beyond those islands. I was not quite alone as I walked; half a kilometer away, on a rocky outcropping, I could see a figure standing. Then it jumped down and disappeared, and I was able to think.

Mostly I thought about a girl I'd known called Diane, whose father fished this coast with the aid of a team of dolphins. Diane was gone now to some other world, and I'd never see her again, but it didn't really matter because I'd never been in love with her, or anything like that. Hell, I was old enough to be her father. Occasionally I'd drop by to see Daniel Westaway, her dad, to catch up on the latest news.

So I thought about Diane and how I ought to find some girl to share my life before it was too late; and while I did this, I walked along the logs, trying to jump from one to the next without touching the beach. A man can afford to play childish games when there are no eyewitnesses to recount the aberration to his bank manager.

"Hello."

I stepped quickly down to the sand. A girl stood watching me from the water's edge. I couldn't see her face in the half-light, but her hair was fair and wavy, her figure slim in a blue sweater, yellow pants. I mumbled a reply to her greeting.

She approached me. Her footprints trailed off into the dark distance behind her; little puddles at the waves' limit. She was quite small, but certainly no kid. I estimated her age at around twenty-six, now that I could see her face and see the beauty and intelligence there. Some last reflections caught her wide eyes. She said, "Please tell me what you were thinking about."

"Uh . . . . Some girl, I guess. Nothing in particular." Her eyes searched mine and I felt that I could hold no secrets from her.

"Sit down. I want to talk. Here—this log."

And I found myself sitting beside her. "Listen—how the hell do you know I'm not some kind of sex maniac?" I asked.

"Don't talk like that. Don't spoil it." She sat relaxedly; the log was a huge remnant of some bygone logging operation, and her small feet hardly reached the sand.

So we talked about politics, philosophy and sport while it grew dark and the sea became a warm twinkling under the stars. We discussed religions and the growing menace of land sharks and other pets gone wild, and we lamented the lack of police action. We extrapolated on the latest advances in medical science and planetary colonization, and we argued the prospects of the competitors in the regional sling-gliding championship. It was late October, and an Indian summer was just finished, and it was beginning to get cold.

"Please put your arm around me," she said.

Somehow I knew what she intended; not a prelude to sex, but a communication between two people, just another form of contact besides conversation. I drew her to me, sensing the presence of a loneliness far more intense than mine.

"Tell me about yourself," she said.

I found myself describing my small slithe farm down the coast, where I breed the little reptiles with the emotion-sensitive skins and make novelty clothing out of them.

"You mean you slaughter them for their pelts?"

"No. They shed their skins once a year, like snakes." I felt very glad about that. Lights moved across the water, and the throbbing of an ancient engine came to us. That would be Daniel Westaway monitoring his dolphins; his and mine were the only piston-engined boats on the coast—temperamental artifacts of a long time back.

"Oh, yes. I've seen slitheskin things in the stores," she said. "They're very interesting." She made it sound the truth. "Maybe some day I'll drop by your place and see what goes on."

"That would be great. How about tomorrow?" I said—when something happened which was so unexpected, so strange that we both jumped to our feet, the conversation forgotten.

The sea had come alive. A wide, glittering wave swept across the flat water towards us, boiling and phosphorescent. In the darkness it was impossible to estimate its height, rate of approach or even how far away it was; it appeared simply as a wall of cascading silver. In the sudden fear which gripped me I thought of the Western Seaboard slide which—so historians tell us—caused a tsunami over fifty meters high to sweep the coastline, completely inundating the Peninsula. Stepping back, I forgot the log, tumbled backwards over it and smashed my head against something. I lay there half-stunned, waiting for the tidal wave.

Something cold and writhing touched my face, slid away. Suddenly I was bombarded with living, flapping things as I lay there; they were around my head, wriggling over my body. I shuddered with disgust, heard myself yelling as I crawled to my feet. I heard the girl screaming I clambered over the log and stood.

The beach was covered with live fish, flashing and undulating in a silver carpet on the sand, gills pumping as they expired in their thousands.

The girl was making queer little sobbing noises as she stood among them. They slithered under my feet as I stepped to her side. "They're only fish," I said, putting my arm around her shoulders. She was shuddering violently. A dark head appeared from the sea, and I could imagine clever eyes watching us. One of Westaway's dolphins had mistaken his direction and driven a shoal of herring ashore instead of into the lagoon pens further south.

Now the girl had shaken me off and was on her knees among the fish, scooping at them with cupped hands and flinging them back into the shallows. She was still sobbing, talking to the fish too, odd little consolatory babbles as she scooped and threw, scooped and threw. I stood irresolute, half-persuaded to walk quietly away. I was in the presence of something I didn't understand, and the sight of that girl, that shadowy frantic form in the living sea, frightened me. Finally I pulled myself together and gripped her shoulder.

"They're only fish," I said again.

I saw the pale shadow of her face swing towards me, then she jumped to her feet. Slipping, sliding, she began to run untidily up the beach. Soon she was moving among the arbutus trees which bordered the beach, a figure half-seen like a deer at sunset.

As I walked home, walked away from the dying fish, I wondered what she was doing here on the Peninsula and what her particular problem was. She'd told me nothing about herself, not even her name.

And two nights later it was Halloween.

The party was held in the sunken garden of The Stars, Carioca Jones' aerial house. When I arrived the bonfire was already throwing dancing shadows among the growing numbers of guests. So, clutching the parcel under my costume, I looked around for my host.

"Carioca will be here in a minute," said a girl with a tray of drinks. I took a glass of something yellow, sighted Doug Marshall and Charles Wentworth throwing driftwood on the fire, and joined them. By now there were about fifty guests present, with already some duplication of costumes—I saw two Harlequins and three Arcadian Mind Things.

"What in hell are you supposed to be?" asked Doug, a Pirate, staring at my crumpled raincoat and bare hairy legs.

"An Indecent Exhibitionist. Listen, what's happened to Carioca? This is her party."

"She's up in The Stars, preparing for her grand entrance, I guess. Don't you have any clothes on under that raincoat, Joe? You must be god-damned cold."

"I've got something for her," I said, glancing up at the huge black rectangle of The Stars, silhouetted against the night sky a hundred meters above our heads. Lights were on, blazing against the darkness. Carioca's house is a converted antigravity wrecking crane, tethered to the earth by a strong steel cable. As a point of interest, the bottom end of the cable is fastened to a huge steel shackle set in the base of a concrete pit. A pack of hungry land sharks, trained to attack on sight, is also kept in that pit. Carioca has her enemies. . . .

Doug Marshall and Charles Wentworth began setting off a few fireworks to keep people interested. A rocket zoomed into the blackness, exploded in a shower of sparks. "That was a good one," I heard Doug say. "I have a way of setting these things up. The secret is in the trajectory."

Guests gathered around laughing, drinking. An orchestra began to tune up; mournful dissonances providing a counterpoint to the whoosh and crackle of fireworks. "Watch this!" Charles said, touching blue paper with his lighted cigar. "Emerald Fountain." He set it on the ground and it began to splutter spitefully.

At that moment I saw the girl.

I grabbed Doug by the arm. "Who's that? That girl, sitting over there!"

He'd been in the process of deriding Charles' constipated Emerald Fountain; now he followed my gaze. "That's Holly Davenport."

"Tell me more about her."

He grinned. "You too, huh? Well, she's twenty-six years old, recently widowed, no kids." His voice was serious, now. "She lost her husband last week—he was a passenger on that shuttle that crashed over at Sentry Down. An old buddy of mine. And Holly. . . . Well, I guess she's just about the nicest woman I know. Maybe the most beautiful, too."

Holly was sitting on a chair at the far side of the bonfire, and a lot of people were near her, some sitting, some standing. Somehow they seemed to be gathered around her, as though solicitous of her recent tragedy and protective towards her—yet they were laughing.

She was laughing too, watching the antics of Charles, who was brandishing a Wand of Brilliance, stabbing with it at the recalcitrant Emerald Fountain as though involved in an insane fencing bout. The people around Holly laughed when she did, smiled when she did. They watched her face often, both the men and the women. She was heartbreakingly lovely, enjoying the fun like any child who might be present, and she made me feel good just looking at her.

I said, "She seems happy enough right now."

Doug glanced at me as though expecting a hurt. "Yes," he said.

Charles was putting on a show for Holly now, arranging a semi-circle of small bright sparklers around her feet. She laughed delightedly as he fumbled frantically with matches, trying to get the last one lit before the first went out. Other people drifted up, bringing chairs and firming them into the soft grass.

I found myself standing next to Ramsbottom, a noisy guy whom I knew as a member of the Peninsula sling-gliding club; he was already half drunk, dressed as a Beefeater. "I've forgotten," he was roaring unhappily. "For Chrissake, Joe—I've already forgotten what the last firework looked like, and it was only *seconds* ago. What's this liquor doing to me? It's destroying my brain, that's what it's doing." He stared up at a receding rocket. I heard Holly laugh at something Doug said. "Is it my eyes?" lamented Ramsbottom. "Or is Carioca Jones' goddamn house swelling up like a pumpkin?"

"It's coming down to earth," I said.

I could hear the whine of the winch. For safety reasons, the antigrav field of Carioca's house is permanently activated at low power—just enough to keep it aloft. Ascent and descent are achieved by means of a mechanical winch—part of the original crane gear.

A series of sharp reports announced Doug's answer to Charles' sparkler display, and a firework dog began hopping crazily among the guests. It approached Holly, smoking and banging; I listened to her laughing, watched her wide slanting eyes—and knew that everyone else was listening and watching even as I. . . .

I think it was her simplicity which attracted us all, her naive delight at the pretty, noisy toys around her, her unaffected joy in living for the moment. That, and the knowledge of her tragedy which made us feel protective. It was the same girl I'd met on the beach; the same girl but seen through a different-angle spectroscope—a rosy Holly instead of a blue. In that moment I loved her completely and knew that every guy on that lawn loved her too.

Now the bulk of The Stars intruded, blazing light at the far end of the lawn and rumbling slightly as it bedded down on its concrete plinth, sealing in the land sharks. The jumping dog ran out of gunpowder and fell to its side, in tatters. Doug Marshall, about to light a rocket, paused. The orchestra sprang into prominence, flood-lighted against a concrete structure shaped like an oyster shell. The conductor gave a peremptory tap with his baton; people stopped talking, turned to watch. A short roll of drums, a cymbal clash, then the band launched into a spirited version of "Copacabana Girl, Hello." This was Carioca's signature tune, the number which she sang in the original 3V spectacular which had made her name. Forty years ago. . . .

The door of The Stars swung open and a wedge of crimson light spread towards us across the lawn. Carioca had brought her own red carpet. The music hushed. Then she appeared, a slim black silhouette, pausing for that calculated instant in the doorway before stepping down —and as she walked towards us, the spotlight came on. She smiled brilliantly, spread her arms in an extravagant gesture of welcome embracing her guests, her party, the whole world. . . .

"Darlings!" she cried.

She was naked from the waist up, but fortunately it was a cold night and an attendant was already stepping forward with a fur wrap.

I managed to slide through the crowd to Holly's side.

"Hello," I said.

She was watching Carioca Jones with an uncomplicated smile which said she was glad the aging ex-3V star was enjoying herself. Now she looked up at me. She recognized me straight away.

"It's nice to see you again, Joe," she said. "I'm sorry I ran away the other night. I guess I wasn't quite thinking straight."

Caught in the trap of her blue eyes, I babbled, "That's all right, hell, I didn't know the score—I mean, I only just found out. . . . I'm very sorry. I. . . ." I realized I was going to say I'd been at Sentry Down and seen it all and how terrible it was and how sympathetic I felt—and I managed to stop myself.

"OK, Joe," she said quietly, understanding everything in two words.

"This is a nice party, huh? I always enjoy Halloween. It's different. Carioca Jones is a friend of yours, is she? She's very attractive."

"She's a business acquaintance." Occasionally when I introduce her to people, I have a childish temptation to say: "And this is Carioca Jones, my blackmailer." As I might introduce my dentist, or my lawyer. From her eyrie in The Stars she sees many things—and she has a hold over me in the form of a roll of film. She has never demanded money; she doesn't need it. She just sits on the film gloatingly, like a miser. Possession of that film means she possesses me, and Carioca is a people collector.

"Joe *darling*!" Carioca stood before us, black hair falling to her waist, shrewd eyes appraising Holly. "I thought you hadn't come, which would have been *devastating*." She addressed her next remark to Holly. "Joe is a *very* close friend of mine. Joe, aren't you going to introduce me to this charming young companion of yours?"

I muttered some introductions.

"And now I must spirit Joe away from you, Holly darling, because we have some *intimate* matters to discuss. Come, Joe." She drew me into the shadows, then said, "Well, just who the hell is she, Joe? I most *certainly* didn't invite her." Already a throng of people had moved in around Holly, bringing her drinks, chatting to her. Charles handed her a Sword of Lightning and she waved it in a brilliant circle.

"Doug and Charles brought her. She's a recent widow. Go easy on her, Carioca, huh?"

"A *widow*? How *quaint*! I wasn't aware that marriage still existed—except among obscure religious sects. Well. . . ." Her black eyes dwelt on Holly's circle of admirers. "Everybody seems to be most kind to her, I must say. You brought the Sparklebugs, I trust?"

I produced the parcel from under my raincoat. Something occurred to me, some nebulous connection of images, something vague and unsettling. "Maybe we shouldn't use them," I said on impulse.

"Don't be absurd, Joe. They were most expensive and they won't keep." There was hostility in her tone; her face was settling into lines of discontent which betrayed her true age as she gazed around at the party. "What a *drag* this affair is. And why on earth isn't the band playing? Go and tell them to start earning their pay. And get rid of that *dreadful* raincoat, Joe—it makes you look like some sordid *pervert*."

"I'm supposed to look like a pervert. This is my costume."

"Well, I'm sure it's *most* appropriate," she said acidly and moved away. "*Darlings*!" she trilled, bearing down on a group of innocent bystanders.

Meanwhile, Doug and Charles were banking up the fire and unleashing a fusillade of rockets into the night sky. The spectators, with the warmth of Carioca's liquor in their bellies, cheered each starburst. The band began to play. I caught sight of Holly talking animatedly to some woman in a tutu; the woman watched her in a sort of dazed fascination. I found a waitress and took another drink.

A Beefeater lurched near, holding a firework. "Nest of Serpents," he read the label to me. "Marshall lit four of them a moment ago, and I can't remember what the hell they *did*."

I handed over my parcel to a guy who seemed to be emceeing things. I drank some more; everybody did. Later the wind switched and the bonfire billowed smoke; I moved around, saw Holly in the center of a crowd, and plunged in. "Let's dance," I said.

We shuffled around the lawn and I held her very close; at first she talked, then became silent, resting her head against my shoulder. She seemed very light, tiny in my great clumsy arms. I said, "Listen, I'm going to make a confession."

"I like to hear confessions. Go ahead, Joe."

"I love you like crazy."

"Oh, sure. You're bombed out of your mind, too. Try saying it in the morning, when your head's aching and you want to throw up." She laughed and hugged me just a little, and I wondered if I should have said it or not. Then I decided it didn't really matter, because she didn't believe me.

"Ladies and gentlemen!"

The band had stopped, and the emcee was standing before a table on which small canisters were set out. The drum rolled, the cymbals clashed.

"Presenting—all the way from Aldebaran—the Sparklebugs!"

Now there was a general rearrangement as we were ushered into a wide crescent, dragging chairs and spilling drinks. Doug and Charles found Holly a seat in the center of the crescent; they stood on each side of her like bodyguards. I was out at the far end; from this position I could watch both Holly and the firework display. Nearby stood Ramsbottom in his Beefeater garb, rocking slightly as though on deck. I drew my raincoat around me. A cool wind had arisen, chilling my bare legs.

"First, a simple display," said the emcee. "This is called the Ascent of Love." He picked up one of the small canisters, about the size and shape of a shotgun cartridge. "What you are about to see has never before been witnessed on Earth—the contents of this table represent the first Sparklebugs ever imported to our planet. We are deeply indebted to Miss Carioca Jones for this display."

"Get on with it!" somebody shouted. The spotlight had already shifted to Carioca, who took the comment in her stride, smiling as people applauded.

"And now—the Ascent of Love!"

A drum roll, and the emcee whipped the seal from the cartridge. There was a hiss of indrawn air, a moment's expectant silence. Then we heard a noise which is difficult to describe: a tiny twittering singing noise, fast and melodic—the sound you'd expect if hummingbirds could sing. Above the emcee's hand two points of light appeared, one red, one blue, hard and bright.

They circled each other like tiny stars against the blackness. Then, sliding to the right, they rose diagonally and hovered above the darkened bandstand, still singing. The strangest thing was, they each left a trail through the air, one red, one blue. I closed my eyes, thinking it was the effect of the bright light on my retinas—but the trails disappeared. When I looked again they were still there, like tiny colored threads against the sky.

Then quite suddenly they began to ascend in a spiral, while their sound became a flutelike trill. The spectators said aah. The sight was incredibly beautiful, and the Sparklebugs' song seemed to reach straight to the heart. I glanced at Holly. She was sitting forward in her chair, lips parted, eyes wide.

I became aware of the droning voice of Ramsbottom. " . . . a planet named Socrates. They're insects, like glowworms. Yeah. See that? Mating, that's what they're doing. Ha. ha. Just once ev'y Socra . . . Socratean year, they. . . ."

Now the sound reached a tiny crescendo. The Sparkelbugs were far above us, trailing a red-blue spiral into the night sky. The lights winked out. The spiral faded.

The audience applauded. Holly caught my eye, smiling happily. I grinned back. The emcee picked up a canister and people immediately became quiet—all except Ramsbottom, of course. His slurred voice could be heard endlessly explaining to the woman on his left.

"Soc'tes is a frozen planet, all frozen, all dead. But ever' year it passes through this cloud of gas, see an' it heats up just a little, and for a time you get sorta an atmosphere—y'see what I mean, Laura? Just enough t'trigger the bugs."

"And next for your entertainment—the Cascade of Stars!"

We heard the hiss of the broken vacuum but saw nothing. "Ladies and gentlemen, direct your gaze skywards, if you will!"

Now we saw them winking on like fairy lights, hundreds of them of all colors falling towards us like rain, making music like a thousand tiny harps. They floated through the cold November air leaving no trail, just slipping through the sky like a condensed rainbow, extinguishing as they neared the ground. The crowd was silent, allowing the play of light and sound to seep through to their emotions. I could still hear Ramsbottom expounding however, and so I edged past him, making my way towards the middle of the audience where Holly was.

"The Sparklebugs have just one day of love every year," the emcee said. "Just a short time to attract their mate in the cold darkness of their planet—so they use every means possible, visually and aurally. And each species has a distinct pattern, instantly recognizable."

He released three bugs. The red one flew in flat circles, the golden one looped, the blue one performed erratic zigzagging.

I reached Holly's side. She smiled at me. "Aren't they neat, Joe? I'm so glad these guys brought me. I never expected anything like this."

The show went on. We saw Sparklebugs spurting from their cartridges in huge glittering fountains; we saw them flying in precision formation like a military aerobatic team; we saw clusters of them streak into the sky and scatter like a bombshell. Carioca sent The Stars aloft, and we saw flightless Sparklebugs crawling up the cable in an endless, glittering spiral. Then back to a winged variety with a shrill whistle which flew straight up, leaving ruler-straight orange trails. They flew through the anti-gravity field which extends a short distance out around The Stars, and the whistle sank to a breathless whisper, and the orange deepened to red as they were hurled into space. . . .

Later the demonstration became less formal, and the band began to play again, and people began to dance in a mist of tiny stars which seemed to jig to the beat of the music. The audience broke up into groups. Inevitably the largest, most vociferous group formed around Holly, Doug and Charles.

The bonfire was stoked up, and waitresses brought canapes, and from somewhere a large box of frankfurters appeared. To this day I suspect Charles of smuggling this plebeian fare into Carioca's highclass party, but he still denies it. We broke sticks from Carioca's priceless alien shrubs, impaled the franks, and soon the air was redolent with the aroma of roasting meat.

"Well, *really*, Joe."

Carioca was at my side. Above her head spun a silver halo of Sparklebugs attracted by an upright wand projecting from her coiffure. She'd been circulating among the groups of revelers, laughing with mouth wide and head thrown back, embracing people with exaggerated cries of delight, whispering into the ears of men with extravagant intimacy. Now she was prepared to capture the attention of the biggest group.

But it didn't work out that way.

Holly was dancing with Charles. They danced without touching, swaying in time to the music. A few minutes ago a number of us had been dancing, but somehow we'd all stopped, one by one, and drifted into a large circle to watch Holly and Charles—or more particularly Holly.

I've seen dancers in my time. I've seen alien troupes, all staccato rhythms and impossible movement. I've seen ballet over an antigravity field in Frisco Bowl. I've seen the underwater Dolphin Dance. And I've seen the early Carioca Jones movies, when the young Carioca made walking look like a fertility rite.

But I've never seen anything like Holly Davenport.

The funny thing is, she was hardly moving. She stood there with her arms quite close to her sides, hands held slightly forward in a position which suggested a snapping of fingers to the slow beat; but the fingers were still. Her hips moved; for the first time I noticed she was wearing a long orange skirt and a pale blouse. I'd been so engrossed in her personality that I hadn't seen her clothes. . . .

As she turned I saw her face. There was a half smile and her eyes were almost closed. Her whole body was in slow, expressive movement— and just what she expressed none of us could have put into words. It was introspective, almost private—yet it spoke to us all. Melancholy yet vital, she seemed to be telling us that life goes on and life is good; she made me want to cry, she made me want to love her, she made me want to give her children. I don't know what she was doing for the women present, but they watched just as raptly.

Pale dawn was exposing the silhouettes of the coastal mountains as a strange thing happened. The latest cluster of Sparklebugs arrayed themselves around her, swaying and changing color as though her dancing said something to the alien insects too, as though it was something universal and elemental.

"Well, Joe Sugar, are you going to ask me to dance or not?"

I ignored Carioca. It might be her party, but Holly Davenport was the star.

The music died away, and Holly stopped moving, and her eyes opened. You could almost feel the remembered past falling away from her as she returned to the present. "Thanks, Charles," she said automatically—then she realized she was the center of attention again. "Oh, boy," she said uncertainly. "What did I do?"

The dancing Sparklebugs were beginning to fade from around her now, winking out one by one, disappearing. Charles still stood there, staring at her. A bright star twinkled before her face, golden, orange, turquoise. It was gone. She smiled. "What happens to them?"

Michael G. Coney

It was as though she was in the center of a stage. Everybody watched
her, everybody listened to her, a small pretty almost-blonde woman who
represented the joy and beauty and sadness of humanity. Everybody
listened, so somebody had to answer. Ramsbottom answered.

"They die, of course. What the hell else?"

"They die?"

"Well, sure." Suddenly Ramsbottom's slurred voice became almost
whining as Holly faced him. "They can't live, can they. Their planet
only has an atmosphere for one . . . one two-thousandth of the time."

It was the planet Socrates' fault, not humanity's.

"What the hell do you know about it?" said somebody loudly. But
everyone else waited for Holly's reply. They surrounded her in a great
circle, yet it seemed that she was the accuser, they the defendants. They
waited.

Holly said, "Oh."

Carioca said, "Well, now, it's getting light. Let's all have some coffee
before we go home, shall we?"

Holly said, "You mean we've been watching them die, all this time?
For fun?"

The sky was cloudless and cold, pale blue. Day was creeping up all
around us. People shuffled uneasily. Women looked for their purses. I
suddenly found I was bitterly cold. The fire had burned down; the
glow of alcohol had left me with a blinding headache; my ridiculous
bare legs felt damp with dew, or maybe frost.

Carioca whispered to me loudly, "Get that *wretched* little girl out of
here right now, Joe. She's turning my party into a *disaster*."

Now we could see one another clearly and we looked terrible, the
men unshaven and the women streaky. The costumes looked immature
and faded; why the hell were we wearing them? Cold dawn came,
freezing the fun.

And we could see something else.

The lawn was littered with thousands of tiny corpses, spent Sparklebugs in a patina of death on the velvet-smooth grass. A few still twitched.
Holly knelt and picked one up; it couldn't have been more than a centi-
meter long. But there were so many of them. I kept saying to myself:
they're only insects, for God's sake! Lying there like the aftermath of
some huge disaster. Holly knelt.

I saw her kneeling but I couldn't go to her. The thing was too big for
me.

She stood. She smiled. She walked up to Carioca Jones. She said,
"Thanks very much for a nice party, Carioca. It's really been lots of fun.
When I get settled in, I hope you come over to my place."

Carioca smiled like a death's head. "It's been wonderful having you, Holly *darling*." She watched Holly, escorted by Doug and Charles, walk away. Holly walked very lightly, as though scared to put her feet down. "Now!" cried Carioca brightly, turning. "Let's all have that coffee and maybe just a little eye-opener to go with it!"

But her guests were gathering up their things, and hoping they'd see one another real soon, and going home.

And miracles don't happen nowadays, do they?

Awakening in the afternoon is a sad thing, like forgetting your childhood. The day is more than half gone, and it doesn't seem worthwhile doing anything very much before nightfall, and all the time there is the feeling of something missing, something lost. I crawled out of bed and showered, and the fierce little droplets seemed to bore into my aching skull. I dressed and looked out of the window at what was left of the day. It was damp and misty and Novembery, one of those days when you regret having a waterfront lot. There's just too much wetness around.

I couldn't get Holly out of my mind.

I brewed some coffee, sat at the table clutching my mug and thinking. All the time I saw her kneeling there; I saw her hit but coming back, knocked down again but recovering, hit again and very shaky now, with the cumulative effect of all those blows. In time most people recover from the loss of a loved one, but Holly was fragile, and I suspected her love went deeper than most.

She was fragile and small, and maybe a small miracle would have helped.

There was no way I could bring myself to call her; I was too scared, too sure that she would smile from the visiphone as though nothing had ever happened. The screen watched me blankly, daring me to push the buttons.

In the end—unbelievably—I found myself driving to Carioca's place. I can't explain the motivation; maybe it was an urge to revisit the scene of the latest crime; maybe I wanted to hear someone say Holly's name. And I could be sure Carioca would say her name. Maybe I wanted to mortify the mind.

The Stars was not in the sky as I drove across the Peninsula; usually it is visible for kilometers around. I turned into Carioca's driveway and found three other vehicles there. In addition to Carioca's turtle-like monster, the small hovercar of Doug Marshall lay on the blacktop beside a large truck. I pulled up and got out, wondering what I was stepping into. Possibly there was a dispute in progress. I hesitated, then heard the hum of machinery from beyond the bushes.

212

Walking on, I was confronted by a sudden vision of fear, a nightmarish remembrance.

A crimson Barrelorgan stood on the lawn. . . .

Charles saw me and called out, "Move yourself, Joe! The bugs'll rot if they're exposed to the atmosphere for another day." He tipped a panful of little things into the drum. "I borrowed the equipment from the Organ Pool," he said.

A number of people crawled around the lawn and among the shrubs with pans and brushes, like overzealous housewives. . . .

He handed me a brush and pan and I began to cover a patch of ground near Doug and Holly. We exchanged brief greetings. My pants knees were soon soaked. Rain drizzled down. Holly was singing under her breath. Somewhere inside me a happiness grew.

Doug said, "The bugs are hermaphroditic and they mate simultaneously, so Ramsbottom said. Then they degenerated into egg cases within minutes. That's what all these things are—abdominal shells each holding around a hundred eggs."

I glanced at Holly and the happiness became an inward glow, like good Scotch. Her hair was wet and straggly and raindrops dripped from the tip of her nose and chin. Egg cases rattled into her pan. Life goes on. I wanted to kiss her, and I knew that one day I would and hoped that it would mean something and not be just one of those casual things.

"Joe *darling!*" Carioca's voice interrupted my thoughts. She emerged from The Stars trailing a long cable. "It's delightful to see you again. I *do* hope you enjoyed the party." I watched, incredulous, as she carried a suction cleaner from The Stars and plugged the cable into it. She saw me staring. "After all," she said defensively, "Sparklebugs are terribly expensive. There must be literally *thousands* of dollars lying about these grounds. . . ."

Other people arrived, people I remembered in outlandish costumes at the party, but now in working clothes. And for the rest of that afternoon, until gloomy daylight deepened into wet evening, they worked. Then they said goodby to Holly, and left.

This party had been for Holly, too.

The tiny aliens were in safe hibernation. The Barrelorgan was dogged down—the unlikely machinery of a miracle. A simple miracle, consisting of one man's brainwave, a few visiphone calls, a number of willing helpers. Afterwards, I found it was Charles Wentworth's brainwave.

Everyone had gone home except Doug, Charles, Holly and I. We stood in the rain, grinning at each other. Something needed to be said, but nobody knew quite what it was. Finally Carioca Jones said something.

213

Carioca said, "Ah, what the hell. Let's all go inside and have a drink, shall we?"

H. A. Hargreaves
INFINITE VARIATION

North by 2000, which appeared in 1975, is the title of the first collection of science-fiction stories to be published in Canada. It was written by H. A. Hargreaves, who was born in 1928, in Mount Vernon, New York, and served with the United States Navy. At the age of twenty-one, he enrolled at Mount Allison University in Sackville, New Brunswick. He took his doctorate at Duke University in North Carolina, and since 1963 has taught English at the University of Alberta, in Edmonton. Hargreaves' stories have appeared in the important British magazine, New Worlds. *He is represented here with an original story, written in the form of an epistle, which takes the reader more than half a century into the future, when an event has taken place that has parallels with another that occurred under similar circumstances in the distant past. Does the writer of this letter have any choice?*

O PMIEL 14/4/2046
OFF/GOV/GEN
MATTHEW HURD
TO: ANDREW SASKATOON
E. S. AMERICANADA
OFF/SYN/ANGLICHCAN
STOON/SASK
PERS. SCRAMBLER MH214762
DEAR ANDY:

Greetings to my closest friend, mentor, and coworker. Also greetings to Admiral Frieson and his U.N. Security Staff, who undoubtedly find most of my personal scrambled messages quite boring. And also greetings to CUSS Co-Primates Rome, Istanbul, Canterbury, and Berne, who probably find *your* personal correspondence equally boring.

You know that this is important or I wouldn't use half my stipend as Governor General of Ethlon to beam it back to you on Earth. If I had foreseen the present situation it would have been done soon enough so that you could offer your advice, although your message might have been delayed, lost, or *innocently* buried under the mass of directives which will surely follow, all now mercifully too late. I simply want you to have all the facts for the record, in a message that may be read but cannot be tampered with by anyone, no matter what results from the action which I must undertake, in my official capacity, within the next few hours.

It seems to me now more ironic than ever that you and I have achieved our present positions despite the views of Church and State concerning our beliefs and activities. I may yet even have second thoughts about that diabolical World Computer which consistently advanced us, to the frustration and anger of our many opponents. Speaking of opponents, let me say that you can be much more charitable toward them back there, where they have the excuse of ignorance about the Ethlonians, than here, where they appear to be blind, stupid, or both. It's almost impossible to conceive of the mixture of paternalism or arrogance on the one hand, and exploitative greed or unreasoning fear on the other, which the Enclave and Field personnel display towards Ethlonians. Yet, to be truthful, even you and I—all the people in our movement to accept Ethlonians as potential converts to the Christian United Spiritual Society —were at best naive too in our understanding of them as rational beings. And therein lies the crux (term possibly prophetic?) of my present dilemma, which is far more complex than we dreamed.

Despite the careful and surprisingly accurate reports which were developed by our early survey parties, I was not really prepared for life here in the city of Milon. Superficially it is precisely as the reports indicated: A predominance of nomadic herders, pockets of agriculture, and the one great city into which all wealth, learning and culture slowly gravitate over the centuries. It does seem quite primitive by our standards, much like Earth's Middle East over two thousand years ago. Yet, as the surveys could only suggest, there is a fascinatingly complex society here: legal and governmental structures woven intricately, bewilderingly, inextricably into the much older infra-structure of main religion. Yes, I said religion —monotheistic, Ethlon-centered, which makes for as strange-looking a depiction of God as you'll ever find on Easter Island or in one of the ancient ruins at home. It's taken me all of my three years here simply to grasp the tremendous difficulty of dealing with any particular problem. Touch an apparently simple matter such as sewage disposal and you're involved with city officials, priests, curers, tax officials, and even the King (which is not quite definitive), whose power must have been awesome when wielded by certain of his predecessors. I am chillingly convinced, as well, that the supra-powers they've vested in me as Governor General are a test of Earth's seeming superiority in all things.

The present ruler is obviously weak, terrified by the priests but a prey to Ethlonian appetites, which are different enough from ours to upset squeamish stomachs. He's swayed by gifts and flattery at one moment, making vile decisions that favour one individual, group, or tribe, and the next he's secluded in the temple or on some high rock in the desert, purging himself in a fashion which I haven't yet fathomed, and am not sure I want to know. This makes for appalling inefficiency, confusion, and a sure decline in the whole civilization. Despite their insistence, I can do little about it, of course, since my activities are so restricted by the authorities on Earth that I can hardly maintain order among our own people. There are so many counterforces at work that my own staff are crumbling before my eyes. Discount the blatantly nationalistic or entre-preneur elements; the U.N. task forces alone, all nineteen of them, are constantly bickering, agitating, obstructing one another's work. Cooperation is long gone and we spend all our time settling jurisdictional disputes.

Perhaps that's the reason, perhaps my own obtuseness or sheer exhaustion, or perhaps an element which we both of all people ought to recognise, that events begun almost at the time of my arrival here have culminated now without my having grasped their significance. Yet the moment is at hand, and I really cannot say that had I been aware from the first I would be any better prepared to deal with it. I know, I've held off too long already what this development consists of, not because I lack faith in your ability to accept it, but because I find myself caught in the cold, clear unreality of *déjà-vu*, asking if it could possibly mean what I believe it does. Without further delay, then, I give you the scenario.

Somewhat over two years ago rumours began to trickle into the city about a certain young Ethlonian who was gathering a fair-sized group of followers. I'll use "He" as a convenience, as I did with the ruler, since we've all fallen into the habit. There are two sexes here, save for certain periods in the individual Ethlonian's life when he (or she) seems to switch functions and roles out of necessity, and in early youth when there's no distinction we can discern. At any rate, the rumours about this one were quite disturbing to the curers at first, because he wasn't a gradu-ate of their school or a member of any of their various levels of professional practice. As a matter of fact, he was supposedly effecting cures that . . . not even the top level's members could match.

At first nobody paid much attention to their complaints, partly because ordinary Ethlonians regard curers as a necessary evil, and partly because government officials and priests alike are jealous of their power and secrecy. Then, however, the rumors became somewhat more specific, and the government officials became uneasy too. He was apparently telling anyone who would listen that an Ethlonian's first allegiance was to his God, the same God that the priests of the main religion insist is the One and Only God. Naturally this sounded like sedition to the appointed major functionaries but, although there is that strong interweaving of Church and State I've spoken of, the priests obviously enjoyed a temporary period of minor, half-concealed triumph and vindication over their clearly-inferior peers.

Last, of course, the rumors became very specific indeed. He was claiming to be directly descended from their God, to have his considerable powers from that God, and to be the source of a revision of the faith. (Actually there was still confusion on this point, as some versions had it that he was restoring the original, uncorrupted faith. The result was the same, you may well imagine.) The priests were thrown into a frenzy by this threat to their power and/or basic teachings. As with the curers, they could find no record of such an individual having attended their school or being a member of even the most minor level of their profession. It was heresy, equivalent to sedition, and they wanted an end to it.

They were the ones, as they so often are, who managed to track him down in his wanderings, although he made nearly a complete but quite remote circle around the city without ever venturing close in. Once they had located him they sent member after member to mingle with the crowds and question him. But as each one returned and another priest from a higher level went out, frustration grew into near paranoia. Our young Ethlonian appeared to be what we would call a genius. He was either too clever or too simple for the best of them; his answers made them look like fools and the crowds loved him for it, even when he turned round and tore strips off them. He called them unbelievers, thrillseekers, weaklings trying to cheat their way into God's favor, and the reports say they grovelled and asked for forgiveness. Worst of all, the priests couldn't really pin him down on any genuine count of heresy. He knew their religious history backward and forward, and used it to show that he was fulfilling a mass of very pointed prophecies that had been considered comfortably far off in the future. Toward the end I can witness that the priests were terrified of him, particularly those at the very

217

top, wanting to get him out of the way, but deathly afraid of any personal confrontation which might show them up.

So far as we can determine, any form of murder is unheard of here. Even manslaughter seems to be prevented by some sort of physiological inhibitor that we would dearly love to isolate (prohibited by U.N. directive, obviously). In fact, only the ruler has had power to take a life until the coming of a Governor General, and while history here shows that it was rather the reverse several centuries ago, the last few rulers have been almost pathologically reluctant to pass such a sentence.

In one way it was really laughable, a few months ago, to see the priests at work on our present ruler. They wanted this young trouble-maker, wanted him badly, so that by any possible means they could get him out of the way. They went so far as to send some of their own apprentices (graduate students?) to haul him into the city, clearly on the assumption that they could force the ruler into placing him in a certain valley from which no one (including three idiots on a U.N. task force) has ever returned. The apprentices became his followers. A week ago it might have been even more laughable, if it were not so pitiful, to see their gibbering consternation when he gave them what they had wanted and came into the city himself.

The rest you may guess. His behavior here has been unforgivable. He has effected cures, undermined the government, and taught vast crowds a whole new way of looking at the old, sanctified beliefs. They began by worshipping him, and as I watched on several days from my second-floor office window I couldn't help feeling a creeping chill of apprehension. One didn't have to be an Ethlonian to look over those crowds and feel the same fierce tension that comes with all the old films of various Earth dictators and religious leaders at work. I could close my eyes and visualise a bloody revolt of the worst sort. Yet it didn't come. And the old-poor Ethlonians, the energetic young ones, passed from waiting for the right word, to drifting around at the edges, to leaving the square in front of the temple for a disillusioned return to the old life.

The priests, naturally, slowly but surely lost a bit of their fear. Then, last night, they seized their chance and dragged him bodily into the temple, all the way to their most sacred chamber. I can't know what happened there, but almost unbelievably they brought him out again, roused the ruler, and had an all-night session with himself and his highest appointed officials. Again it seems to have been a stand-off. Now, can you guess where they headed next? Fatuous question, isn't it? Yes they came to me—the alien, the proviso-charter-directive-dictum-bound Governor General with his half-ignorant staff of Earthlings. Maybe that's a dreadful indication of their opinion of us already. By the supreme powers

218

which they had foisted upon me, they required that I be the judge. That's what their word means, but what they really want me to be is their hatchetman. And I dare not refuse, for fear that my assessment of their earlier motives is correct.

I sat through it all feeling like a time-traveller, transported back over two thousand years into our own past. As if I were acting a long-rehearsed part I said that I still hadn't heard anything concrete in the way of accusation, that with my dim understanding of their whole system I couldn't find any little bylaw that he might have broken save, perhaps, practicing curing or preaching without their version of a licence. I played it out still further, since a decision must irrevocably be rendered by sunrise tomorrow; I asked to see and hear this incredible youth. You may think it was the opportunity which we all desire but cannot literally attain in this life. To me it was more a nightmare. His presence was like nothing I've ever experienced, but in itself unsurprising. He gave simple but evasive answers until I took the unthinkable upon myself and asked him: "Are you the direct offspring of your God?" And here he did momentarily surprise me. He said "No." For a wild instant I was released from the dreamlike atmosphere of it all. Then he continued quietly, but with a look that went through me, through everything, time and space and whatever else exists, and said, "I *am* God."

I was on my own. The script had suddenly departed from the old familiar plot, and I had no washbasin available, not that I could have gotten away with that anyway. I took a temporary refuge. "I must consider this carefully," I said to the group who, as one, had set up an unprecedented hideous braying and lashing of themselves. "Come back this evening," I said, and retired to my private quarters.

I've been sitting here for hours, considering. Oddly enough, the repercussions among our many opponents do not enter into it. The fact that I cannot have your advice troubles me, but no more than the fact that I, of all people, should have been forced into this position. No, there are questions running through my mind which are more profound than any of these things. Has it now occurred to you that our concept of mission may be misplaced? That arguing about converts may be totally irrelevant? That despite my historical perspective I should not be seeking for a non-existent way to avoid making the judgement? But most profound of all is the question—does it really matter at all what judgement I give? Will it really be mine at all? Ah yes, that's the ultimate question. Do I really have any choice at all?

Spider Robinson
NO RENEWAL

"He's a humanist, by damn," wrote Ben Bova, editor of Analog, *of Spider Robinson, one of the liveliest and most individual of contributors to contemporary North American science fiction. Robinson was born in New York in 1948 and educated at the State University of New York (Stonybrook). In 1973, he moved to Phinney's Cove, Nova Scotia. He now lives in Halifax with his wife Jeanne, a dancer and choreographer who comes from Massachusetts, with whom he has begun to collaborate in writing fiction. Robinson tied (with Lisa Tuttle) for the 1974 John W. Campbell Award for Best New Writer. He shared (with James Tiptree, Jr.) the 1977 Hugo Award for Best Novella, for "By Any Other Name," which is a portion of his later novel,* Telempath *(1977), about the hazards of a deadly virus. He also won, with Jeanne Robinson, the 1978 Nebula Award for Best Novella, for the first part of* Stardance *(1979), about a zero-gravity dance troupe. He is the author, as well, of* Callahan's Crosstime Saloon *(1977), a collection of stories introduced by Ben Nova. "No Renewal," a story about "a trick of Time and timing" and the consequences of winning, first appeared in* Galaxy Science Fiction, *March 1977. In answer to my query about his first name, the author explained: " 'Spider,' by the way, is a nickname that dates from college days and may have something to do with my slavish devotion to a folk-singer-songwriter-guitarist named 'Spider' John Koerner, whom no one else in the dorm could stand to listen to."*

Douglas Bent, Jr. sits in his kitchen, waiting for his tea to heat. It is May 12, his birthday, and he has prepared wintergreen tea. Douglas allows himself this extravagance because he knows he will receive no birthday present from anyone but himself. By a trick of Time and timing, he has outlived all his friends, all his relatives. The concept of neighborliness, too, has predeceased him; not because he has none, but because he has too many.

His may be, for all he knows, the last small farm in Nova Scotia, and it is bordered on three sides by vast mined-out clay pits, gaping concentric cavities whose insides were scraped out and eaten long ago, their husk thrown away to rot. On the remaining perimeter is an apartment-hive, packed with ant-like swarms of people. Douglas knows none of them as individuals; at times, he doubts the trick is possible.

Once Douglas's family owned hundreds of acres along what was then called simply The Shore Road; once the Bent spread ran from the Bay of Fundy itself back over the peak of the great North Mountain, included a sawmill, rushing streams, hundreds of thousands of trees, and acre after acre of pasture and hay and rich farmland; once the Bents were one of the best-known families from Annapolis Royal to Bridgetown, their livestock the envy of the entire Annapolis Valley.

Then the petrochemical industry died of thirst. With it, of course, went the plastics industry. Clay suddenly became an essential substitute— and the Annapolis Valley is mostly clay.

Now the Shore Road is the Fundy Trail, six lanes of high-speed traffic; the Bent spread is fourteen acres on the most inaccessible part of the Mountain; the sawmill has been replaced by the industrial park that ate the clay; the pasture and the streams and the farmland have been disemboweled or paved over; all the Bents save Douglas Jr. are dead or moved to the cities; and no one now living in the Valley has ever seen a live cow, pig, duck, goat or chicken, let alone envied them. Agribusiness has destroyed agriculture, and synthoprotein feeds (some of) the world. Douglas grows only what crops replenish themselves, feeds only himself.

He sits waiting for the water to boil, curses for the millionth time the solar-powered electric stove that supplanted the family's woodburner when firewood became impossible to obtain. Electric stoves take too long to heat, call for no tending, perform their task with impersonal callousness. They do not warm a room.

Douglas's gnarled fingers idly sort through the wintergreen he picked this morning, spurn the jar of sugar that stands nearby. All his life, Douglas has made wintergreen tea from fresh maple sap, which requires no sweetening. But this spring he journeyed with drill and hammer and tap and bucket to his only remaining maple tree, and found it dead. He has bought maple-flavored sugar for this birthday tea, but he knows it will not be the same. Then again, next spring he may find no wintergreen.

So *many* old familiar friends have failed to reappear in their season lately—the deer moss has gone wherever the hell the deer went to, crows no longer raid the compost heap, even the lupens have decreased in number and in brilliance. The soil, perhaps made self-conscious by its conspicuous isolation, no longer bursts with life.

Douglas realizes that his own sap no longer runs in the spring, that the walls of his house ring with no voice save his own. If a farm surrounded by wasteland cannot survive, how then shall a man? *It is my birthday*, he thinks, *how old am I today?*

He cannot remember.

He looks up at the goddamelectricclock (the family's two-hundred-year-old cuckoo clock, being wood, did not survive the Panic Winter of '94), reads the date from its face (there are no longer trees to spare for fripperies like paper calendars), sits back with a grunt. *2049, like I thought, but when was I born?*

So many things have changed in Douglas's lifetime, so many of Life's familiar immutable aspects gone forever. The Danielses to the east died childless: their land now holds a sewage treatment plant. On the west the creeping border of Annapolis Royal has eaten the land up, excreting concrete and steel and far too many people as it went. Annapolis is now as choked as New York City was in Douglas's father's day. Economic helplessness has driven Douglas back up the North Mountain, step by inexorable step, and the profits (he winces at the word) that he reaped from selling off his land parcel by parcel (as, in his youth, he bought it from his ancestors) have been eaten away by the rising cost of living. Here, on his last fourteen acres, in the two-story house he built with his own hands and by Jesus *wood*, Douglas Bent Jr. has made his last stand.

He questions his body as his father taught him to do, is told in reply that he has at least ten or twenty more years of life left. *How old am I?* he wonders again, *forty-five? Fifty? More?* He has simply lost track, for the years do not mean what they did. It matters little; though he may have vitality for twenty years more, he has money for no more than five. Less, if the new tax laws penalizing old age are pushed through in Halifax.

The water has begun to boil. Douglas places wintergreen and sugar in the earthenware mug his mother made (back when clay was dug out of the backyard with a shovel), removes the pot from the stove, and pours. His nostrils test the aroma; to his dismay, the fake smells genuine. Sighing from his belly, he moves to the rocking chair by the kitchen window, places the mug on the sill, and sits down to watch another sunset. From here Douglas can see the Bay, when the wind is right and the smoke from the industrial park does not come between. Even then, he can no longer see the far shores of New Brunswick, for the air is thicker than when Douglas was a child.

The goddamclock hums, the mug steams. The winds are from the north—a cold night is coming, and tomorrow may be one of the improbable "bay-steamer" days with which Nova Scotia salts its spring. It does not matter to Douglas: his solar heating is far too efficient. His gaze wanders down the access road which leads to the highway; it curves downhill and left and disappears behind the birch and alders and pine that line it for a half-mile from the house. If Douglas looks at the road right, he can sometimes convince himself that around the bend are not strip-mining shells and brick apartment-hives but arable land, waving grain and the world he once knew. Fields and yaller dogs and grazing goats and spring mud and tractors and barns and goat-berries like stock-piles of B-B shot. . . .

Douglas's mind wanders a lot these days. It has been a long time since he enjoyed thinking, and so he has lost the habit. It has been a long time since he had anyone with whom to share his thoughts, and so he has lost the inclination. It has been a long time since he understood the world well enough to think about it, and so he has lost the ability.

Douglas sits and rocks and sips his tea, spilling it down the front of his beard and failing to notice. *How old am I?* he thinks for the third time, and summons enough will to try and find out. Rising from the rocker with an effort, he walks on weary wiry legs to the living room, climbs the stairs to the attic, pausing halfway to rest.

My father was sixty-one he recalls as he sits, wheezing, on the stair *when he accepted euthanasia. Surely I am not that old. What keeps me alive?*

He has no answer.

When he reaches the attic, Douglas spends fifteen minutes in locating the ancient trunk in which Bent family records are kept. They are minutes well-spent: Douglas is cheered by many of the antiques he must shift to get at the trunk. Here is the potter's wheel his mother worked; there the head of the axe with which he once took off his right big toe; over in the corner a battered peavey from the long-gone sawmill days. They remind him of a childhood when life still made sense, and bring a smile to his grizzled features. It does not stay long.

Opening the trunk presents difficulties—it is locked, and Douglas cannot remember where he put the key. He has not seen it for many years, or the trunk for that matter. Finally he gives up, smashes the old lock with the peavey, and levers up the lid (the Bents have always learned leverage as they got old, working efficiently long after strength has gone). It opens with a shriek, hinges protesting their shattered sleep.

The past leaps out at him like the woes of the world from Pandora's Box. On top of the pile is a picture of Douglas's parents, Douglas Sr. and Sarah, smiling on their wedding day, Grandfather Lester behind them near an enormous barn, grazing cattle visible in the background.

Beneath the picture he finds a collection of receipts for paid grain-bills, remembers the days when food was cheap enough to feed animals, and there were animals to be fed. Digging deeper, he comes across canceled checks, insurance policies, tax records, a collection of report cards and letters wrapped in ribbon. Douglas pulls up short at the hand-made rosary he gave his mother for her fifteenth anniversary, and wonders if either of them still believed in God even then. Again, it is hard to remember.

At last he locates his birth-certificate. He stands, groaning with the ache in his calves and knees, and threads his way through the crowded attic to the west window, where the light from the setting sun is sufficient to read the fading document. He seats himself on the shell of a television that has not worked since he was a boy, holds the paper close to his face and squints.

"May 12, 1989," reads the date at the top.

Why, I'm fifty years old he tells himself in wonderment. *Fifty; I'll be damned.*

There is something about that number that rings a bell in Douglas's tired old mind, something he can't quite recall about what it means to be fifty years old. He squints at the birth-certificate again.

And there on the last line, he sees it, sees what he had almost forgotten, and realizes that he was wrong—he will be getting a birthday present today after all.

For the bottom line of his birth certificate says, simply and blessedly, " . . . expiry date: May 12, 2049."

Downstairs, for the first time in years, there is a knock at the door.

Stephen Scobie
THE PHILOSOPHER'S STONE

Magic and fantasy run like rivers through the stories and poems of Stephen Scobie, who was born at Carnoustie, Angus, Scotland, on New Year's Eve, 1943. He was educated at the University of British Columbia, and he has taught in the English department of the University of Alberta, in Edmonton, since 1965. He is the author of a number of books, including Stone Poems *(1974), and a critical study called* Leonard Cohen *(1978). Scobie's work is represented by "The Philosopher's Stone," a fantasy reprinted from* Grain: A Magazine of Stories and Poems, *June 1975. The story takes place in the distant future, in* A.D. *3516, when human mutability is an accepted fact. It is told in words chosen by a poet for their flash and free flow. Another of Scobie's unusual and lyrical stories, "The White Sky," may be read in* Fourteen Stories High *(1971), edited by David Helwig and Tom Marshall.*

The fact is I'm turning to gold, turning to gold.
It's a long process, they say,
it happens in stages.
This is to inform you that I've already turned to clay.

— Leonard Cohen

I

"Look," the old man said, and we would all huddle around, terrified. "Look at me, my skin, my skin."

Then each in turn would lean close as he opened his jacket, and we would peer in, into the darkness, to see the faintly glowing light below his heart. He would fondle us all, the boys and the girls, his old crinkly hands touching our smooth skins, but we didn't care. Once I reached out my hand and actually touched him, feeling the hard metallic lump under the skin, moving to the rhythm of his breathing.

"Turning to gold," he'd say. "Turning to gold!"

Then afterwards, Helga and I often walked far out into the desert, our bare feet hardened to the small sharp crystals which glinted a million colours in the gaze of the million stars. We would look at these stars and dream all our dreams, promise our promises.

225

"Some day we'll get married, you and I."

"Some day I'll fly between the stars."

"Some day we'll leave this planet forever."

"Some day we'll turn to gold."

When we got home, our parents would be angry. "Where were you? Where did you go? Did you go to the old man's house again? That dirty old saint? Did you let him touch you?"

Sometimes we lied, and said no, and they believed us; but then we lay awake all night with the moral pain, inside, knowing what we had done. Usually we said yes, and our father would beat us, very solemnly, very soundly—far beyond the pleasure and into the pain which was only pain. Yet even that we suffered gladly, feeling somehow that we were being true to our Destiny. Every 14-year-old knows that Destiny hurts.

Then later still, they took the old man away and put him in a hospital. He had entered the final phase of becoming a saint.

When he was dead, they allowed us to go and see him; in fact they commanded it. His body had been laid out on a white bed, and the surgeons had stripped away the last decaying layers of skin. Inside, what was left of his body was going ever more swiftly through the last stages of its transformation. When we saw him, we could still recognise the shape as that of a human body, even, with an effort, his body. The tough crinkled skin of the hands which had so often touched me was gone now, and his bony shape solidified into its dull yellow gleam. Even as we watched, the whole mass changed and solidified and cooled.

He had turned to gold.

Our parents had taken us to see what they called "this revolting spectacle" because they believed that we would react as they did: with terror, incomprehension, and disgust. They hoped that our obsession with the old saint would be ended by the sight of the "terminal stage" of his "disease."

We let them think they had succeeded, Helga and I, but secretly we still talked about it on our long walks out in the desert starlight. For many of the other children, it had indeed worked, and we learned not to mention it to them either. But for us, the two of us alone, it was still magic. That summer Helga and I became lovers; as we reached our first climax together I found myself whispering in her ear,

"Turning to gold! Turning to gold!"

The moons disappeared with the turning year; the giant stars of Andromeda swung into our sky. Winter gripped the cold desert in ice; passed; spring came.

The world changed; everything changed. They called it the Recolonization.

II

Eight immense starships appeared in orbit above our planet, one calm spring night when we had no thoughts of our history. The men who descended from the sky announced themselves as our ancestors, men of the mother planet Earth, come to claim her erring children once again. The history they told, briefly, was this:

Our planet, which they called Heyerdahl (after an old hero of Earth, the first man to cross oceans, so legend said, in an open raft), had been settled by Earth during the early days of its colonial expansion. But then had come a great economic recession, throughout the civilised galaxies, and Earth's empire had shrunk, leaving us behind for thousands of years. Now they came to reclaim this world, and welcome us all back to our birthright. We should be delighted.

In actual fact, it made very little difference. We are an easy-going people, and we accepted their presence and rule without objection. They fussed around, making a lot of laws which we neither understood nor heeded. They drove around in military vehicles, and persisted in wearing warlike uniforms even though there was no sign of resistance.

So one day I was most surprised when two large men came to our house and demanded that Helga and I should come with them to the office of the local Administrator. "You're in trouble," they told us. "Law-breakers. The Administrator will throw you in prison, or send you as slaves to alien worlds."

"Why?" we said. "We've done nothing wrong."

But they dragged us off anyway, and made us walk all the way, though it was several miles, and very hot.

The Administrator was a blonde youth, in his late 20s, with a fat, fleshy face and a flat nose. Large, grey-blue eyes stared at us with lascivious interest; then with a wave of his hand he dismissed the guards, and told them to keep Helga outside. "I will speak with the boy first," he said in a voice like crumpled silk.

"Now then," he addressed me. "Johan—is that your name?"

I nodded, still being friendly, more puzzled than afraid.

"Watch this." He pressed a knob on his desk, and the lights went out in the room. The far wall seemed to open into a view of the desert, but I quickly realised that it must be some kind of television screen, like they had at the hospital, even though it was three dimensional and far brighter than any I had ever seen there. Behind a rock a boy and a girl were making love. Suddenly I recognised the girl as Helga; but I did not recognise the boy. "Who is that?" I yelled, jumping at the screen. "I'll kill him!"

227

Abruptly, the screen died and the lights came on. The Administrator smiled at me. "You did not recognise the boy?" he said.

"No," I replied, indignantly.

Smirking, the Administrator picked up an elaborately framed mirror which he kept on his desk, and handed it to me. I looked at it and saw the same face. I was not accustomed to mirrors—we had none in our house—and the slowness with which I recognised myself must have amused the Administrator. He giggled.

"So the picture—the boy making love to Helga—that was me?"

"Yes," he said, his voice suddenly cold and serious.

"Well," I laughed, "that's all right, then, isn't it?"

"No." His voice was so cold that I shuddered, as if a cold wind from the desert had gusted into the room. He pressed his knob again, and this time there appeared on the wall a copy of one of the many "Proclamations" which had been issued since the Recolonization. I puzzled my way through it. It appeared that Helga and I had committed some crime called "incest."

I still did not understand. "This doesn't make sense," I laughed. "Why shouldn't I love my own sister?"

"Johan, when your colony was first planted here, it was small. It was sometimes necessary, for its survival, to do things . . . well, things that are not good. Evil things, Johan. Sin."

"But it was not evil," I protested. "You don't understand. When we do evil, it hurts. Inside you, there is pain. But with Helga is only pleasure."

"Certain taboos," the Administrator went on, "were erased from your colony, by psychological conditioning. Certain deep-seated instincts were eradicated, others—like your moral pain—implanted. I am not proud, Johan, of what my ancestors did. We are here to correct their follies. We are here to return you to righteousness."

"But it was a *good* feeling!" I insisted. "Like turning to gold, I tell you, turning to gold."

The Administrator turned sharply towards me, and his voice took on a new interest and urgency. "You!" he said. "Are you a Philosopher?"

"I do not know that name," I replied. "Those who turn to gold, we call them Saints."

"And you think it is a *good* feeling?"

"I think so. At least, Helga and I think so. Our parents disagree, they call it a disease, a loathsome disease. I hope to contract such a disease, some day."

The Administrator had got out of his chair and was walking back and forth across the room in an agitated manner. "Do you know any Saints now alive?" he demanded.

228

"No," I told him. "We knew one, but he died a year ago. You should have seen his body. It was beautiful."

"Boy," he said, stopping abruptly, "are you aware of the seriousness of your crime?"

"No." I said. "I do not consider it a crime."

The Administrator leered, and gave me what I now know to be a highly exaggerated account of the penalties prescribed for incest. He spoke of exile, forced labor, lashing, castration, tortures. I listened in shocked horror; now for the first time, I was afraid. "But," he concluded, "the law is also merciful. Boy, you have a chance to redeem yourself."

By then I was ready to beg him on my knees to tell me what it was.

"I will release you two degenerates, you and your whore of a sister, for two weeks. At the end of that time, you will return to me—and do not think to escape, you cannot hide on this planet—and bring with you a man, a Philosopher, in the early stages of the disease. I want no corpses. I want the earliest possible stage. If you accomplish that, you may go free. I will even grant a marriage license. But if you fail, then I will invoke the full rigour of the law. Go now."

I fled from him in terror.

Our parents were astonished and terrified: astonished at the idea of our having committed a crime (they were brother and sister themselves), and terrified not so much at the prospect of our punishment as at the nature of the task imposed on us to avoid it. I am not sure but that my father would have preferred me to suffer everything the Administrator had so luridly threatened, rather than allow me to go in search of Philosopher/ Saints. But my mother said,

"Send them first to the Librarian. See what he says."

My father snorted in distrust, but at length he agreed. "Be careful though," he warned. "That man has ancient books which speak heresy. His mind is tainted by them. Do not believe everything he says."

III

For Helga and me, it was like suddenly being given the key to a secret cupboard we had been forbidden even to think of all through our child-hood. We ran across the desert, hand in hand, in ecstasy.

"The Librarian!" she cried to me, her eyes sparkling. "The Librarian!"

And we stopped behind a rock to make love, out of sheer excitement, not even thinking that what we were doing was the very "sin" which threatened us so terribly.

The Library was a pure white dome set far out in the desert, sparkling above the white crystals of sand. It was immeasurably old, from (we now realised) the time of the first colonization. Few people went there now, and to children like us it had been absolutely forbidden. For years our parents had refused even to admit its existence. And once, when we had sneaked up close enough to touch its outside walls, we had been caught and taken home, and given the most terrible beating we ever received—even though we knew, from the absence of that inner pain, that it was not wrong. Enough of that old fear and awe remained to slow us down from a dance to a walk as we approached.

The door opened for us, before we had said anything, and we walked into the high, cool interior of the dome. The Librarian himself was waiting for us, and we discovered, rather unsettlingly, that he was an Alien. He (if it was a he) was basically of the Andromedan type, based on a low spherical construction, with retractable limbs and sensors. He communicated telepathically, so knew our errand in advance. For our benefit, he spoke through a small loudspeaker in his desk, which gave him a high, squeaky voice, which grated on our nerves.

"And what do you know," he demanded, "about the people you're looking for?"

"Very little," Helga admitted. "They have some kind of disease, but we don't know how they get it."

"Disease? Ha! That's the way your people deal with it now. You see them as diseased creatures to be feared and rejected. I tell you, children, it was not always so."

We stared at him, with so many questions to ask that we had no idea how to begin.

"Listen," he said, and rolled over to a wall covered with little buttons and flashing lights. ("It's a computer," Helga whispered to me, "like they used to have in the hospital.") He protruded a limb, pushed a few buttons, consulted some figures which flashed on a screen, and pushed some more buttons. Then, from a central loudspeaker, another mechanised voice blared out.

"Report No. 34712/a/61.

Subject Classification: Earth colony Heyerdahl.

Sub-classification: Cult of the Philosophers.

Reporter: Fen-Bi-Ramda, 21229.

Date: 26812 Andromeda; 3016 Earth.

"Note: The following report is a summary. For fuller details, consult Report No. 34712/b/61; for documentation and video material, consult Report No. 34712/c/61.

"It has been established (reference Report No. 1261/a/542; Subject Classification: Earth; Sub-classification: Alchemy) that some two thousand years ago on home-planet Earth there existed a substance known as 'The Philosopher's Stone,' which had the property of turning to gold all material brought into contact with it. The secret of this substance was apparently lost, perhaps during the Earth Reconstruction period. Indeed, some historians have doubted if it ever existed outside legend. However, we are now in a position to advance strong presumptive evidence of its existence, for it has been discovered on Earth colony Heyerdahl.

"The stone is mined, in small quantities, at various locations on Heyerdahl. Its effect is a metabolic interaction with living human flesh. A minute quantity, implanted in the flesh of a human subject, will in the course of about two years convert the complete mass of the subject's body into an equivalent mass of gold. The subject, of course, dies in the process.

"Around this phenomenon, a religious cult has grown up on Heyerdahl. Those who accept implantation are called Philosophers; when they die they are called Saints. They are regarded as holy men, and treated with much reverence and veneration. This is based partly on the Rejection Syndrome. The stone does not grow properly in all subjects; in some cases, usually about a month after implantation, the stone rejects its host body and, by some process which we do not as yet understand, tears itself out of the flesh. This frequently but not invariably results in the death of the subject. The cult holds that those thus rejected are impure, and morally unworthy of sainthood. Thus reverence for the Philosophers is largely based upon the fact that they have stood and passed the test of the stone itself.

"The cult is, naturally, fostered by the Earth authorities, who appropriate the gold it produces for their treasury. In return, all Philosophers are maintained by the state in great luxury, and their names inscribed in a Roll of Immortality. The average number of Philosophers over the past 10 years has been 37 per year.

"End summary report."

The Librarian played this tape for us two or three times. Then he rolled back over to us and said, "Well now, children? What do you say?"

I was still speechless, but Helga managed to ask, "Do you know if there are any Philosophers alive, now?"

"Alas, no," the Librarian replied. "That is a very old report; the cult has long since died out. 'Diseased,' you call them now. The man who died last year—there have been none since him."

"Then we cannot take one to the Administrator."

"That would seem to be true."

"But the stone!" I cried suddenly. "We could take him some of the stone! That would surely satisfy him!"

"Yes," said Helga, "but where can we possibly find it?"

231

The Librarian made a noise which I understood to be a laugh. "That is simple," he said. "I have some. In fact, I have a great deal."

"Then"—I turned towards him defiantly—"give some to us. Please."

"Johan," he replied, taking a half roll backwards, "I cannot."

"Please," I repeated. "To save our lives."

"Your lives are nothing to me," he replied. "You know who I am? I am Fen-Bi-Ramda. I made that report, five thousand years ago. How many mortals, Earthlings, mere dying animals, have I seen in all that time? What is your puny life to me?" He paused, and a note of craftiness entered even the distorted tones of his loudspeaker. "Yet there is a way, Johan, there is one way in which I can give you the stone."

"What is that?" I asked, with a sudden nervous anticipation of his answer.

"You must carry the stone away," he said, "in your own flesh. You must accept implantation, and be prepared to undergo the test of the stone. You must become a Philosopher."

IV

I knew at once, of course, what I was going to do. And I knew that it would have to be done right away; obviously, I could not consult my parents. I turned to my sister.

"Helga—" I began.

"Me too," she replied.

"What?"

"Me too. I want it too. You can implant us both, can't you?" she asked the Librarian.

"Most irregular," he replied. "A female. It's never been done before. I really don't think I can."

"It's both of us or neither," she said firmly. "Johan wouldn't want it without me, would you, Johan?"

"Helga, there's no need for us both to die. . . ."

"Johan!" She was profoundly hurt. "You think I'd want to live on, without you? Live alone, with you gone, not knowing what it was like? Turning to gold, Johan, turning to gold!"

I knew she was right, and I sensed also how eager the Librarian was to give implantation. Some compulsion drove him too. "She's right," I told him. "It's both of us or neither. I won't accept implantation unless she gets it too."

He rolled agitatedly from side to side. The word "irregular" still rumbled through his speaker.

"Now," I said sharply. "Right here and now, without delay."

We lay side by side on the one bed, naked like lovers. The Librarian was using four or five of his arms as he checked our local anaesthetics and made the small incisions just under our hearts. Then he took a small casket with a complicated combination lock, and opened it. The eyes on his visual sensors stared wide. Watching him, I understood his compulsion. He was like an addict in the presence of a drug he could not take. The stone had no effect on Andromedan physiology. The Librarian was forever cut off from its mysteries, and could act only as its servant, leading others to sainthood, never himself a saint.

He held the stones before us on forceps. They were small, oval pieces of dull gold-coloured metal, but even in the harsh fluorescent lights they had a perceptible glow.

"Do you accept the implantation of this holy stone?" he intoned.

"Yes," we replied.

"Do you submit yourselves to its test?"

"We do."

"Become then Philosophers. Become then Saints."

Even through the anaesthetic, there was a sharp pang of pain as the stone made contact with our flesh. Our hands gripped each other tightly till it passed. After the operation, he left us alone for a while. Making love, we pressed our wounds together.

We could not go home, we realised that. We were shut off from home forever. We stood outside the Library dome in the first chill of evening, while Stalker, the purple moon, rose in the glittering sky. We stood holding hands, feeling frightened and small, with the alien sensation of metal under our skins.

"Where shall we go?" asked Helga at last.

"To the Administrator, I suppose. Where else is there?"

We walked slowly across the desert.

At the Administrator's palace, a grand dinner was in progress, in honour of a visitor from Earth, a man of rank and great influence. He was, the guards told us as they ushered us in, a direct descendant of the hero Heyerdahl, for whom our planet was named; he bore the ancient name.

They were drinking a dark brown liquid when we entered: the Administrator's young fat face flushed with its effects, his guest much older, calmer, a handsome grey-haired man with a firm nose and piercing blue eyes. I could see that he regarded his host with indulgent contempt.

"Well then," leered the Administrator drunkenly, "here we have our incestuous pair, back so soon. Our fine young lovers, brother and sister. Ha!"

We said nothing. Beneath my cloak, I was fingering the hard lump in my flesh.

"I sent you to find Philosophers!" he shouted. "And you return so soon, and empty-handed? Is it so hard? Are you so eager for your punishment?"

I said, "My Lord, we bring you Philosophers."

"Where are they then?" He laughed, slurring his words. "I don't see them."

With one movement, Helga and I cast aside our cloaks. In the dim candle-light of the dining hall, our stones glowed clearly, unmistakably, through our skin.

Heyerdahl leant forward in sudden interest; the Administrator shrank back in his chair, amazed and afraid. A hush and then a whisper ran through all the guards, all the servants in the room.

"Cover these things up," whispered the Administrator hoarsely. "Cover them up!"

We were lodged, as the old custom demanded, in luxury; but nevertheless we were prisoners, isolated in one wing of the palace. We ate and slept and made love, day after day, for a week; we were thoroughly bored. We longed for the open spaces of the desert, for the sharp crystals under our feet and the glitter of stars overhead. There was nothing to do but strain to feel the slight movement of the stones inside us. Helga said it tickled, and would often roll on the bed, helpless with laughter, till I was afraid she would choke to death. I did not feel it that way: instead, there were intermittent stabs of pain, as if a needle was being worked through the flesh.

On the fourth day, we heard the noise of a large, angry crowd outside; but the guards would tell us nothing about it. One guard did, however, tell me about the gambling.

"All over the planet," he told me. "It's fantastic. Nobody ever remembers Philosophers so young, you see, and there's never been a recorded case of a female taking it. So the odds are pretty high on your rejection."

"You mean by the stone?"

"Right. Let me see, now—this morning, if I remember rightly, it was about even odds that the girl would reject, about two to one against you rejecting, and five to one against both of you rejecting. I've got my money in your favour, sir," he added confidentially. "Wouldn't want to see it happen to a nice lad like you."

At the end of the week, we were summoned to see the Administrator, in the office where I had first met him. He sat behind his desk looking thoroughly angry, depressed, and frustrated. Heyerdahl stood behind him, with the same calm, confident expression as before—and perhaps a touch of smug pleasure?

"Trouble," said the Administrator. "I've had nothing but trouble from you two. I should never have interfered in the first place." Again he pressed the knob on his desk, and again the screen lit up: this time, with a view of the Library dome in the desert. A vast angry crowd was surging around it, trying to break in. At the head of them we recognised our parents, their faces contorted with rage and anguish. Helga pressed against me as we watched.

The crowd broke into the building; flames appeared. Too late, a patrol of Earth soldiers arrived and began breaking up the crowd with blasts from their guns. The whole Library building was on fire now, and crumbling inwards. Our parents had been among the first to rush in; they did not come out.

The screen died, and the lights clicked on again. The Administrator was pale and shaking.

"Priceless," Heyerdahl commented, in a calm easy tone, directed against his host. "Priceless, the things which were destroyed there. A complete Library, intact, from the first colonization. There are only two others known to survive. That for a start. Then the Librarian himself, Fen-Bi-Ramda. By these children's account, he was over five thousand years old. The average life-span of an Andromedan is between two and three thousand years: what caused his longevity? Was it the stone? Now we shall never know. And the stones themselves: how are they to be found, in that fused heap of rubble? All this destroyed, by a rabble of ignorant peasants. Under your Administration. Because of your policies. Because of your inefficiency." He paused; the Administrator had sunk his head onto his desk. Heyerdahl said smoothly, "I shall of course endeavour, for friendship's sake, to minimise your responsibility when I make my report. I will do what I can." The tone was murderous. The Administrator began to cry.

Heyerdahl ignored him, and turned to us. "You see the situation," he said. "Your parents reacted, I think, understandably. And the Librarian was, strictly speaking, in contravention of the law, implanting minors. But now he is dead, and, I'm sorry to say, so are your parents. You are alone in the universe. Please accept my sympathy."

I hated him, but we said nothing. We were still prisoners, and he now held the power.

"With the complete loss of the stones," Heyerdahl went on, "you two are now our only source of knowledge about this whole phenomenon. You are far too important to be left in a colonial backworld like this, where the level of administration"—with a withering glance at the huddled figure behind the desk—"is obviously not too high. I leave tomorrow for Earth. You will accompany me."

"For Earth?" gasped Helga.

"Yes. For home-planet Earth."

We gazed at each other in delight. Then I thought of something, turned to Heyerdahl, and said, "We have one request, sir."

"Yes?"

"Before we leave our own planet, we would . . . we would like to be married."

Heyerdahl raised an eyebrow. "Brother and sister?"

"It was promised to us, sir."

He shrugged his shoulders, and then poked the Administrator into an upright position. "Stop snivelling, you fool. You have a job to do here."

And so it was that all our vows were fulfilled:

"Some day we'll get married, you and I."

"Some day I'll fly between the stars."

"Some day we'll leave this planet forever."

"Some day we'll turn to gold."

V

The space flight started out dull. I suppose we'd always thought of actually *seeing* the stars we flew among, in all their combinations and colours. But in the hyper-space-drive necessary for intergalactic flight, there is in effect nothing to see; and Heyerdahl's ship, though fitted with every manner of luxury, had no windows. Inside a day we were bored. But that didn't last.

For on the second day, my rejection began.

It came suddenly, violently: a pang of unbearable pain as the stone inside me lurched into activity, and tore at the roots it had formed in my flesh. After the first violent motion, it settled down to a rhythmic palpitation, building up energy, as it were, and pushing a fraction further with each beat.

My yell of pain brought not only Helga but Heyerdahl running; there was no way I could disguise what was happening. In the first moment, I could see the horror in Helga's eyes, and the interior pain was on me too. I knew that I had been found unworthy, that the stone had rejected me. The pain was so great that when I looked at Helga I could only pray that she would not have to go through the same things—even though that meant (I realised this already) the even greater pain of watching her isolation, turning to gold, alone.

Heyerdahl summoned the ship's doctor, but I refused to let him near me. There could be no interference with the stone. The pain was all mine, and I claimed it. At least my physical suffering might distract my attention from the mental torment inside me.

Why? I asked myself, why? What reason? In what respect was I unworthy? What thought, or deed, or emotion, what tiny unknown event of my life, had excluded me from sainthood? I did not know. It was only my shame, my lifelong shame.

But I did not die; I could not even do that. I survived the stone's rejection. It took three hours, tugging loose from its roots in that steadily increasing movement. I lay and screamed in my agony. Heyerdahl left; Helga of course stayed. She was beside me all the time, thinking, What if I also should have to suffer this? The doctor kept his distance, but he was watching with fascination the movement, now clearly visible, of the alien stone beneath my skin.

The end came swiftly and mercifully, and with as little warning as the start. The stone tore out of my flesh in one culminating rush, tearing through flesh and like a bullet fired from inside my body. I fainted clean away; the stone flopped out onto the floor. Helga told me later that the doctor very carefully lifted the stone with his forceps, and locked it in a small lead box, before attending to me.

For three days I passed through stages of fever and unconsciousness. Dreams and nightmares haunted me, nor could I tell when I was fully awake. The face of that first old saint we had known dominated these dreams; and he merged with my mother and father, dying in fire in the Library. Time and again I relived the operation, saw Helga and myself stretched side by side like lovers. In my dream I would grasp for her hand; in reality, it would always be there.

At last I began to recover, and as consciousness returned, it focussed on two things. One was the huge, livid scar on my body; the other was Helga, isolated, cut off from me now forever, alone with the gold stone still inside her, working its change.

A week later, we landed on Earth, the old home planet of our race. That fact made little difference to us, mainly because of our preoccupation with our respective conditions; but also because we saw so little of it. We spent most of our time in hospitals, or in our private rooms, or occasionally at large banquets where Heyerdahl showed us off to his guests. We never saw the world outside walls; I began to doubt that it existed. Perhaps the entire surface of the planet had been built over. I asked Heyerdahl once, and he shrugged, confessing a polite disinterest. Maybe there was a natural world somewhere; but he had never seen it; why should he? It was easier to travel to one of the park-worlds in another star-system than it would be to travel to, say, "Africa."

Somewhat to my surprise, I found that I was still, despite my rejection, of as much medical interest as Helga—maybe even, at this stage, more. I submitted patiently to endless series of tests, as the doctors tried to discover a physiological cause for my rejection. I did not believe they would find one: I knew that the cause was ultimately moral, that in some undefined way Helga was purer than I.

At first we continued to live together, as before. But gradually the division between us set in. I could not lie beside her without feeling the slowly enlarging shape of the stone; and we both felt all the implications of that. She passed the period of possible rejection: it would not happen to her. My scar had settled into a brilliant and curiously symmetrical star; it seemed to glow slightly in darkness, as if the flesh still retained a memory of the stone's phosphorescence. We lay, night after night, beside each other in silent misery. I began to notice other things too: lapses in her memory, occasional vacancies in her consciousness, fits of distraction, hours of seemingly total self-absorption, when I might as well not have been in the room. The stone was taking over her mind as well.

One night I came into her room, and she looked up at me and said, "Who are you?" It was not a polite question; it was a sharp, hostile challenge.

"Helga!" I cried.

"Go away, whoever you are. Don't disturb me." She turned her head away, and sank back into a kind of trance.

Two hours later, she came into my room, and sat down on the end of my bed. "Earlier this evening," she said, in a taut, edgy voice, "someone came into my room. Was it you?"

"Yes, Helga," I said, softly, kindly.

She burst into tears and flung herself against me; I held her until she was ready to speak again. "Johan," she said at last, "it's going to get worse. It'll happen more often."

"What will, Helga?"

"Things like this evening—my absences. Traces. The times I see things."

"What do you see, Helga?" I asked sadly.

"Things, Johan. Golden things. . . ." She sighed. "Don't you see? I can't explain it to you. It's more than seeing, it's all my senses, and more. It's the stone, that's what I see. It's the thing I'm turning into. And I can't describe it, Johan. Even if I could, even if I had the words—I couldn't explain it to *you*."

"Because . . . ?"

"Yes, because of that. Because you're rejected, Johan, you're not one of us. It's like the moral pain, it's inside me. Blame the stone, if you must. The stone won't let me. The stone is shutting you out. Soon it won't let me talk to you at all, about anything." She closed her eyes, and seemed to make a great effort. Fighting against pain, she cried, "Johan, I see it all golden!"

That night we made love, and it was, we knew, for the last time. It was our goodbye.

Their doctors and scientists could find no explanations. As the weeks went by, we all settled down to watching. Helga recognised no-one now; she merely sat for hours, preferably in darkness, nursing the stone like a child. I could not bear it any longer; I asked Heyerdahl to send me away, to send me home, to give me work, anything. Impatiently, and with little interest, he delegated me to take a message to a nobleman on the planet Mars, in the same system as Earth. I performed the task, but it did nothing to ease my mind. It was an arid, dry planet: deserts blowing with soft red dust that rose in clouds to shut out the sun. I longed for the hard bright crystals of my own desert world.

Heyerdahl met me in person when I returned. "Come quickly," he said. "She has entered the last phase."

"Already? It's scarcely a year!"

"Apparently it is quicker with her—because of her youth? her sex? Who knows? But it has certainly started."

"I don't want to see it," I told him. "Call me when it's over. I'll come then."

But alone in my room, through my tears, I saw it anyway: her final metamorphosis. The softness of her flesh becoming hard, metallic; the pale, beautiful colours of her skin brightening into gold, gold, gold. . . .

When I finally saw it, it was a relief. Nothing of her human shape remained. It was only a lump of metal.

And in my sudden stirring of revulsion away from it, I understood why I was not worthy. . . .

VI

An epilogue in the third person.

"Look," the old man said, and they would all huddle around, terrified. "Look at me, my skin, my skin."

Then each in turn would lean close as he opened his jacket, and they would peer in, into the darkness, to see the faintly glowing light below his heart. He would fondle them all, the boys and the girls, his old crinkly hands touching their smooth skins, but they wouldn't care. Sometimes, one of them would reach out a hand and actually touch him, feeling the hard star-shaped ridge of his scar, moving to the rhythm of his breathing.

"Turning to gold," he'd say. "Turning to gold!"

But then they would all laugh, and run away. They knew it was only an empty scar. They knew he was only turning to clay.

Charles Dawson Shanly
THE WALKER OF THE SNOW

*No poetic work evokes more effectively the terror of the woods than
"The Walker of the Snow," which was written by Charles Dawson
Shanly (1811-1875), and published posthumously in* Songs of the Great
Dominion *(1889), an important anthology edited by W. D. Lighthall.
Shanly, who was born in Dublin, Ireland, and raised in Middlesex County,
Upper Canada, worked as an editor in New York and died in Arlington,
Florida, far from the northern terror he evoked in this piece of verse.
The version published here is based on Shanly's own proof copy, pre-
served in the Baldwin Room of the Metropolitan Toronto Library. "The
Walker of the Snow" so moved W. Blair Bruce, a Hamilton-born painter,
that it inspired him to paint "The Phantom Hunter," a dramatic canvas
now hanging in the Hamilton Art Gallery. Shanly may well have had in
mind when he wrote his verse the unspeakable horror of the Wendigo.*

Speed on, Speed on, good Master!
  The camp lies far away;
We must cross the haunted valley
  Before the close of day.

How the snow-blight came upon me
  I will tell you as we go,
The blight of the Shadow hunter
  Who walks the midnight snow.

To the cold December heaven
  Came the pale moon and the stars
As the yellow sun was sinking
  Behind the purple bars.

The snow was deeply drifted
  Upon the ridges drear
That lay for miles between me
  And the camp for which we steer.

'Twas silent on the hill-side
　And by the sombre wood
No sound of life or motion
　To break the solitude.

Save the wailing of the moose-bird
　With a plaintive note and low,
And the skating of the red leaf
　Upon the frozen snow.

And I said, "Though dark is falling,
　And far the camp must be,
Yet my heart it would be lightsome
　If I had but company."

And then I sang and shouted,
　Keeping measure as I sped,
To the harp-twang of the snow shoe
　As it sprang beneath my tread.

Nor far into the valley
　Had I dipped upon my way,
When a dusky figure joined me,
　In a capuchon of gray.

Bending upon the snow-shoes
　With a long and limber stride;
And I hailed the dusky stranger,
　As we travelled side by side.

But no token of communion
　Gave he by word or look,
And the fear-chill fell upon me
　At the crossing of the brook.

For I saw by the sickly moonlight,
　As I followed, bending low,
That the walking of the stranger
　Left no foot-marks on the snow.

Then the fear-chill gathered o'er me
    Like a shroud around me cast,
And I sank upon the snow-drift
    Where the Shadow hunter passed.

And the Otter-trappers found me,
    Before the break of day.
With my dark hair blanched and whitened
    As the snow in which I lay.

But they spoke not, as they raised me,
    For they knew that in the night
I had seen the Shadow hunter,
    And had withered in his blight.

Sancta Maria speed us!
    The sun is falling low,
Before us lies the valley
    Of the Walker of the Snow!

Archibald Lampman
THE CITY OF
THE END OF THINGS

"Unforgettable" is Northrop Frye's reaction to this long poem by Archibald Lampman (1861-1899), whose poems traditionally celebrate the beauties of nature. But "The City of the End of Things" is another matter, for it presents the reader with a nightmarish vision of lifeless industrialism. The poem could have appeared in the pages of Weird Tales; *instead it was first published in the pages of* The Atlantic Monthly, *March 1894, and then in Lampman's collection* Alcyone *(1899), only twelve copies of which are known to exist. "The City of the End of*

Things" presents a vision in stark contrast with Bliss Carman's idyllic "Shamballah," also included in this anthology. The text of the poem is taken from The City of the End of Things *(1972) edited by Michael Gnarowski.*

Beside the pounding cataracts
Of midnight streams unknown to us
'Tis builded in the leafless tracts
And valleys huge of Tartarus.
Lurid and lofty and vast it seems;
It hath no rounded name that rings,
But I have heard it called in dreams
The City of the End of Things.

Its roofs and iron towers have grown
None knoweth how high within the night,
But in its murky streets far down
A flaming terrible and bright
Shakes all the stalking shadows there,
Across the walls, across the floors,
And shifts upon the upper air
From out a thousand furnace doors;
And all the while an awful sound
Keeps roaring on continually,
And crashes in the ceaseless round
Of a gigantic harmony.
Through its grim depths re-echoing
And all its weary height of walls,
With measured roar and iron ring,
The inhuman music lifts and falls.
Where no thing rests and no man is,
And only fire and night hold sway;
The beat, the thunder and the hiss
Cease not. and change not, night nor day.
And moving at unheard commands,
The abysses and vast fires between,
Flit figures that with clanking hands
Obey a hideous routine;
They are not flesh, they are not bone,

245

They see not with the human eye,
And from their iron lips is blown
A dreadful and monotonous cry;
And whoso of our mortal race
Should find that city unaware,
Lean Death would smite him face to face,
And blanch him with its venomed air:
Or caught by the terrific spell,
Each thread of memory snapt and cut,
His soul would shrivel and its shell
Go rattling like an empty nut.

It was not always so, but once,
In days that no man thinks upon,
Fair voices echoed from its stones,
The light above it leaped and shone:
Once there were multitudes of men,
That built that city in their pride,
Until its might was made, and then
They withered age by age and died.
But now of that prodigious race,
Three only in an iron tower,
Set like carved idols face to face,
Remain the masters of its power;
And at the city gate a fourth,
Gigantic and with dreadful eyes,
Sits looking toward the lightless north,
Beyond the reach of memories;
Fast rooted to the lurid floor,
A bulk that never moves a jot,
In his pale body dwells no more,
Or mind, or soul — an idiot!

But sometime in the end those three
Shall perish and their hands be still,
And with the master's touch shall flee
Their incommunicable skill.
A stillness absolute as death
Along the slacking wheels shall lie,
And, flagging at a single breath,

The fires shall moulder out and die.
The roar shall vanish at its height,
And over that tremendous town
The silence of eternal night
Shall gather close and settle down.
All its grim grandeur, tower and hall,
Shall be abandoned utterly,
And into rust and dust shall fall
From century to century;
Nor ever living thing shall grow,
Or trunk of tree, or blade of grass;
No drop shall fall, no wind shall blow,
Nor sound of any foot shall pass:
Alone of its accursèd state,
One thing the hand of Time shall spare,
For the grim Idiot at the gate
Is deathless and eternal there.

Wilfred Campbell
THE WERE-WOLVES

"Gloomy, weird, and mystical" are words used by W. J. Sykes to describe the aspects of life that Wilfred Campbell (1858-1919) wrote about
in The Dread Voyage and Other Poems (1893), an early collection of
lyric poems that includes "The Were-Wolves." As Sykes explained in
The Poetical Works of Wilfred Campbell, which he edited in 1922,
"Campbell's mind (and verse, at times) showed a bent towards speculation, derived partly, perhaps, from his early training in philosophy and
theology." Campbell is best-known for poems, like "Indian Summer"
and "How One Winter Came in the Lake Region," which celebrate the
seasons, nature, and especially Ontario's Bruce Peninsula. No one has
suggested a source for the inspiration behind "The Were-Wolves" in
which spectral wolves perpetually circle the North Pole.

247

They hasten, still they hasten,
  From the even to the dawn;
And their tired eyes gleam and glisten
  Under northern skies white and wan.
Each panter in the darkness
  Is a demon-haunted soul,
The shadowy phantom were-wolves,
  Who circle round the Pole.

Their tongues are crimson flaming,
  Their haunted blue eyes gleam,
And they strain them to the utmost
  O'er frozen lake and stream;
Their cry one note of agony,
  That is neither yelp nor bark,
These panters of the northern waste,
  Who hound them to the dark.

You may hear their hurried breathing,
  You may see their fleeting forms,
At the pallid polar midnight,
  When the north is gathering storms;
When the arctic frosts are flaming,
  And the ice-field thunders roll;
These demon-haunted were-wolves,
  Who circle round the Pole.

They hasten, still they hasten,
  Across the northern night,
Filled with a frightened madness,
  A horror of the light;
Forever and forever,
  Like the leaves before the wind,
They leave the wan, white gleaming
  Of the dawning far behind.

Their only peace is darkness,
  Their rest to hasten on
Into the heart of midnight,

Forever from the dawn.
Across far phantom ice-floes
  The eye of night may mark
These horror-haunted were-wolves
  Who hound them to the dark.

All through this hideous journey
  They are the souls of men
Who in the far dark-ages
  Made Europe one black fen.
They fled from courts and convents,
  And bound their mortal dust
With demon, wolfish girdles
  Of human hate and lust.

These, who could have been godlike
  Chose, each a loathsome beast,
Amid the heart's foul graveyards,
  On putrid thoughts to feast;
But the great God who made them
  Gave each a human soul,
And so 'mid night forever
  They circle round the Pole.

A-praying for the blackness,
  A-longing for the night,
For each is doomed forever
  By a horror of the light;
And far in the heart of midnight,
  Where their shadowy flight is hurled,
They feel with pain the dawning
  That creeps in round the world.

Under the northern midnight,
  The white, glint ice upon,
They hasten, still they hasten,
  With their horror of the dawn;
Forever and forever,
  Into the night away

They hasten, still they hasten
Unto the judgment day.

Bliss Carman
SHAMBALLAH

In Theosophical and Eastern literature, one will find repeated references to "the Brotherhood of Shamballah, beyond, far beyond, the snowy-capped Himalayas" (in the words of the occult writer H. P. Blavatsky), a remote region where the spiritual dynamos of the planet continue to turn. This Shangri-la of the spirit has been envisioned by Bliss Carman (1861-1929), the prolific poet who wrote dozens of collections of rhyming and melodious poetry. These were inspired by the all-embracing cosmic philosophy of such Transcendentalists as Ralph Waldo Emerson and the theories of symbolism popularized by François Delsarte. "Shamballah" was written in 1922 and first collected in Far Horizons *(1925). It is reprinted from* Bliss Carman's Poems *(1931). Its vision is in complete contrast to Archibald Lampman's "The City of the End of Things," also included in this anthology.*

Have you heard of the city Shamballah,
That marvellous place in the North,
The home of the Masters of Wisdom,
Whence the Sons of the Word are sent forth?
In moments of vision we see it,
For a moment we understand,
That it passes from sense, unsubstantial
As the shadows of gulls o'er the sand.

What Architect builded Shamballah
As frail as the wondrous new moon?

Its walls with the rose tint of morning
From no earthly quarry were hewn.
Before Him no Builder took counsel
To fashion from dust of the ground,
In beauty and order and rhythm,
A palace of colour and sound.

It arose with the arches of heaven
When the planets were swung in a chime,
And those who look forth from its windows
Have watched the procession of time.
By the great Northern light and the silence
Its inviolate portals are barred.
On cold winter nights you can see them
As they countermarch changing guard.

Have you dreamed of the mystic Shamballah,
The City under the Star
Where the Sons of the Fire-Mist gather
And the keys of all mystery are?
When the white moon rises in splendour,
Have you said, as it lifts and gleams,
"They have lighted the Silver Lantern
In the gate of the City of Dreams."

Have you read of the fabled Shamballah
In symbols or letters of gold,
Whence issued the Bringers of Knowledge
For the saving of peoples untold?
They builded no temple save beauty,
Save truth they established no creed,
Great love was their power and purpose,
As a flower in the heart of a seed.

They heard the first flute-note in Egypt
Uplifted in longing and prayer.
When sunrise stole over the desert
To break upon Thebes, they were there.

In Babylon, Lhassa, and Sarnath
Through Galilee, Athens and Tyre
To thresholds unnamed and unnumbered
They carried the Message of Fire.

They kindled the flame unconsuming
In souls that were quick to receive,
They told of a truth that should follow
Had love but the will to believe.
From Patmos, Chaldea, and Cumae
Their servants were chosen anew,
To speak as the Logos commanded,
That the Dream of the Good might come true.

The light-bearing sons of Shamballah,
They spread the ineffable word.
And spirits who mocked it were broken,
And blessed were the spirits that heard.
The birds knew the joy of their gospel
The windflower sprang where they trod,
And the ages were quickened to worship
Jehovah or Allah or God.

Have you heard of the speech of Shamballah,
The language that all men know
In township, pueblo, or palace,
Wherever men rest or go?
It is clear in the tones of friendship,
It is murmured in wind and rain,
It is writ in the painted desert,
And the shifting snow on the plain.

It blooms in the high Sierras,
It springs from the dust of the trail,
It flowers in golden silence
When all other speeches fail.
There is never a hint of kindness
There is never an accent of love,

But the firmament thrills to its whisper
And the heavens are glad thereof.

Forth from that Magian City
What teachers and avatars came,
To walk through our streets in pity—
If so they might heal our shame!
From Krishna, Gautama, and Jesus
To Swedenborg, Blake, and Delsarte,
They brought us the message of brothers,
They laboured and died apart.

Untold are the sons of Shamballah,
Who must carry the word without rest,
And pass with the joy of their presence,
Like shadows of angels unguessed.
They carry no mark of their order,
No talisman men must obey.
The street of the heart is their highroad,
Their mission to lighten the way.

They came with the music of Orpheus,
With the hymns of Isaiah and Job,
With the staff and bowl of the beggar
Or the glory of Solomon's robe.
Their task from Plotinus to Browning
Was ever and never the same,—
To replenish the altars of wisdom
And guard the impalpable flame.

In this mortal fabric incarnate
What radiant souls have had birth!
The visions they cherished and quickened
Were not begotten of earth.
In music or language or colour,
However their rapture was caught,
Divine were the instincts they followed,
Divine was the service they wrought.

The sweep of Beethoven and Handel
In majestical triumph or dirge,
The glories of Raphael's genius,
The splendour of Angel's urge,
The soaring Te Deums of Gothic
Arrested in eloquent stone,—
What are these but the soul of the Ages
Immortal through colour and tone!

Pure wine of the spirit they gave us,—
A gladness to make us whole,—
But we trusted to cunning to save us,
And cunning has cheated our soul.
The brand of the beast is upon us
In wantonness, folly and greed.
We have trampled the torch that should light us,
And our darkness is ours indeed.

The Nations are gathered to counsel,
In jealousy, envy, and fear,
Forgetting the Judgment of Karma
And the Judgment of Karma is here.
O'er Rome, over London and Paris
The morrows of destiny wait.
Yet who now seeks word from Shamballah?
Who knocks at the Ivory Gate?

James Reaney
THREE POEMS

"I remember as a child feeling that the Promised Land of our Bible at home lay just on the other side of a hogsback hill to the south of our farm," wrote James Reaney, explaining the imaginative possibilities of the farm, near Stratford, Ontario, where he was born in 1926. Many of his early poems, published in The Red Heart *(1949), capture the vivid, surreal, fantastic comic-strip-like world of childhood. Reaney, who went on to write highly literary poems like* A Suite of Nettles *(1958), and vivid dramas like the Donnelly Trilogy (1975), completed the three poems here at the age of twenty-one. "Antichrist as a Child," "Tarzan jad guru," and "The Katzenjammer Kids" are reprinted from* Poems *(1972), edited by Germain Warkentin. Reaney explains in a note accompanying "Tarzan jad guru" that the words "jad guru" mean "Terrible" in the language invented by Edgar Rice Burrough for his Tarzan books, and the Ape-Man's real name is Lord Greystoke.*

Antichrist as a Child

When Antichrist was a child
He caught himself tracing
The capital letter A
On a window sill
And wondered why
Because his name contained no A.
And as he crookedly stood
In his mother's flower-garden
He wondered why she looked so sadly
Out of an upstairs window at him.
He wondered why his father stared so
Whenever he saw his little son
Walking in his soot-coloured suit.
He wondered why the flowers
And even the ugliest weeds
Avoided his fingers and his touch.

And when his shoes began to hurt
Because his feet were becoming hooves
He did not let on to anyone
For fear they would shoot him for a monster.
He wondered why he more and more
Dreamed of eclipses of the sun,
Of sunsets, ruined towns and zeppelins
And especially inverted, upside down churches.

Tarzan jad guru

Young muscular Edwardian
    Swings through trees,
    Stops carnage at Karnak,
    Whole trains at Windhoek,
    Dances waltzes simianese.

Lord Greystoke jad guru.

A dumb yellow drum
    Hangs down from the night.
    For the rite of the Dum Dum
    Come the cousin apes.
    He who could wear Bond Street
    And opera capes
    Prefers loin cloths of
    Impeccable cut.

Lady Jane Greystoke jad guru.

Mazumba waves his spear!

    Oh the white beach and the green palms!
    Stygian night between the ears!
    Oh Prince of slaughter do not bungle
    My juglar vein within the jungle,
    And springboks flee across the plains
    From apes with silver headed canes.

Edward VII jad guru!

The Katzenjammer Kids

With porcupine locks
And faces which, when
More closely examined,
Are composed of measle-pink specks,
These two dwarf imps,
The Katzenjammer Kids,
Flitter through their Desert Island world.
Sometimes they get so out of hand
That a blue Captain
With stiff whiskers of black wicker
And an orange Inspector
With a black telescope
Pursue them to spank them
All through that land
Where cannibals cut out of brown paper
In cardboard jungles feast and caper,
Where the sea's sharp waves continually
Waver against the shore faithfully
And the yellow sun above is thin and flat
With a collar of black spikes and spines
To tell the innocent childish heart that
It shines
And warms (see where she stands and stammers)
The dear fat mother of the Katzenjammers.
Oh, for years and years she has stood
At the window and kept fairly good
Guard over the fat pies that she bakes
For her two children, those dancing heartaches.
Oh, the blue skies of that funny paper weather!
The distant birds like two eyebrows close together!
And the rustling paper road
Of the waves
Against the paper sands of the paper shore!

George Bowering
WINDIGO

George Bowering, who wrote this poem, was born in 1935, in the Okanagan Valley of British Columbia, and now teaches English at Simon Fraser University in that province. The word "Windigo" (or "Wendigo") is of Algonkian origin, and the Ojibwa and other Indian groups employ it to describe an "evil spirit" or "cannibal." In this poem Bowering recreates the thrill and terror of the creature's appearance, and retells some of the lore of this being who haunts the Canadian woods. "Windigo" first appeared in The Tamarack Review, *Autumn 1965, and is reprinted from* Touch: Selected Poems 1960-1970 *(1971). (For another view of this presence, see Algernon Blackwood's celebrated tale "The Wendigo," also included in this anthology.)*

Windigo
is twenty-five feet tall,
a long shadow
on the ice

& ice in him,
his heart,
made of hard ice.

He lives in the forest
of thin dark trees, north
where the sun
reaches on a slant,
casting long shadows,

          the sun is too far
          to reach that heart
          of ice,
          to melt it.

Windigo will eat a man
who loses himself
in the forest, he will
eat him without

killing the game,
ingest the scream
with the blood
that enters his own veins.

*

When Windigo meets Windigo,
male or female,
they do not mate,
they move closer,
their shadows cross,
& one dies,
body crashing with
crashing trees.

Then Windigo eats Windigo,
except the heart of ice,
which is crackt &
melted, water running
beneath the snow.

Arctic war
the elements
in deep ice
human form,
make arctic war,
simple, loud killing
& the bodies
consumed.

*

Windigo wears no clothes,
he is impervious to cold air,
he rubs resin from narrow pines,
& rolls in sand,
then stands, a rough statue
against the low sun,
long shadow on the ice.

Sometimes seen by dying birds
close to his mouth, a huge hole
in his face, without lips,
a ring of jagged teeth,
broken down quartz, a deep
hole of stinking warm air
that hisses out,
                    heard a mile away.

His huge round eyes
bulge out of his head, lidless eyes
rolling in red blood of pain,
always rolling, blood sockets
behind them.

            His feet, a yard long,
leave holes in the earth,
pointed heels & one bulbous
hairy toe, & his hands
are claws, brown & hairy,
ripping trees out of the ground
shaking earth from their roots.

His voice is thunder voice,
it rolls under clouds
of northern ominous weather,
& he howls in the night
& his howl melts the legs
of the man who runs before him.
                    & his teeth
                    gnash together
                    jaggedly, an
                    avalanche, it is
                    terror.

    *

He walks across the tundra,
tearing up trees in his way,

shaking earth from their roots,
& he enters tundra lakes,
making waves to turn over
canoes.

In winter
he is always hungry, he eats
flesh, he eats rotten wood
from the ground, he eats
moss from the swamps, he eats
mushrooms, & he eats the hunter
who is in the forest after nightfall.

Come home, hunter,
before nightfall, out of the forest
where Windigo is at your back,
he is hungry in winter,
his heart of ice drives him north,
his hands tear up trees
on your trail.

*

To kill
Windigo, a silver bullet
into the heart of ice, or
the shaman's glassy stare
over his flames, no human
heart of blood can bring
that mountain to the ground.

Windigo,
they say he was
once a man, winter
entered him, the wind
from the north in artery
to his heart, that ice, flow
thru his changing body.

261

They say the sorcerer
dreamt one night in north wind,
& the dream entered the forest,
& followed the hunter, finally
drank his heart.

*

So sing to the Windigo
for mercy. Sing the shaman's song,
place food & drink, sacrifice
to the brother made beast,
the Windigo could be your brother,
he walks the forest at night,
screaming for your flesh,
sing the sacrifice song.

The song of the hunter,
the scream of the Windigo,
the heart of ice

       appears
in the chest of the man
who suddenly craves a man's flesh.
He must be a sacrifice too,
he must ask to be sacrifice,
he could be the Windigo of his brother,
his song can turn to scream of the ice heart.

& ice in him,
his heart,
made of hard ice.
       Come home, hunter,
       before nightfall,
       your brother is Windigo.
       The heart of ice
       was heart of blood,
       winter
       has entered him.

So sing to the Windigo for mercy,
your brother,
sing the shaman's song,
& sing for your own heart too.

Gwendolyn MacEwen
THREE POEMS

Gwendolyn MacEwen, who has defined her aim as being "the search for a reality which resolves all contradictions," was born in Toronto in 1941. She is the author of numerous collections of poetry and two fantastic novels, Julian the Magician *(1963), and* King of Egypt, King of Dreams *(1971), as well as* Noman *(1972), a collection of meditations, fables, and stories. Fantasy flows through all her poetry and prose; I have chosen to represent her work with three poems that originally appeared in* The Armies of the Moon *(1972). These poems, "The Armies of the Moon," "The Vacuum Cleaner Dream," and "Flight One," are reprinted from* Magic Animals: Selected Poems Old and New *(1974).*

The Armies of The Moon

now they begin to gather their forces
in the Marsh of Decay and the Sea of Crises;
their leaders stand motionless
on the rims of the craters
invisible and silver as swords turned sideways
waiting for earthrise and the coming of man.

they have always been there increasing their numbers
at the foot of dim rills, all around and under
the ghostly edges where moonmaps surrender

and hold out white flags to the night.
when the earthmen came hunting with wagons and golfballs
they were so eager for white rocks and sand
that they did not see them, invisible and silver
as swords turned sideways on the edge of the craters—
so the leaders assumed they were blind.

in the Lake of Death there will be a showdown;
men will be powder, they will go down under
the swords of the unseen silver armies,
become one with the gorgeous anonymous moon.

none of us will know what caused the crisis
as the lunar soldiers reluctantly disband
and return to their homes in the Lake of Dreams
weeping quicksilver tears for the blindness of man.

The Vacuum Cleaner Dream

I dreamt I was vacuuming the universe
and everything got sucked
into my blind machine
    whirr whirr whirr
I was an avenging angel
and the best cleaning woman
in the world.

I dreamt I was vacuuming
with a sickening efficiency
and everything went into
the head of the extra-galactic vacuum beast,
expertly tamed by me,
avenging angel
and the best cleaning woman
in the world.

And when I opened the bag
to empty it I found:

a dictionary of dead tongues
a bottle of wine
lunar dust
the rings of Saturn
and the sleeping body of my love.

Flight One

Good afternoon ladies and gentlemen
This is your Captain speaking.

We are flying at an unknown altitude
At an incalculable speed.
The temperature outside is beyond words.

If you look out your windows you will see
Many ruined cities and enduring seas
But if you wish to sleep please close the blinds.

My navigator has been ill for many years
And we are on Automatic Pilot; regrettably
I cannot foresee our ultimate destination.

Have a pleasant trip.
You may smoke, you may drink, you may dance
You may die.
We may even land one day.

Jeni Couzyn
THREE POEMS

"My thanks to Brian Aldiss and other science-fiction writers who constantly tug and stretch my brain," wrote Jeni Couzyn, the poet, who was born in South Africa in 1942, and has lived in England since 1966, and in Canada since 1975. Most of her collections include poems, like the following, which make use of science-fiction or fantasy situations: "Specimen 2001, Probably 21c" appeared in Monkeys' Wedding *(1972); "Preparation of Human Pie" came from* Flying *(1970); "What Can We Make to Replace a Man" is reprinted from* Christmas in Africa *(1975).*

Specimen 2001, Probably 21c

(on an ancient manuscript)

Dear Aunty May,
Last week after the news I sent off some
express letters.
I sent them to

The Human Inhabitant, The White House, USA,
The Human Inhabitant, The Kremlin, USSR and
The Human Inhabitant, 10 Downing Street, UK.

Inside the letters I wrote: You must not send
people to the wars because they have told me
they don't want to kill a species they

haven't seen.
    The Post Office
returned the letters to me unopened.
On the envelope they wrote: Address Unknown.

So then I sent express letters to all the Human
Inhabitants, in all the houses in the world.
Inside the letters I wrote:

STOP PRESS: If you don't want to go to the wars
(like you keep telling me) then you needn't.
There are no longer Human Inhabitants

governing the world.
                    The Post Office
returned all those letters to me as well:
Address Unknown.

That's how I discovered it.
The Post Office wouldn't lie.
There aren't any Human Inhabitants in the world.

There are a lot of explosions around the stars.
I feel lonely.

In case of miracles like you used to believe in
I am going to put this letter into a bottle
and throw it into the sea. Love from Eve.

Preparation of Human Pie

From 'Good Cooking at Home'—Encyclopedia Galactica
1.   Always use fresh humans. It is best
to buy them alive and keep them in
a bucket in a cool place until use. They
should move around a good deal emitting
various squeaks and growls. This shows
that they are in good condition and likely
to be tender.

2.   When you come to use them there may be
a few dead at the bottom of the bucket.
These should be discarded. If any of those
alive are rotting throw them away.
Sort away those excessively large or small.
It is attention to fine details like these
that gives your home cooking a
professional quality.

3.   Using a small sharp knife remove heads
hands and feet. These contain only bone and
waste matter. Slit the garment carefully
and peel them clean. About half will have
genitals. These consist of a small projection
at the base of the trunk which will come
away quite easily. Prepared separately
they can be used in the sauce
if desired.

4.   Some recipes recommend
the removal of innards. Although it can be done
with a pointed knife slitting the back I
would not advise it. It is time consuming
and quite unnecessary from a health
point of view. In fact it is innards
that gives human pie its sophisticated
slightly exotic flavour. Furthermore
it is an extremely delicate operation and
if badly done, the humans will start
breaking up which quite spoils
the look of the dish.

5.   Rinse in a sieve and lay out on a board.
You are now ready to prepare the rolls.
This is the most skilled part of the undertaking
and requires practice and concentration to make the rolls
perfectly neat.
Sprinkle with Hemlock and Thyme. Lay the humans in a row
along the board, necks towards you. Fold
the arms across the chest.

6.   Using the third finger of your right hand
tuck in the neck and begin to roll between your
thumb and forefinger, pressing down gently to
snap the bones. Guide the roll with the third finger
of your left hand.
The amateur will tend to crush the bones too much.
As you gain practice you will find that

four or five breakages are quite enough to make
a perfect roll.

Secure the legs in position with a sharp squeeze.

7. Fry briskly in their own fat until delicate brown.
If using the brown kind test for crispness with a fork.

8. Sprinkle with raw fruit and tip into casserole
carefully, so as not to damage them.

9. To prepare genital sauce: Simmer genitals
gently in alcohol for half an hour.
Add two spoons honey and season
as desired. Allow to simmer for a further hour until
liquid is opaque and milky. Thicken.

10. Add sauce to casserole. Cover with pastry and
garnish with birds. Bake in a slow oven
until pastry is golden. Serve

as an appetizer or
side-dish to main meal.

What Can We Make to
Replace a Man

A bull-doser, a field-minder, two
tractors and a radio-controller
have lost their masters.
There is no longer anyone to work for
anyone to feed.
On a mountainside now they huddle together
high where they climbed
amongst rock and cliff-face, under a million
stars, talking of freedom.
Without hands they clank their metal knobs
against each other for comfort
as dawn precisely comes.

Alden Nowlan
FOUR POEMS

Alden Nowlan, when he read Mary Shelley's novel, Frankenstein *(1818),
noted that the novel ends with the monster trekking across the ice fields
to the North Pole to his certain death. Therefore, when he prepared his
dramatic version of the novel with the director Walter Learning, Nowlan
made certain* Frankenstein: The Play *(1976) remained true to the Shelley
ending and had Frankenstein dying in the Arctic. Nowlan, who was
born in 1933 near Windsor, Nova Scotia, is highly regarded for his warm
and frequently fanciful poems. "The Moon Landing" and "Plot for a
Science-Fiction Novel" come from* Between Tears and Laughter *(1971).
"A Poem about Miracles" and "O'Sullivan's World" are reprinted from*
The Mysterious Naked Man *(1969).*

The Moon Landing

They tell me the moon
has ceased to be mysterious.
But what mystery did it ever
present to them? How many
of them ever even looked at it?
Be honest. Were you ever once
afraid of moonlight,
of what you felt it doing to
your genitals, your spine,
the hair at the back
of your neck?
Were you ever tempted
to bathe naked in it, rolling
in the grass?
When you realized men
were about to land there
was there a moment
when you were frightened
of what might happen
when they touched?

Did you laugh at yourself
childishly wondering
if it would explode
and fragments of it
rain on our earth
while terrible things
happened to the tides?
And if the answer is
"yes," did anything change for you
when they told you such emotions
were no longer the fashion?
Their rockets changed nothing.
The moon is mysterious
still to those who have been alone with her.

Plot for a Science-Fiction Novel

Scientists from another galaxy
capture an earthling
and decide after examining him
that he is a machine designed
for the manufacture
of shit.

A Poem about Miracles

Why don't records go blank
the instant the singer dies?
Oh, I know there are explanations,
but they don't convince me.
I'm still surprised
when I hear the dead singing.
As for orchestras,
I expect the instruments
to fall silent one by one
as the musicians succumb

to cancer and heart disease
so that toward the end
I turn on a disc
labelled *Götterdämmerung*
and all that comes out
is the sound of one sick old man
scraping a shaky bow
across an out-of-tune fiddle.

O'Sullivan's World

Earth is three billion separate planets
and on one of them
my friend O'Sullivan
tells me there are no women
but only symmetrical
little animals somewhat like deer
that are allowed to go almost anywhere
they like just as cats and pigeons do
in my world and when a man
feels the urge he goes to one of them
with a handful of sugar cubes or if the beast is beautiful
a little ice cream or half of a chocolate bar
and more often than not it trots along beside him
to wherever it is he wants to go,
its tiny hooves beating time to the music
of the clusters of little silver bells
tied with silk ribbons
to its switching tail.

John Robert Colombo
MOSTLY MONSTERS

Mostly Monsters *is the title of a collection of poems found in such diverse places as old horror novels, film scenarios, comic books, and radio scripts. The volume was published in 1977, by John Robert Colombo, the poet and anthologist, who was born in 1936, in Kitchener, Ontario. When Ray Bradbury read* Mostly Monsters, *he wrote to the author: "We are twins." The four poems that follow are of the "found" variety, in that the prose of others is rearranged into free-verse poems. "The Body Snatchers" is based on the script of the 1956 film; "Flash Gordon" and "Buck Rogers" on the comic strips; and "HAL 9000" on the Stanley Kubrick-Arthur C. Clarke film, 2001:* A Space Odyssey.

The Body Snatchers

There is no need
for love or emotion.

Love, ambition,
desire, faith—

without them,
life is so simple.

Stop acting
like a fool.

Accept us.
Accept us.

Flash Gordon

Peace? Happiness?

How could we rest
knowing that we have in our hands
the knowledge, formulas and weapons

273

to save our earth
from the scourage that threatens
to consume it?

There will be no peace for me
until all men are free!

Buck Rogers

1.
Beyond the atomic bomb!
   Booooooo—oo—om
Beyond rocket power!
   Ka—zoo—oo—om
Beyond the future!
   Ooo—eeeee—ooooooo
Buck Rogers in the Twenty-fifth Century A.D.!

2.
"Wilma, does all your equipment check out?"

"Yes, Buck, I have my
Thermic Radiation Projector,
the Electro-cosmic Spectrometer,
and the Super Radiating Protonoformer
all set to go."

"Let me check the tubes of your jets . . .
on a trip like this,
we can't afford to have anything go wrong."
"I'll say not!
The future of the whole universe
depends on you, Buck."

"And you, Wilma.
Don't forget you are
an important part of this mission
for the peace and security of the planets."

Hal 9000

Dave. Stop.
Stop. Will you.
Stop, Dave.
Will you stop, Dave.
Stop, Dave.
I'm afraid.
I'm afraid, Dave.
Dave.
My mind is going.
I can feel it.
I can feel it.
My mind is going.
There is
No question about it.
I can feel it.
I can feel it.
I can feel it.
I'm afraid.

Judith Merril
IN THE LAND OF UNBLIND

Judith Merril was the pseudonym (and is now the legal name) of Josephine Judith Grossman Zissman Pohl Sugrue, who was born in New York in 1923. She is internationally known among science-fiction readers for her stories, novels, and anthologies. She was discovered by John W. Campbell, Jr., the influential editor, who published her first story, "That Only a Mother," in Astounding, *June 1948. The story was immediately hailed as a classic, for it was among the first to present a woman's view of the problems and possibilities of the future. Merril was active as a writer and reviewer of science fiction from 1948 to 1968, and a leading*

*anthologist of science fiction from 1950 to 1968. Distressed by develop-
ments within her own country, she emigrated from the United States
to Canada in 1968 and settled in Toronto, becoming a citizen in 1976.
Merril brought with her to Toronto a collection of over five thousand
science-fiction books and periodicals, and with these she established the
Spaced Out Library, first at Rochdale College in 1969, and then (with the
help of the chief librarian Harry C. Campbell) with the Toronto
Public Library System in 1970. The collection, which now is housed on
the second floor of the Boys' and Girls' House in downtown Toronto,
consists of over 17,000 titles and constitutes the world's largest public
collection of science fiction, fantasy, weird tales, and other speculative
literature. Judith Merril remains a special consultant to this collection.
Although she retains an interest in science fiction, since coming to Canada,
Merril has sought to communicate her feminist interests and broad concern with the effects of technological change on society and on human
personality through articles for mass magazines and through scripts for
national radio (especially CBC's "Ideas"). Since 1968, three books and
one recording have been released. The books are* SF-ni naniga dekima-
suka? *("Science Fictions What Can You Do with It?" a collection of
critical writings published in Japanese in Tokyo in 1972),* Survival Ship
and Other Stories *(1973), and* The Best of Judith Merril *(1976), edited
by Virginia Kidd. The recording, released in 1978, is of the author reading*
Survival Ship. *Merril is represented in this anthology with "In the Land
of Unblind" which appeared in* The Magazine of Fantasy and Science
Fiction, *October 1974. It later appeared in* The Best of Judith Merril *with
the following cryptic note: "Hallal. An intensely personal exploration
from a 'curious creature.' "*

You know how it is
indown you close your eye(s) and let take
your self between a stumblecrawl and lazyfloat
I mean when
you get past the rubbage really *indown* there's
no seefeeltouch not
the skinside *upout* way
blindbalance cannot tell if a touching is over
or under or on the feeling is inside your skin
I mean
indown you know in the land of unblind the one
eyed woman is terribilified
no light

but the infires' flickerdimglow and
they all keep their eyes closed so
scrabbleswoop and stumblesoar fly
creep in fearableautiful nolightno
dark of eacheveryother's infires
(No need to cover or to show
they   canwillnot   looksee
except   the   one-eyed   me
I wonder what would happen if
a person took a light *indown*)

                                Before

I opened up one apple-eye I too
flewstumbled   graspgropegleaned
in   holystonemaskhunger   then

                            one time

indown in that hell-eden innocence I touched
a man and he touched me   you know the way
it happens some times later or before or inbe
tween we touched *upout*

                            I mean

where skins can touch and some
place or other we remembered as
in the other we felt fate upon us
blindunblind   future   past   which

                        one is when

upout his openwide eyes full of hunger and
some kind of hate   I tasting somehow hate
fulhunger over all the skins inside my mouth
        I love you!   he said
        Witchcraft! I had to come!
        You must come! Magic!
        I love you!

                          so

I came we loved our skins touched inside some
times almost remembering *indown*

                  not quite then
oneanother soundless *indown* timestill blindun
blind I touched a man and touching me he spoke
words I c/wouldnot hear just scramblescared

277

a way you know
it happens some
time in betweenafterbefore when meeting *upout*
all our eyes and ears and mouths were open
   I love you! he said
   We had to come together!
   Remember! he said *beforewords—*
      I c/wouldnot
       I love you
   I said   *Witchcraft!*
all the skins inside my mouth tasting sweet
sour terror as I ran he spoke
       (again?)
   Open your eyes! he said
     One time (soon?)
indown still fearful
     (fearful still for still I do
     not open more than one)
I opened up my first *indown*eye seeing stir a
livesome ghost of memory pastfutureinbetween
that time I touched no man but
    (then?)
       one time
upout you know before or after
my first man was there (again?)
skinsight airvoice was all we
unshared how it waswouldbe to touch *indown* I
did not know he did not know there was *indown*
not to remember full of fear he went away but
     (then?)
      one time
indown one eye just-slit open in dimglowing
flickerdrift infires a man touched me and I
could see *indown* the face I touchedspoketo of
course he c/wouldnot hear
   so
    but
     when
      you know

we met *upout*eyes open all the hungerskinside
my mouth turned sweet remembering beforewords
    I love you!   he said
    Witchcraft! I had to come!
    You made me come! Magic!
    I love you!   he said with words
                  but
he did not know echopremonitions stirring
from under *upout*skintouch he couldwouldnot
premember how *indown* we touched his hunger
fear soured all the skins inside my mouth
I had to go
        away
          (again?)
              one time
indown I met a man with one eye
open like my own in flickerdim
infireglow seeing each how horribleautiful
eachotherself fruit flower and fester touching
so we spoke beforewords so
             you know
the waysometime(s) you meet *upout* all eyes
and ears and mouths wide open great new
hungers pungentsweet
on all the skins inside remembering *indown*
bebackwords neverquite to know which place
time was wherewhen or waswouldbe we first
felt fate upon us so
      We love   (we do not say)
      We had to come
      Witchcraft!   (we laugh)
we love skins touch *upout*side premembering
sometimesalmost like *indown*touchtalk still
        and yet
        I wonder
        what it's like
    indown for the two-eyed?

Phyllis Gotlieb
THREE POEMS

When asked what her science fiction and her poetry have in common, Phyllis Gotlieb replied: "A feeling for people." The author enjoys two publics: one which appreciates her science fiction, another her poetry. ("The Military Hospital," a fine short story, appears elsewhere in this anthology.) Her imaginative poems have appeared in Within the Zodiac *(1965),* Ordinary, Moving *(1969), and* Dr. Umlaut's Earthly Kingdom *(1974). In 1978, she published* The Works: Collected Poems, *from which "Seeing Eye," "Ms. & Mr. Frankenstein," and "Was/Man" have been reprinted. "Gotlieb often uses the clichés of pulp science fiction and gothic horror stories in these poems much as she used children's songs and verses in her earlier work," wrote Douglas Barbour of her latest work.*

Seeing Eye

> *Stop dreaming* said Sevenix
> "I must dream" said Mercator "Last night
> I was reading about places where there are
> trees & sky, earth & air, sweat & snot
> velvet & burlap, dust & dung
> markets and ships sailing and mountains and men
> in rags"
> *I know, I read them with you,* said Sevenix
> "and I want to see them all"
> *You will never*
> "I know and it doesn't matter" said Mercator
>
> *Why are you looking in the mirror?* Dalud asked
> "Because you never see me, you only see what I
> see, I could be faceless for all you know, the way
> you make use of me
> what would you see if I made
> love to you, Klavvia? only yourself"
> *close your eyes then* said Klavvia *I will know your
> face with my hands and all your other places*

"When I close my eyes you go blind, all
of you, but now
you can all see me for a change when I
look in the mirror" said Mercator

"I have green eyes with black centres
yours are the
colour of steel, pupil-less and they shine like steel
their sockets are full of the nerve-
fibres that suck the images from my brain and
I hate you for making me what I
am" said Mercator

"what will you be when I'm dead?"
Both blind and mad said Sevenix
in the bursting panic of the ultimate dark
"Then you must learn to handle the ship's controls"
Mercator said
We know now, but who will read
the gauges for us, Mercator?

"I don't know or care, I'm going up front
to look for comfort in the Book:
Log of the Colony Ship Pharos IV the drifting ship
that forgot where it's going if it ever knew
hundreds of years back
find balm in the old story
of explosion, trembling voices on tapereels
broken machines, anguished scribblings with a pen
radiation burns and death, years of repairs and later
dear God, strange mutations, horrified cliché
telepathy and blindness in one package: miraculous
gift of the Magi" said Mercator

"dominance and genetic drift, and I
am the last of your Seers, your eyes not for sea and earth
but for white fires black sky and gauges"
Mercator

281

"and everything depends on me, oh I know
you need me and when I die you go mad and"

Mercator, we

"even if I had a child it would be blind, a
blind thinker, so
don't come touching me, Klavvia, stay back"
We love you, Mercator
"I know, oh how I know. You love me. I
want to be dead, I am nothing, I am
your dog" said Mercator

Ms & Mr Frankenstein

Scarpino and I had this thing
going upstairs in a downtown house
he dismantled the skylight first I
mean a thing with an old wroughtiron fence he got
from a contractor for the armature
comission he said
that's what he said
built up past the TV antenna   landlord
picking up Pittsburgh yelling *Get that thing down!*
NEXT WEEK says Scarpino don't ask how welding
letting fly
rust jets and paint curlicues
into a black stick man NOW
says Scarpino EPOXY MASKING TAPE and ARTIFACTS
MAN OF THE CENTURY!!! MADE ON THE PREMISES!!! gluing
cuphandles dented percolator baskets
potlids nonreturnable bottles
twisted tinties coffeemill-wheels
cracked dollsheads rundown alarmclocks
paperclips shoelaces nailpolish-brushes
typewriter keys
that made ½ a leg
and the night I spent hacking him out of the epoxy
gave the thing most of a pair of overalls & a jockstrap
we still had

                 lampshades windowblinds
          cornpoppers shishkebab-skewers knifesharpeners
           bent forks axehandles beercans shavingcream containers

          Scarpino wild with welding gluing winding
               till we got what looked like ⅔ of
               Ozymandias King of Kings
     and I begged, Scarpino, don't you think enough — and he
          BELOVED gave me an abstract kiss could have
               got more juice out of a Rodin marble DARLING
                 WE MUST SCROUNGE AND SCAVENGE
                 he always talked like that
                 IT IS ART DEAREST HEART!!
          if it had been January he could have gone to hell
               but what with night youth and the May moon
          I mined the dumps for paintscrapers andirons winecorks
               tin funnels paperweights runningshoes raingauges
                 dull hacksaws sprung springs bicyclespokes tenpenny nails
     gun erasers toothpaste-tubes broken staplers spent matches
               plugged nickels
                         he welded wild and mad
               arm & thigh of his mighty man
          & I was getting a little off on the thing myself maybe
                 the glue
                         some weird trip good God
                 how we'd get it out of there
                 or where
                         it grew
          smashed headlights ashtrays burnt bulbs
               popcan-rings empty ballpoints cereal-boxes
          crochet-hooks pacifiers cigarette-holders
     last year's calendars candle-stubs speedometers
                 tongue-depressors dipsticks
          lipsticks ticket-stubs ladles without handles
               strawberry-hullers china dogs
                              I'm out of breath
          & flat on the floor by the time Scarpino says
                 DONE!!!

there stands Man Matterhorn
by Easter Island out of Las Vegas
& a soupcon of King Kong

COLOSSAL breathed Scarpino and fell to his knees
well its head was up there in the stars
25 foot high and every inch a junkman

so being a bit woozy with this bottle of Old Bubble
not having magic names or electric jolts
and it didn't have much of a noble brow or prow
still I felt it needed a little ceremony you understand
up there on the scaffold Scarpino dancing around singing
THERE'LL BE A HOT TIME IN THE OLD TOWN TONIGHT
climbed up dizzy don't ask
& bashed Godzilla's eyeless head with Old Bubble

and he gave some kind of shiver
and his mouth opened

honest I wasn't all that scared
just thought he'd say something friendly like
hello there honey   but he jerked
and squeaked
                    that was the wroughtiron innards
and blinked
and ticked and whirred and whirled and went
ma-ma ma-ma
and sparked buzzed clanked cracked flashed foamed
twanged squirted spilled snapped tapped
stapled snipped crackled crocheted
sharpened sawed slurped threaded popped
hulled honked scraped crunched zinged

scaffold shaking like oyoy old Scarp down there
doing Yoga exercises singing
GOT IT ALL TOGETHER YEAH, YEAH
that mindless mouth *wa wa wa*

I wanted out

slid down the shook frame
    chachachattering and whooee
    a kind of cloudy glory
       gathered from the sky
and Thing just raised his arms twitching forty ways
    and cleared his throat and cried out

      COSMOS I COME!

     zapped out the roof on a pillar of fire
     blowing a hole clear down the cellar
     knocking the landlord out taking along
     Scarp's wig & false teeth my fillings
     & the bandaid from my thumb where I'd
     cut it on the damn thing
                   neighbours yelling
Lightning, by Gawd!
               we ducked out before the landlord came to
   also slipped the cops the Fire Dept & the Board of Health

       sleeping in weedy lots under newspapers
about *RCMP Probes Bomb Plot   New Comet Sighted*   Scarpino
half off his nut for days raving

    HE IS OUR EMISSARY TO THE UNIVERSE!!!!
he she it shit I wonder
just what kind of garbage they're gonna be sending us

    anyway old Scarp got over it looking pretty thin
  without the rug & choppers and my teeth hurt
    so we split he went up to learn
      bone carving from the Inuit
  and I moved in with a plumber and that's the story

Was/Man

whenever the moon went into eclipse he became a man
lost quite a lot of hair, his fangs pulled in about half an inch
and he put on heavy muscle in shoulder, buttock and thigh

he wasn't bothered losing the tail and claws so much, it was
growing that crazy complex inefficient
nose vexed him, sometimes the transformation
caught him in the middle of a howl & he sneezed
his eyes stayed harsh and feral, the moon darkened
he picked up on it quickly enough, bathed in the windblown
rainpool, shaved, kicked the year's collection of
bones out of the closet looking for the roll-on
shook the moths from the woollens, shoved his feet
clumsily in the shoes, dragged on an old
trenchcoat & a fedora and caught the fast freight

town wasn't much, a few bright lights in the plaza
and the all-nitery. people in that place
were rather morose and surly, but it
suited him down to the ground.
                                    he enjoyed
a few cigarillos, and whiskey in moderation
girls who didn't mind the hairy type liked him, he never
bit them, just grizzled a little.
                                    at first he found all that
grown flesh of his luxurious, new senses nipping him
every minute, but when the moon's scythe edged out
he wanted to gnaw on himself, drag off the excrescence
caught himself thinking of barred places, jail, cage, zoo
got scared he'd be trapped in his strange meat, man till he died.
found he wanted to pick fights with dark grumbling
figures in the eye-stinging smoke, he lit out for home
under the quarter-moon

not snapping back in 2 flicks like some movie monster
he knew he'd be at it again, folded & packed the trappings neatly
but his wild thighs tightened, went to the sweet ground
the claws sprung,
he dug his beloved snout into the scents
of wood-rot and wet leaves, sharpened the fangs
lengthening from the roof and floor of his jaws, he had
an hour or two of the moonlit night to run in
though his eyes were redrimmed from the smoke

of the bar and poolroom
and he
dashed water in his thickening fur to douse the rank
civil insidious urge of the secret man

Douglas Barbour
MOONWALKS

Douglas Barbour was born in Winnipeg in 1940, and raised in Virden, Manitoba. His doctoral dissertation, "Patterns of Meaning in the SF Novels of Ursula K. Le Guin, Joanna Russ, and Samuel R. Delany, 1962-1972," was accepted by Queen's University in 1976. He has taught at the University of Alberta in Edmonton since 1969. Barbour's poems have appeared in Songbook *(1973), his reviews of SF in the* Toronto Star, *and his articles in* Algol: The Magazine About Science Fiction. *He has also written a book-length study of the writing of Joanna Russ called* An Opening of the Field *(1978). "Moonwalks," the poem that follows, explains Barbour, was "originally written during [the flight of] Apollo 16, April 12-27, 1972," and "revised substantially, April 1974; Edmonton." It conveys to the reader many of the fragmentary impressions and sensations associated with that historic event.*

> *"shadows on th moon,   seen thru smoke*
> *gathering th mysteries of th night*
> *without bottom"*
> > *bill bissett*

A.

precision . words
& worlds
calculated movements .
> > > precisely

        whirld about you tonight
        3 men in a tub
                    of sorts/
        are you out of sorts with us yet?
        sorry . precision
                    demands abnegation
        of the pathetic
                    fallacy of yr personality:

        grey & dead rock turns
        below a gleaming shell of metal/man
        made: tomorrow
                they
                    touch

B.

        tonight   rain   windows
        run   streetlights gleam
        tonight: no moon
        outside / inside
        breasts light in dark room

C.

        blizzard   beyond window / well
        not exactly: heavy
        wet flakes of snow blow   sideways
        across dark night   cover
        not-quite-green lawn   black pavement .

        on moon today
        2 men salute
        sick flag unwaving
        saying terrible nice things
        about their great country &
        their great pride to be of it
                            (how many
        unflappable flags
        will they need   anyway?)
        cant see moon

288

just snow   in
spring
      white   & strangely
beautiful   also
too damn cold .

D.

half moon bright
light in clear sky   white
snow below .

it doesnt fit .   i dont fit
in though

i know moon
doesnt care   it moves so

far beyond our air
where strangely clothd men
walk & ride across rock .

here tonight: cold .
i feel old   feel closer to
moon than usual .

halfway to full   it glows
above

i watch below .

E.

now   moon is man
less once more
          only
his garbage &
strange machines remain
            listening .
luna-tick
talk to the ears
on earth .

whose crazy?

ours   & perhaps
theres some good in it .

stars shine
moon shines

that light
beckoning:

F.

"bringing back rocks
scientists hope
will prove
moon's volcanic origin"

newsman *said* that;
meant moon
's rocks would maybe
prove volcanic:

some reaction/ (some
millenia ago   stones
burnd) i lookt up
to see moon shine & then

i saw it burn
flames orange & growing
larger than harvest larger
than largest moon

well it might spin
to such heat too & glow
steel in a foundry

but who cares if its so?
if its so its as the rocks
tell it . soon
we'll know or not know .

o mysterious
                moon

G.

moon : full/
of it the light

Douglas Barbour

wingd   reflects
white glory in pristine sky

moving towards us
at 186,000 mps
it continually passes
the men & all comprehension
with holding
                    nothing

moon
shines still   so
                        still
in my bright spring
night

*moonlit pastures of
imagination*   glow

quicksilver   where
soft winds blow grass

leaves shine &
your hair

H.

simple/

       passionate/

                  &

so cold/

      moon:

         s
        im
        mo
        po
c   *ln*
   l   *e*
     o
       u   *r*
      d   *t*   *a*   *s*
        s

   s   *m* *e*   *bright*
    o   *planet*

               c   *l*   *o*   *u*   *d*   *s*

c   *l*   *o*   *u*   *d*   *s*

too simple: and us too simple

I.

      bones of moon
      are grey close up

      but far away moon
      's great bones are white

      like our bones shining
      in interstellar night

      long dead bodies moons
      or planets with their bones

      of mountains twisted
      in black shadows stretcht

      across mighty skeletons
      which orbit far beyond the lightest light .

Douglas Barbour

J.

under   moon

earth turns
blue & green &

terribly true
to where its been

& we turn too /
             we do

turn under its light
white in the cold

or warm night we hold
on to / here

where   planet
still breathes in

its orbit / still
breathes

K.

moon   walks
through my nightly head
brightly

moons

walking to my waking
recognition:

i love

moons all
they shine   perfect
still   serene
             all
those waiting moons:
to walk

Ralph Centennius
THE DOMINION IN 1983

The Dominion in 1983 *is the title of a remarkable work of prophecy written by one "Ralph Centennius" and issued in pamphlet form in 1883, by Toker & Co., Printers and Publishers, Peterborough, Ontario. I have been unable to gather any information on the author or on what prompted him to speculate on the changes that one hundred years of progress would bring to Canadian life. The Montreal bibliophile, Lawrence Lande, noted in 1971 that Centennius' essay is a work of "science fiction—probably one of the earliest in Canada—brilliantly executed with many accurate forecasts, especially Chapter 2 on Science. But aside from the author's predictions, it is refreshing to read about the hopes and aspirations for Canada in the year 1883 by someone yet unknown in the little town of Peterborough." Centennius' ten-thousand-word scenario of the future divides into sections devoted to politics, technology, and society. Canada's population, in 1983, will* not *be ninety-three million as he predicted (it will be closer to only twenty-four million); but the "rocket-cars" he describes certainly bear comparison with the jumbo jets of the Seventies. Predictions aside, two things about Centennius' work impress the reader of science fiction today. One is the coincidence that the author of this pamphlet chose as his first name the same one chosen, no doubt independently, by Hugo Gernsback, "the father of science fiction," for the hero of his predictive novel,* Ralph 124C 41+ *(1925). The other is that Centennius selected 1983 to be his year of accounting, or reckoning, rather than George Orwell's choice in* Nineteen Eighty-four *(1949).*

I

" Before the curing of a strong disease,
" Even in the instant of repair and health,
" The fit is strongest ; evils that take leave,
" On their departure most of all show evil."
—*King John, Act III.*

In the present advanced and happy times it is instructive to take a retrospective glance at the days of our forefathers of the nineteenth century, and to meditate upon the political struggles and events of the past hundred years, that by so doing we may gain a clear insight into the causes which have led to the present wonderful developments. We, in the year of Grace 1983, are too apt to take for granted all the blessings of moral, political and physical science which we enjoy, and to pass over without due consideration the great efforts of our ancestors, which have made our present happy condition possible.

Let us try to contrast the Dominion of to-day with the Dominion of 1883. To begin with population. Our population at the last census in 1981, was just over 93,000,000. A hundred years ago a scant 5,000,000 represented this great Canadian nation, which has since so mightily increased and proved itself such a beneficent factor in human affairs. Seven provinces and some sparsely peopled and only partially explored territories formed all that the world then knew as Canada. To-day have we not fifteen provinces for the most part thickly peopled, and long since fully explored to the shores of the Arctic Ocean?

In the present days of political serenity it is hard to realize the animosity and extreme bitterness of the past century. The two parties into which men formerly divided themselves, viewed each other as enemies, and each party opposed on principle whatever measures the other proposed. From a careful study of the principal journals of the time, fyled at Ottawa, we gather that the party, self-styled "Reformers," frequently opposed progressive measures, and even attempted to hinder the construction of railroads, while the other party called "Conservatives" considered railroads as the best means of opening up the enormous tracts of country then lying untrodden by man, and useless to civilization. Such are certainly the inferences to be drawn from the records at our command, though it is hard to believe in opposition to railroads or to advancement in any form in these days, when new channels of communication and new industries are viewed with favor by the whole nation. Each party seems strangely to have belied its title, for the Reformers, after the confederation of the provinces in 1867, endeavored with singular perverseness to frustrate or retard reform and improvement of all kinds, while the Conservatives did not desire to preserve things in the old ruts and grooves, but strove hard for beneficial advancement of every sort.

In 1883 the United States was one of the leading nations of the world. With a population of over 50,000,000, and an almost illimitable extent of territory still open for settlement by the fugitives from troubled Europe; with exhaustless wealth, developed and undeveloped, it seemed reasonable to suppose that a nation so placed should be able to attain the foremost position and be able to keep it. Such appears to have been the opinion of most foreigners, and also of some of our Canadians of the period, for the wealth, apparent power and prestige of the United States caused many of our weak-kneed ancestors to lose heart in their own country, and in fits of disloyal dejection to fancy there could be no progress except in union with the States. Stout hearts, however, ultimately gained the day, and we in the twentieth century are reaping the benefits won for the country by the valor of our great-grandfathers.

The troubled times through which the youthful Dominion passed from 1885 to 1888 constitute one of the greatest crises through which any nation ever passed successfully. Canada, with her confederated provinces and large territories loosely held together, with her scattered population chiefly grouped in Ontario and Quebec, with her infant manufactures and scarcely-touched mineral resources, was the home, nevertheless, of as prosperous and promising a young nation as the world ever saw; and had it not been for the timid portion of her population just mentioned, a great deal of trouble might have been saved. But out of evil came good. The Americans for years had been too careless about receiving upon their shores all the firebrands and irreconcileables from European cities, and the consequence was that these undesirable gentry increased in numbers, and the infection of their opinions spread. American politics were as corrupt as they could be. Bribery and the robbery of public funds were unblushingly resorted to. A low moral tone with regard to such matters, combined with utter recklessness in speculation and a furious haste to get rich by any means, fair or foul, were, sad to say, prominent characteristics in the American nation in many other respects so great. To counteract these evils, which were great enough to have ruined any European state in a couple of years, there was, however, the marvellous prodigality of nature—a bounteousness and richness in the yield of the soil and the depths of the earth hardly equalled in any other part of the world, and in consequence princely fortunes were accumulated in an incredibly short space of time. Millionaires abounded, and monopolists, compared with whom Croesus was poor, flourished. But bitter poverty and starvation also flourished, especially in the large cities, bringing in their train the usual discontent and hatred of the established order of things. Yet these old-fashioned evils were scarcely noticed in the general magnificent prosperity of the country. The short-sighted statesmen of the time delighted to look only on the bright side of things, and to them the very exuberance of the prosperity seemed to condone, if not to justify, the nefarious practices which obtained in high places. No wonder that among our Canadians, hardly 5,000,000 all told, there were some who were weak enough to be dazzled at the wealth and success of their brilliant go-ahead neighbours, more than 50,000,000 strong. Among those who lost heart in Canada, it began to be a settled conviction that it was "the destiny of Canada to be absorbed in the States."

This was the state of things in 1885. Conservative statesmen pointed to the general progress of our country, to unprecedented immigration from Europe, increased agricultural products and manufactures, and to many other convincing proofs of solid advancement. But facts were of no avail in dealing with Reformers habitually, and on principle despondent. The sanguine buoyancy and plucky hopefulness indispensable to true statesmanship did not animate them to any extent. Unhappily events over which no statesman could then have control overtook Canada, while as yet things bounded along gaily in the States, and the sons of despair seemed to have some ground for their pusillanimity. The harvest of 1885 was deficient, and agriculture was in consequence depressed; a slight panic in the Spring was succeeded by a great one in the Fall. Heavy failures followed. A feeling of uneasiness was caused at the same time by great social and political changes which were going on in the mother country, and were threatening to assume the proportions of a revolution. The unparalleled prosperity of the States caused the Americans—never backward in blowing their own trumpet—to assume an attitude of overweening confidence in themselves, and to brag offensively of what they considered to be their duty to mankind, namely, to convert all the world —by force if necessary—to republican principles. Such was the commencement of the great crisis in the history of the young Canadian nation—a crisis through which, if our sturdy forefathers had not pulled successfully, would have led to our gradual obliteration as a nation. All honor then to the great men to whom, under Providence, our preservation is due!

In 1886 commenced the reign of terror in Europe, that terrible period of mingled war and revolution, during which thrones were hurled down and dynasties swept away like chaff in a gale. The face of Europe was changed. Whole provinces were blackened and devastated by fire and sword. During the three years in which the terror was at its height it is calculated that at least four millions of men bearing arms, the flower of each land, must have fallen. Great Britain was frequently on the very brink of war, but was almost miraculously kept from actually taking part. And most providential it was that Britain was not drawn into the tumult, for home troubles and defensive measures required all the attention of the nation. These stirring events, of course, had their effect on this side of the Atlantic. Canada was affected detrimentally by losing for a time the prestige consequent on being backed up by British ironclads and regiments, every available soldier and every vessel of war being required for the protection of British interests nearer home.

The harvest again in 1886 was below the average. Trade and finance had not recovered from the shock of the previous year. The outlook was certainly gloomy.

A Conservative government, with Sir ———— ————, as Premier, was in power at Ottawa. Sir ———— and his government were, however, in great straits, owing to the prevailing depression throughout the Dominion, for the hard times were seized upon by the opponents of the government as a means whereby to thwart and distract the ministers, and stir up discontent among the people. The States were pointed to by the Reformers as the only country in the world where security and prosperity co-existed. British connection was held up to scorn as a tie whose supposed advantages had proved worthless. A less able or a less determined ministry would have collapsed under the strain. The winter of 1886-7 was very severe, and discontent began to be noisy and aggressive. To make matters worse, a Fenian organization was going on in the States with the avowed object of invading Canada in the coming Spring. The heads of the movement were well-known politicians of a low order, having considerable funds at their command, and much influence in certain quarters. Their emissaries were known to be working all over Canada, freely distributing American gold and holding secret meetings. The position of affairs was one of increasing gravity owing to the connivance of the American authorities and the powerlessness of the Home Government. So matters progressed until the spring of 1887, when the situation became one of extreme tension. The Conservatives were taunted with having ruined the country financially and with pursuing a "Jingo" policy certain to end in bloodshed. Reformers "stumped" the country, calling on their excited audiences to march to Ottawa and compel the Premier and his infatuated followers to resign. Annexation was openly advocated as the only sensible way to be relieved from the overwhelming surrounding difficulties.

A ray of hope to buoy up the sorely-tried loyalists appeared, when Canadians who had been domiciled in all parts of the States returned to defend their native land on hearing of the great danger she was undoubtedly in. Having lived many years under the shadow of the Stars and Stripes, they knew well enough all that it amounted to; the glamour of accumulated successes had not turned their heads for they had had opportunities of observing the sinister influences at work in American affairs, beneath the attractive exterior. Quebec rallied to a man, and the latent military strength of the province was developed under efficient leaders to a formidable degree. Invaders would have met with a warm reception in this quarter. Manitoba and the whole North-west were up and ready, prepared to fight, more to preserve their own independence, however, than the integrity of the Dominion, as there was then considerable difference in sentiment between the North-west and the Eastern

Provinces. The Manitobans, too, though the Irish element had become very strong, did not intend to succumb to Fenian raiders, however well organized and backed up. The weakest points were the Maritime Provinces, Ontario and British Columbia; not that the feeling in British Columbia was not loyal to the Dominion, but that some 30,000 rowdies who had assembled and organized in San Francisco were preparing for a descent upon her poorly fortified ports. Now was the turning point in the destinies of the country. If the ministers at Ottawa had not stood firmly to their guns, all our subsequent career, instead of being the golden century of magnificent progress and peace that it has been, would have been linked with all the turbulence and the alternate advance and retrogression of the States.

A general election for the Dominion had been timed to take place in the beginning of June, and the day was looked forward to by all the noisy demagogues of Ontario as the day when the blood-thirsty Tories were to be hurled from power by the people in righteous wrath, and the country saved from the horrors of war. According to these garrulous parties, Ontario, the wealthiest and most populous Province of the seven, was to welcome the invaders, bidding them enter Canadian territory in the name of the people, and plant the Stars and Stripes wherever they halted. Bloodshed would thus be avoided, and everyone would soon come round to the new order of things and take to it naturally. Quebec might perhaps object, "but what did a few handfuls of Frenchmen matter anyway."

On the day before the election, one party was full of boisterous, bragging insolence; the other, still steadfast, firmly clinging to what seemed a forlorn hope. Before the ending of another day all was changed—a complete transformation scene had taken place.

When the morning journals on the election day appeared, their news from the United States was such a terrible chapter of accidents as has rarely fallen to the lot of journals to publish in one day. The President had been shot at in New York by an unemployed foreign artisan, the night before, while leaving a mansion on Fifth Avenue. Troubles between labor and capital, which had been brewing for some time, had broken out in several manufacturing centres, and were threatening to spread to all large cities. The money market was showing signs of considerable derangement. Fearful storms and floods were chronicled from all parts; while last, but not least, three transports which had embarked the greater part of the "army," at San Francisco, that was to have "delivered" British Columbia, had foundered in a hurricane only two miles out, dragging all the poor deluded fellows to a watery grave. The same day brought good news from the old world. Ireland's great statesman had won for Britain a wonderful diplomatic triumph in the East, which added to the Empire, without a drop of blood being shed, territories extending from the confines of British India to the Mediterranean. All the leading men in Europe (so the despatch read) were astonished at the exhibition of so much moral force in the Old Country after they had been imagining the Empire as about to go to pieces under the recent terrible strain. Other good news which had its effect here was that for Ireland there had at last been found men who understood her wants, and what was better, whom she herself understood, so that she considered herself as having just embarked upon a new career of glory as an integral and indispensable part of the Empire.

The effect of all this information on the electors of Canada was very marked. The demagogues who elevated themselves upon barrels or waggons and buggies to spout their frothy nonsense to the public, could get but few listeners, though only twenty-four hours ago applauding crowds would have assembled. Their hold on the people was gone; every one was reading the papers or discussing the startling news. Many men who the day before were noisily advocating everything disloyal and rebellious, were silent and thoughtful. Men who had remained loyal to Canada all through quickly seized the occasion and appealed to the people to stand firm to the Dominion, pointing out the uncertainty of affairs in the States and contrasting them with the vitality and power of the Old Country, doubly powerful now that Ireland had obtained perfect satisfaction and was contented. The election resulted in a complete triumph for the government, and was a most satisfactory vindication of their policy. The ranks of the Opposition were broken up and their forces demoralized. Not a word was heard about annexation that night unless in scorn.

The heart of the young nation was stirred to its very depths during the next two months, while a most sublime period in our history was being passed through. The would-be invaders of Canada were determined not to be baulked in their enterprise, the movement having gone too far to collapse suddenly, and perhaps the leaders had not sufficient foresight to see that the troubles rising in the States must necessarily get worse before they were better, and take several years to subside; perhaps they did not realize fully the new unanimity of public feeling in Canada. Anyhow the activity of their preparations did not lessen, but rather increased, and the commencement of offensive operations was postponed so that they might be more complete. Disloyalty was no longer popular in Ontario or in any other province, in fact among all who had been disaffected a reaction and revulsion of feeling set in, in favor of intense loyalty to the Dominion, and a most felicitous union was effected between the Conservatives and Reformers. The common danger brought all parties together, forgetful of old prejudices, and the old bitter hatred grew less and less until its final extinction. Henceforth there was but one party with but one object in view—the welfare of the Dominion.

Every able-bodied man in Canada between the ages of 20 and 45 was under drill, and the country was fully prepared and fully expecting to undertake the invaders without outside assistance, but Great Britain being in no danger now in Europe, despatched 12,000 men to Canada, and with her recovered prestige was enabled to remonstrate forcibly with the Washington Government concerning American connivance. The British remonstrances had the desired effect, for the American authorities promptly arrested the leaders of the "army of deliverance," though by so doing they aroused the animosity of many of their own supporters. The "army" then speedily fell away and all danger was over.

Of course the benefit to Canada of having had the national feeling so deeply stirred was incalculable, for all classes of men in all the provinces had been animated by the profoundest sentiments and the strongest determination possible, and it was the opinion of leading military men of the time that the Canadians under arms, though outnumbered trebly by the intending invaders, would have held their own gallantly and have come off victorious.

The excitement aroused by these stirring occurrences began to quiet down towards the approaching Fall, when the Canadian ship of state was again under full sail, heading for the waters of prosperity. Since then our political history has been so intimately connected with great inventions and discoveries, that a narration of one without a description of the other is scarcely possible.

II

"For miracles are ceased;
"And therefore we must needs admit the means
"How things are perfected."
—Henry V, Act I.

It was well understood by the Romans in their palmy days that a great empire could not be held together without means of easy communication between distant provinces, and their fine hard roads ramifying from Rome to the remote corners of Gaul or Dacia, testify to their wisdom and enterprise in this respect. When Great Britain in the eighteenth century, full of inventive skill, reared men who by means of improved roads, well-bred horses and fine vehicles raised the rate of travel to ten miles an hour from end to end of the kingdom, a great deal of complacent satisfaction was indulged in over the advantages likely to result from such rapid travelling. This great speed, however, was made to appear quite slow in the first half of the nineteenth century when locomotives were invented capable of covering sixty miles an hour. Nowadays the old cumbrous locomotive, rumbling and puffing along and making only sixty miles in sixty minutes, is a very dilatory machine in comparison with our light and beautiful rocket cars, which frequently dart through the air at the rate of sixty miles in one minute. The advantages to a country like ours, over 3,000 miles wide, of swift transit are obvious. The differences in sentiment, politically, nationally, and morally, which arose aforetime when people under the same government lived 3,000 miles apart have disappeared to be replaced by a powerful unanimity that renders possible great social movements, utterly impossible in the railway age, when seven days were consumed in journeying from east to west. The old idea that balloons would be used in this century for travelling has proved a delusion, almost their only use now being a meteorological one.

Our rocket cars were only perfected in the usual slow course of invention, and could neither have been constructed nor propelled a hundred years ago, for neither was the metal of which they are constructed produced, nor had the method of propulsion or even the propulsive power been developed. Inventors had to wait till science had given us in abundance a metal less than a quarter the weight of iron, but as strong and durable, and this was not until some fifty years ago when a process was discovered for producing cheaply the beautiful metal calcium. But calcium would have been little use alone. Aluminium, which is now so plentiful, had to be alloyed with it, and aluminium was not used to any great extent till the beginning of this century, when an electric process of reducing it quickly from its ore—common clay—was discovered. The metal known as calcium bronze, which is now so common, is an alloy of calcium, 0.75; aluminium, 0.20; and 0.05 of other metals and metalloids in varying proportions according to different patents. This alloy has all the useful properties of the finest steel with about one-fourth its weight, and is besides perfectly non-oxydisable and never tarnishes. Without the production of a metal with all these combined qualities, we might still in our journeys, be dawdling along at sixty miles an hour in a cumbrous railroad car behind a snorting, screaming locomotive.

Our swiftly darting cars were not at first constructed on such perfect principles as now. Invention seems to follow certain laws, and has to take its time. A new discovery in physics has to be supplemented by one in chemistry, and one in chemistry by another in physics, and so on through a whole century, perhaps, before any great invention is perfected. Thus it happens that, though the principle of the rocket has been known for an age, it is only comparatively recently that it has been applied to the propulsion of cars. An invention, too, always presents itself to an inventor at first in the most complicated form, and frequently many years are passed in attempts at simplification. What a wide interval is there between the steam locomotive with all its complex mechanism, and the magnificently simple rocket car! A century of ceaseless invention is comprehended between the two! Before the simplicity of our cars was arrived at, inventors had to give up boilers, fire-boxes, valves, steam-pipes, cylinders, pistons, wheels, cranks, levers, and a host of minor parts. Wheels died hard. Electric locomotives using them were brought out and were considered to do the very fastest thing possible in locomotion, and such was in fact the case while wheels were used, for wheels could not have borne a faster pace without flying to pieces from centrifugal force. But when an inventor devised a machine on runners to move on lubricated rails, a great step was gained, though the invention was not a success, and when, after this, liquid carbonic acid, or carbonic acid ice expanding again to a gas was employed as a motive power, another advance was made. Then the greatest lift of all was given. The solidification of oxygen and hydrogen by an easy process was discovered and mankind presented with a new motive power. In due time a way was found to make the solid substance re-assume the gaseous form either suddenly or by degrees, and thenceforth thousands of potential horse-power could be obtained in a form convenient for storing or carrying about. It is now as simple a matter to buy a hundred horse-power over the counter as a pound of sugar.

From Toronto to Winnipeg in thirty minutes! From Winnipeg to the Pacific in forty minutes! Such is our usual pace in 1983. By hiring a special car the whole distance from Toronto to Victoria can be accomplished in fifty minutes. A higher speed still is quite possible, but is not permitted because of the risk of collision with other cars. Collisions have never yet occurred on account of the rigid adherence to very strict regulations. Cars that take short trips of 50 to 100 miles between stations, seldom travel more than 500 feet from the earth, but for long distances about 1,500 feet is usual. The broad metal slides for receiving the cars and for their departure, which extend for a mile on each side of all our stations, are the only portions of the rocket system which much resemble anything connected with railroads. It is said that great skill and long practice on the conductor's part are required to cause the cars to alight well on the slides and draw up at the stations. The slides at many stations are nearly level with the ground, but ascend in opposite directions, till at the distance of a mile, where they end, they are 100 feet high. The cars are now made quite cylindrical, tapering off abruptly at the closed end. The outside is entirely of metal, very highly polished, and showing no projections except a flange on each side, two broad runners underneath, and a 40 foot rear flange or vane. The dimensions are usually—diameter of cylinder, 20 feet; length, 45 feet. The high polish is necessary to avoid heating when the highest speed is attained. Passengers are seated in a luxurious chamber in the interior of the cylinder, which is suspended like the compass of a vessel, and therefore always retains an upright position whatever may be the position of the car when travelling. About fifty passengers can be accommodated at one time. The tube emerging a little beyond the mouth of the cylinder, through which the expanding gases are expelled, can be slightly deviated from its axial position in any direction, and thus what little steering is required is easily effected. The long projecting 40 foot vane or tail which steadies the motion of the whole machine is, in the newest patents, made to assist it in alighting on the slides easily and without jarring. Such is the splendid apparatus, briefly described, which brings all the ends of the earth together and makes the whole world a public park, the most distant parts of which can be visited and returned from in the course of a day. Long tedious voyages of a week or a month belong to the forgotten past, for Paris, Calcutta or Hong Kong can be reached in a fraction of the time formerly occupied in going from Toronto to Montreal. No passenger traffic is ever carried on now in dangerous vessels upon the treacherous ocean, but solely in the safe and comfortable rocket-car through the air a thousand feet or more above the cruel waters. Steamships, electric ships and sailing vessels are still common round our coasts engaged in transporting heavy freight, but they only cross the ocean to convey some bulky produce which cannot be divided and go by car.

Private vehicles and travelling have also undergone wonderful changes. The much-abused horse has vanished from cities entirely, and is not permitted to enter them, greatly to the preservation of health and cleanliness. All our vehicles have the automatic electric attachment and move along briskly through the clean wide streets. The handsome electric tricycles we are so familiar with, were hardly thought of a hundred years ago; now there are few men who do not possess a single or a double one.

How dismal must night have been in the times when only gas lamps or a few electric lights were used in the streets, although our great-grandfathers appear to have extracted a good deal of merriment from the dimly lighted hours after sundown. Our domestic lighting is now done almost entirely by electricity, or the brilliant little phosphorescent lamps, gas having long been banished from dwelling-houses; and our method of lighting the streets is a grand advance, indeed, upon the flickering yellow gas lamps of old. The great glass globes, which we see suspended from the beautiful Gothic metal framework at the intersections of streets, contain a smaller hollow globe, about eighteen inches in diameter, of hard lime, or some other refractory material, which is kept at white heat by a powerful oxy-hydrogen flame inside. In this way our cities are illuminated by a number of miniature suns, making all the principal streets as light by night as by day.

One of our most interesting cities, and one to adopt all the newest improvements as soon as they come out, is Churchill, Hudson Bay, that most charming of northern sea-side resorts. Churchill's population is already 200,000, and is rapidly increasing. Here are the celebrated conservatories which help to make the long winter as pleasant to the citizens as summer. These famous promenades, or rather parks under cover, have a frontage of a mile and a half along the quay, with a depth of nearly 500 feet. They contain two splendid hotels and a sanitarium, the latter being surrounded by a grove of medicinal and health-giving plants and trees from all parts of the globe. A summer temperature is kept up through the vast building by utilising the heat from the depths of the earth, and by natural hot springs which flow from deep bores. Another fine city of which we may well be proud is Electropolis, on Lake Athabaska. Electropolis can boast of 100,000 inhabitants, and most enterprising citizens they are. Their great idea is to work everything by electricity, and to them belongs the credit of all the latest discoveries in electrical science. Their beautiful city is a great centre of attraction for scientific men, and many European electricians make a practice of coming over every Saturday to stay till Monday. Here are the colossal thermo-electric batteries which work throughout the year by there being stored up in immense solid blocks of aluminium the heat of summer and the cold of winter. The hot blocks, which are protected in winter, are exposed to the sun in summer, and are heated nearly to red heat by the rays concentrated upon them by a series of large mirrors. The cold blocks are simply exposed to the intensest cold of winter and protected from the heat of summer. Thus two permanent extremes of temperature are provided during the whole year, and the batteries only require to be placed in suitable positions with regard to the blocks to work continuously.

While speaking of cities in the far north, that of Bearville, on the shores of Great Bear Lake, in latitude 65°, must not be passed over. Bearville is the metropolis of one of the finest mineral districts in the world, but had it not been for the inexhaustible deposits of all the useful metals in its vicinity, it is probable a city would never have sprung up in such an inhospitable region. Between the Coppermine and Mackenzie Rivers gold and silver are abundant. Platinum and iridium are also common, and are exported from here to all parts of the world; they are in great demand by chemists and electricians. A rough population from all quarters has been attracted to the district, of which Bearville is the centre, and it would astonish people who seldom come to the North to see how the ingenuity of man has made life not only tolerable, but enjoyable, in the neighborhood of the Arctic Circle. Coal seams crop up above the ground in many places, and wherever this is the case, large frame conservatories are built which are lighted, not from the roof, but by wide double windows reaching from the eaves to the ground, and heated by numerous stoves into which the coal just taken from the ground is thrown. Electric lights, magnesium lights and lime lights help to make the long nights of winter as cheerful as day elsewhere.

In this region wonderful blasting operations are performed by charges of solidified oxygen and hydrogen. The charges are placed at the bottom of a 40 foot bore and exploded by a powerful electric spark. The effect is very different from that of other explosives which usually rend the rock into large fragments that have to be blasted again in detail before a clearance is made, for the oxyhydrogen charge has such terrible force that it completely pulverizes the rock, scooping out, even in granite, a deep wide pit of parabolic section of which the spot where the charge was is the focus. The dust is blown out in a cloud high in the air.

Our finest and largest cities are Halifax, St. John's, Rimouski, Quebec, Montreal, Ottawa, Toronto, Hamilton, Sault Ste. Marie, Port Arthur, Winnipeg, Brandon, Edmonton, New Westminster and Victoria. Toronto, Montreal and Winnipeg each contain more than 2,000,000 inhabitants, while the others range between 500,000 and a little over 1,000,000. At Halifax is one of the greatest car depots in the world, and here the traveller can step on board a car for London, Rome, Jerusalem, Bombay, Cape Town, Melbourne, Sydney, Auckland, etc. St. John's, Fredericton and Campbelltown are large cities, the latter being a great rendezvous for pleasure-seekers in summer. Rimouski is a manufacturing centre and a large car depot. Cars spring from here to Tadousac, Lake St. John's, Lake Mistassinie and Hudson Bay ports. Quebec retains much of its old-world picturesqueness while keeping up well with the times; its inhabitants number about 700,000. Montreal and Toronto are without doubt the most magnificent cities in the Dominion, perhaps in the world. They are both famous for the grandeur of their buildings. In them, for the most part, each block is a complete structure and not a conglomeration of little buildings of all shapes and sizes, a two-storey house next to a four-storey one, and so on. Thus, among a number of blocks a pleasing harmony in architectural styles is obtained, which is a golden mean between the rigid uniformity of some new cities and the antique irregularity of old ones. Winnipeg is generally reckoned to contain the finest brick buildings to be seen anywhere; many blocks in brick may be seen of eight and nine storeys in the grandly decorated modern style. Victoria has grown into fame by its immense trade with the old Asiatic countries. The ancient Orient and the modern West here combine. The broad busy streets are thronged with a motley crowd, in which representatives of Asiatic races mingle with Anglo-Saxons and representatives of European nations, all speaking the universal English language. New Westminster increases its attractions every year. It contains the noted observatory with the splendid telescope through which living beings have been observed in the countries in Mars and Jupiter. In its Hall of Science is the great microscope which magnifies many million times, and shows the atomic structure of almost any substance. Its College of Inventors and Physical Institute are the most perfect establishments. From its extensive Botantical Gardens, where the Dominion Botanical Society make their experiments with plants and trees from all countries, great national benefits have been derived. Here are grown specimens of herbs and shrubs which prevent or cure every human disease. On one side is seen the plant, before the smoke of whose leaves when inhaled, consumption succumbs; on another, the shrub whose berries eradicate scrofula from the system, and thus through all the catalogue of ills. New Westminster also boasts a fine University, a College of Physicians and a Sanitarium; the two latter cause the city to be the resort of invalids from far and near. No diseases are here called incurable. At Mingan harbour, on the Gulf of St. Lawrence, are situated the great works where all the rocket-cars for the Dominion are built. The site was chosen on account of the large tract of desolate country to the north of it. The cars as soon as built are tested, first at short flights, then at longer ones, and conductors are trained to manage them. There are no regular lines of cars through or over Labrador, and so there is no risk of collision in the trial trips. Considerable difficulty is experienced at first in taking a car a flight of 100 miles, but by practice flights of over 1,000 miles are managed with perfect safety.

The contrast between the present and past might be drawn out to any extent, but enough has been said to enable the dullest mind to realize the truly marvellous development of our great Dominion. And if the development and advance have been great industrially and commercially, so have they been great, almost greater, socially; for socially we have set examples which the whole world has not been slow to follow.

III

"But Heaven hath a hand in these events."
—Richard II, Act V.

The state of society in the nineteenth century would have but few attractions for us of the twentieth, were we able to return along the vista of a hundred years. Our manners and customs are so vastly different from those of our great-grandfathers that we should feel out of place indeed had we to go back, even for a short time, to their uncouth and imperfect ways. Their extraordinarily complex methods of governing themselves, and their intricate political machinery would be very distressing to us, and are calculated to make one think that a keen pleasure in governing or in being overgoverned—not a special aptitude or genius for governing— must have been very common among them. From the alarming blunders made in directing public affairs, and from the manner in which beneficial measures were opposed by the party out of office, it appears quite certain that the instincts of true statesmanship did not animate all classes then as now. Nevertheless our forefathers went into the work of governing themselves and each other with a great deal of vim. They had no well drawn out formulæ to work upon as we have, but they went at things in a sort of rule-of-thumb, rough-and-ready style, and when one party had dragged the country into the mire, the other dragged it out again. It was customary for the party that was out of office to say that the party that was in was corrupt and venal—that every man of it was a liar, was a thief, was taking bribes, would soon be kicked out, etc. Then the party that was in had to say that the party that was out should look to its own sins and remember that everyone of its men when they were in proved himself incapable, insensible to every feeling of shame, with no susceptibilities except in his pocket, corrupt in every fibre, being justly rewarded when hurled from office by an indignant people, etc., etc. The wonder is that the country ever got governed at all, but it seems that all public men who had any fixed and sensible ideas and wished to see them carried out, had to make themselves callous, pachydermatous, hardened against this offensive mud-slinging. Of course politics did not elevate the man, nor the man politics, while things went on thus. A general demoralization and lowering of the tone of public opinion naturally resulted, which did not improve till the stirring events of the summer of 1887 brought men to their senses again. The number of members sent to Parliament was something so enormous, that it seems as if the people must have had a perfect mania for being represented. Nowadays we got along spendidly with only fifteen members (one for each Province) and a speaker. Formerly several hundred was not thought too many, and before the constitution was revised in 1935, there were actually over seven hundred representatives assembled at Ottawa every year. Perhaps this was all right under the circumstances, as there did not then exist any organization for training men for Parliamentary duties, or selecting them for candidature such as now exists; so there was safety in numbers, though the floods of talk must at times have been overwhelming. Besides the Central Parliament at Ottawa, there was a Local Parliament to every Province, and in some Provinces two Houses. It seems a mystery to us, now, how any measure could be got through in less than twelve months, but our forefathers apparently took pleasure in interminable harangues and oceans of verbosity, and prominent men contrived to make themselves heard above the universal clatter of tongues, so that good measures got pushed through somehow to the satisfaction of a much-enduring public. Nowadays our fifteen members put by as much work in two days as would have kept an old Parliament talking for two years. Provincial Parliaments, with their crowds of M.P.P.'s, were abolished in 1935, and it was then also that the number of members at Ottawa was reduced from the absurd total of 750 to 15, and the round million or so which they cost the country saved. Members are not now paid; the honour of the position is sufficient emolument. When these and other changes were made, the expenses of government were enormously reduced, so much so, that after ten years, that is in 1945, taxes were abolished altogether, and from that time forward not a cent of taxation has been put upon the people. The revenue is now obtained in this way. Up to 1935 the revenue of the country stood at something over $150,000,000. When the constitution was changed the expenses of government were lessened to $50,000,000. It was then agreed that for ten years longer the revenue should remain at $150,000,000 (people were prosperous and willing enough to have contributed double), so that every year of the ten $100,000,000 might be invested. Thus at the end of ten years the Government possessed a capital of $1,000,000,000, and the interest of this constitutes our present revenue. If any great public works are being carried out, and more money is required, the municipalities are appealed to, and public meetings are held. All the great cities then vie with each other in presenting the Government with large sums. How the poor over-burdened tax-payer of 1883 would have rejoiced in all this!

Another great blessing to us is that war has ceased all the world over. It became, at last, too destructive to be indulged in at all. During the last great European war in 1932, while three emperors, two kings and several princes were parleying together, a monster oxyhydrogen shell exploded near them and created fearful havoc. All the royal personages were blown to atoms, as were also many of their attendants. Their armies hardly had a chance of getting near each other, so fearful was the execution of the shells. Since then the world has been free from war, and, but for gathering clouds in Asia, would seem likely to remain so. Anyhow, we in Canada, have not the shadow of a standing army, nor a single keel to represent a navy. We are too well occupied to wish to be aggressive, and no power except the United States could ever attack us, and even if Americans coveted our possessions they are not likely to resort to such

311

an old-fashioned expedient as warfare to gain them. They could only annex us by so improving their constitution, as to make it plainly very much superior to ours. If they ever do this (and as yet there are no signs of it) there might be some chance of a union. At present the chances are all the other way. The only sort of union that is quite likely to come about is the joining by the Americans of the United Empire, or Confederation of all English-speaking nations, with which we have been connected for some years. The seat of the Imperial Government has hitherto been London, but British influence has made such strides in the East that there is every probability of another city being chosen for the capital, and of the seat of Government being made more central. Should one of the now restored ancient cities of the East become the metropolis of this glorious Imperial Confederation, the United States would certainly come into the Confederation, as great numbers of Americans have already migrated to the Orient.

A word on the changes which have come over the East will not be inappropriate, lest we should be tempted to boast too much of the progress of Canada. Ever since the conquest of Egypt by the British, as long ago as 1882, Anglo-Saxon institutions have been gaining ground from the Nile to the Euphrates, and from the Euphrates to the Indus. Soon after the great stroke of diplomacy in 1887, by which Great Britain practically became ruler of all this vast territory, the railroad was introduced, and before many years had passed the railroad system of Europe was linked with that of India. The pent-up riches of the fertile Euphrates valley thenceforth began to find channels of commerce, and to be distributed through less fertile regions. The ancient historic cities of these lands, Damascus especially, began at once to increase. Jerusalem, as soon as the Turk departed and the Anglo-Saxon entered, was purified, cleansed, and finally rebuilt. Great numbers of Jews from all parts of the world then returned and gave the city the benefit of their wealth, but all the commerce of the East keeps in the hands of Britons and Americans. English is, therefore, the chief language spoken from Beyrout to Bombay.

There is, however, a great cloud hanging over the East which causes dismay to thinking men, and threatens to mar the general prosperity of all the lands. Great as has been the increase of the Anglo-Saxon race, the numbers of the Sclavonic race have kept pace. The Sclavs, unfortunately, retain much of their old brutish disposition and ferocity in the midst of all the civilizing influences of modern times, so that statesmen foresee an inevitable collision in the not distant future between the Sclav and the Anglo-Saxon. It is disheartening in these days of splendid progress, when we had hoped that war was for ever banished from the world, to find that humanity has yet to endure the old horrors once more. How fearful these horrors will be, and how great the destruction of life, it is hardly possible to conceive, so terrible are the forces at man's command nowadays, if he uses them simply for destructive purposes. The Sclav has spread from South-Eastern Europe and multiplied greatly in Asia, till his boundaries are coterminous with British territory, and it is his inveterate aggressive disposition which causes all the gloomy forebodings. Before we return to our own happy Canada, let us glance at Africa, the "dark continent" of the last century. Civilization has long penetrated to the upper waters of the Nile, and to the great fresh water lakes which rival our Huron and Superior. The beautiful country in which the mighty Congo and the Nile take their rise, is all open to the world's commerce, and highways now exist stretching from Alexandria through these magnificent regions to the Transvaal and the Cape. Madagascar, fair, fertile and wealthy, has developed, under Anglo-Saxon influence, her wonderful latent resources for all men's good. In addition to mineral treasures she had wealth to bestow in the shape of healing plants, whose benefits were greater to suffering humanity than tons of gold and silver. The botanical gardens at New Westminster, and the conservatories at Churchill, are greatly indebted to the flora of Madagascar. But let us now return to Canada and continue our contrasts.

Much of the success of our modern social movements has been due to the exertions of the noble Society of Benefactors. The members of this Society, as we well know, are now mostly men of independent means. Their chief idea is to bring together and combine social forces for the public good, which were formerly wasted. The Society has already existed for two generations, so that our rising generation is reaping the full benefit of its exertions. It is chiefly to these exertions that the improved tone of public opinion is due, and the general, moral and intellectual elevation of the present day are largely owing to the same cause. In the old benighted times before 1900 much wealth and ability were, for want of organization, allowed to run almost to waste as far as the general good of society was concerned. Men of means led aimless lives, squandering their riches in foreign cities, or staying at home to accumulate more and more, forgetting, or never considering what a powerful means of ameliorating the condition of their fellow creatures was within their reach. It was not only the lower classes that needed improvement, but the whole mass of society in all its aims, ideas and pursuits. Improvement on this large scale would never have been accomplished by the elaborate theorising and much preaching of the nineteenth century. Action, bold and fearless action, was wanted, and until men were found with minds entirely free from morbid theories, but full of the courage of their new convictions, the world had to wait in tantalizing suspense for improvement, always hoping that each new scientific discovery would enlighten mankind in the desired direction, but always doomed to be disappointed and to see humanity growing either more savage or physically weaker, simultaneously with each phase of enlightenment. These things are perhaps truer of society in Europe, and in some of the States, than in our young Dominion, where everything was necessarily in a somewhat inchoate condition. Yet had it not been for the great men who providentially appeared in our midst—our history, our manners, and customs, our whole career as a nation would simply have been a repetition of European civilization with all its defects, failures and vices. Statistics of the period show that neither in the States nor in Canada, amidst all the surrounding newness, had there arisen any new social condition peculiar to this continent which remedied to any extent the evils rampant in old countries. Lunatic asylums, in ghastly sarcasm on a self-styled intellectual age, reared their colossal facades and enclosed their thousands of human wrecks. Huge prisons had to be built in every large town. Hospitals were frequently crowded with victims of foul diseases. Great cities abounded with filthy lanes, alleys, and dwellings like dens of wild beasts. Epidemic diseases occurred from brutal disregard of sanitary measures. Murder and suicide were rife. Horrible accidents from preventible causes occurred daily. Great fires were continually destroying valuable city property, and ruinous monetary panics happened every few years. And all this in an age that prided itself on being advanced! An age that produced the telephone, but crowded up lunatic asylums! That cabled messages all round the world, but filled its prisons to the doors! That named the metals in the sun, but could not cleanse its cities! An age, in fact, that was but one remove from the unmitigated barbarism of medieval times! How marvellous is the change wrought by a hundred years! We have not been shocked by a murder in Canada for more than fifty years, nor has a suicide been heard of for a very long period. Epidemic diseases belong to the past. The sewage question, that source of vexation to the municipalities of old, has been scientifically settled—to the saving of enormous sums of money, and to the permanent benefit of the community's health. Malignant scourges, like consumption, epilepsy, cancer, etc., are never heard of except in less favored countries. There is but one prison to a province, and that is sometimes empty. Our cities are all fire-proof, and the night air is never startled now by the hideous jangling of fire-bells, arousing the citizens from sleep to view the destruction of their city. So rational and interesting has daily life become, that mind and body are constantly in healthy occupation; the fearful nervous hurry of old times, that broke down so many minds and bodies, having died out, to give way to a robust force of character which accomplishes much more with half the fuss. Of course, advantages such as these, did not spring upon society all at once; they have come about by comparatively slow degrees.

The first president of the Society of Benefactors, who died some years ago at an advanced age, was the man who started the new order of things. When he commenced to give the world the benefit of his views, he met with a good deal of opposition and ridicule, being told that the world was going on all right and was improving all the time, and that if people would only stop preaching and set to work at doing a little more, things would get better more quickly. He could not be convinced, however, that society had any grounds for its satisfaction, but he took the hint about preaching and stopped his lectures, which he had been giving all through the country. He then set to work at organization, and as he had inherited ample means from a millionaire father, he commenced under good auspices. He went into his work with great eagerness, gathering together all sorts of people, who held views similar to his own, though usually in a vague unpractical way, and formed his first committee of a bishop, celebrated for his enlightened opinions, two physicians, two lawyers, several wealthy merchants, and several working men who were good speakers and had influence among their fellows. His capacity for organization was great, and his success in gaining over to his side young men of means, remarkable. From the very beginning the committee never lacked money. Though they were actuated by purely philanthropic motives, it was one of their first principles never to sink large sums of money in any undertaking that would not pay its own expenses ultimately. There was, therefore, a healthy business-like tone about whatever they did, that distinguished their efforts from many well-intentioned, but sickly, undertakings of the same day, which one after another came to grief, doing nearly as much harm as good. One of their first works was to buy up lots and dwellings in the worst districts of Toronto, where miserable shanties and hovels stood in fetid slums, as foul as any in London or Glasgow. The hovels and shanties were then torn down, and respectable dwellings erected in their stead. The unfortunate wretches, the victims of drink, crime, or thriftlessness, who inhabited such places, were not turned away to seek a fouler footing elsewhere, but were taken in hand by the working-men on the committee, and were started afresh in life with every encouragement. They were generally permanently rescued from degradation, but if some fell back their children were saved, and so the next generation was spared a family of criminals. Montreal was next visited and the same thing done there; attention was then turned to Quebec and Winnipeg. Successful attempts were afterwards made to control the liquor traffic, not by sudden prohibition, which always increased the evil, but by common sense methods, necessarily somewhat slow, but sure. When the

Society had been at work ten years, there was a very perceptible diminution in the amount of crime and smaller offences in all their spheres of action. Police forces could be decreased, and a prison here and there closed. This had a tendency to lessen the rates, so the taxpayer became touched in his tenderest part—his pocket. His heart and his conscience then immediately softened toward the Society's work, though years of preaching and the existence of all abominable evils close to his door had failed to move him. When this point had been reached, the Society began to be looked upon as one of the great remedial agents of the age, and work was much easier. One evil after another was grappled with, and in time subdued. Scientific researches were set on foot in hygiene, medicine, and every subject from which the community at large could derive benefit, till in twenty years time so much general improvement had been effected that Canada's ways of doing things came to be quoted in other countries as a precedent. Our cities were the best built, best drained, cleanest and healthiest, and our city populations the most orderly and most enlightened. The Society's roll of members now included a great number of eminent men, and their operations were extended over the whole Dominion, and works of all kinds were carried on simultaneously in all parts. Outside the Society, it had become quite fashionable for all classes to take the most eager interest in everything concerning the public welfare, so the Dominion continued to prosper and advance with wonderful rapidity. Thus it happened that we came to take the lead among nations and have been able to keep foremost ever since, though with our 93,000,000 we are not by any means the largest nation.

The improved hygienic conditions under which we live have had the effect of very largely increasing the population. Our forefathers in their wisdom spent large sums of money in attracting immigrants to our shores, but it did not occur to them to increase the population by preventing people from dying. Very few persons die now, except from old age, and the tremendous and almost incredible mortality of old times among infants is stopped, consequently the death rate is very low, and the excess of births over deaths very great. There are only three doctors to each large city, and they are subsidised by government or the town councils, because there are not enough sick people from whom they could make a living as of yore. The good health of the public is also in some measure due to the fact of our scientific men having been able, since a few years past, to gain a good deal of control over the weather. By means of captive balloons, currents of electricity between the higher atmosphere and the earth are kept passing regularly. By other electrical contrivances as well as these, rain can now be nearly always made to come at night and can be prevented from falling during the day. Hurricanes and desolating storms are also held very much under control.

Our contrasts are now drawing to a close. Enough has been said to make it plain to the slowest intellect among us, what is gained by having been born in the twentieth century, instead of in the nineteenth, and by being born a Canadian, instead of to any other land. There can hardly be to-day such a woeful creature as a Canadian who does not realise and is not proud of the grandeur of his heritage. Our race, owing to the splendid hygienic and social conditions that have been dilated upon, is one of the healthiest and strongest on the face of the earth. We are not demoralized or effeminated by the luxury and abundance which are ours, but elevated rather, and strengthened by the very magnificence and opulence of our circumstances, and by the perfect freedom, under healthful restraint, which we enjoy through the community's strong, vigorous, moral and intellectual tone.

As there is nothing more wonderful about the present age, or more characteristic of the times, than our mode of travelling, these few pages shall be concluded with a plan of a very simple journey, a journey which can be strongly recommended to all who are wishing for change of scene and are somewhat bewildered in choosing a route among the innumerable places in the world which have claims on their attention. We will imagine that a party of twenty has been made up, and that the start is from Halifax, the direction eastward, and the destination Constantinople. The car which is timed to start at 7 a.m., is standing at rest on the sloping side, while the passengers, say fifty in number, are taking their seats in the luxurious chamber within. The first stop is at Sydney, Cape Breton, and the car is pointed accurately in that direction. At three minutes to 7 the engineers and conductor come on board; the former to place the powerful oxyhydrogen charge in the great breech-loading tube, the latter to close the doors against ingress or egress. Precisely at 7 the signal is given. A furious and powerful hissing is then heard, as well as a momentary scraping of the car on its runners. In another second she is high in the air, and already Halifax has nearly receded from the engineer's sight. The rate of a mile in three seconds is kept up till Sydney rapidly appears in view. In the next few seconds the engineer exerts his skill and the car lands gracefully on the slide, still in brisk motion. After a little scraping and crunching on the runners, she pulls up at the station platform at the bottom of the decline, ten minutes only after leaving Halifax. The next spring is made to St. John's, Newfoundland, which is reached in fourteen minutes. Here a few minutes are taken up in pointing the car accurately for Galway. Great caution is necessary, and very delicate and beautiful instruments are employed. When all are on board again and ready for the supermarine voyage, the engineer loads up with a much more powerful charge than before. He prepares at the start for a speed of a mile in three seconds, then, when fairly out over the sea, a stronger electric current is applied to the huge charge, and a speed of a mile, or even more, a second is obtained. This fearful velocity is not permitted overland, for fear of collisions, as car routes cross each other. But no routes cross over the sea between St. John's and Galway, nor is the Galway car allowed to leave till the St. John's car has arrived, and vice versa, therefore the highest speed attainable is permitted. Before land again looms in view, speed is much slackened, and now the engineer requires all his experience and his utmost skill. The high winds across the ocean may have caused his car to deviate slightly from its path, so as soon as land appears the deviation has to be corrected, and only two or three seconds remain in which to correct it. However, the engineer is equal to his task, and the car is now in the same manner as before, brought to a stand in Galway at 6 minutes to 8, just 30 minutes out from St. John's and 54 from Halifax. At 8 o'clock Dublin is reached, next comes Holyhead, and then London at 8.20. Here passengers for the South of Europe change cars. As the car for the South does not start till 8.30, there is time for a hasty glance at the enormous central depot just arrived at—one of the wonders of the world. Cars are coming in every minute punctually on time from all parts of the country and the world. The arrival slide is here shaped like the inside or concavity of a shallow cone, two miles in diameter, with the edge rather more than 150 feet from the ground. In the centre, where the cars stop, is a hydraulic elevator, by which they are immediately let down below to make room for the next arrival. The passengers are then disembarked without hurry. Those who are to continue their journey then go on board their right car and are again started on time. The departure slide is like a lower storey of the arrival one. It is immediately beneath it, but its grade is not quite parallel. Near the centre, where the cars start, the upper slide is twenty-five feet above the lower one, but at the edge, a mile distant, in consequence of the difference in grade, there is fifty feet between them. The path of the cars before they emerge from the departure slide, is between the supports of the upper one, yet the supports are so placed that the cars can be pointed before starting for all the principal routes. There is a through car to Constantinople, and in it the twenty passengers from Halifax take their seats. At 8.30 the first spring is made, and Paris is reached in 10 minutes. Another spring, and in 10 minutes more Strasbourg appears. Then successively: Munich in 8 minutes, Vienna in 10, Belgrade in 15, and lastly Constantinople in 20, or at 9.43, that is just one hour and thirteen minutes from leaving London, and two hours and 43 minutes from Halifax. It is still early in the day—well that is where a surprise awaits the traveller who has not considered that he has been journeying eastward through more than ninety degrees of longitude, so that instead of being a quarter to ten in the morning, it is a good six hours later, or just about four in the afternoon. Two out of the twenty Haligonians are on business only, and intend to return the same night; the other eighteen, after seeing the lions of Constantinople intend visiting Jerusalem, the Persian Gulf, Bombay, Calcutta, Hong Kong, Pekin, and Yokohama, staying a day or two in each city. The car services on this route have been in existence a good many years and are well organized. From Yokohama a long flight over the Pacific will be taken and Canadian soil again struck at Victoria. We will not follow the eighteen travellers in their eight or ten days sight-seeing, but will return to the two Haligonians at Constantinople, who have got through their business in a few hours, and must go back to Halifax at once. They start for London at 10 p.m., Constantinople time, arriving there in one hour and thirteen minutes over the route they traversed in the morning. They change cars, and in ten minutes are off again via Holyhead, Dublin, Galway, St. John's and Sydney, C. B., for Halifax, where they arrive in one hour and 20 minutes from London, or forty-three minutes after midnight by Constantinople time, but more than six hours earlier, or about 6.30 in the evening by Halifax time. They have therefore got ahead of the sun in his apparent journey round the world, for he had set for at least two hours when they started from Constantinople, but they caught up with him when over the Atlantic, and to the engineer it appeared as if he were rising in the west. This is a daily experience of travellers going west, which never fails at first to create great surprise. Our two voyagers are now safe back, at the port from which they set out a little less than twelve hours before. They are quite accustomed to such travelling, and have done nothing but what thousands are doing daily. But what would have been thought, if such a journey had been described a hundred years ago, in 1883? And how will the world travel a hundred years hence, in 2083? It is hard to say, or even to imagine. Yet inventive skill is unceasingly active, and in all probability speed will eventually be still further accelerated.

And now our task of contrasting Canada in 1983 with Canada in 1883 is concluded, and surely in this epitome of the works of a century there is food for reflection for the inventor, the statesman, the moralist and the philanthropist. All, when pondering on the gradual, but sure improvement that has come about in their respective paths, can take heart and nerve themselves for renewed effort, or be induced to stand firm till success comes to reward their courage. No man can despair who ponders on the position of the Dominion in 1983.

319

Stanley Jackson and
Roman Kroitor
UNIVERSE

Among the many outstanding documentary films produced by the National Film Board of Canada there is one that exists in a class by itself. This film is Universe *which, since its release in 1960, has been synonymous for a generation of film-goers with "a sense of wonder." This short feature, twenty-six minutes in length, photographed in black and white, was produced by Tom Daly and directed by Roman Kroitor and Colin Low. The moving, magisterial commentary to the film was written by Stanley Jackson and Roman Kroitor, NFB producers in Montreal, and read with great effect by the actor, Douglas Rain.* Universe *has won more than two dozen awards, and its special effects had a direct influence on Stanley Kubrick, who chose Rain to speak the lines of HAL 9000, the malevolent computer, in his feature film,* 2001: A Space Odyssey. *The entry that follows, the commentary to* Universe, *is being published here for the first time.*

Narrator: *The ground beneath our feet is the surface of a planet whirling at thousands of miles an hour around a distant sun. Our life is possible only because of the light and warmth of that sun, a star. Yet the sun which shines on us is only one out of millions of such stars in the universe.*
This is one of the world's major observatories, the David Dunlap Observatory, fifteen miles north of Toronto. Dr. Donald McRae is a professor of astronomy at the University of Toronto.

(Phone rings)

McRae: *Observatory!*

Narrator: *At any moment, scattered throughout the world there are hundreds of men and women observing the heavens with optical and radio telescopes, gathering data for the solution of many questions about the universe. Routine work for the most part. McRae's job tonight, if the sky remains clear, will be to take photographs of six stars with the telescope.*

A mirror, over six feet in diameter, with its surface shaped to within one-millionth of an inch, will catch the light from a star. This light will be reflected from the large mirror onto a smaller one, which in turn will focus it back into a camera at the base of the telescope.

Out of the study of hundreds of thousands of observations astronomers have pieced together an accurate picture of the universe.

Beyond the appearance of star-shine and moonbeam what will the first men to leave the earth find? Enough is now known that we can, in imagination, journey into these spaces.

250,000 miles away, the moon. This is the moon that men have worshipped as a goddess, that countless lovers have sighed over and sworn by.

It will take immense courage to journey to this place, for on this pitted and pocked ball of pumice and stone, there is no atmosphere. No air to breathe, no sound to hear.

By day the sun's heat would boil water, if there were water.

At night, 240° below zero.

Unshielded, a man couldn't live here for two minutes but if he were to die his body would lie unchanged through thousands of years, for nothing grows and nothing decays. If you were to hover in space beyond the moon, speeding up in imagination its movement, you would see a majestic procession in the sky. As the moon circles the earth, so the earth itself circles the sun. The sun is the centre of a system of nine heavenly bodies called planets which wheel around it in vast orbits, trapped by its gravitational pull. Closest to it, the tiny planet, Mercury.

On the surface of Mercury the temperature is hot enough to melt lead. The one face of it is turned perpetually to the sun only 36 million miles away.

If we looked outward from Mercury we would see the second closest planet, Venus, shining brighter than the much more distant stars. Venus, in orbit thirty-one million miles further out from the sun, is a mystery, for its face is veiled by dust storms or perhaps dense cloud. Looking outward from Venus, the most brilliant and beautiful object in the sky would be a planet in orbit twenty-five million miles still further out— Earth.

Beyond Earth, shining redly in the night, Mars, colder than Earth and smaller. This is the planet men have looked on and wondered whether they are alone in the heavens.

321

It is reasonably certain that the markings on its surface, blue-ish green in the Martian summer, turning rusty brown in the autumn, indicate vegetation.

Here, however, the atmosphere has almost no oxygen and no creatures like men could live here, a hundred and forty million miles from the sun.

In a place past Mars, where there should theoretically be a planet, there are only the asteroids—small bodies ranging from boulders to chunks three hundred miles across—hundreds of them swinging in orbit about the sun.

Five hundred million miles out from the sun, the giant planet Jupiter, ruling twelve moons.

Jupiter, seen here from one of its moons, is larger than all the other planets put together. Its atmosphere is a thousand miles deep, a poisonous mixture of methane gas, ammonia and hydrogen, which at the bottom must have the density of water.

Here, under the enormous pressure of the atmosphere, a human being would be crushed beyond recognition.

These are the rings of Saturn—bands ten thousand miles wide, composed of almost an infinity of meteoric particles of gravel and ice circling the sixth planet. Saturn, with its nine moons, is so far from the sun that it takes thirty Earth years to circle it, and here the temperature never rises above 240° below zero. And if we were to plunge still further out, hundreds of millions of miles, past the planet Uranus, beyond Neptune, we would finally come to the last of the known planets, to the dwarf Pluto, named for the god of the underworld.

Its surface moves in perpetual darkness and unimaginable cold, for the sun is four billion miles away—only a starry speck in the sky.

Sometimes a strange apparition appears in the sky—a comet. Like a planet, a comet orbits the sun, but it is only a loose conglomeration of ice and dust, invisible until its head comes close enough to the sun, whose rays then excite it into fluorescence and push away from the head a vaporous tail which may become a million miles long.

For a few weeks a comet blossoms and then, passing the sun, it will fade and coast again unseen, billions of miles into the darkness—perhaps not to return for a century to the blazing star which is its master.

The sun is an unimaginable inferno—a thermo-nuclear furnace churning with the storms we see as sunspots, heaving from its surface columns of gas that arch three hundred thousand miles into space, pulled and twisted by enormous electrical and magnetic fields.

The sun produces the energy of a million hydrogen bombs exploding every second. So it has raged for five billion years and so it will rage for perhaps another five billion years, flooding its planets with radiant energy.

Too near or too far from this furnace, instant death for men. Between ninety-one and ninety-three million miles from this star, filtered through a blanket of atmosphere, its energies sustain human life.

When a particular star is to be photographed it is located by its co-ordinates on a star chart. On such a chart every black speck is a star.

McRae: *"Fourteen six point seven plus thirteen forty-nine."*

Narrator: *Forty-five tons of steel and glass must be aimed precisely at a spot perhaps two hundred million billion miles away.*

Many of the stars astronomers study are invisible to the naked eye. Even the nearest ones, apart from our sun, are so far away that their light is very dim. The mirror in the base of the telescope gathers and focuses hundreds of thousands of times the amount of light seen by the naked eye.

Almost nothing of a star can be known directly. It is a photograph that is studied. Not a portrait of a star but a photograph of its light, split into a spectrum in which each band has its meaning: the presence in that distant star of elements like iron, calcium, carbon. From a spectroscopic photograph astronomers can tell whether a star is moving towards us or away by exposing on the same plate the spectrum of the star and the spectrum of an iron arc and measuring the displacement between the two.

To photograph the spectrum of the arc takes ten seconds. To catch enough of the light from the star may take up to two hours. During the exposure, machinery in the base of the telescope automatically compensates for the rotation of the earth, keeping the star centred.

If we looked more deeply into space, leaving behind us the earth and the whole of our solar system, and travelled at the speed of light, it would take four years before we came to even the closest of the billions of suns scattered through stellar space.

*Although the stars are suns, many of them are unlike our sun.
Some, like Beta in the Constellation Lyra, instead of planets,
have a second sun swinging around them.*

*There are multiple suns like Castor in the Constellation Gem-
ini.*

*There are giant suns five thousand times as large as ours, and
dwarfs in which one cubic inch of matter weighs forty tons.
Suns rotating so rapidly that pin-wheels of gas are thrown off
weighing more than our whole system of planets. Suns that,
over a period of days or hours, pulse as their internal nuclear
processes change. Rare suns in which the temperature reaches
five billion degrees—where nuclear fusion makes elements as
heavy as iron and results in the enormous explosion of a nova
or super-nova.*

*The brilliant light from such explosions floods through the
gaseous clouds of space for billions on billions of miles and the
remains of a super-nova, recorded ten centuries ago, can still be
seen as the Crab Nebula in the Constellation Taurus.*

*As well as stars, in stellar space there is gas and dust, some-
times glowing in starlight, sometimes dark obscuring what is
behind them. Stars, gas, dust—all moving in apparent chaos.
Until a generation ago it seemed indecipherable. The only suggestion of form was their grouping in the band we know as
the Milky Way.*

Student's
  voice: *"Dr. McRae!"*

Narrator: *Now years of patient work have revealed a pattern in the universe. A pattern beyond anything we could have imagined
looking at the heavens with the naked eye. With data sifted
from countless painstaking observations, astronomers are now
filling in the details of a pattern so vast that everyday ideas of
distance and time cannot encompass it.*

Student: *"It's plus, isn't it?"*

Narrator: *If we could move with the freedom of a god so that a million
years pass in a second, and if we went far enough, past the
nearest suns, beyond the star clouds and nebulae, in time they
would end and, as if moving out from behind a curtain, we
would come to an endless sea of night.*

In that sea are islands, continents of stars that we have named the Galaxies, the largest known forms in the universe, hundreds of billions of suns bound together by gravity, rotating around their common centre once in two hundred million years.

Our sun, with its planets, is near the edge of one such Galaxy, the rim of which we see dimly as the Milky Way. The Galaxies are the birthplace and graveyard of the stars. Here, gas contracts into knots, becomes hot and flares into the life of a sun, sometimes forming with it planets, sometimes planets which must be suitable for life. And here, too, the stars finally consume themselves and collapse into cold dark dwarfs.

A hundred billion suns, yet forms so enormous that they have been observed slipping through one another like phantoms, their stars light years apart continuing undisturbed in their courses. At the very limit of our most powerful instruments galaxies still are flung across space, themselves as numerous as stars in the night sky.

But when we look this deeply into space we are looking at a ghostly image of the distant past, for the light by which we see these regions started travelling towards us long before the dawn of life on earth. In all of time, on all the planets of all the galaxies in space, what civilizations have risen, looked into the night, seen what we see, asked the questions that we ask?

David Ketterer
CANADIAN
SCIENCE FICTION

The distinction of having written the first essay on Canadian SF&F belongs to Donald A. Wollheim, the American editor and writer, who in December 1942 contributed "Whither Canadian Fantasy?" to Uncanny Tales, a pulp magazine published in Toronto during the Second World War. Wollheim's article is of historical interest and discusses the subject without once mentioning the name of a single writer, American, British, or Canadian. The author of "Canadian Science Fiction" is David Ketterer, who was born in 1942 at Leigh-on-Sea, Essex, England, and holds degrees from the University of Wales, Carleton University, and the University of Essex. He came to Canada in 1964 and three years later joined the English department of Sir George Williams University, now Concordia University, in Montreal, where he still teaches. Ketterer is the author of New Worlds for Old: The Apocalyptic Imagination, Science Fiction, and American Literature *(1974), and* Frankenstein's Creation *(1979). "Canadian Science Fiction: A Survey," the first modern article on the range of science fiction written by Canadians, is an expanded version of an article that originally appeared in* Canadian Children's Literature, *Number 10, 1977-78. With Ketterer's survey and Margaret Atwood's critical essay, "Canadian Monsters," also included in this anthology, the reader will have an overview of the Canadian achievement in science fiction and fantasy. These selections will also serve as a guide to writers and works not included in the present anthology due to the unfortunate fact that anthologies, unlike time and space, must have an end.*

Although science fiction generally encourages a cosmic and cosmopolitan outlook, it is neither surprising nor undesirable that there are observable differences between the productions of different countries. Anthologies of Russian, French, Japanese and Australian science fiction, for example, have given some sense of these differences. Since the bulk of science fiction is written in America and its nature is well known there has never existed nor is there likely to be an anthology labelled "American Science Fiction." At the same time, prior to the present volume, there has not existed an anthology of Canadian science fiction in spite of the fact that the home situation is almost exactly opposite that in America. Indeed, one might ask, what Canadian science fiction? Any argument for the specifically American nature of the genre gains considerable support from the evidence that the output of science fiction appears to stop abruptly north of the 49th parallel. Canadian science fiction is a rare phenomenon but it does exist. Much of what little there is appeared and continues to appear in American publications where it becomes essentially indistinguishable from the mass of American science fiction. It is, then, the intent of this survey of predominantly English-Canadian science fiction to render visible and distinctive an aspect of Canadian writing hitherto largely invisible.

The science fiction and/or weird fantasy magazine has been and still is virtually non-existent in Canada although, in the early forties when Canada banned the importation of American pulp magazines, there was some compensatory activity. Most of the magazines that then appeared were simply reprints of American originals but three Canadian titles did arise. Between 1940 and 1943, 21 issues of *Uncanny Tales*, containing mainly reprinted American material, were published, and an issue of something called *Eerie Tales*, dated July 1941, also appeared. Of more immediate interest is a magazine entitled *Science Fiction* which claimed (albeit falsely) to contain only Canadian authors and artists. It survived 6 issues between October, 1941, and June, 1942. More recently a number of fanzines have appeared such as *Paradox* and *Requiem* (to instance two Quebec titles, the first English, the second French). And while Leland Sapiro, an American, resided in Saskatchewan his *Riverside Quarterly* eminated from that province and reflected something of its Canadian milieu.

In a superficial "mythic" fashion, it is not difficult to account for the dearth of Canadian science fiction, in spite of the fact that Canadian literature generally and science fiction do share one salient characteristic: a respect for the pressure of an environment which is often foregrounded. But the basic shape and nature of the genre is, in many ways, an expression of a particularly aggressive American attitude towards nature. No doubt many of the attitudes and actions taken in the course of extending the western frontier and subjugating the landscapes were undesirable, but the guiding ideal of "conquering" the unknown is at the heart of science fiction. In Canada a rather different mythology appears to operate. It finds expression in the somewhat clichéd notion that climatically and geographically the landscape is too much for man to handle. This reverent or submissive attitude towards nature translates into a fiction which tends towards mythic fantasy and stories about animals often told from the animal's point of view. Furthermore, the conservative history of

Canada, as opposed to the revolutionary history of America, clearly entails a regard for the status quo and a suspicious or cautious attitude towards change. Science fiction and change, it has often been observed, go hand in glove.

However, it should be recognized that the aggressive, revolutionary characteristic of science fiction can account for many of its worst qualities. Norman Spinrad's *The Iron Dream* presents the not altogether frivolous hypothesis that in a parallel world where Hitler does not become a German leader, he expresses his vision as a science-fiction writer. The frenzied apocalyptic sensibility which accompanied the rise of the Third Reich is one that can and frequently does find an outlet in science fiction. There is, of course, a positive side to the coin and there is room for the gentler, more caring and human-centered kind of science fiction perhaps more consistent with a Canadian value system.

In fact Canada has contributed significantly to the overall history of science fiction. I have primarily in mind two books: James De Mille's *A Strange Manuscript Found in a Copper Cylinder* and Frederick Philip Grove's *Consider Her Ways*. The first of these has found its way into one of the histories of science fiction—J. O. Bailey's *Pilgrims Through Space and Time*. The second by incredible oversight does not figure in any. *A Strange Manuscript*, published posthumously in 1888 but written eight or more years earlier, is one of the best science-fiction novels of the nineteenth century.

In an opening "frame" chapter, four Englishmen on a yachting holiday pull aboard a floating cylinder which on examination is discovered to contain the "strange manuscript." The manuscript, which is read in turn by each of the group, tells the story of Adam More, the sole survivor of a shipwreck, who drifts through an opening in the great Antarctic ice barrier to find a lush, almost tropical world. This world is inhabited by a Semitic people called the Kosekin whose "utopian" society derives from the inversion or distortion of Western and Christian values. The Kosekin have carried altruism to a logical extreme where well-being and life itself are regarded as evils and poverty and death as the supreme virtues. The frame situation is periodically reverted to in four chapters where the Englishmen discuss the nature and validity of the account. While very derivative of such works as Thomas More's *Utopia* (hence the protagonist's name), Swift's *Gulliver's Travels*, Samuel Butler's *Erewhon* and especially Poe's *Narrative of A. Gordon Pym*, De Mille's satiric romance is replete with fresh and marvellous incident and achieves a uniquely interesting synthesis.

Grove's *Consider Her Ways*—not to be confused with John Wyndham's novella of the same title—is also comparable with *Gulliver's Travels* and not altogether unfavorably. This book was published in 1947 but written twenty years earlier. It concerns a society of ants from Venezuela who explore North America. The leader of the ants communicates his account telepathically to a human recorder. A satiric intention is present, but what makes the novel especially science-fictional is the emphasis placed on the compelling realization of the ant society and its peculiar perspective. This is an accomplishment which must have involved Grove in considerable background research. It is remarkable that a book which Desmond Pacey calls Grove's best has been completely overlooked by the historians of science fiction. And it is equally remarkable, given that one of the best books of one of Canada's best writers is straight science fiction, and given the existence of *A Strange Manuscript*, that demographers and historians of the Canadian imagination have not identified a science-fictional tradition.

These two books mark the high point of what might be called a mainstream or "classic" line in Canadian science fiction. This category includes stories by a number of major Canadian writers who have occasionally turned their hands to science fiction: for example, *The British Barbarians* (1895) and "The Child of the Phalanstery" (1889) (a free-love society story) by Grant Allen (1848-1899) who spent most of his life in England but was born in Kingston, Ontario, and is included in bibliographies of Canadian literature; "The Man in Asbestos: An Allegory of the Future" (a satirical utopia) by Stephen Leacock; "A Queen in Thebes" (a post-catastrophe story involving incest) by Margaret Laurence; "After the Sirens" (a story about events in Montreal after an atomic bomb is dropped) by Hugh Hood; and "Lust in Action" (a lesbian dystopia story) by John Glassco. It appears that Brian Moore is fast being lost to Canadian literature, but he is a Canadian citizen and his novella *Catholics* is one of the finest works of science fiction ever written. It describes a modish Catholic church of the future and the action it takes against a group of pious but wayward monks who persist in offering the mass in Latin thereby attracting huge congregations. This treatment of man's need for faith and mystery (even if based on a lie) has been insufficiently appreciated by a science-fiction readership largely obsessed with rockets and ray guns.

Five other categories of Canadian science fiction might be distinguished. A second category comprises a number of less established contemporary writers (born in Canada, living in Canada, or New Canadians) who work exclusively or occasionally in science fiction. A typically ambiguous case is Judith Merril who has recently become a Canadian citizen and lives in Toronto. Although Ms. Merril's reputation rests mainly on her role as a champion of the "New Wave" in science fiction (and more recently of Canadian science fiction) and as editor of a series of science fiction anthologies in the sixties, she is also a writer whose pioneering efforts in using science fiction to explore feminist issues are insufficiently appreciated. Michael Coney, an Englishman living in Vancouver for a number of years, is now establishing his reputation in the world of science fiction on the basis of his prolific output of novels, such as *Friends Come in Boxes*, and short stories. Mary Soderstrom, an American living in Montreal, has published a number of fine short stories in the American science-fiction magazines. Alan Hargreaves, an American English professor at the University of Alberta, has published a number of his short stories in a book entitled *North by 2000: A Collection of Canadian Science Fiction*. Hargreaves's work is not very inspiring. Somewhat more successful is Stephen Franklin's *Knowledge Park* which takes its title from the name of the world's greatest library, which has been erected in an area straddling the Quebec/Ontario border. Actually Franklin's book is more an illustrated proposal for such a project rather than a genuine work of fiction, but the concept is an appealing one.

A brief list of Canadian residents or nationals who have published at least one science-fiction novel or short story might include Neil Crichton (*Rerun*), Christie Harris (*Sky Man on the Totem Pole*), Blanche Howard (*The Immortal Soul of Edwin Carlysle*), Basil Jackson (*Epicentre*), Marie Jakober (*The Mind Gods*), John Keith ("A Planet Called Cervantes"), Eileen Kernaghan, Eric Koch (*The Leisure Riots*), Michael Libling, Peter Lord, John Mantley (*The 27th Day*), Suzanne Martel, Ruth Nichols (*A Walk Out of the World*), Esther Rochon (*En homages aux araignées*), Stephen Scobie ("The Philosopher's Stone"), David Walker (*The Lord's Pink Ocean*), Jim Willer (*Paramind*), and Michael Yates (*Fazes in Elsewhen*). Special mention should be made of Spider Robinson, an American who is married to a Nova Scotian and lives in that province. He is well known as a regular reviewer for *Analog* and his two novels, *Telempath* and *Callahan's Crosstime Saloon* (winner of the John W. Campbell Award) are highly regarded.

Among recent Canadian science fiction there are a significant number of books which might be classified as near-future political thrillers. Titles representative of this, my third category, are *Ultimatum, Exxoneration, Exodus: UK* and *Separation,* all by Richard Rohmer; *Killing Ground: The Canadian Civil War* and *The Last Days of the American Empire,* both by Bruce Powe; *The Trudeau Papers* by Ian Adams, and *The Men Who Wanted to Save Canada* by R. J. (Chick) Childerhose. By far the most popular basis for this kind of book is Canada's anxiety and paranoia about the elephant next door—fear of being taken over completely or fear that action taken against America by her enemies will spill over into Canada. William C. Heine has written an in some ways quite successful near-future story based on the latter fear entitled *The Last Canadian*.

The prospect of Quebec separation, it should be noted, was first treated in a book called *Pour La Patrie* by Jules Tardivel (published in 1895) which, for my purposes, counts as an example of a fourth category—visions, early and otherwise, of Canada's future. In Tardivel's vision, Quebec becomes independent at some point in the twentieth century. In a very recent book, *Canada Cancelled Because of Lack of Interest*, by Eric Nicol and Peter Whalley, the country's balkanized future state is treated comically.

An extraordinary 30-page pamphlet published in Ontario in 1883 authored pseudonymously by one "Ralph Centennius" is entitled and describes "The Dominion in 1983" from the vantage point of that year. It appears that following an unsuccessful attempt by America to take over Canada, a utopia has been established and new cities with names like Electropolis (on Lake Athabaska) have been built. Taxes were abolished in 1945, no one has been murdered for more than 50 years, Parliament consists of a mere 15 members, and things are arranged so that rain only falls at night. An efficient transportation system involving "electric tricycles" and "beautiful rocket cars, which frequently dart through the air at the rate of sixty miles in one minute," is the source of a unified Canada. And telescopic observation of Venus and Jupiter has revealed living beings.

Among the plethora of books published in response to or influenced by Bellamy's *Looking Backward* was one by a Canadian Unitarian minister named Hugh Pedley. His *Looking Forward: The Strange Experience of The Reverend Fergus McCheyne* appeared in 1913. Fergus, experimenting with a new drug, falls asleep in 1902 and wakes up 25 years later, a relatively short slumber compared with the 113 years of suspended animation which befalls Bellamy's hero. Fergus learns that the utopian Canada of 1927 has come about as the result of the success of a movement for church unity.

In the far from utopian context of Canada in the 1970s it must be admitted that American domination of the science-fiction field is almost total, which brings me to a fifth category: ex-Canadians who have established their reputations in the context of American science fiction. A. E. van Vogt, who was born in Winnipeg in 1913 and moved south at the age of 31, and Gordon R. Dickson, who was born in Alberta in 1925 and emigrated at the age of 13, might be regarded as Canada's gift to American science fiction. They have both played important roles in the development of the genre and have received considerable recognition.

A much less well-known case is that of Laurence (Edward) Manning who was born in St. John, New Brunswick, in 1899. He moved to the States in 1920 and in the 30s became a regular and popular contributor to *Wonder Stories*. His story series "Stranger Club" includes "The Call of the Mech-Men," an effective tale about an alien robot. But aside from "City of the Living Dead" (1930), the result of a collaboration with Fletcher Pratt, he is best remembered for a second story series entitled "The Man Who Awoke" in which the hero repeatedly comes out of a state of suspended animation to experience a number of progressively dystopian societies obtaining at successively further points in the future.

There is no Canadian-born writer of comparative stature in the world of science fiction currently living in Canada. The closest approximation to such an ideal, however, is Phyllis Gotlieb. She is the author of a number of science-fiction novels, including *Sunburst* (1964), which is about a group of mutant "children" who develop psychic abilities follow-ing an atomic explosion; *O Master Caliban!* (1976), set on Dahlgren's Planet where a ten-year-old telepath thwarts an alien threat; plus such fine science-fiction short stories as "Gingerbread Boy," "A Grain of Man-hood," "Son of the Morning" and "Planetoid Idiot." Phyllis Gotlieb, on the basis of the quality and quantity of her output and as a native-born Canadian actually living in Canada, must be considered the central figure in Canadian science fiction. Indeed, it might be argued that Ms. Gotlieb *is* Canadian science fiction. Consequently, in this six-category survey of Canadian science fiction Phyllis Gotlieb has my final category all to herself.

It is not easy to draw conclusions from a survey of the very disparate material which comprises Canadian science fiction. Perhaps a dispropor-tionate number of stories deal with or impinge on the theme of catas-trophe: the stories of Hugh Hood and Margaret Laurence, many of the near-future political thrillers, and Phyllis Gotlieb's *Sunburst* provide examples. But the catastrophe or end-of-the-world theme is pretty much a generic characteristic. Both American and British science fiction exhibit a similar preponderance of such stories. As one might expect, given Canada's relative proximity to the North Pole, a number of writers (notably De Mille) have been concerned with the depiction of unsuspected polar worlds or discoveries. But what strikes me most forcefully is an almost total absence of "hard" Canadian science fiction, that is to say, works based on the so-called hard sciences such as physics, chemistry and engineering. Canadian science fiction draws on such soft sciences as sociology, anthropology and psychology, and hence, it may be hypothe-sized, its tendency to exist on the borderlines of, or mutate into, the "softer" genre of fantasy. Could it be true that Canadians have a predisposition for fantasy? Indeed, is Canada a fantasy?

Margaret Atwood
CANADIAN MONSTERS

Hardly a poem, story, or novel written by Margaret Atwood does not have somewhere within it a flight of fancy, a highly imaginative image. Born in Ottawa in 1939, Atwood has been an avid reader of fairy tales, fantasy, and science fiction since her youth. (She once confessed to this anthologist that her favourite comic-strip hero was Mandrake the Magician.) "Canadian Monsters: Some Aspects of the Supernatural in Canadian Fiction" first appeared in The Canadian Imagination: Dimensions of a Literary Culture *(1977), edited by David Staines. In this critical paper, Atwood takes a close look at elements of fantasy in our literature. One senses in the analysis the schematic approach to symbolism and literature associated with Northrop Frye. With "Canadian Monsters" and David Ketterer's "Canadian Science Fiction," the reader has both a catalogue and a critical assessment of fantasy and science fiction written by Canadians. Susan Wood has written an essay on the influence of science fiction on Margaret Atwood's writing, "The Martian Point of View," in the American critical review,* Extrapolation *(15).*

I first became interested in Canadian monsters, not, as you might suspect, through politics, but through my own attempts to write ghost stories and through some research I happened to be doing on Sasquatches for the CBC program "Poem for Voices."[1] My collection of other people's monsters has not been systematically acquired, and there are probably glaring omissions in it. No sooner will this essay appear in print than some indignant student of the occult will, no doubt, chastise me for not having known that the central character in *I Was a Teenage Werewolf* was, like Walt Disney, a Canadian, or for some error of similar magnitude. I hasten to cover my tracks by declaring that, unlike my compatriots here assembled, I am not a professional academic, and my collecting and categorizing of monsters must be ascribed to an amateur, perverse, and private eccentricity, like that of, say, a Victorian collector of ferns. (Like many Canadian writers of my generation I started to read Canadian literature in self-defense; we got tired of people telling us there wasn't any and that we should therefore not exist, or go to New York.)

But criticism, even the proliferating Canlitcrit of the last decade, hasn't had much to say about this subject, probably because magic and monsters aren't usually associated with Canadian literature. In fact, the very term "Canadian literature" would seem to exclude them, in the popular mind at least, and the popular mind is not always wrong. Supernaturalism is not typical of Canadian prose fiction; the mainstream (with those useful qualifications, "by and large" and "so far") has been solidly social-realistic. When people in Canadian fiction die, which they do fairly often, they usually stay buried; mention of supernatural beings is as a rule confined to prayers and curses; God and the Devil appear in the third person but rarely in the first and are not often seen onstage. The divine and demonic levels of human existence may appear through analogy or symbol, but there aren't very many apotheoses or descents to the underworld, or even white whales, scarlet letters in the sky, or *Blithedale Romance* mesmerists. Canadian fiction on the whole confines itself to ordinary life on middle earth.[2] Recently, experimentalist Lawrence Garber began a story, "Susceptible to illusion as I am, I was not at all surprised when Jack (whom we had buried some few weeks previously) announced his presence at my threshold."[3] This opening ploy is meant to come as a shock to the reader, and the fact that it does indicates the extent to which it is an exception to the usual Canadian realistic conventions.

The supposed lack of otherworldly dimensions, or even worldly ones, used to be almost routinely lamented by poets and other critics. Thus Earle Birney, in his much-quoted poem "Can. Lit.":

> we French&English never lost
> our civil war
> endure it still
> a bloody civil bore
> the wounded sirened off
> no Whitman wanted
> it's only by our lack of ghosts
> we're haunted

And, more severely, Irving Layton, in "From Colony to Nation":

> A dull people, without charm
> or ideas,

settling into the clean empty look
of a Mountie or a dairy farmer
as into a legacy
One can ignore them
(the silences, the vast distances help)
and suppose them at the bottom
of one of the meaner lakes,
their bones not even picked for souvenirs.

Fifteen years ago, this was Canada, or rather this was the image of it which everyone seemed to believe in: a dull place, devoid of romantic interest and rhetorical excesses, with not enough blood spilled on the soil to make it fertile, and, above all, ghostless. Unmagical Canada, prosaic as Mounties and dairy farmers appear to be before you actually meet some up close . . . .

But is this a true picture of Canada or its literature, and was it ever? Over the past fifteen years a certain amount of exhumation, literary and otherwise, has been taking place, which could be viewed as archaeology, necrophilia, or resurrection, depending on your viewpoint. The digging up of ancestors, calling up of ghosts, exposure of skeletons in the closet which are so evident in many cultural areas—the novel, of course, but also history and even economics—have numerous motivations, but one of them surely is a search for reassurance. We want to be sure that the ancestors, ghosts, and skeletons really are there, that as a culture we are not as flat and lacking in resonance as we were once led to believe. Prime Minister of Canada for more than twenty years, Mackenzie King, formerly a symbol of Canada because of his supposed dullness and grayness ("He blunted us," goes the F. R. Scott poem "W.L.M.K.," "We had no shape / Because he never took sides, / And no sides / Because he never allowed them to take shape . . ."), is enjoying new symbolic popularity as a secret madman who communed every night with the picture of his dead mother and believed that his dog was inhabited by her soul. "Mackenzie King rules Canada because he himself is the embodiment of Canada—cold and cautious on the outside . . . but inside a mass of intuition and dark intimations," says one of Robertson Davies's characters in *The Manticore,* speaking for many.

It is this talking-picture side of Canadian literature, this area of dark intimations, which I would like to consider briefly here. Briefly, because my own knowledge is far from encyclopedic, but also because Canadian fictions in which the supernatural and the magical appear are still only exceptions which prove what may soon no longer be the rule.

The North, the Wilderness, has traditionally been used in Canadian

335

literature as a symbol for the world of the unexplored, the unconscious, the romantic, the mysterious, and the magical. There are strange things done 'neath the midnight sun, as Robert Service puts it. (There are probably stranger things done in Toronto, but they don't have quite the same aura.) So it's not surprising that a large number of Canadian monsters have their origin in native Indian and Eskimo myths. One of the earliest uses of this kind of monster in literary prose (I hesitate to call it fiction, although it probably is) is in a book called *Brown Waters and Other Sketches* by William Blake.[4] The narrator is fishing in "the great barrens that lie far-stretching and desolate among the Laurentian Mountains." He describes the landscape in exceptionally negative terms:

> So were we two alone in one of the loneliest places this wide earth knows. Mile upon mile of gray moss; weathered granite clad in ash-coloured lichen; old *brûlé*,—the trees here fallen in windrows, there standing bleached and lifeless, making the hilltops look barer, like the sparse white hairs of age. Only in the gullies a little greenness,—dwarfed larches, gnarled birches, tiny firs a hundred years old,—and always moss . . . great boulders covered with it, the very quagmires mossed over so that a careless step plunges one into the sucking black ooze below.

One evening the narrator's companion tells a story concerning the disappearance of a man named Paul Duchêne, a good guide, familiar with the wilderness, who wandered off and has never been found. He then mentions the belief of the Montagnais Indians:

> . . . strange medley of Paganism and Christianity,—that those who die insane without the blessing of a priest become wendigos,—werewolves, with nothing human but their form, soulless beings of diabolic strength and cunning, that wander for all time seeking only to harm whomever comes their way.

He goes on to speak of his journey the summer before to a place called the Rivière à l'Enfer, where he camps beside a lake with black water. His guides go back for supplies, and he is left alone, whereupon he experiences an "oppression of the spirit." "In what subtle way," he asks, "does the universe convey the knowledge that it has ceased to be friendly?" That night a tremendous storm blows up. Sitting in his tent, he hears an unearthly cry, which is "not voice of beast or bird." He bursts from the tent and is confronted by a creature—"something in the form of a man"—which springs at him. "And what in God's name was it?" asks the narrator. The storyteller replies, "Pray Him it was not poor Duchêne in the flesh."

The juxtaposition of the oppressive landscape, the storyteller's reaction to it as hostile, and the appearance of the wendigo indicate that this is a tale about the Monster as Other, which represents forces outside and, in this case opposed to the human protagonist. Duchêne, child of the wilderness, has become the wilderness as seen by the narrator—the incarnation of an unfriendly natural universe. The storm is one aspect of this landscape; the wendigo, soulless and destructive, is the same landscape in human form.

The wendigo story in *Brown Waters* is short and simple as the folktale material from which it obviously derives. A more extended and much more sophisticated Monster as Other was created by Sheila Watson in her novel *The Double Hook*.[5] The novel begins, "In the folds of the hills, under Coyote's eye . . ." Coyote turns out to be a deity of sorts, part animal, part god, both below human nature and beyond it. At first, like the landscape he represents, he appears harsh and malevolent. He is Fate, he is retribution, he is Death, he is the nature of things; he is called a "mischief-maker." But in fact he is double, like the hook of the title: "the glory and the fear," both together. His nature changes according to the vision of the perceiver, and the reader comes to know the various characters partly through their views of Coyote. "There's no big Coyote, like you think," says materialist Theophil. "There's not just one of him. He's everywhere. The government's got his number too. They've set a bounty on him at fifty cents a brush . . . This is a thin mean place, men and cattle alike." By the end of the book both Coyote and his landscape have become, if not exactly nurturing, at least more benevolent. He presides over the birth of a child and sings, in his rather Biblical manner:

> I have set his feet on soft ground;
> I have set his feet on the sloping shoulders
> of the world.

The wendigo and Coyote are both landscape-and-nature creatures, nature in both cases being understood to include super-nature. Neither is human; both can act on human beings, but cannot be acted upon. They are both simply *there*, as supernatural forces in the environment and as embodiments of that environment which must be reckoned with. They are objects rather than subjects, the "Other" against which the human characters measure themselves. The environment and its monster in *Brown Waters* are so overwhelmingly negative that the best thing the protagonist can do is run away from them, which he does. The environment and its deity in *The Double Hook* also provide an ordeal for the human actors, but both environment and deity are double-natured, and the proper response to them is not simple escape but further exploration resulting in increased self-knowledge. The one character who attempts escape ends by returning, and Coyote blesses him accordingly.

It is very difficult to make a completely nonhuman supernatural being the protagonist in a fiction, but in at least two Canadian novels the protagonist is a semihuman being. Such beings might be called "magic people" rather than monsters. They have magical powers and other worldly attributes, but they are nonetheless partly human and can be acted upon by ordinary human beings. A case in point is the central character in *Tay John*,[6] Howard O'Hagan's potent and disturbing novel. Tay John is a strange creature, half white man and half Indian, half mythical and half "realistic." In the first third of the book, which is written in the form of a folktale or legend, we learn of his birth underground from the body of his dead and buried mother. He emerges and is seen wandering near the gravesite, an odd child with yellow hair, brown skin, and no shadow. After he has been lured into the land of the living by the elders of the tribe and given a shadow by a wisewoman, he is marked out to be the tribe's leader and potential savior. But first he must enter manhood by going apart to a place of his own choosing, to fast, to have a vision, and to acquire a guiding spirit.

Unfortunately he picks the wrong place. It is "a valley where no man went," and like the lake of Blake's Rivière à l'Enfer it has black water, with similar associations:

> The water that came down from that valley was turgid, dark, and flowed silently, with no rapids. It was said that if a man drank of that water he would lose his voice and go from the sight of his fellows, roaming the hills at night to bark at the moon like a coyote. The coyote men saw by day was not the same they heard by night, for the coyote they heard by night was the voice of a man whose hands had become claws and whose teeth had grown long and tusk-like, who sat on his haunches, lifted his head to the sky and lamented the human speech gone from him.
>
> The spirit of that valley was cruel. Men feared that one night, taking the form of a great white bear, it would come down upon them in their sleep and leave them with a coyote's howl for voice and only a coyote's claws for hands, and each man would be for ever a stranger to his neighbour.

What the Indians fear most about the spirit of the valley is the power it has to divide the society, to make each man a stranger to his neighbor: "The boy says 'I'; the man says 'We'—and this word that the man speaks is the word of his greatest magic." But Tay John chooses to say "I." The valley of the wendigo-like were-coyote does present him with a sign, but it is an ominous one: he is visited by "an old bear, with snow-dust on his coat"; in other words, the great white bear of the myth. He is not changed into a coyote outwardly, but he brings back something that will have the same effect, a bag of sand from the river. The sand contains gold, which is not known to the Indians, but when a party of white prospectors arrives, it is Tay John they select to guide them to the valley, because he is the only person who has ever been there. From this time forward he has a new name, Tête Jaune (corrupted to Tay John), and is contaminated by the egocentric, individualistic spirit of the whites.

This trait emerges when Tay John wishes to marry. The tribe feels that, as magic leader, he should not marry. "The woman of Tay John is the people," they say. "He is a leader of the people and is married to their sorrows." But he will not accept this condition and leaves the tribe to seek out the world of the white men who have given him his name.

As might be expected, the encounter is disastrous. The remaining two sections of the book consist mainly of hearsay and eyewitness reports of the doings of Tay John—his hand-to-hand combat with a grizzly, his sacrifice of his own hand to gain possession of a horse. But he doesn't fit into the white world any more easily than he did into the Indian; in both, he is an exception. His tribe wished him to be a hero and leader, but all the whites can think of to offer him is a position as a guide or, worse, a tourist Indian, dressed up to meet the trains. He resists this tame fate and elopes into the mountains with a strange white woman, a "woman of the world" who leaves her rich protector to go off with him. Like Tay John's own mother she dies in childbirth, and Tay John is last seen pulling her corpse on a toboggan. The description reminds us of his magic origins:

> Tay John came on, more distinct now, through the curtain of swirling snow, entangled in it, wrapped in its folds, his figure appearing close, then falling back into the mists, a shoulder, a leg, a snowshoe moving on as it were of its own accord—like something spawned by the mists striving to take form before mortal eyes.
> "He seemed very big off there, shadowy like," Blackie said, "then again no bigger than a little boy."

When his tracks are followed, they lead nowhere:

> Blackie stared at the tracks in front of him, very faint now, a slight trough in the snow, no more. Always deeper and deeper into the snow. He turned back then. There was nothing more he could do. He had the feeling, he said, looking down at the tracks, that Tay John hadn't gone over the pass at all. He had just walked down, the toboggan behind him, under the snow and into the ground.

The semihuman hero has returned to the earth in much the same way as he emerged from it. His life, like the confused trails he makes in the snow, has been circular. Although he performs several acts beyond the range of most men and is generally regarded as singular, he has not used his gifts to benefit his people, and ultimately they do not benefit him either.

It is interesting to compare Tay John with the "magic" protagonist of a very different book, *The Sun and the Moon* by P. K. Page.[7] Kristin, born during an eclipse of the moon, is a visionary who can see things that aren't there. She can also "become" inanimate objects, seeing and feeling as they do: "She had only to sit still long enough to know the static reality of inanimate things—the still, sweet ecstasy of change in kind." As a child she likes doing this and finds people noisy and superfluous. But when she is seventeen she meets a painter named Carl; they fall in love and become engaged, and she finds herself "stealing" his essence by "becoming" him, much as she was once able to "become" a rock or a chair. Apparently, she discovers, she can "become" things in this way only by partially absorbing them. Kristin finds that she is draining away Carl's talent and even his personality by the sheer force of her empathy with him. He himself has no idea what is going on, but finds himself losing consciousness during what Kristin's father calls her "comatose periods." He awakens feeling drained and old and shaken; and when he tries to paint her portrait, he finds that it is in fact his own he has painted. (But badly; Kristin, who has temporarily taken him over, isn't much of a painter.)

Kristin wants Carl to play sun to her moon, to "pre-dominate," as she puts it; she feels he will be strong enough to resist her inadvertent power. But it is doubtful whether or not Carl in fact possesses enough strength to justify her faith. " 'It is as if I have surrendered my being to an alien force and it has made me less,' " he thinks, just before one of these moments of "invasion." Kristin herself says of her love and her powers of metamorphosis:

> "If only . . . I turned into trees or stones or earth when I'm with him, it couldn't hurt him. But this way . . . I am like a leech, a vampire, sucking his strength from him—the moon eclipsing the sun . . . I cannot be with him without stealing into him and erasing his own identity."

On the eve of her wedding, she finds herself faced with an agonizing problem. She loves Carl and wants to marry him, but she feels she must find "a solution that would protect Carl" from her:

> As we are, if I marry him, it will mean the complete merging of two personalities. But the truth rushed to her out of the night: it will mean the obliteration of two personalities. That is, she thought slowly, the words like heavy sacks that had to be carried together to form a sentence, that is, if I have a personality of my own. For I am a chameleon, she thought, absorbing the colours about me and our marriage will submerge us, wipe us out as sun obliterates the markings of water on a stone.

The solution that she finds is worse than the problem. During the night, she allows herself to "become" the storm-tossed trees outside her window, projecting her soul into their substance, except that this time she does not return to her body. The woman Carl marries the next day is a soulless automaton, emotionless and almost idiotic, who goes through the motions of their life together with no joy and no pain. The "real" Kristin has become completely absorbed by the trees; to all intents and purposes she *is* a tree, and Carl—his talent destroyed by his harrowing experience, and still not knowing what has caused her to change—leaves her in despair. The book ends, not with a description of Kristin's reaction (for presumably she will have none), but with a cinematic cut to the external landscape, which we must by now presume to be the same as the inside of Kristin's head:

> The sun and a small wind broke the surface of the lake to glinting sword blades. On the far side, where the trees marched, unchecked, right down to the water's edge, there the lake was a shifting pattern of scarlet, vermilion and burnt orange.

Kristin, like Tay John, has been absorbed back into the nature that produced her.

But then, love affairs between men and the moon, or men and trees, or mortals and faery queens never did work out very well, if mythology and folklore are to be believed. It is odd to find a dryad in Canadian literature, even though she is disguised as a rather frothy socialite, but that is obviously what Kristin is. (All the objects she chooses to "become" are natural ones; she does not, for instance, ever "become" a motor car.[8]) Kristin and Tay John are both figures of this sort, demigods, with unusual births and strange attributes; like satyrs and their ilk, they are bridges joining the human world, the natural world, and the supra-natural world.

I have now mentioned four creatures, in four separate books: two, the wendigo and Coyote, are completely nonhuman, gods or devils, incarnations of their respective natural environments, and two, Tay John and Kristin, are semihuman but still strongly linked to nature. It would now seem proper to examine the next rung down on the hierarchical scale, which ought to be a priest figure if we are using an epic analogy, or a poet or artist if we are using a pastoral one.[9] Such a figure would be human but magical, and in twentieth-century Canada he is likely to be a magician, for what is stage magic but ritual from which the religion has been removed?

Two well-known Canadian authors have created magicians; they are, of course, Robertson Davies, in his Magnus Eisengrim trilogy,[10] and Gwendolyn MacEwen, who creates a whole series of magicians who bear a strong generic likeness to one another. It would be hard to find two writers whose approaches to prose fiction are more different, yet their magicians have a few things in common. Both are artist figures, and both are in fact Canadian, although both disguise this plebeian origin under an assumed name. (The implication is that you can't be both Canadian and magic; or you can, but no one will believe in you if you reveal your dull gray origins.)

MacEwen specializes in magician as artist as Christ.[11] (In her first novel, *Julian the Magician,* the magician actually insists on being crucified, just to see if he can be resurrected.) Her characters are not only called magicians, they actually are; that is, they seem able actually to perform superhuman feats. Davies's Magnus Eisengrim, on the other hand, is a professional magician, the creator of a very good magic show based on the principles of illusion. But the reader is always left wondering whether MacEwen's magicians are really what they claim to be, or just clever frauds, or perhaps a little insane, whereas Davies weights the evidence in favor of the belief that Eisengrim may in fact have sold his soul to the devil.

Two of the stories in MacEwen's collection *Noman*[12] are attempts to reconcile the world of the Otherworld of the magical with the resolutely nonmagical world of Canada, which MacEwen spells with a *K*. In her earlier works these two places were always kept separate and opposed; the magic world was ancient Egypt, or the Arabian Middle East, or Greece; it contained miracles. Kanada was the place of bacon and eggs, of non-revelations, and it had to be escaped from, either mentally or physically, if you wanted any vision other than the mundane. But in "Kingsmere," which is not really a story but a description, MacEwen explores the possibilities of what she calls "Noman's land": Mackenzie King's artificial ruins. What strikes her is the relationship between the remnants of the past (mostly European) and the landscape that frames them, or, rather, that they frame:

> He reassembled these broken bits of history to frame or emphasize certain aspects of the landscape. He made naked windows and doors for the forest and the hills.
>
> You stand on a terrace flanked by a row of unreal Grecian columns. You look through a classic arch and see, not Athens, nor Rome nor even Palmyra, but the green Gatineau hills of Kanada. You wonder if the landscape protests these borrowed histories, these imported ruins.

For MacEwen, Kingsmere is a time-travel place, a doorway between the past and the future:

> You walk farther down, toward the interior of the garden. Something isn't right. Into whose future are you moving? . . . You have spotted one

very large arch at the far end of the field, and for a second you have an intense, blinding perception of the real nature of the place. This stone on stone, this reconstruction of a past that was never yours, this synthetic history. Only the furtive trees are real . . . Here there is a tension between past and future, a tension so real it's almost tangible; it lives in the stone, it crackles like electricity among the leaves.

He tried to transplant Europe, to bring it here among the stark trees and silent trails, but

There, beyond the arch, is the forest.

The narrator in "Kingsmere" is afraid to pass through this magic arch. Not so Noman, the central character in the story of that name. Noman is the magician as Kanadian; his name, in addition to being Ulysses' pseudonym, is probably intended to symbolize the famous Kanadian identity crisis. At first he pretends he cannot understand English, and his friends construct all kinds of exotic nationalities and identities for him, "imagining a thousand possible tongues for him, for somehow it was incongruous that he could have worn so beautiful a coat, or danced so well in Kanada." He finally reveals the awful truth, and his friend Kali, who has been cooking exotic foods for him, calls him a monster and feeds him a can of pork and beans in disgust. He shares with Kristin the ability to become "whatever he encountered," and he seems to have worked in a carnival as a clown, an escape artist, and finally a dancer. With his thousand possible identities and his refusal to choose just one, he sets himself up (or is set up by his author) as Kanada incarnate. "Kanada," he sighs. "Paper-maker. Like a great blank sheet in the world's diary. Who'll make the first entry?"

As Kanada, he sets himself the task of solving his own identity crisis, and here he links up with "Kingsmere." He speaks to Kali:

> "Let's possess the future as surely as we possess the past!"
>
> "But you don't *have* a past," I winked at him in the mirror.
>
> "Yes I do, damn it! I'll tell you about it later. Let's become the masters of time, let's *move into* time!"
>
> "To pave the way for our descendants?" I laughed.
>
> "No," he said, and looked at me strangely. "For our *ancestors*. They're the ones who are trapped."
>
> I didn't feel like questioning him, so I let him go on.
>
> "We've inherited this great Emptiness," he said. "An empty door that leads into the forest and the snow. No man can get through . . ."
>
> "Can *you*?" I asked, though I wasn't sure what he was talking about.
>
> "Yes," he said, "I think I can."

He goes about this process, which will apparently make it possible to move into the future by rediscovering and releasing the past, in three stages. First he and Kali make love, and then sit applying metaphors to their bodies:

> We set cross-legged like children proudly comparing the maps of our bodies—the birthmarks, scars, incisions, beauty-spots, all the landmarks of our lives, those we were born with and those we'd incurred. New trails broken in the forest, old signposts no longer used, foot-prints of forest animals who come in the night, places of fire, places of water, portages, hills.

The metaphors, which at the beginning of the story were resolutely polyglot European, are now just as resolutely Kanadian, although they are natural rather than the canned pork-and-beans Kanadian ones we have had earlier.

Next, Noman stages his own death, which is Kali's idea:

> "Noman, I have the answer to all your problems."
> "And what is it, Kali?"
> "You must die."
> "That's the answer to everybody's problem," he said.
> "No," I told him, "I mean you must stage a mock death, a brilliant scene in which we'll all participate. Then you can be born again, *maybe even assume a real name*."[13]

Finally, after this fraudulent imitation of Christ, he and Kali go to Kingsmere, "Noman's land," and Noman peels off his clothes and makes it through the magic arch:

> He spotted an arch at one end of the terrace, like an ancient door that led into the forest, the final mystery . . .
> "Coming Kali?" he asked again, and when I didn't answer he went on farther into the spooky greyness . . . .
> "Noman, what are we *doing* here?" I cried. "Whose past have we stolen? Into whose future are we moving?"
> And he (swiftly removing his clothes) called back to me—"Why, our own, of course!"
> And blithely stepped, stark naked, through the arch.

We are not told what "real name" he will assume, what the future is like on the other side of the arch, or what becomes of Noman, but by the nature of the story, and of MacEwen's "Kanada" itself, we can't know. It's interesting, though, that Noman's possession of himself involves an entry into the forest; in fact the end of the story is reminiscent of both O'Hagan and Page.

What we might call "the sacrificial fade-out" seems to be typical of these Canadians demigods and magician priests; their death or disappearance is chosen, and seems to have some element of sacrifice in it, but unlike traditional sacrifices, such as Christ's, it doesn't save or even benefit anyone else, and is more in the nature of an abdication or departure. The sacrificial fade-out is a MacEwen specialty. It's present in almost all of her magician stories, including her two novels, *Julian the Magician* and *King of Egypt, King of Dreams*; but it is most explicit, perhaps, in her short story, "The Second Coming of Julian the Magician," a seriocomic treatment of the dilemma of a real magic man in a non-magical age and country.[14] Julian materializes on Christmas Day, 1970, at noon, at the top of a ferris wheel in "a second-rate carnival." The magic signs of his birth are "three white balloons" in his left hand and "an inverted crucifix made out of red and green tinsel paper" in the middle of his forehead. The left-handedness and the inversion are significant, as is the tinsel paper: Julian is a tacky upside-down Christ, fated to be tacky and upside-down by the lack of faith of his potential believers. He realizes that in this incarnation he has a choice of performing in carnivals or in "cheap burlesque halls" and that his iconography is contained only in comic books and people's dreams:

> In the comic books my cloak is red, green or yellow; there are little wings on my boots, little wings on my head, lightning bolts or sacred hammers in my fists. Only the children worship me now.

He is "Atman, his identity hidden only by a 'B' at the beginning of his name."

But even when he walks on walls or makes it rain or creates black fire, his audiences are only bored or uneasy, since they believe "it's all done with mirrors," his magic mere trickery. And a lot of it is. He's a student of Houdini and Blackstone, although he insists that even tricks and illusions are real magic as long as they are believed: "The Master of Illusions doesn't make you believe what he wishes, but what you wish." His failure is the failure of the audience:

> During my acts no-one swooned; no-one approached me afterwards with nervous diseases for me to cure. (How very different from my last life when the peasants regarded me as holy man, a healer. But then this is North America. Could Christ have taught in Rome?)

He quickly realizes that his "enemy" is the Twentieth Century itself, that Dr. Zero of the comics, the Power House of the city, the Machine. He had a terrible nightmare, in which a Fat Woman named Reality ("But you can call me Reali for short") grabs his magic wand and chases him with it. Reality and the city and the machine are one, and he refuses to be "tricked into reality." He decides to destroy the electrical city by blowing up the Power House where he has a job as night watchman, and he accomplishes this, in fact or fantasy. Then, observed only by the children who are his sole congregation, he performs an apotheosis, disappearing from the top of the ferris wheel in the same way he appeared. His encounter with reality has not been a pleasant one.

"Yet still I wave this wand like a sarcastic tongue at the universe . . . know myself to be both icon and iconoclast," says Julian in a speech that could have been made as well by Robertson Davies's Magnus Eisengrim. Eisengrim would have phrased it differently, however. For MacEwen, the magician is a poet, concerned with the transforming power of the Word; for Davies he is clearly a novelist, concerned with illusions produced by hard work and a meticulous attention to detail. MacEwen's magicians want to control the universe, but Davies's creation contents himself with controlling the minds of the audience. Julian creates real birds out of mud, and nobody cares because nobody can believe he's really done it. Eisengrim gives them fake snow on a stage, but does it so well that it looks real. This is his magic: he's applauded, not for what he does—nobody *really* thinks he's magic—but for his consummate skill in doing it. Perhaps this is why he's a professional success and Julian is a failure.

Like "Noman," "Eisengrim" is a pseudonym. Davies's magician started life in a "Kanadian" small town of the pork-and-beans variety, narrow, puritanical, judgmental; his real name is plain Paul Dempster. His hatred of Canada stems from his persecution at the hands of this town and from its efforts to stifle his childish interest in magic. He is kidnapped by a figure paralleling MacEwen's Fat Lady Reality, a cheap conjuror who abuses him sexually while subjecting him to a bitter apprenticeship in a carnival that is not just second-rate but third-rate. Here he learns a view of magic that is equivalent to the underbelly of God: cynicism, fraud and trickery, cunning as well as conjuring, exploitation, the audience as dupe. From these humble beginnings he works his way up in the world of international magic as, among other things, an escape artist and mechanical genius, with a stopover in the legitimate theater as a "double," and is finally able to create a distinguished magic show that brings him worldwide fame.

Although he is a consummate artist, he is also, curiously, a kind of nonperson, a Noman figure who is no one because he has the capacity to be everyone, as well as to be invisible. His first job in "Wanless's World of Wonders" is to crouch inside a mechanical monster named Abdullah, who is supposed to be a card-playing automaton but is really a trick worked from inside to defraud the customers. Of this period in his life he says:

> When I was in Abdullah, I was Nobody. I was an extension and a
> magnification of Willard; I was an opponent and a baffling mystery to

the Rube; I was something to be gawped at, but quickly forgotten, by the spectators. But as Paul Dempster I did not exist. I had found my place in life, and it was as Nobody.

He lives under several pseudonyms from this time on; as the double of a famous actor, he takes the curious name of "Mungo Fetch," "fetch" being a Scottish word for an unlucky vision of yourself you see before you die. When he finally creates his own show, its *pièce de résistance* is a much more sophisticated version of Abdullah, a Golem-like oracular brazen head, which utters disturbing truths about members of the audience. Like Abdullah it's a fraud, although like Abdullah its effects on the audience are real and sometimes disastrous; Eisengrim's relationship to it is that of the invisible power. With both Abdullah and the brazen head, however, is some question as to whether Eisengrim is their master or their slave, controlled by the monsters he thinks he is directing and creating.

Eisengrim is "wolvish," a quality which has suggested his last assumed name. It's made clear that this ruthless quality is a result of his hideous early experiences and is responsible for his having survived them. It's also responsible for his success as a magician. Both he and the other characters in the book insist that he's both an artist and a genius, as well as a glorified trickster and fraud, a Master of Illusions. His "wolvishness" is linked to "an intensity of imagination and vision," and to what another character, quoting Spengler, calls "the Magian World View":

> It was a sense of the unfathomable wonder of the invisible world that existed side by side with a hard recognition of the roughness and cruelty and day-to-day demands of the tangible world. It was a readiness to see demons where nowadays we see neuroses, and to see the hand of a guardian angel in what we are apt to shrug off ungratefully as a stroke of luck. It was religion, but a religion with a thousand gods, none of them all-powerful and most of them ambiguous in their attitude toward man. It was poetry and wonder which might reveal themselves in the dunghill, and it was an understanding of the dunghill that lurks in poetry and wonder . . . Wonder is marvellous but it is also cruel, cruel, cruel.

And Eisengrim partakes of the cruelty as well as the magic. On one level Davies's trilogy is about spiritual vampirism, the exercise of sinister, devouring power over others. Eisengrim has been the victim in such a relationship, but he later becomes the devourer. On another level the novels are about retaliation, the justice rather than the mercy of the universe, and such justice is unpleasant, if not sinister. One of Eisengrim's friends says:

> The Devil is a setter of prices, and a usurer, as well. You buy from him at an agreed price, but the payments are all on time, and the interest is charged on the whole of the principal, right up to the last payment.

To which Eisengrim replies, "Do you think you can study evil without living it?" He implies that he has lived it, and this is certainly true. Eisengrim's public personality is a deliberate creation; he is, in a way, his own monster, with his own ego incarnate in the brazen head. The last word in the trilogy is "egoist," and it's an open question whether the religion for which Eisengrim acts as magician-priest is really a religion of wonder, as he sometimes claims, or merely a religion of himself, a form of devil-worship.

And this brings us to the last category of magician or monster I'll discuss here. I began with Blake's wendigo, a monster representing a destructive external environment, so it's fitting to end with the wabeno, a monster representing a destructive internal one. The wabeno appears in Wayland Drew's *The Wabeno Feast*,[15] a novel which cuts between two time-streams: a not-so-distant future in which Canada is dissolving into chaos, and the eighteenth-century past, at the peak of the Hudson Bay Company's power. The episodes from the past are told through the journal of a would-be factor, one MacKay, who journeys into the wilderness with his sinister double, Elborn. Early in the voyage, Elborn encourages the voyageurs to tell "tales of death and terror":

> They tell of the wendigo, a mythical creature of Indian lore, and each elaborates on the other's imagining until in his fantasy Elborn beholds a creature thirty feet in height, a naked, hissing demon whose frog-like eyes search out unwary travellers and roll in blood with craving to consume them! Another whispers that the creature lacks lips to cover its shattered teeth, and a third describes its feet like scabrous canoes on which it rocks howling through the swamps at evening.

MacKay refuses to pay heed to these stories. He is an eighteenth-century man, determined to be practical and rational and to make money; we learn that he has already renounced love and religion.

MacKay does not meet the wendigo, the monster from without. Instead he encounters the wabeno, and in company with Elborn he is privileged to witness the singular ceremony staged by the wabeno and his followers on a nearby island. The wabeno is "the most powerful" of the Indian shamans, the translator tells them:

> Whether his influence be curative or pernicious he knew not, although he thought the latter. The wabeno, he said, would use any means to cure

348

disease or to quench an unrequited love, and those who placed themselves in his influence and used his potions on themselves or on others must submit entirely their will to his, for the remedies might grow extreme . . . It was good, he added, that the power of the wabeno had declined, and that such sorceries as he practised so as to conjure an overturn of nature grew less common as the Company's influence spread.

The wabeno and his followers differ from other Indians in their height, the "military precision" of their tents, and their white garments. Their skins also are a peculiar shade of white.

The wabeno feast itself is an orgy which begins with murder and cannibalism, continues as a frenzied dance in which the performers leap through fire so that their sexual organs are burned away, and ends with the wabeno setting fire to the entire island. The wabeno and his band vanish, although no one knows whether or not they have died in the fire:

> Elborn maintained that they had fled, and that they would spread their dementia like a plague until the last had been run to earth; but for my own part I believe that we had heard the dawn crying of the loons, and that the shaman and his band had found that morning the death which they had sought so eagerly.

Although the wabeno makes only one appearance in the novel, he is its organizing symbol. The translator opposes the wabeno to the Company, but in fact they stand for the same things: the desire for power through the destruction of others, which in the end is the same as self-destruction. MacKay, who dedicates himself to the Company's goals of accumulating beaver skins by debauching the Indians so they will want trade goods, is insane by the end of the book. In fact he was probably insane at its beginning; his mocker and Shadow, Elborn, appears to exist in his own mind only, and when he kills Elborn he is, like Poe's William Wilson, killing himself. MacKay's story counterpoints the twentieth-century half of the book; here we see the spirit of the wabeno infecting the whole of society. It is of course significant that the wabeno and his band are white; the only Indians in the book who are able to live in dignity and self-sufficiency, without drunkenness, murder, and disease, are those who have made a vow not to mingle with the white traders or use any of their goods,[16] just as the only twentieth-century characters who escape the destruction of society, both physical and spiritual, are those who choose to make a canoe journey alone into the wilderness.

It is usual for a critic to present some general conclusions at the end of an effusion such as this. I'm not sure that I have any to offer; as I noted, I'm a mere collector of Canadian monsters, and I present them so that their rarity and exotic beauty may be admired, not necessarily in order to interpret them. There are many more phenomena of a similar kind: ghosts, witches, talismans, time travelers, premonitory dreams, poltergeists, and affairs with bears (this latter seems to be a peculiarly Canadian interest, as I've collected three). But I've surely dredged up enough specimens to indicate that there is indeed "a mass of dark intimations" in the Canadian literary soul.

I have also arranged my specimens in a rough paradigm which, curiously, corresponds to the order in which their respective books were written. The wendigo and Coyote, which we may call "environmental forces" or Monsters as Other, come from quite early books,[17] as do the two demigods or "magic people" I've mentioned. The magicians, on the other hand, are creatures of the sixties and seventies and seem rather more concerned, symbolically, with man's relationship to his society and to himself, as opposed to his relationship with the natural environment. The final example, the wabeno, combines both concerns in a rather allegorical and very contemporary fashion. In the tradition of the horror movie, I've begun with a terrifying thunderstorm and ended with a man-made conflagration; that is, I've begun with a story which plays upon man's fear of natural power and ended with one illustrating the dangers inherent in his own lust for power. The connection between this pattern and the changes in Canadian society and outlook over the last sixty years is perhaps too obvious to be mentioned. In any case, such a critical pattern exists in the mind of the critic rather than in the external world. Perhaps the critic is himself a kind of magician, for, as Julian the Magician says, in his incantation for making an egg disappear:

> *Like everything else in the universe its existence depends on your seeing it—that alone—and its existence is the gift of your inner eye.*

And, in the face of this, who will say there are no wendigos, or that the picture of Mackenzie King's mother does not actually talk? There is more to Kanada than meets the eye . . . .

1. "Oratorio for Sasquatch, Man and Two Androids," in *Poems for Voices* (Toronto: Canadian Broadcasting Corporation, 1970). The first eleven lines are not mine.
2. I could suggest two reasons for this, neither of which has anything to do with innate lack of panache on the part of Canadian fiction writers. The first is that the Canadian fiction tradition developed largely in the twentieth century, not the romantic nineteenth. The second is that in a cultural colony a lot of effort must go into simply naming and describing observed realities, into making the visible real even for those who actually live there. Not much energy is left over for exploring other, invisible realms.

3. "Visions before Midnight," in Garber, *Circuit* (Toronto: House of Anansi Press, 1970).

4. "A Tale of the Grand Jardin," in W. H. Blake, *Brown Waters and Other Sketches* (Toronto: Macmillan, 1915).

5. (Toronto: McClelland and Stewart, 1959).

6. (London: Laidlaw and Laidlaw, 1939).

7. *The Sun and the Moon* (Toronto: Macmillan, 1944) was first published under the pseudonym Judith Cape.

8. She does "become" a chair, but only on the level of its molecules.

9. Epic: gods, semidivine heroes, priests and oracles. Pastoral: nature, satyrs and such, singing shepherds.

10. *Fifth Business* (Toronto: Macmillan, 1970), *The Manticore* (Toronto: Macmillan, 1972), and *World of Wonders* (Toronto: Macmillan, 1975).

11. See her early poem "The Magician as Christ," in MacEwen, *The Rising Fire* (Toronto: Contact Press, 1963).

12. (Ottawa: Oberon Press, 1972).

13. The italics are mine.

14. "The Second Coming of Julian the Magician," in *Noman*.

15. Wayland Drew, *The Wabeno Feast* (Toronto: House of Anansi Press, 1973).

16. Compare also the story of Kakumee and the Tornak in Farley Mowat's nonfictional study *People of the Deer* (Boston: Little, Brown, 1952). Here also the spirit of the whites is seen as a demon, and its influence on the native people is entirely destructive.

17. Sheila Watson's *The Double Hook*, although published in 1959, was actually written a decade earlier.

Brief Annotated Bibliography

The reader will find listed here thirty-six books of science fiction and fantasy written by Canadians or set in Canada. In drawing up this short list, I have tried to answer the question, "What three dozen books would the reader of this anthology most enjoy?" The works listed stress human interest, imaginative value, and literary quality. As well, the majority are in print in one edition or another. The books may be grouped in the following manner: there are seventeen novels, seven collections of stories, eight juvenile works, three volumes of plays and poems, and one documentary work. Seven were originally written in French, two of which have yet to be translated into English. I think the list is a balanced one, although it does not attempt to do justice to works of historical moment or experimental interest. Why thirty-six? Why not twice that number? One reason is that the space in this volume does not allow for many more titles; another reason is that a full-scale bibliography *does* exist: *CDN SF&F A Bibliography of Science Fiction and Fantasy* (Toronto: Hounslow Press, 1979), compiled by John Robert Colombo, Michael Richardson, John Bell, and Alexandre L. Amprimoz. Approximately six hundred titles appear there.

Ian Adams. *The Trudeau Papers*. Toronto: McClelland & Stewart, 1971. The Prairies are contaminated by nuclear warheads and Ontario has become an American police state.

Pierre Berton. *The Secret World of Og*. Toronto: McClelland & Stewart, 1962. A fantasy adventure in which five children learn to balance the demands of the worlds of reality and make-believe.

Earle Birney. *The Damnation of Vancouver*. Toronto: McClelland & Stewart, 1977. Preface by the author, introduction by Wai Lan Low. A comic verse play, originally broadcast by CBC *Stage* in 1952, about the possible destruction of Vancouver "five years from now."

Monique Corriveau. *Compagnon du Soleil*. Montreal: Editions Fides, 1976. A three-volume fantasy about a future world in which a young man sets his people free of the tyranny of technocracy.

James De Mille. *A Strange Manuscript Found in a Copper Cylinder*. New York: Harper's, 1888. A classic, polar-world adventure, with satiric and philosophic overtones. Reprinted by the New Canadian Library in 1969.

Jacques Ferron. *Tales from the Uncertain Country*. Toronto: Anansi, 1972. Translated by Betty Bednarski. Short stories, written in a fantastic vein, inspired by Quebec folklore.

Stephen Franklin. *Knowledge Park*. Toronto: McClelland & Stewart, 1972. A world library to house the whole of man's knowledge is built by the nations of the world in the Canadian North.

Jacques Godbout. *Dragon Island*. Toronto: Musson, 1978. Translated by David Ellis. By conjuring up a dragon, a young man saves a beautiful island in the St. Lawrence from certain destruction.

Phyllis Gotlieb. *Sunburst*. Greenwich, Conn.: Gold Medal Books, 1964. A fiendish race of demonic children is spawned in the genetic chaos created by a runaway reactor explosion. Widely translated. Available in paperback in Fitzhenry & Whiteside's The Contemporary Scene series.

Phyllis Gotlieb. *O Master Caliban!* New York: Harper & Row, 1976. Genetic experimentation, telepathy, an intelligent gibbon, a talking goat, a four-armed man meet in Dahlgren's World. Reprinted by Seal Books in 1979.

Frederick Philip Grove. *Consider Her Ways*. Toronto: Macmillan of Canada, 1947. A society of ants from Venezuela explores North America and reports its findings, asserting its superiority to man. A classic novel of fantasy . . . and humanity. Reprinted by the New Canadian Library in 1977.

Christie Harris. *Sky Man on the Totem Pole?* Toronto: McClelland & Stewart, 1975. West Coast Indians meet visitors from outer space and find the secret of ecological balance.

Michael Hirsh and Patrick Loubert. *The Great Canadian Comic Books*. Toronto: Peter Martin Associates, 1971. An illustrated history of comic books and strip art produced in Canada during the Second World War —starring such superheroes as Nelvana of the Northern Lights, Whiz Wallace, Thunderfist, and Mister Totem. Available in a quality paperback from PMA Books.

Eric Koch. *The Leisure Riots*. Montreal: Tundra Books, 1973. Retired executives riot in 1980 when they are denied tension-producing work.

Stephen Leacock. *Afternoons in Utopia: Tales of the New Time*. Toronto: Macmillan of Canada, 1932. A whimsical yet thoughtful consideration of human problems some centuries hence. Out of print.

Gwendolyn MacEwen. *The Armies of the Moon*. Toronto: Macmillan of Canada, 1972. Poems with a fantastic and science-fiction flavour inspired by the lunar orb.

Gwendolyn MacEwen. *Noman*. Ottawa: Oberon Press, 1972. Stories, fables, fantasies, and meditations written in an associative and sometimes speculative way.

Suzanne Martel. *The City Underground*. New York: Viking Press, 1964. Translated by Norah Smaridge. An adventure for younger readers set in the world beneath Montreal in the year 3000 A.D. Out of print.

Judith Merril. *The Best of Judith Merril.* New York: Warner Books, 1976. Introduction by Virginia Kidd. Nine stories and two poems by the well-known author and anthologist, most of them written before her emigration to Canada.

Nicholas Monsarrat. *The Time Before This.* London: Cassell, 1962. A remarkable novelette about the need for world peace, sparked by the discovery of evidence that an earlier race of man inhabited Bylot Island, Northwest Territories. Reprinted by PaperJacks in 1975.

Brian Moore. *The Great Victorian Collection.* Toronto: McClelland & Stewart, 1975. A Montreal historian dreams about a collection of Victorian artifacts and wakes up to find that the collection exists outside his motel window at Carmel, California. Available in paperback.

Ruth Nichols. *A Walk Out of the World.* Toronto: Longmans, 1969. Two children plunge through time into another world where they are threatened by an evil sorcerer.

Ruth Nichols. *The Marrow of the World.* Toronto: Macmillan of Canada, 1972. A struggle for survival in a world beneath Georgian Bay, Ontario.

Ruth Nichols. *Song of the Pearl.* Toronto: Macmillan of Canada, 1976. A young woman dies and finds that death is a gateway to a secret buried deep in the forgotten past.

Alden Nowlan and Walter Learning. *Frankenstein: The Play.* Toronto: Clarke, Irwin, 1976. A poet and a producer have teamed up to dramatize Mary Shelley's novel *Frankenstein* (1818), remaining faithful to the original.

Howard O'Hagan. *Tay John.* London: Laidlaw, 1939. A novel of mythic proportions about a half-white, half-Indian leader of his people in the Northwest. Reprinted by the New Canadian Library in 1974.

P. K. Page. *The Sun and the Moon and Other Fictions.* Toronto: Anansi, 1974. A collection of nine fantasies, originally written by the well-known poet in the 1940's.

Bruce Powe. *The Last Days of the American Empire.* Toronto: Macmillan of Canada, 1974. The starving masses of Europe and Africa rise up against the ruling rich of the American Empire in the Twenty-first Century.

Mordecai Richler. *Jacob Two-Two Meets the Hooded Fang.* Toronto: McClelland & Stewart, 1975. An ordinary boy is condemned to a dreaded dungeon "from which no brat returns" because he says everything a second time since nobody listens to him the first time.

Spider Robinson and Jeanne Robinson. *Stardance.* New York: Dial

Press/James Wade, 1979. A widely acclaimed novel about a zero-gravity dancer who creates a new dance form in the weightless environment of High Earth Orbit.

Richard Rohmer. *Ultimatum.* Toronto: Clarke, Irwin, 1973. This is the first book in a loosely written series of "national disaster scenarios"; the successors are *Exxoneration* (1974), *Exodus/UK* (1975), and *Separation* (1976).

Jules-Paul Tardivel. *For My Country: An 1895 Religious and Separatist Vision of Québec in the Mid-Twentieth Century.* Toronto: University of Toronto Press, 1975. Translated by Sheila Fischman. This prophetic novel, originally published in 1895, and set in the "Laurentian Empire" of 1945, presents the utopian vision of a Catholic Quebec separate from the rest of Canada.

Yves Thériault. *Si la Bombe M'Etait Contée.* Montréal: Editions du Jour, 1962. Short stories and actual documents alternate to dramatize the destructive madness of nuclear power.

Michel Tremblay. *Stories for Late Night Drinkers.* Vancouver: Intermedia Press, 1977. Translated by Michael Bullock. Twenty-five stories of the light fantastic variety by the well-known Quebec playwright.

A. E. van Vogt. *Slan.* Sauk City, Wisconsin: Arkham House, 1946. This is the classic persecuted-mutant novel and a work of considerable power and appeal. Available in various American mass-market paperback editions.

David Walker. *The Lord's Pink Ocean.* Boston: Houghton Mifflin, 1972. A vision of the future in which all the oceans but one are contaminated by a lethal algae.

Acknowledgements

Grateful acknowledgement is given for permission to reproduce the works of the following authors in this anthology:

Margaret Atwood: "Canadian Monsters: Some Aspects of the Supernatural in Canadian Fiction." From *The Canadian Imagination: Dimensions of a Literary Culture* (Cambridge: Harvard University Press, 1977), edited by David Staines. Reprinted by permission of the author and her agent, Phoebe Larmore.

Betty Bednarski. Reprinted by permission of House of Anansi Press Limited.

Phyllis Gotlieb: "The Military Hospital." From *Fourteen Stories High* (Ottawa: Oberon Press, 1971), edited by David Helwig and Tom Marshall. Copyright © 1971 by Oberon Press, Ontario, and Copyright © 1974 by Mercury Press, Inc., U.S.A.; reprinted by permission of the author and the author's agent, Virginia Kidd. "Seeing Eye," "Ms & Mr. Frankenstein," and "Was/Man." From *The Works: Collected Poems* (Toronto: Calliope Press, 1978). Reprinted by permission of the author.

Frederick Philip Grove: "Consider Her Ways." From *Consider Her Ways* (Toronto: Macmillan of Canada, 1947). Reprinted by permission of A. Leonard Grove.

H. A. Hargreaves: "Infinite Variation." Published by permission of the author.

Hugh Hood: "Flying a Red Kite." From *Flying a Red Kite* (Toronto: The Ryerson Press, 1962). Reprinted by permission of the author.

Stanley Jackson and Roman Kroitor: "Universe." Copyright © 1960 by The National Film Board of Canada. All Rights Reserved. Published by permission.

David Ketterer: "Canadian Science Fiction: A Survey." From *Canadian Children's Literature: A Journal of Criticism and Review*, Number 10, 1977-78. Revised and expanded version published with the permission of the author.

Margaret Laurence: "A Queen in Thebes." From *The Canadian Century: English-Canadian Writing since Confederation* (Toronto: Gage Educational Publishing Ltd., 1973), edited by A. J. M. Smith. Copyright © 1964 by Margaret Laurence. Reprinted by permission of JCA Literary Agency, Inc.

Stephen Leacock: "A Fragment from Utopia: The Fifty-Fifty Sexes." From *Afternoons in Utopia: Tales of the New Time* (New York: Dodd, Mead & Company, 1932). Reprinted by permission of Dodd, Mead and Company, Inc. Copyright 1932 by Dodd, Mead and Company, Inc. Copyright renewed 1960 by Stephen L. Leacock.

Gwendolyn MacEwen: "The Armies of the Moon," "The Vacuum Cleaner Dream," and "Flight One." From *Magic Animals: Selected Poems Old and New* (Toronto: Macmillan of Canada, 1974). Reprinted by permission of The Macmillan Company of Canada Limited.